A Proper Country Funeral

Tony Read

SPINETINGLERS
PUBLISHING

A Proper Country Funeral
By Tony Read

ISBN - 978-1-906657-32-1

Spinetinglers Publishing
22 Vestry Road
Co. Down
BT23 6HJ
UK
www.spinetinglerspublishing.com

This book has been formatted by
Spinetinglers Publishing
UK

To Shirley John and Paul with my love.

To my friends Dr Graham Brodie, Martin Mulliss and Ian Brew for their support and encouragement, and to Caroline Brew for reading the manuscript of this book and correcting so many errors.

CHAPTER ONE

Some said afterwards that it had been *a proper country funeral*, but in truth it had not. The coffin had been carried to the church by pony and trap, and a procession of 10 vintage tractors had followed on behind, each one painstakingly restored by its proud owner. Paintwork had sparkled in the early autumn sunlight, and people had commented that this was the true spirit of the countryside, but they were wrong. What they had witnessed was an undignified parade of affluence; none of these old work horses had ploughed a field in anger or sweated in a baking meadow for more than 30 years. They were playthings, mechanical toys of the rich and idle, and the man who was to be laid to rest that afternoon was the richest and most idle of them all. Inside the packed church there had been many suntanned faces, but not one that had been sculpted by decades of exposure to the elements and to the seasons. There were plenty of people in attendance, who claimed the virtue of hard work, but they all had slender elegant fingers and beautifully manicured nails. Calluses and blisters were nowhere to be seen and nobody had struggled in vain to remove deeply engrained dirt from gnarled and battered hands. *A proper country funeral,* at least one that Will Hammond would have described as *proper* would have had a sincerity and a simple dignity that this elaborately stage-managed performance entirely lacked; perhaps that was one reason why his mind had been constantly dragged back to an earlier time, two decades before, when he had sat miserably with his family, in a cold, uncomfortable chapel to mourn the passing of Jacob Farrington. The memory of that dismal occasion was as potent and as powerful today as it ever had been, and as Will knew for sure as it always would be.

Jacob had lived a good life, nobody doubted that fact, and his untimely death on the day of his 40th birthday had been a tragedy that should never have occurred. Will remembered the overwhelming grief of his bewildered wife and the uncomprehending despair of his children. A giant oak had been felled, the rock upon which so many lives had been built had crumbled into dust, and it was all so unnecessary and so very reprehensible.

Feelings of guilt never really leave you, Will had learnt that lesson well; although sometimes, for a short while, they can be concealed under a blanket of forgetfulness when the happiness of the moment overwhelms all other emotions, but it never lasts. At times when they are least expected memories return to pierce the flimsy armour of contentment with steely shafts of regret and self-loathing. Will knew those memories well, he had lived with them throughout his adult life and they had wounded him and left him damaged and scarred. His first marriage had ended in bitterness and in recrimination and he had had only himself to blame. He had become convinced that he was destined to spend a life alone; then, against all the odds, he had found Julia. Somehow she had seen the decent man he could have been. She had recognised his inner gentleness, and his overwhelming desire to do good and she had made him hope there could be a future. He had asked her to marry him, and even though his mind had screamed at him *if she only knew,* and he had experienced the fear of discovery and rejection, he had stood firm in his resolve, and she had come to him as his wife and he had felt cleansed. When first Victoria and then Richard had been born his joy was immeasurable, but even then his brain had taunted him with the fear of exposure: *when they find out, and they will inevitably find out, they will hate you* it had mocked him. He had persuaded himself that this need never happen, and that the boy who had played such a tiny part in a terrible crime was long since dead, but he couldn't smother the ever present doubts that continually breathed new life into the embers of his self loathing. How he had tried! He was a devoted husband and a loving father, and his generosity towards others was widely noted; but nothing could erase the past. Then miraculously first Jeremy and then Timothy Eggleton had died and at last the ghost that had tortured him since childhood seemed about to be exorcised. He had attended the over-choreographed funeral to assign to the dustbin of forgotten history the memory of a terrible deed; that had been a terrible mistake. His eyes had not seen the gilded casket that contained the mortal remains of the millionaire but rather the stout oak box in which the body of Jacob had been lowered into the grave. His senses had played tricks; he hadn't smelt costly cologne and expensive French perfumes, but instead had breathed in the smells of animals and of agricultural land; and when the congregation sang he had heard the diverse dialects of rural England not the refined accents of privilege that rose to the rafters of the church. The spectre that haunted him throughout his life refused to die. Like the Phoenix rising from the ashes it had become immense and strong, and then when ashen faced, and in a state of panic, he had looked around, wanting nothing more than to flee he had seen a face gazing at him intently: at that moment the past had fused with the present and the future; there could be no escape for him; and only one end.

At the Devonshire Arms at Beeley well dressed men and women drank Rioja and Chardonnay and recalled episodes in the life of "Dear Timothy" Will was not one of them; his BMW would not have been out of place among the Jaguars, the Audis and the Porsches, and his well tailored suit would have stood comparison with any elegant garment on display, but he didn't belong there. Twenty years ago he had sacrificed everything to be accepted, and what good had it done him? On this, which would be the last day of his life, he wanted to be alone and to think of the people who truly mattered, and to make his confession to a higher being. In Bakewell he found a hardware shop, and from there he purchased ten metres of rope, a penknife and a small ball of string. The pretty postcard he bought in the little bookshop was of Bakewell Bridge in springtime, daffodils danced amidst green grass and the picture was a eulogy to a cycle of new life and hope. On a bench by the riverside, just downstream from the scenic view depicted, still instantly recognisable, even though the season's colour had taken on different, less vibrant hues, he sat and wrote his last message to his beloved Julia.

I'm so sorry, he wrote. *I love you so much. Tell the children their daddy adored them more than they could ever know and that he so much wanted to watch them grow up. If there is a merciful God maybe someday we will be permitted to meet in Paradise. Don't ever weep for me, one day you will realise that this was for the best: men like me do not deserve someone as beautiful as you.*

My angel and my eternal dream

Will.

There were tears in his eyes when he posted the postcard to his wife, and there were tears in his eyes when he sat alone in the churchyard at Ashford in the Water and there made his peace with God. Nobody came near, nobody intruded on his sadness, and for the first time in a generation he felt unthreatened. Dusk was beginning to fall as he drove onto the car park at the old Millers Dale Station; only one car was still parked there, and even as he opened his driver's door an elderly man, with a black Labrador dog, returned to reclaim his modest conveyance, and soon Will's was the only vehicle remaining.

No doubt he presented an incongruous sight; a well dressed man with highly polished shoes wearing a smart suit and a black tie, his jacket pockets bulging with hidden objects, and with a length of blue rope coiled over his shoulder; but there was no one there to take notice. Purposefully he strode out towards Cheedale, only stopping when he reached the viaduct that straddles the fast flowing river far below. His mind was now set, closed to all thoughts except of that which he had to do. He took the rope from his shoulder and uncoiled it, and tied one end of it to the locked metal gateway through which children on Outward Bound courses, under the strictest supervision abseil down to the footpath in the valley bottom. Fumbling slightly, he took the other end of the rope and fashioned it into a noose for his own neck, drawing the slip knot tight under his Adam's apple. Finally, he removed the ball of string from his pocket, and cutting off a short section of twine, he threaded this under his belt and then tied his left wrist to his side. If at the very moment he jumped he lost his nerve there would be nothing he could do, one hand alone would not rescue him; and so, secure in the knowledge that he could not save himself he climbed onto the low wall on the other side of the track bed and leapt from the present into the past tense.

CHAPTER TWO

When Will hadn't returned home by five o'clock Julia Hammond was not worried, although she was a little surprised. She hadn't expected he would be so late, but personal experience had taught her that funerals frequently brought people together who may not have met each other in years, if not decades, and when that happened often the need to talk was irresistible. She remembered that when her Aunt Emily passed away, two of her old school friends, who hadn't set eyes on each other for more than 40 years, had never-the-less instantly recognised each other, and when they had done so the flow of conversation had been unstoppable. Taxis had been sent packing to return at a later hour, train times had been put back and back, and it was only when they were in imminent danger of being stranded overnight that these two elderly ladies had finally torn themselves away from their historic revelations and reluctantly returned to their present day lives, but promising each other that they would never lose touch again. Julia hoped that Will might have met a long lost friend, he didn't have enough friends, and if somehow he could rekindle a boyhood acquaintanceship, that would be a really good thing.

She recalled her silly cousin Alistair, also at Aunt Emily's funeral, falling in with a group of middle-aged men, who were all her auntie's former pupils: so much beer had been drunk and so much whiskey that Alistair had collapsed in the ladies' toilet, incapable of movement, or coherent speech, and he had been taken home in, disgrace, in the back of her Uncle Michael's car, a plastic washing up bowl on the floor, and the rear seats covered with newspaper to protect them from his overflowing stomach. She had no worries about Will on that score: he had not drunk alcohol since he was a teenager; there had been some very bad experience which he never talked about, and since that day, no beer, wine or spirits, had ever passed his lips.

When six o'clock came and still no Will, the first seeds of anxiety were beginning to germinate, but the children needed feeding, and surely to goodness he would arrive home soon: he had his mobile phone with him, if something had gone wrong he would certainly have telephoned her: she convinced herself that it had to be for the best if for once he had broken out of his normal everyday routine.

At seven o'clock she telephoned his mobile, it was switched off, and at ever decreasing intervals thereafter she tried again and again to make contact with him.

By eight o'clock she was really worried: the children had been put to bed without their daddy's goodnight kiss that meant so much to him; something had to be seriously wrong; at 8.22 pm she telephoned the local police station.

"Has he gone missing before?"

"Has there been some sort of argument?"

"Has he seemed worried about anything, or has he been behaving oddly in any way at all?"

Julia answered every question in the negative. The lady on the phone was very kind; she said she was sure that there would be an innocent explanation. There had been no reports of any serious road traffic accidents within the Peak District, or any reported incidents of violence or disorderly behaviour. Perhaps he had had too much to drink after all, and if he didn't normally drink that could have affected him badly; maybe he was now ashamed, and afraid to return home until he sobered up. Eight hours was a very short time for a person to be adjudged to be missing, the likelihood was that soon he would return safe and sound, although perhaps more than a little the worse for wear. The hours continued to crawl by.

CHAPTER THREE

The noise on the mini bus carrying twelve children from inner city Manchester to Miller's Dale was no louder than was to be expected, although had the coach time travelled and detoured to drive beneath the ancient walls of Jericho, the continued existence of these would have been put at serious risk. All was not harmony; whilst the majority of the eleven and twelve year olds were enjoying their first taste of the "great outdoors" there were several who found the youth hostel at which they were staying too Spartan for their tastes, and they also resented the embargoes that had been placed on the playing of computer games and using mobile phones.

"It's all fuckin shit!" complained a sullen eleven year old girl, defiantly ignoring demands to moderate her language, "I ain't jumpin off no fuckin bridge". The *street cred* that she gained for refusing to submit to the demands of her teachers successfully diverted attention away from her innate and very real fear of heights.

Wearing brightly coloured helmets, the noisy crocodile of kids followed their instructors along the old railway line, ignoring requests from the adults to help carry the abseiling equipment. Jack Bond had seen it all before, and had long since given up expecting any willing volunteers. After they had spent a couple of hours abseiling it would be different; for almost all of the children the excitement of the day would have finally overwhelmed them; that was his reward. On the way back to the bus they would be much more cooperative, and the chatter would be enthusiastic; it was always thus, and there was no reason why today should turn out to be any different; but Jack would soon be in for an unpleasant surprise.

The first thing he saw as he approached the old railway viaduct was the length of blue rope that sagged loosely between the two edges of the bridge. It was not entirely unknown for fool hardy individuals to risk abseiling without a permit, but it was unusual for ropes to be left in situ after the reckless adventure had ended. The stupidity of people prepared to risk life and limb on a whim, or as an act of bravado never failed to appal him; but very soon he realised that something far more disturbing than irresponsible abseiling had happened there last night. The length of rope was far too short, descending as it did no more than twenty feet below the pedestrian walk way before coming to an abrupt end; and alarmingly it was knotted into a noose. With a growing feeling of trepidation he pulled it back over the parapet. His naked eye did not spot the flakes of skin, or of body tissue, but the red staining on the top side of the cord could not be missed.

"Ugh! What's that down there in the water?" shouted one of the kids. Jack knew instinctively what the boy had seen.

"Take them all back as far as the old lime kiln now!" he ordered, "and don't let any of 'em come back here!" There was urgency in his voice that demanded instant and total compliance.

When everyone except him had withdrawn to a safe distance, Jack steeled himself to look over the side, knowing, but not wanting to see the sight that had caused the disgruntled child's reaction.

There was no doubt. The headless body of a man lay half in and half out of the rapidly flowing river. He remembered reading somewhere about the extraordinary care Albert Pierrepoint had taken to work out the precise length of drop that a condemned man or woman needed to make to ensure the instantaneous demise of the person concerned: too little and the victim would be garrotted; too much and the rope could sever the head from the body: he knew that that had happened here. Somewhere in the river, or on the bank, a human head was waiting to be found, unless it had been dragged away by foxes, or bowled along by the current to some distant reed bed or ox-bow lake. With shaking hands he dialled 999 on his mobile, the signal was weak, but it was just sufficient: at more or less the same time Jack was making his phone call, the postman was delivering a pretty postcard to the home of Mrs Julia Hammond.

CHAPTER FOUR

The on-call detective inspector is expected to be able to deal with whatever crime, catastrophe or cry for help Fate happens to toss in his direction during his stint on duty. The on-call detective inspector at the time of the discovery of Will Hammond's body was D.I. Mark Hobson. It isn't a requirement that the duty officer attend every sudden death that occurs on his watch. If a 90 year old lady passes quietly away in her sleep, with no obvious suspicious circumstances, a senior police officer is not needed at her home address; but with any violent death that is an entirely different matter. It doesn't matter if the violence is suspected to have been visited on the deceased by external forces, or inflicted upon himself by his own hand, to begin with the D.I. has to be there, and a headless corpse screams loudly for his prompt attendance. Within minutes of being notified of the discovery of the body Mark Hobson was on his way to the Cheedale viaduct.

He was not a local man. A single lifetime was sometimes not long enough to confer on a resident the status of belonging, and there were villages in the remoter bits of the Peak District where it took two, or even three generations to earn that particular description. It was barely three years since Mark had transferred from the

South Yorkshire to the Derbyshire Constabulary, his personal journey towards acceptance had hardly begun, but at least he was no longer considered to be a complete stranger which was a good beginning.

He wasn't universally liked; no decent policeman could ever expect to be: sections of disaffected youth detested his hard approach towards anti-social behaviour and the local drug dealers hated the vigour with which he pursued them; but to many of the old time criminals he was OK because they saw him as being straight. Amongst the victims of crime his compassion, commitment and common sense were widely acknowledged; to the men and women who worked with him he was recognised as being "a good copper."

The initial information that Mark had received was that this was probably a suicide. He wondered what it was that had driven a fellow human being to take his own life. As yet he knew nothing about the man who had died. Had he had some terrible argument with his wife or partner? He didn't know. Was he overburdened by debt or by worry? He couldn't yet say. Were there mental health or other medical difficulties? It was too early to speculate. Was there something in his past life he feared would be uncovered? It was premature even to begin to consider such a motive for his actions. Of one thing though, Mark was already sure. The possibility that his head would be ripped from his body, like the top of some deep rooted weed anchored in heavy ground could never have occurred to him. Had he understood that the people closest to him would have to cope with the psychologically damaging discovery that a person they cared deeply about had been literally torn apart by his own actions, and had he remembered that one of his loved ones would have to perform a truly distressing identification of the body, the manner of his entry into another world must surely have been modified to spare them just a little of the horror that this ill thought out decision to quit life in the way that he had, would inevitably heap upon them.

By the time Mark arrived at the old railway station, the entire western part of the car park had been cordoned off for the use of police and emergency vehicles only. No ramblers or dog walkers were being allowed to wander towards Wormhill or Miller's Dale, but it was still permitted to cross over the railway bridge and stride out towards Litton Mill or to climb the steep paths over the hills to Priestcliffe. Notices had been put up closing the footpaths nearest to Cheedale Bridge to public access, and the only people Mark saw as he walked the few hundred yards to the scene of the tragedy were police personnel. Just before the commencement of the viaduct itself he stopped by a set of limestone steps that lead from the track bed to the valley bottom below. They were worn and uneven. Mark thanked his lucky stars that it was not damp. Wet limestone he knew could be as slippery as ice, and the grips on his work day shoes would have been no match for that natural hazard.

The police pathologist Dr Gerald Grimshawe, universally known as "The Grim Reaper" to the officers of the Derbyshire Constabulary, had no such fears; the tweed suits and stout country brogues he habitually wore might look old fashioned in town, but they were entirely right for the wild outdoors and for this large, lugubrious man who was blessed with a brain the size of a minor planet. His initial examination of the body had already been completed.

"No mystery about this one Hobbo" he said, calling D.I. Hobson by his widely used nickname. "The silly bugger tried to hang himself, and managed to wrench off his own head in the process. I'll give you a full report when I've examined the body properly, but I can tell you now the daft sod meant business; he wasn't taking any chances; he tied his left hand to his belt, just to be sure he couldn't save himself.

"Can you rule out completely the possibility that he was set upon, trussed up like a chicken and chucked over the side by people who wanted his death to look like a suicide?" asked Mark. The Grim Reaper gave him a scornful stare.

"Don't you think that if he had been seized by a gang of assassins intent on hanging him that he would have struggled? So far as I can tell, from what I accept has been a fairly cursory examination to date, the dirt on the footpath hasn't been disturbed in any significant way. There is no evidence of ripped clothing or any finger bruising that I can see, and although there's no head, so I can't be absolutely certain until it's found, there is nothing as yet to suggest he was murdered. I know you police officers look for foul play under every stone, and you get very disappointed when there isn't a collar to be felt, but I tell you, this one is simple, he "did himself in" as Eliza Doolittle might have said, nobody to my mind has "done him wrong", but if I do come across any suspicious injuries, which I won't, I'll be sure to let you know." With that parting salvo, Doc Grimshawe turned his back on the Detective Inspector and grumpily climbed back to the footpath up above. He needed a pee and a cup of strong tea; the "Wriggly Tin" was now open, it could fulfil both those needs.

"I think the Doc might be right about this one Sir," said P.C. Seddon. "We've found a B.M.W. motor car in the car park that P.N.C's to a William Hammond; his wife reported him missing last night, and she was apparently very worried about him. We recovered this chap's wallet, there is a photo card driving licence and several cash cards all in that name; I think Mrs Hammond is going to be receiving some very bad news."

"I suppose they're still looking for the head" said Mark, keen to move onto safer ground.

"As you can see Sir, frogmen are searching the river as we speak. The Doc says that it could have bounced like one of Barnes-Wallis's bombs. They're confident they'll find it, but sadly they haven't had any joy yet."

"Let me know as soon as they do. My next job has to be to go and talk to his wife; God, how I hate being the bearer of bad news.

CHAPTER FIVE

"Oh my God it's awful! Why would he do such a terrible thing? There must be a mistake. Will loved me, I know that, and he worshipped the children, and we loved him so much! It's got to be a mistake! Tell me it isn't true! It can't be him! It can't be him! This is a nightmare, an appalling, dreadful, terrible nightmare!"

Mark Hobson shook his head. "I'm so sorry, so very sorry, but there is no doubt. Will's father has identified the remains. There is a birth mark on his right forearm, and Will's wallet was recovered from the dead man's pocket. His car was found abandoned in a car park a few hundred yards away from where the body was discovered, and sadly you have received a note. I wish I could say otherwise, but it wouldn't be true. I'm so dreadfully, dreadfully sorry."

The emotion that overwhelmed Julia was real: her whole body shook and her tears were unstoppable. Two things were immediately obvious to Hobson: Will Hammond had been loved by a beautiful caring woman; and secondly his death had come as a total shock. He would need to ask in depth questions about the marriage and about Will's business interests. Were there any financial or other problems? Had there been any rows or disagreements with anyone that Julia was aware of? Had Will ever talked about killing himself? Was he depressed or taking medication, or receiving any psychiatric counselling? And was there anything in his background that might give a clue as to why he had so tragically taken his own life? But all these questions would have to wait. Right now Julia needed somebody to comfort her and hold her tight; that person should have been Will, but he was the one person who would never, ever hug her again. Mark left Julia in the arms of her father, knowing that words were inadequate at this time, and apologising that he would have to return to talk to her at a later date. Children's toys had littered the living room floor and the house had been full of flowers and family photographs; Mark felt sure that Will had been happy there: why would a man with so much to lose, and apparently so much love to give, and to receive, throw it all away? It made no sense; there had to be a reason for this sad train of events; something must have been said or done to trigger the suicide of this prosperous, contented family man.

"There's not much I can tell you about him." Alan Nadin sipped his pint of Robinson's bitter and considered the question that Mark had asked him. Retirement suited Alan, although there were times when he longed to be back working with his former colleagues, and when he missed the excitement of a police career. There was not much the former detective sergeant didn't know about the town of Burrdale and its inhabitants, so his less than encouraging reply to Hobson's initial question didn't seem to offer the possibility of much enlightenment.

"Tell me what you do know," said Mark, "I've yet to speak to his wife in any detail, and understandably his parents are also too distraught to be of much help at present, but from what I've seen it looks as if he was a much loved husband, father and son, living in comfortable circumstances, without any obvious problems. Why such a man would want to kill himself, I don't have the foggiest idea!"

"Well, he's a local boy who's done well. His father was a gamekeeper on the Coverdale Estate. The family didn't have a lot of cash, but they appeared to be content enough, and when Will were a lad he were a pleasant enough kid. He played football with our Jamie. Will were a born natural, there were plenty of people predicting that he could make a career out of the sport; he lived and breathed the game, then all of a sudden he dropped it like a hot potato, and to the best of my knowledge he never pulled on a football strip, or kicked a football ever again."

"Do you have any idea what made him do that?"

"I haven't a flippin clue; it could have been simply that Man United got dumped out of the F.A. Cup by Watford, that were a shock result; I remember him telling our Jamie that it was his first away game and that Jerry Eggleton's dad had given him a brand new number ten shirt, which he'd worn every day for a week, but just two or three days after the match I was told that he'd ripped that shirt to shreds. He'd never struck me as being a mardy kid till then; but after that match his whole personality changed."

"In what way?"

"Well, he stopped hanging about with the other kids. From then on he just kept himself to himself, and he worked and worked at his school work and there's no doubt about it he did very well. And while I think on there's summat else. When Will were a happy kid he got into a few scrapes, same as all lads do. He got our Jamie drunk as a skunk when they were both just thirteen years old, and even though his dad walloped him for it, it didn't stop him swallowing the odd can of cider when he could get hold of it, but after that shirt episode he never touched another drop of drink. He changed from being a lad who were up for anything into a proper killjoy all in the course of a single week."

"What happened when he left school?"

"You'd have to ask his parents about that Mark. All I know is that he went to a red brick university somewhere and reputedly worked his socks off, and then he got a good job as a financial adviser with a firm in Manchester, and judging from that house he lived in he made a fair bit of money, although some of that may have been down to his first wife."

"So, he's been married twice then?"

"His first marriage only lasted three years. She were the daughter of a Manchester barrister. She left him because she said that she couldn't live with such a cold emotionless type of bloke. It was a huge shock when a few months later he turned up with a cracker like Julia."

"They seem to have been happy."

"So everybody says, and certainly he did unwind when he were with her. He started to come out of his shell a bit more and to take an interest in the things around him. I do know he started to give a lot of money to the Cricket Club and to the local hospice.

"Have there been any rumours circulating about him recently?"

"Not that I'm aware of. Since that cider drinking episode I've never heard anything bad about him."

"And what about friends, do you know who they might be?"

"He ain't got any Mark. He used to be friends with our Jamie and with Jerry Eggleton, and there were a couple more lads in that crowd who he knocked about with, but apart from Jamie they were all a bit out of his league, and it must be nigh on twenty years since he last spoke to any of them."

"How very strange! Anyway, enough of Will Hammond for the time being, let's talk about you, how are you keeping? You're looking pretty good; it seems like retirement is suiting you."

"It's not bad Mark, it's not bad, and I'm still pottering about doing the odd thing here and there, and I've got a few irons in the fire that I'm keeping warm."

"Is one of those irons Jackie Skinner Alan? Word is that you've been seeing a bit of her lately."

"You can't keep anything secret in this bloody town can you Mark? Yes I have been seeing a bit of Jackie, and to tell you the truth it feels good. She needs a man about the place with those three kids, and I've not had too many people to talk to since Liz passed away. The last seven years haven't actually been a bed of roses."

"Good on you Alan. You must come and have dinner with Helena and me, and bring Jackie with you, she's a nice girl and she deserves a decent fellow like you."

"We might well do that Mark, it sounds a nice idea, and talking about Helena, how is the delectable Mrs Hobson bearing up these days?"

"She's very well Alan, she's very well indeed, although she's got her hands full with our Christopher. I'll let you into a secret, she's pregnant again, and this time so far, without any of the problems there were last time, and of course there's no Paul Burgess waiting in the wings to cause trouble."

"That's great news!! Congratulations Mark, you've got an absolute treasure there, look after her well, you're probably the luckiest bloke in Burrdale by a country mile!"

CHAPTER SIX

"They still haven't found his head; God knows what condition it will be in when they eventually do! Judging by his wedding photographs he was a pretty good looking bloke too!"

"His poor wife must be devastated." Helena finished spooning the last morsels of food into Christopher's gaping mouth and wiped the sticky residue from around his lips. Christopher tried to pull his face away from the bib, and snorted a little to express his displeasure; he was, however generally speaking a happy soul and his moment of disgruntlement soon passed. Helena beamed a radiantly happy smile, life was good and she felt contented.

Mark watched his wife as she lifted the baby out of the high chair. Even after four years of marriage he never tired of looking at her, and there many times when he found it hard to believe that such a beautiful woman had agreed to marry him. To his mind, she scored the perfect 10. Her face, her eyes, her figure (when she wasn't pregnant) couldn't be faulted, and she was so intelligent and so gentle. Mark was sure that she had been the million dollar prize that miraculously he had somehow managed to win for himself. He looked at the pile of toys that Christopher was gleefully distributing all over the living room carpet, and at the flowers Helena had picked from the garden, which sat in a vase on the oak dresser, well out of reach of inquisitive fingers, and the thought struck him that in a much grander house than this, a little more than twenty four hours before, the atmosphere must have been quite similar to the one he now felt so happy in his own cottage.

"He had a lovely wife and two gorgeous little kids, why would he choose to throw everything away? I'm certain he thought the world of them, why would he kill himself in such a dreadfully brutal way; there isn't any sense in any of this love?"

"There has to be a reason, and I'm sure you'll find out what it is, and if its personal then it won't involve you will it? You'll only really be involved if there's been a crime won't you? And perhaps that's not very likely is it Mark?"

"Likelier than you may think Love. I can't remember off hand what percentage of suicides occur because the deceased had a finger in the till, but I do know that it's quite high, and I can't explain why, I've got a feeling about this case that worries me. I went to see Alan Nadin after I'd visited the widow, we had a pint together, and I hoped that he might be able to give me a bit of background information, but there wasn't much he could tell me except that when Will Hammond was a lad he got his boy Jamie drunk, and that he once ripped up a brand new football shirt in a fit of pique because his team lost. He's not been in any trouble since, and he's obviously done very well for himself. He didn't go to the pub; socially he was a bit of a recluse. Incidentally, nothing at all to do with what we've just been talking about do you remember me telling you about the wife of the man Paul Burgess shot dead, and how sorry I felt for her, well guess what! She's seeing Alan Nadin, and he seems pretty damned chuffed about the whole idea. I hope you don't mind, I've given them a non-specific invitation to come and have dinner with us sometime."

"No, that's fine sweetheart. Providing you give me sufficient notice when you fix a date I'd like that very much. It will be lovely to see Alan again, but it does mean that everybody will know that I'm expecting another baby."

"I'm afraid I told Alan this afternoon, I couldn't resist it. He's very, very pleased, and he won't gossip, but it's probably time we did tell our friends, it's sixteen weeks now and the lovely bump inside your tummy can't be kept hidden for much longer. You look so well my darling, so very different from the last time when you were pregnant with Christopher."

"Yes, I suppose I am, but let's not tempt fate, there's still an awfully long way to go yet."

At the self same time Helena was glancing down at her expanding tummy with a sense of satisfaction Sharon Farrington was being kicked by the unwanted life form rapidly maturing inside her womb. It shouldn't have happened, she didn't want to be pregnant, and she had definitely not planned to have a child so soon after her marriage, but the accident had happened and David had insisted that she keep it, probably under intolerable pressure from his over-interventionist mother. God knows how they would afford to live when there was another mouth to feed; farming was at an all time low, the future looked bleak, and it didn't help to say that things could have been worse and that mercifully they had escaped the scourge of Foot and Mouth disease that had so devastated many parts of the country. Yes, it was true that the clean Peak District air had not been polluted by the smell of diesel and the stench of burning flesh that had risen in plumes of black smoke from the mass funeral pyres seen in Cumbria and elsewhere, but Derbyshire farmers had not been immune to hardship. Normal movements of livestock had been prohibited and that had led to animals having to remain on the farms and to soaring feed bills, and just like the rest of the farming community the Farrington family had felt itself to be a family under siege. Even though that siege had now been lifted, its after effects continued to make life very difficult. The "Bed and Breakfast" business her domineering mother-in-law carried on remained depressingly subdued, utility bills were rocketing, and there had not been the big upturn in the price of lamb that had been forecast in some quarters. Pennies needed to be pinched in a vice like grip. The talk at the dinner table was always of mounting debt, and night after endless night comparisons were drawn between the state of affairs now, and the more prosperous times that had existed when her father-in-law was alive. "Jacob did this", "Jacob did that", "Jacob did the other"! There were times when Sharon wanted nothing more than to put her fingers in her ears and scream loudly to block out for a second the homilies to the Sacred Jacob's name. If she had known before she agreed to marry David that things would turn out like this she might have married Tommy Baxter instead, and traded David's rugged good looks for Tommy's thick glasses and secure salary as an I.T. consultant, but Sharon hadn't realised that even twenty years after his death in the year before she was born, Jacob Farrington would still be casting a long shadow. The dead control the living, well certainly they did in the family she had married into, and whilst Brenda, the arch disciple continued to rule the roost, and to be a conduit for Jacob's thoughts and opinions, it was inevitable that they would continue to do so.

CHAPTER SEVEN

I have become Lazarus. Death held my hand, but I broke free and now I am invincible. I have returned to walk down familiar streets and gaze upon once familiar faces, but there is no joy. I am not recognised, that much is good. With eyes firmly averted from the past they think only of the future, but they will learn that the past can still bite. I shall reveal myself, but not yet: why would a predator want to advertise his presence to his quarry? But oh the pickings look meagre now. When Timothy was alive, that fat and foolish man, he was a milch cow for me to suck on, and I drank deep. He paid me well, and he could well afford it. We had an understanding, a little of his money bought a lot of my silence, and the deal was a good one. It benefitted us both. He used my talents well, and many times, at his command I have leeched the life blood from his enemies, and he has rewarded me well for my self-indulgence. We all have secrets that are best left hidden. I have a snout for secrets, and sharp teeth and claws, and in the guise of trusted friend or confidante I can strip away the flesh of deceit to reveal the rotten organs hidden deep within. When men have panicked, I have laughed, and I have seen their hands shake and their lips grow pale, and I have taken a pride in my work. I am a dispenser of fear, but often on a sugar coated pill. The slag who conceived Jerry's child was greedy, she wanted a slice of the Eggleton cake, and would not be bought off with crumbs. Ten thousand pounds to terminate an unwanted accident of creation was not ungenerous, but she demanded more, and had she followed my advice more could have been obtained to the advantage of us both. When she decided to stand alone, she made a big mistake. The pursuer became the pursued, the exposer was herself laid bare. The miscarriage was an unkind joke played by God, the mental disintegration that brought her to her knees was a product of her own weakness; still Timothy was pleased and my reward was handsome. Now Timothy the gluttonous parasite is dead, and I shall not be remembered in his will. There will be no specific bequest for me, no annuity, no capital sum, no pension to protect me in old age, and I have been robbed of my inheritance. It's my own fault. I should have known that the overweight sack of offal's life hung by a thread, that sooner rather than later that frail pump imprisoned in a cavernous ribcage would explode under the extreme pressure of his wanton greed, but I did not think. Pole-axed by a massive heart attack, dead within seconds, there was nothing anyone could do. I was a careless fool, and now somebody has to pay the price for my stupidity.

I needed fresh carrion to gorge on; the Fat One's funeral seemed to be the place to look. What a show stopping theatrical performance it was; a shallow piece of frippery, in which cosmetic emotions made every cheek blush. With my hawk's eyes I gazed on all their faces. Nobody noticed me, their eyes were too full of crocodile tears to see; nobody that is except one, but he saw me so very clearly. Why was I invisible to everybody else but not to him? I think it was because he looked at me with the eyes of a boy and through them saw the boy I once was too. How he had changed! How prosperous he had become! I remembered the shabby child who stuck to us like a bluebottle on fly paper, and who we found it impossible to pull away from. He wanted all the things that Jerry had, he wanted to be just like us, but what right had he to expect to be our equal? He was desperate to be accepted, and in the end we tolerated him because I sensed that one day he might turn out to be useful. He became cocky then, and dared to overplay his hand, and we had to slap him down. How pathetically he pleaded to be allowed to make amends, and how willing was he then to sacrifice all his rough hewn scruples to achieve absolution! Thirty pieces of silver wrapped in a football shirt and a cup tie ticket, a reward for services to be rendered, and never was Judas more cheaply bought, yet even then he couldn't see. In Nature there is always a price to pay, and inevitably the magnitude of the sin will be uncovered. I thought the final realisation of his guilt would destroy him, and that he would drown in a raging sea of grief, but there in church he sat with the elite, and my snout sniffed riches. I sharpened my talons so that I could dig them deep into my quarry.

I should have guessed that at heart he would turn out to be a coward. He realised straight away that there would be no place to hide, and that like a bloodhound following a trail my pursuit of him would be remorseless. He had no stomach for the fight. He saved his trembling skin by ripping off his own head. Even in death he got it wrong! But once again I look starvation in the face, and the thought of that appals me.

But no game is lost until it's lost. I am used to set backs in my life and I will survive. I am blessed with a hunter's brain, and am not at all constrained by fetters of compassion. If I cannot threaten the guilty I will prey upon the innocent and the vulnerable and ultimately achieve a prosperous end. Many times my shoulders have been wet with salt tears, and I have dispensed re-assurance in tender loving measures, and thus I have been freely given that which otherwise I had planned to seize. The grieving widow makes a pleasant morsel, if devoured gently; the helpless child is a fine dessert if sweetened with a dash of pity. I choose my moments well and I have killed with kindness when the time was right. I have a vixen and her cubs to savage, and on the way a few more old scores to settle. The scent of death is still upon the wind. The smell overpowers me and is perfume to my soul. A new game commences, the hounds have been unleashed. There is no time to lose, and nowhere for my prey to find a safe hiding place.

CHAPTER EIGHT

"I know that when he went to that funeral he had no thought of killing himself. Oh, how I wish he hadn't gone; he'd be at home with me now if he'd stayed away, and I encouraged him to go! I thought he might meet an old friend. It's all my fault! I killed him! If I could turn the clock back I'd beg him on my knees not to go, but it's too late, it's too, too late! He's gone forever; he's never, ever coming home". Julia Hammond's body was in spasm, and but for the strong arms of her late husband's father, Mark Hobson felt she might have fallen to the floor. It was the second time in two days that he had witnessed her distress, and the sight was a moving one.

"I know it's difficult for you Mrs Hammond, and I know that there's nothing I can do or say which will bring you comfort, but we do have to try to find out why Will took his own life. If you're right in what you say, and I've no reason at all to doubt you, then something happened at that funeral to cause Will to do this terrible thing. We're getting a list of all the people who attended the service from the undertakers, and maybe that will give us some sort of clue, but can you tell me if there was anybody Will was hoping to meet, or if there was anybody he particularly wanted to avoid?"

Julia shook her head, she was making a desperate effort not to cry, and she clung to Will's father for support.

"Will never talked about his past life to me; it was a closed book. He always told me his life began when we met. Maybe Bob can help you. I would if I could, but I can't. I just can't! I only know that the man that I married was sweet and loving and gentle; I know nothing about the man he was before that." The tears burst through Julia's pathetically inadequate defences, and were uncontrollable.

"I'll tell you all about me son Inspector, but not just at this minute. Julia comes first, I can't leave her alone. Her Dad's had to go to a meeting, her Mum's on her way here, when she arrives then I'll talk to you, but I'm not leavin her by hersel, you can see that her heart's breakin: I ain't walkin away from her until she's got someone else to lean on."

The old man's jaw was solid rock, Mark knew that he could not be shifted and that he would be as good as his word, and he knew that he was right. Julia Hammond was so very fragile; he could not be the one to smash her into smithereens.

It took the best part of two hours for Charlotte Metcalfe to arrive: road works on the A6 at High Lane had caused a two mile traffic jam, and an elementary error at Disley, undoubtedly caused by anxiety, had further added to the delay. It was only when mother and daughter were in each other's arms that Bob Hammond felt able to detach himself from his daughter-in-law and speak to the detective inspector from the Derbyshire Constabulary. Before he felt up to answering questions, however, the former gamekeeper had a question on his mind that cried out for an answer.

"Is my son complete yet Inspector? Have your men found his head?" The words stuttered like an ice cold internal combustion engine; Mark shook his head,

"Not yet Mr Hammond but we're still looking." Bob Hammond groaned, he had spent a lifetime picking up the remains of vulpine murder, and the thought that his only son's face might have fed the rapacious appetite of foxes was more than he could bear; and even if the head had avoided the razor sharp teeth and snarling rage of the carnivore, by now maggots and flies would be stripping the skull of its last vestiges of humanity: his distress was all too obvious to Mark Hobson.

"We're doing everything we can. I promise you we will find Will. He will be a whole man when he's laid to rest, on that I give you my word."

Bob Hammond shrugged; a hopeless, fatalistic, and sceptical raising and dropping of his broad shoulders.

"Ask me whatever you want to know about my son Inspector, I'll tell you everything I can, "the truth, the whole truth and nothing but the truth", nothing can hurt him now can it Mr Hobson?"

"Well to begin at the beginning, what was Will like as a boy? Alan Nadin tells me that he was a happy go lucky kid who was exceptionally good at football; I also think he was best mates with Alan's lad Jamie."

"That he were Mr Hobson, and Alan's dead right, he were brilliant at soccer. He'd been in Derbyshire youth teams and caused quite a stir; scouts from Sheffield Wednesday were definitely sniffin around him; a few more weeks and I'm certain that they would have tried to sign him up as a junior at Hillsborough."

"But he didn't just live for football did he Bob? I'm told he was a normal high spirited lad who occasionally got into a few minor scrapes, I mean no more than any other red blooded lad, but he wasn't always an angel was he? Alan's told me about Will getting Jamie drunk on cider."

"What normal boy is Mr Hobson? What normal boy is? And when he stepped out of line he was punished for it, but he never caused me any real headaches."

"Then suddenly something strange happened to Will didn't it? He gave up playing football altogether, and he ripped up a brand new football shirt that he'd been given; do you know why he changed so completely and what it was that caused him to destroy the shirt?"

"I think a lot of things came together at the same time. He got in with a group of kids whose families were a lot better off than we were, and I think he started to resent the fact that we were poor. He was always mithering me to take him to watch Manchester United, and I couldn't afford to do that; I didn't have the time to go in any event. Then he got given this ticket by Jerry Eggleton's dad and he were over the moon. He talked non-stop about the match for over a week, and he kept telling me how much United were going to win by, and then Sod's law made 'em lose 2-0 and he were gutted, but there were more to it than that: I never did get to the bottom of it. I think that summat must have been said by Jerry or by one of his posh friends which hurt him very much. They dropped him, or he dropped them, I don't know which, but he tore up the football shirt that he'd worn to the game, and he never played in another football match. I think that maybe eventually I might have been able to talk him round, but that same week Jacob Farrington died: he were like an uncle to Will, and the shock of the accident really knocked him for six. And then that were it. He were never the same lad after that, and although he started to do much better with his schoolwork than he'd ever done before, the price he paid for success was loneliness and regret.

Then by some miracle he finally discovered Julia, and at least she was able to give him a few years of happiness."

"So you think it's likely that Jerry Eggleton, or one of his friends did or said something that wounded Will. I think that I will need to pay them a visit, can you tell me just who those lads were?"

"There were Jamie Nadin of course, he were a good lad and I don't blame him in any way, but the others I didn't really take to. Jerry Eggleton was a stuck up little prick, and Ralph Ambridge and Justin Barnes weren't much better. Ralph Ambridge is still knocking about somewhere, but Jerry's dead, of course, and I believe Justin Barnes is also dead. His dad were a marketing director for some sort of pharmaceutical company. I think the family emigrated to South Africa in the mid 1980's, and I believe Justin was killed in a car crash a couple of years later, the rumour was that he hit an elephant head on, but I really don't know if that's true or not. There were a couple more lads who I can't remember at all, but they were just like Jerry and Ralph. What happened to them, and where they ended up I ain't got a clue."

"And Will never mixed with any of them ever again after the football shirt incident?"

"Yes, except for Jamie Nadin, who he bumped into every now and again, but Jamie had left that group just before all this happened;

I think his dad had managed to show him what a shallow, selfish bunch they were: I wish I'd been able to do the same with Will."

"But Will did finally get the message didn't he? So what I can't understand is why, after all this time, did he go to Jerry Eggleton's father's funeral?"

"I don't know, maybe he thought he were cutting a final link with a part of the past he wanted to forget; he never said owt about it to me, so I could be entirely wrong, but to my mind it does sort of make sense."

"Just one more question Bob, and then I'll let you get back to Julia and her mum. You told me just now that Jacob Farrington died in some kind of accident, and that Will was very upset by this. What sort of accident was it? How exactly did Jacob Farrington die?

"It was a bit bizarre really. He slipped on rocks at Elmton Crags. Wet limestone's lethal as you know Mr Hobson, but why he were clambering up that hillside nobody knows. There were a theory that one of his sheep had got stuck, and that he'd climbed up to free it, but it weren't still trapped when they found his body. There were a big chunk of rock close to his head, his skull had been stove right in, he'd obviously crashed down on to it as he fell; his skull had splintered like an eggshell struck wi' a ten pound lump hammer."

CHAPTER NINE

"They've finally fished his head out of the river somewhere just outside Litton Mill; it had travelled a fair way down stream; it's barely recognisable as human: even his mum wouldn't know him, and you couldn't show it to anyone who loved him, they'd have nightmares for decades if you did do. There's no doubt that it's him though, D.N.A. conclusively proves that it is;" so spoke Detective Sergeant Peter Bennett as he explained the latest developments to Detective Inspector Mark Hobson.

"Some anglers spotted it close to the river bank. They apparently thought that it was an old football with its outer casing in shreds; that was until they had a closer look. It's not a pretty sight, as you can well imagine; when they saw what it really was one of the fishermen was so upset that he puked up in the river. Now that did excite the ducks and the fish, and so far as I'm concerned it means that locally caught rainbow trout is off the menu for at least the next couple of weeks."

"Poor Julia and poor Bob," said Mark, "if Will had known it would end like this then I'm bloody certain that he wouldn't have taken his life in the manner that he did."

"He obviously weren't thinking right Boss. Bakewell police have traced the shopkeeper who sold him the rope; it's not every day that a well dressed bloke in a suit and black tie walks into a shop to buy ten metres of thick cord."

"Is he sure that it was Will Hammond?"

"Absolutely no doubt: he recognised him from the photograph in the newspaper. He remembered him because he seemed very emotional, and he paid cash for the rope and the other bits and pieces that he bought, but he didn't wait to collect his change."

"Was he by himself?"

"He was definitely alone. The shopkeeper watched him as he walked to his car, he were parked on a double yellow line and the traffic warden had been prowling around. Luckily for Will he hadn't issued him with a parking ticket, so the shopkeeper saw him just get into his car and drive off. There were nobody with him then, and the man walking his dog at the old railway station says he was alone at Millers Dale a bit later on."

"What man is that Pete?"

"Some old geezer who lives in Tideswell. He takes his dog for a walk along the trail three or four times a week. He remembers seeing this big car pull up, and a smartly dressed bloke getting out. He thought it was odd, he hadn't got a dog with him you see, and when he saw him slip a coil of rope over his shoulder then he thought it was damned strange, and so the memory stuck."

"Was there anybody else about?"

"Not a soul, he weren't being followed if that's what you're thinking. I don't believe that there's a shadow of a doubt that he topped himself, and I don't think for a moment that he did it at the point of a gun."

"So why did the poor sod do it then? Have you had any joy from the undertakers yet?"

"Well they've given me a list of names that makes the London telephone directory look like a bleedin "Jane and Peter" book. The World and his wife were at that bloody wake: it amazes me that the Queen decided to give it a miss. Everybody who thought that they were anybody crammed themselves into that church; and for bloody what? Timothy Eggleton was a conceited overbearing twat, or at least he was in my book. He gave greedy fat bastards a bad name, and yet they were all there in their finery saying what a wonderful chap he was. You needed dark glasses not to be dazzled by the bling, and there was I thinking we're all progressive socialists now in Tony Blair's "Cool Britannia."

"You didn't like him very much did you Pete?"

"He was the fat slug who got my lad fired from his part time job because he didn't drop everything to serve him first and made him wait his proper turn. My son showed real character, and he got kicked in the teeth for doing so."

"Are there any names on the list that stand out?"

"Dozens and dozens, but there are one or two which I think you'll especially like."

"Try me," said Hobson, and settled back in his swivel chair to listen to his detective sergeant.

The list was longer than the detective inspector had anticipated. D.S. Bennett didn't include the Lord Lieutenant of Derbyshire, or the Chairman of the West Derbyshire Bench, although both had been present at the funeral. He didn't specifically mention the local M.P. or the leader of the Liberal Democrats on the County Council, because he thought it unlikely that such high profile figures were likely to have had any connection with William Hammond. He did mention the Assistant Chief Constable Ashley Prendacott, purely to have the pleasure of seeing his D.I. wince; the detective sergeant then warmed to his task.

"Try these for size," he said, and reeled of a catalogue of names that certainly did attract his D.I.'s attention.

"Roderick Mann and Nigel Shilton, didn't they both do time for tax evasion and insider trading?"

"They did two years apiece, and they're not the only ones who have dined out on porridge at Her Majesty's expense.

"Who else are you talking about?" asked Hobson, now hanging upon every word that D.S. Bennett had to say.

"I'm going back a fair while, but in the mid-eighties Tommy Cassidy served a stretch for attempted murder. Back in those days he owned a string of night clubs in Greater Manchester: most of 'em were dives; all sorts of dodgy things went on and, without doubt, Tommy was at the centre of most of 'em. He wasn't a man to mess with back then was Tommy Cassidy, but in fairness to him, I don't think that he's been in any sort of bother since he got out on licence."

"But we don't believe any of those three had any link with Will Hammond do we Pete? And at the moment we've no idea what connections they all had with Tim Eggleton. I'm sure there's a can of worms waiting to be opened, but as yet we haven't found a bloody tin opener."

"Give it time Gov, give it time. Sooner or later we will prise the lid off, and then I'll bet you a pound to a penny that we'll be overwhelmed by the stench of corruption."

"Who are the people at the funeral that we can directly link to Will Hammond?"

"Well Ralph Ambridge attended in his red Ferrari, and David Boswell and David Gladstone in their flash Porsches; all those lads were in Jerry Eggleton's gang according to Jamie Nadin, and three more annoying little shits you've never seen in your life. I've been in The Feathers when that clique has been holding forth and a more irritating collection of dickheads you'd be hard pushed to meet. Come the revolution they'll be half way up the guillotine steps before anyone has blinked an eyelid, and I'll be there with me knitting, just waiting to see the blade drop."

"I don't think your Mr Blair approves of revolutions, and in any event I believe that all those three have made generous donations to New Labour."

"Blair's head would be the first head to fall. What the hell does he know about working class values? I bet my dad spins in his grave every time Blair talks about protecting the poorest in society. He's more Thatcher than Thatcher, but at least with her you knew what you were getting."

"Yes, Comrade Bennett" laughed Mark, but until your proletarian uprising begins, can we concentrate on the job in hand. Are there any other people I should know about?"

"Well Jamie Nadin mentioned Charles Montgomery and Justin Barnes when I spoke to him, but they're both dead. Montgomery was a nasty piece of work, but I think he died from cancer three or four years ago, and Barnes was killed in a road traffic accident in South Africa, and apart from them he can't remember anyone else. It wasn't a constant group, people dropped in and out, and some were dumped when they had outlived their usefulness. Jamie Nadin left just before he was pushed, the same may have been true of Will Hammond, but it's equally possible that he was squeezed out. When we interview Ralph Ambridge we'll show him the list, and maybe if he's in a good mood, and we're sufficiently servile, he might point out one or two more names for us to concentrate on."

"I'm not holding my breath Pete, but even if he does we won't necessarily have a complete picture will we? Not everyone at the church will have filled in one of those undertakers cards, there will have been people there who won't show up on any list, and unless somebody just happens to mention seeing them we'll be none the wiser. It's a pity that they don't take pictures at funerals in the same way as they do at weddings."

CHAPTER TEN

The judgement of "The Grim Reaper" was not a final judgement, nor was it set in tablets of stone, but it was without doubt a well-considered and carefully thought out one. Doc Grimshawe's initial post mortem examination of Will Hammond's body had revealed few surprises. The serious injuries that he had discovered were entirely consistent with those to be expected if twelve and a half stone of muscle, blood, bone and fat, wrapped up in a thin layer of skin were to hurtle through the air at speed and land on rough and stony ground. The Home Office Pathologist had resisted the temptation to show off his awesome intelligence by calculating the exact velocity at which the headless corpse had struck the limestone boulders to within three decimal points, although had he been asked to work out this figure he could instantly have done so. Once, however he had been accused by a professor who he loathed of being "too clever by half", and that barb had pricked him; as a result, he sometimes tended to conceal a little of his brain power under a cloak of apparent indifference. There was also another reason why his preliminary conclusions were incomplete; when he was arriving at them a vital part of the puzzle had remained mislaid, and until that was found the whole picture couldn't be pieced together; but despite that fact the report he had created still contained a great deal of information.

The fractures that had occurred to both legs, and the severe spinal injury which would have paralysed the man had he been unfortunate to live, were the physical result of his body's bone-crunching impact with the solid rocks that formed the river bed, and although his body had ended up half in and half out of the River Wye, there had been no depth in the water to cushion the blow. There were minimal injuries to the arms and to the upper body, and nothing to suggest that the dead man had been seized or manhandled by others. His clothes were intact, there were no split seams or fabric tears consistent with a violent struggle, and there was no evidence of any puncture or stab wound that might indicate that a weapon had been used to end this man's life. The contents of his stomach indicated that he had eaten little in the hours before his death, and his blood when analysed showed no trace of alcohol or prohibited drugs. The victim was in good physical condition, with no sign of any degenerative illness, and without the untimely intervention of himself or another, he might have expected to live another fifty years. Despite all this certain knowledge, however, Dr Gerald Grimshawe, at the time he wrote this report, could not pronounce on the cause of death.

The later discovery of the severely lacerated head filled in the missing piece, and allowed "The Grim Reaper" to complete an addendum report. There was no silver bullet, or bullet of any other kind lodged in the man's brain, no ice pick or sharpened nail had been plunged into the back of his cranium, and there was absolutely nothing to suggest that the dead man had been the victim of a grisly execution. At last a conclusion could be drawn, and the conclusion Doctor Grimshawe arrived at was the one that he had confidently predicted making when still at the scene of the tragedy. William Hammond had died by his own hand, he had made a noose for his own neck, and he had hanged himself; in his distressed state of mind he had almost certainly never considered the possibility that the rope when it tightened would rip through his flesh like a chain saw, and in a fraction of a second sever his head from his rapidly plummeting body.

"There will have to be an inquest of course, but I think the outcome is going to be pretty predictable, and even though I want my investigation into the reasons why Will killed himself to continue, I don't think they'll be any need for his funeral to be put on hold to await the outcome. It's up to the coroner of course, but there's no law that says you have to wait for his adjudication, and I think it's probable that he will want to do everything he can to avoid causing further distress to the family."

"You're not just saying that, are you Mr Hobson? Both his mother and me, and most certainly Julia want him to be laid to rest quickly. We don't want the waiting to go on and on, it'd be more than any of us could bear if it did."

"Nothing's absolutely certain Bob, but there are only so many verdicts an inquest can come to. Will's death clearly wasn't an accident, it wasn't some fool hardy stunt that went horribly wrong, there's no question of somebody else's negligence, nor is there any suggestion that his death was caused by a piece of badly maintained equipment. Doctor Grimshawe is as certain as he can be that nobody else had a hand in his death. Nobody has alleged that he was with anybody in the last few hours of his life, and the final nail in the coffin is the postcard he sent to Julia. It might have been different if the Doc had found a cocktail of drink and drugs in his blood stream, we could then be trying to find out who it was who supplied him with the stuff, but Will was clean as a whistle, there's no trace of anything nasty inside his body. It may not be a comforting verdict to hear, but I don't think that there's any doubt that the verdict in Will's case will be one of suicide."

"But if there's still an on-going investigation into the circumstances surrounding his death won't that delay matters? I were talking to Alan Nadin, he and Jamie came round to our house last Thursday to offer their condolences. He weren't saying anything for definite, but he did tell us that in his experience it were unlikely that the body would be released for disposal until any criminal investigation were at an end."

"In cases where there's been a murder or manslaughter, then Alan's absolutely right. If somebody has been, or may be charged in the future with causing the death, then it's vital that the defence are able to have access to the body. Pathologists are only human, things can be missed, and they can and do disagree sometimes. Cases have been won and lost on a re-examination of the body, and successful challenges to the prosecution evidence; but that isn't likely to be the case here. Even if we eventually discover that somehow Will was driven to take his own life, and even if it transpired that he had been threatened or blackmailed, or in some other way placed under intolerable stress with malicious intent, it wouldn't change the way in which he actually died. I can't foresee any situation in which there could be a challenge as to the direct cause of his death.

"That's you talking as an experienced policeman Mr Hobson, but what if there's some weirdo on the jury who just wants to make mischief: could somebody like that bugger up the whole process? You read all sorts of strange stories in the papers. I just want to give Will a decent burial and to feel that he's resting in peace. If some dickhead wants to make himself feel important, could he sway the rest of the jury? I don't think neither my wife nor I could stand the strain, and what it'd do to Julia doesn't even bear thinking about."

"There won't be a jury Bob, It'll just be the coroner himself, and he won't want any unnecessary fuss. There'll be no histrionics, no playing to the gallery, no shouting, no emotional outbursts. The coroner's an experienced professional man; he knows exactly what to do. Don't worry about anything going wrong, because I promise you that nothing will."

"I'm not reet sure about that. I'm terrified that when I take the witness stand I'll get mesel into a tizzy, and then I'll forget some vital bit of evidence. As fer poor Julia, I can see her collapsing in floods of tears and not being able to get a single word out."

"You probably won't even be needed Bob. The coroner will probably allow your statement to be read. He's got complete control as to the evidence he calls. In all probability he'll just want to hear from Doctor Grimshawe, and maybe from the chap who actually found the body, and I imagine I'll have a speaking part, but that could well be it. There won't be any lawyers in wigs making opening statements or anything like that. The theatre in cases comes at a later stage if there's a trial, and as I've told you before, I'm as sure as I can possibly be that there won't be one in this particular case, at least not in respect of Will's sad death. You don't even have to be there if you don't want to be, but in some people's eyes it might look better if you, your wife and Julia were all present."

CHAPTER ELEVEN

The thing that Jackie Skinner remembered most about the first time she had gone out on a date with Alan Nadin was that he had made her laugh. She had laughed for the first time in years. The laugh had been totally unexpected, and the sound of it when it broke free had shocked her. Jackie Skinner didn't laugh, Jackie Skinner cried alone, Jackie Skinner coped with screaming children and a family waging civil war upon itself, Jackie Skinner didn't have anything to look forward to except a life of drudgery, and yet there she was, in a nice restaurant, with a man 18 years her senior, and he had made her laugh out loud.

It had taken her a very long time to agree to go out with Alan. Everything about this potential relationship was wrong. He was an ex-policeman, and her late husband had been no stranger to the police. Many were the times that he had verbally abused them, and sometimes in drink he had provoked and fought with them, and they had given as good as they got. Alan Nadin had once felled him with a single blow. Bob Leather had said it had been a fair fight, but that hadn't stopped Mike hating D.S. Nadin above all other police officers. He had regularly called him a "twat", and every four letter word under the sun, and some of his dislike had rubbed off on her because she accepted what he said; but when

Mike was murdered, Alan Nadin had shown genuine concern for her, and when she herself had been threatened and abused by Dick Norton, because he had wrongly believed that Mike had told her something which he thought could unmask the killer of his son, it had been Alan Nadin who had intervened to put a stop to Norton's harassment of her.

When her eldest boy was arrested for shoplifting, and she had had to go to the police station with him so that he could be reprimanded, her other two sons went too because she could find nobody who was willing to look after them while she was away. Because they were bored, they had started to run riot, and the desk sergeant had become increasingly annoyed at their behaviour, and just as it looked as if things were about to get totally out of hand, Alan Nadin had stepped in to calm the children down.

A short while after that, quite unexpectedly, he had visited her house. She had been ashamed of the mess, and of her untidy appearance, but he had been supportive, and had offered to try to get the older boys into local football teams to give them an interest, and maybe also into the cubs and scouts, as he had a friend who was in charge of the Burrdale Scout Group. Alan had said that he was sure ways could be found to take into account her financial circumstances when it came to the question of subscriptions.

Almost without notice his visits to the house had become more frequent, probably because he had now retired from the force and had time on his hands, and she found herself looking forward to them. Before she finally agreed to go out with him he had asked her to do so on quite a few occasions, and she had always turned him down because she thought if she did go her in-laws would see her as a traitor, and even though nothing had happened so far she had found herself already being shunned by them because of the association. On one occasion Bob Leather's evil bitch of a mother had sworn at her in public and called her a "fucking collaborator". Perversely it was this final attempt at discouragement which had given her the courage to say "Yes". An ember of self-respect had been re-kindled and that had made her feel good, even though now everybody seemed to be against her, everybody that was except Bob Leather, Mike's long time best friend.

"Alan Nadin's a decent enough bloke for a copper. He were always straight wi us. He could have busted Mike for that fight, lots of other coppers would have done, but he didn't. He were prepared to let the matter lie. So far as I know, he's never fitted anybody up; Mike could never see that, but Alan Nadin's not bent, it won't upset me if tha' starts going out wi' him."

Jackie broke off from her musing to look into the mirror. It struck her how much she had changed in a relatively short period of time. When she married Mike she had been a very young woman. Mike was the best looking boy in town, with a bit of a reputation, and he had already had a succession of short term affairs. When she told her mum and dad of her plans, they were aghast. They told her Mike was "arrogant" and "cocky" and "unreliable", but he was a boy who understood what turned women on, and she had been dazzled by him. Her stubborn refusal to reject him had led to many family rows.

The sense of reality that eventually strips the gloss from all marriages had come quite early in her case, but by then she was already pregnant, and she had made the conscious decision to stay the course and make the marriage work; and to a limited degree she had succeeded, but only by sacrificing some of her own personality along the way.

Mike had liked his women young, and a little bit tarty, so she had continued to dress in ways that appealed to him, even though her figure was no longer as slender as it once had been. She had dyed her hair and worn a large amount of makeup, because that was the look that attracted him, and everybody had assumed that she was merely a dumb blonde, who in the later years was rapidly approaching her "Best Before" date.

Alan Nadin hadn't type cast her. Alan had treated her as a woman, and over a period of time her true self had started to re-emerge. Money had been an acute problem since Mike's death, and what little of it that there was had been spent on the children, although they were too young to appreciate how great the effort was that was being made, and regularly complained how mean she was when she wouldn't buy them computer games or designer trainers. Out of necessity she had eaten less so the kids could eat more, and her figure had become slimmer as a result. The colour had been allowed to grow from her hair, and now her natural light brown hair had replaced the peroxide sunshine of the Incas; and yes there were some grey ones too. With a very limited income at her disposal she had started to shop in charity shops and she had found that if she shopped carefully good quality clothes could be discovered, sometimes nearly new, and a few nice skirts and blouses had found their way into her wardrobe; even though these clothes were second hand, they showed few signs of wear, and they looked remarkably good.

On the occasion of her first date with Alan she had worn a pale pink sweater and a mid-length, slightly flared white skirt, and the effect had been a pleasing one. She had worn the same clothes a few times since then, and had been embarrassed that she had nothing else but Alan had always complimented her on the way she looked. Tonight however she was able to make a change. She had saved up to buy a black spangley top and some well-cut trousers, which she knew would suit her well. Tonight she and

Alan were going to be the guests of Mark and Helena Hobson, and she wanted so very much to show them that she was worthy of him.

She picked up the clutch bag from the dressing table. She slipped her purse, comb and lipstick into it, and then she searched through the drawers in her bedside table to find something else.

The envelope containing the photographs had been buried under a pile of old bank statements and it took quite a while to find it, but she knew that it was there so she kept on looking until she did. She picked the Truprint wallet from the envelope, and extracted from that the two snapshots she was looking for.

The first photograph had been taken nearly twenty years before. Who had taken the picture she didn't know; she assumed it was one of Beejay's mates, but which one it was she couldn't now remember. The photograph showed a group of six young people. She was standing arm in arm with Bob Leather's little brother, who had been in her class at school. Her best friend Penny was draped all over Beejay, Beejay had a self-satisfied smirk on his face: looking at the photograph for the first time in almost two decades Jackie recalled how much she had disliked him: the chemistry had been all wrong, and even at the age of fifteen she had known intuitively that he was bad news for Penny. Soon after this picture had been taken she recalled that she had successfully steered her friend away from this particular infatuation. The other two youngsters on the photograph were Jamie Nadin and Laura Mycock. They were two or three years younger than the rest of the group: Jamie had a big grin on his face and looked full of mischief: it was because of that expression that she wanted to show Alan and his friends this photograph; she was sure it would make them smile, and could become a starting point for after dinner conversation.

The second photograph that she took out showed Jamie and Will Hammond sitting on a bench in the local park, apparently talking to Mike Skinner and a couple of his mates. Even from the fading print, it was clear that Mike was the "Lion King" and the other boys were just members of the pride. On the extreme edge of the shot stood Jerry Eggleton and Beejay, tolerated but not included, waiting for whatever crumbs of recognition that might be thrown to them. It must have been a painful experience for them not to be leaders; maybe it was to capture Beejay's pain that she had actually taken the picture. She wondered now how they had dealt with Will and Jamie after the big beast had left, she had no way of knowing, but she was sure that they would have been made to suffer for their sins. She stared hard at Beejay, in the photograph; he seemed a very dark figure. The first time she had set eyes on him she had wondered if, despite his fair hair, he was part Indian, and if Beejay was an exotic Tamil name, but later she had been told that this wasn't the case and that it was merely the use of two initials. Why a sixteen year old boy would choose to have a chief executive's style nickname she didn't know. If his Christian name had been Brian and his surname Jones it might have had some validity, but she knew for sure that that was not the case, so in her mind it made no sense whatsoever. She thought that this photograph might be of interest to Mark Hobson, she was prepared to let him keep the print if it was.

CHAPTER TWELVE

The word that was most frequently used to describe Mr Jeremy Mayweather was the word "gentleman", and sometimes the words "of the old school" were added to paint a more complete picture. The coroner for the High Peak was a well respected, well liked man, who had sat as coroner for almost twenty years. The senior partner in the legal firm of Mayweather, Birtles and Swift was a man of scrupulous politeness, and a model of propriety. He was fast approaching his sixty fourth year, small of stature, but with seemingly boundless energy, and when the times demanded it a white hot crusading zeal. In the summer sun his bald head shone like an illuminated pink snooker ball, and his glowing forehead and thick horn-rimmed spectacles could have made him a figure of fun, but Mr Mayweather was never, ever viewed in that light. There was something about his demeanour that demanded respect, and although he was always affable, and the soul of tact and consideration, there was Sheffield steel in his backbone and an unquenchable Yorkshire fire in his soul. Jeremy Mayweather stood up for the little man, often against the might of big business, and he was not afraid to take on Nationalised Industries or even multi-national corporations if the occasion required it. He was a man who strove to uncover the truth, no matter how uncomfortable that truth might be, and always to apportion blame only where it was properly due. In the course of two decades his inquests had exposed dangerously irresponsible work practices and totally unacceptable breaches of Health and Safety legislation, and some people who had thought themselves above the law had found themselves charged with serious offences, including offences of manslaughter, very largely on the basis of his carefully worded reports. He was not a man to be taken lightly was Mr Jeremy Bartholomew Alistair Mayweather, but despite his formidable reputation he was in reality a very kind and generous person.

Detective Inspector Mark Hobson had been told the date of the William Hammond inquest, he had also been informed that he would be required to give oral evidence, as would the Home Office Pathologist Dr Gerald Grimshawe, and that the witness who first found the body lying half in and half out of the River Wye, and the witness who later found the head might also have to answer some questions. None of the family would be needed, and the coroner was anticipating that the inquest was unlikely to last much more than half a day. Mark was pleased that Julia and Bob Hammond were not required, and pleased that as usual Mr Mayweather proposed to deal with proceedings with the minimum of fuss. Mr Mayweather had asked the police to make further enquiries to try to discover if anything had happened at Timothy Eggleton's funeral that might have particularly upset

Will, but so far nobody had been unearthed who claimed to have seen the slightest thing that could have distressed him. One witness had been found who noticed him leaving the church yard at a time when all the other mourners were still at the graveside: all she could tell the police was that he seemed to be in a tearing hurry, and that he was very definitely not with anyone else.

Whilst it is never wise to try to second guess an inquest verdict, everything still suggested to Mark Hobson that the only possible verdict that could be reached, on the available evidence in this case, was one of suicide; and that once that verdict had been reached, common sense, as well as established practice, dictated that his investigation should cease; but something was deeply wrong. If nothing had happened at the funeral that was the immediate cause of Will Hammond's sudden resolve to kill himself, then something must have occurred elsewhere, to unlock memories of events, he had witnessed, or been a part of, that he could not now bear to recall. So far as Mark Hobson knew, the only life changing moment in Will's life seemed to have happened at the same time as, or shortly after, a shock F.A. Cup result. Mark didn't believe that for a normal boy, (and Will Hammond seemed to have been a completely normal boy up until that time), the pain of seeing his favoured team lose would be anything other than transient: there had to be another reason for his dramatic change of character.

Bob Hammond had linked Will's unhappiness, in part at least, to the death of Jacob Farrington, and he had told him that Jacob's death had been a tragic accident, but that nobody really understood how that accident had happened. The coroner's verdict from twenty years ago would be a matter of record. The coroner at the Farrington inquest would have been Mr Mayweather's immediate predecessor. It was unfortunately a fact that that man had been seen by most people as a person who seldom rocked boats, and who rarely if ever had troubled himself to go beyond the obvious. There would be no police file now in existence, partly though the lapse of time, but mainly because Jacob's death was not recorded as a crime. The only contemporary source of information still available to Mark would be contained in the archive material of the Burrdale Advertiser.

Normally a detective inspector would not want to carry out the task of trawling through the back numbers of the local paper, this job was usually done by a detective constable, but Mark Hobson enjoyed looking back at times gone by, and it had been his examination of the same archive material that had led to the discovery of the identity of Virginia Brocklehurst's murderer only a very few years before. He had a little time on his hand, and in a strange way he felt personally involved in this case. Maybe that was because in so many ways Julia Hammond reminded him so much of his own wife, and he couldn't even begin to comprehend why her husband, who by every account clearly adored her, as he adored Helena, would ever choose to inflict so much pain upon her.

The business of wading through back copies of the local newspaper was now a relatively pleasant one. Gone were the days when some ageing custodian of the records opened up a musty smelling cellar to allow an unfortunate searcher to enter and begin the unenviable task of manoeuvring dusty folios of newsprint from tightly packed shelves onto some rickety table, to peer, quite often in vain, at the fading journals; the task barely illuminated by fading 40 watt bulbs.

Everything at "The Advertiser's" office was computerised. In an airy room overlooking the grounds of the local hospital, Mark sat at a modern desk in a comfortable padded chair. After having logged onto the computer, at the click of a mouse, he could call up any back number of the paper he wanted to examine. He started his task by calling up the edition of the newspaper that carried the account of Jacob Farrington's funeral.

The result of that step back into history was a little disappointing, but nevertheless it did provide Mark with a list of the mourners who had attended service; that list was only as accurate as the man from the undertakers had allowed it to be.

The obituary published the week previous to the funeral was much more enlightening, because that told the detective more about the man himself: his character, his life history, his hobbies, his achievements and his family were all touched upon although as Mark realised, this was not a wholly objective portrait of Jacob, and that people other than close friends and relatives might have very different opinions of him.

Above all else Jacob had been a sheep farmer. His pedigree Suffolk ewes had won many prizes at the Bakewell Agricultural Show, and twice in his life he had bred the best animal in the show. He was also an accomplished shepherd, with a string of victories in local, regional and even national sheepdog trials under his belt. He had been tipped as the next United Kingdom champion in the two dogs' event, but as the obituary lamented both of his dogs had died, apparently deliberately poisoned by a jealous rival. He was a leading member of the N.F.U., and a former president of the High Peak Young Farmers club, praised for his knowledge and common sense, but as Mark was to find out a little later he was also a strong willed man with a fierce temper.

Whilst searching under the name Jacob Farrington, Mark found other references to him in earlier editions of the paper, and some of these were far from complimentary. Three times in five years it appeared that Jacob had shot dogs that he claimed had been worrying his livestock. There had been angry letters in the paper from dog lovers accusing Jacob of being trigger happy and heartlessly cruel. The last of these incidents had occurred only a month before his death. A young Great Dane, valued by its owner at over two thousand pounds, had been shot dead. The police had been called to calm down the disturbance that had followed. The owner of the dog hadn't himself been present and it had been his son who had made all the noise, but later the owner himself had threatened to sue Jacob for killing it. Both at the scene of the shooting, and later when the man had threatened to sue, Jacob had responded with a string of profanities, and had also threatened to sue the owner of the dog for the loss of six sheep. The paper didn't say if either of these threats had been carried out. The owner of the dog, who was described by the paper as a local property developer and millionaire, was a certain Mr Timothy John Eggleton.

CHAPTER THIRTEEN

The letters of condolence had started to arrive in the post. Most were written on cards which had pictures of lilies or misty country scenes on them, and which carried the words *With Regret* or *In Deepest Sympathy*, but there were some that bore the tag line *Thinking of you at this sad time* and there were other variations on a similar theme. The senders of these cards, in a wide variety of inks and hand writings, all tried to articulate the same basic thoughts. There were *no words to express their sorrow*, that Julia should try to *remember only the good times*, that *Will wouldn't want his family to weep for him* and many other phrases of comparable sentiment. Undoubtedly, all those words were well meant, and the intent behind these messages of support was to give Julia strength, but at the moment they felt like just one more burden Will's death had piled onto her already overburdened shoulders. The thought that one day soon she would have to sit down and acknowledge them, right now seemed to be an impossibly daunting prospect.

There were letters as well as cards, more than Julia would have thought possible, but people who had known Will as a child now seemed eager to re-assure her that her husband had been a good man, even though few if any of them had spoken to him in nearly twenty years.

One such letter was simply signed Monty. The writer stated that for a short while he had once been a close friend to Will, but that they had fallen out over something, which he didn't explain, and that he now deeply regretted that fact. He accepted full blame for the disagreement, and claimed that he wished with all his heart that things had worked out differently. The letter was full of sadness, and Monty revealed that he had been on a painful voyage of self-discovery. He said that he had been very ill for a very long time, and that that illness had caused him to re-examine his whole life, and to look hard at the choices he had made along the way. He confessed that he now realised that Will had been used and taken advantage of, and that his own treatment of him had been deplorable. Now he said he was racked by guilt, and that he wanted to try to make atonement and to set the record straight. Will *had never wanted to harm anybody*, he was *a good boy at heart*, who despite everything had turned into a *decent man* and in the letter Monty asked to be allowed to visit Julia after the funeral to seek her forgiveness for his past sins. There was no address on the letter. Monty said he realised that Julia might simply wish to throw it away, and if she did so then he would entirely understand. He did say that he would be at Will's funeral, and that if there was an appropriate time he would introduce himself to her. The reason he said he had not put a contact address upon the letter was that he had no idea at the moment where he would be from one day to the next. He swore that he didn't want to cause any distress and said that if she decided she didn't want to speak to him he would go away immediately, and he assured her if that was her wish, thereafter he would never bother her again.

Julia read and re-read the words that had been written. This was a disturbing letter, shrouded in mystery, but instinctively Julia felt, that in some strange way this unknown supplicant might have her best interests at heart.

The letter from the lady who was the manager of the local hospice contained no mystery. It was a straight forward testament to Will's generosity and kindness, but this was a letter that made Julia cry.

"Dear Mrs Hammond", it said, "I'm so dreadfully sorry to hear about your sad loss and the terrible circumstances of William's death. Your husband was a kind and caring man. I don't think that in the twenty five years I have cared for the sick, I have ever met a person who did so much for charity and who wanted so little recognition. As I know you are only too well aware Will was an extremely generous man, both with money and with time. Over the last few years we have had some very lengthy discussions about the needs of the hospice and the way ahead, but not once did he ever even glance at his wristwatch or seek to push the meeting to a close until everything had been properly dealt with. I think Will at heart was a shy man, and certainly he was never domineering, argumentative or unpleasant, but he was absolutely rock solid in the support that he gave to us. There was never an occasion when he let us down, nor did he ever make a promise that he didn't keep. He was so courteous and so charming; it breaks all our hearts to think that we will never see him again.

Many people who stay here have only weeks, or even days to live, and of course some are afraid and many are in pain. Too many people are frightened of being with the dying, and I suppose that that is understandable, but if you are lonely and scared you need company. On every occasion Will visited us he made time for the patients, and he always seemed to know exactly what to say to put them at ease.

We all loved him, and his passing has left a hole in our world, but our loss can't compare to your sad loss. If there is any comfort to be found, please take comfort in this. Will was a good, good man, and all our lives have been enriched forever by knowing him.

Yours with heartfelt sympathy

Susan Moorland

Manager   St Catherine's Hospice.

The final envelope that Julia picked up was different from all the rest. It was smaller than most of the others, and it was edged in black to signify mourning. It looked old fashioned, as if it had come from a different era of time, and for reasons Julia couldn't explain she felt threatened by it. Her hand shook as she slit open the tightly sealed envelope and extracted a small plain white postcard which was also edged in unforgiving Old Testament black. On one side of the card what appeared to a biblical text was printed in bold type.

"The Lord thy God is a Jealous God. The sins of the father will be visited upon the children, even unto the third and fourth generation."

This card was not signed. It seemed to embody an apocalyptic threat to Julia and to her family. When she read these uncaring words, for the second time in the space of a few minutes Julia wept.

CHAPTER FOURTEEN

Helena believed that simple food cooked well was the key to a successful dinner party. Both Mark and Alan had man sized appetites. Detective Superintendent Tim Gratton had told her once that the average copper seldom looked beyond steak and ale pie, washed down with a pint of lager, and that anyone offering a working bobby a small portion of highly priced food served on a square platter and garnished with a miniscule amount of green salad in the cause of haute cuisine would probably find himself arrested for attempting to obtain cash by deception because what he was supplying could not properly be classified as real food!

Not wishing to spend a night in the cells Helena had chosen to start the meal with a thick homemade tomato and basil soup, and had followed that with a venison casserole, slow cooked in red wine, served with dauphinois potatoes and a selection of fresh vegetables. The main course had in turn been followed by "Fruits of the Forest summer pancakes and fresh Jersey cream, and two bottles of an excellent Cabinet Shiraz had been drunk. Alan and Jackie had arrived by taxi so driving wasn't an issue and Mark and Alan had shared a bottle and a half of the wine between them, with Jackie having just two glasses and Helena only the one because she was pregnant and would not drink more. The meal had been briefly interrupted once when Christopher, who had been disturbed by a burst of sudden laughter, woke up with a start, and Helena had had to respond to his urgent demands for "Mummy", but he had settled back to sleep almost immediately and there had been no further problem. The whole evening had been very relaxed, and Jackie had felt herself included and amongst friends. Mark and Helena had been attentive hosts, and the conversation at the dinner table had been free flowing and light hearted. It was as they sat drinking coffee that more serious matters began to be discussed.

"Do you know Jackie" said Mark, "I was just remembering the last time you and I had a long conversation. It was the day after Mike was murdered. You came to the police station with a biscuit tin crammed full with old photographs and letters. I thought you were so brave, and when you left the nick with those three little boys of yours you all looked so lost and scared that I could have wept for you. It seemed so bloody unfair that you had to suffer. I remember coming home and telling Helena how much I thought life stank for some people, and to see you now with Alan, looking so well, and dare I say it so happy, it's as if one of my most disturbing mental pictures has finally been deleted from my brain: I'm so very, very pleased."

"They were bad times Mark and for a long while afterwards things just got worse and worse, then Alan started to look out for me, and everything changed for the better. I know I'm a totally different woman now to the woman I was then."

"I've not really done anything Mark, it's all down to Jackie herself, she'd have got there without any help from me, all I've maybe done is to speed up the process a bit, and if I've given her a bit of joy along the way, it's nowt to the joy that she's giving me."

"Well, one thing's for certain Alan, I've never seen you looking better, you look like a cat that's got the cream, and long may it continue."

Mark's far from original simile reminded Jackie of the photographs that she had hidden away in her bag. Because talk had been so easy, and there had been no awkward pauses the plan that she had had to use these two pictures to stimulate conversation had been entirely forgotten, but now it seemed the time was right to produce them. The father's expression had almost exactly mirrored the son's contented smile of twenty years before. People so often said "Like father, like son", this was a case of "Like son, like father," and the similarity was uncanny. She reached into her bag and pulled out the two snapshots.

"I brought these two photographs with me," she said, "because I thought you might find them interesting. The first one in particular might amuse you, and it's not just me in a ridiculously short skirt and a silly hairstyle that's worth a laugh, just look at the expression on Jamie's face, isn't that exactly the same expression that was on your face a few seconds ago?" and she handed the colour print to Alan to look at.

Alan took the photograph, looked at it carefully, grinned and handed the picture to Helena who did likewise and then passed it on to Mark. It was true; Jamie looked just like his dad, full of impish good humour and Jackie looked like a bright vivacious teenager, there was nothing comical about her at all.

"Who else is in the picture?" asked Mark. "I recognise you of course, and Jamie is unmistakable, but who are the other people shown?"

"The boy next to me is Tony Leather, Bob Leather's younger brother; we were in the same class at school and I had a bit of a crush on him at the time. The girl standing next to me is my best friend Penny Farrington and the lad crushing her in a bear hug and drooling all over her is a lad we called Beejay. I never knew his proper name; he was one of Jerry Eggleton's posh friends. To tell the truth, I never liked him. I thought he was slimy and two faced, and I knew he could be very cruel. I saw him stamp on a big fat toad once, just for a laugh, and I thought what a sadistic bastard you are, but he could look so vulnerable when he turned on the charm: butter wouldn't melt in his mouth, and middle aged women like my mum, always wanted to mother him when he looked like that. Penny thought he was wonderful. I told her he was no good, and we almost fell out big time, but in the end I convinced her to have nothing at all to do with him. I suppose I should feel guilty because I lied to her. I told her he was seeing somebody else when he wasn't, but she believed me and she dumped him. Just to make sure I *accidently* let it slip in front of her dad that she was seeing him. Jacob was no fool, he could see right through Beejay. He went ballistic. He warned him off Penny in no uncertain terms. I know I was sneaky, and I did feel pretty bad afterwards, but I just knew he'd hurt her if she stuck with him. I'm not proud of what I did, but I do think I saved Penny a great deal of pain.

The little girl with Jamie is Laura Mycock, she still lives in Burrdale and I occasionally see her knocking about town. She married Gareth Swain of "Gareth's Taxis" and she's got a daughter the same age of my Andy. She's in his class at school, but they don't play together. She's a girl, she doesn't like football, she tells the teacher when he's naughty and so he doesn't have anything to do with her."

"Typical little lad, eh Jackie? I was just the same when I was seven. I don't want to turn this evening into a cross examination, Helena will kill me if I do, but I don't suppose you know what happened to Beejay do you? At the moment I'm very interested in any of Jerry Eggleton's mates who might have had it in for Will

Hammond when he was a boy, and this Beejay sounds like the sort that could have caused some real trouble."

"I'm sorry I haven't a clue Mark. Somebody told me his dad went to work in the east end of London, which I always thought was the slummy bit, so it seemed to me to be an odd place to go. All I know for sure is that this happened shortly after Beejay's bust up with Penny's dad and that after he left he never set foot in this town again. I've got another photograph of him here, which might be a slightly better picture than the one I've just shown you; you're welcome to hang onto it if you think it's any use."

Mark took the second picture and studied it. "I will keep it Jackie if you don't mind," he said, "It may help me with my investigation. Do you know it's a funny thing how many of Jerry Eggleton's little gang have died or emigrated or moved away or ended up in prison. The rate of attrition is much greater than that which I would have expected to see amongst a group of apparently fit and healthy young men. There was something rotten at the core of that little clique, I'd stake my life on it, and I think in the end Will Hammond was a victim of that festering, systemic badness."

CHAPTER FIFTEEN

"I've got a guessing game for you Gov!" Detective Sergeant Peter Bennett was in an annoyingly cheerful mood; it made quite a change from his normal cynical acerbic self; and as such it was pretty scary.

Detective Inspector Mark Hobson was not in a cheery mood, the late night conversation and the extra glass of wine that had been so enjoyable a few hours ago now conspired to make him feel jaded and lethargic. He wasn't hung over, he had stopped drinking to excess a long time ago, but he was tired and quite definitely a few cuts away from being top notch. He was, however a long way from feeling the intense irritation that he had used to feel when he was invited to *have a nice day* by some wide mouthed, white toothed smiling bimbo the morning after a heavy drinking session when all he wanted was a cup of steaming black coffee. Insincerity was a cardinal sin, and many times Mark had thought that it merited nothing less than a smack across the chops with a blunt implement: D.S. Bennett's uncustomary joviality fell short of deserving such extreme punishment.

"I don't like guessing games Pete; in fact, I fucking hate 'em. Why don't you give me a break and go and find somebody else to annoy?"

"You'll like this one Gov, I guarantee it," and without pausing to allow his D.I. time to protest, the D.S. launched straight into his theme.

"This is your starter for ten," he said. "Can you tell me the name of the dickhead who sat on his fat arse and did absolutely nothing for most of his over long life, and yet still left an estate valued at well over seventy five million pounds for his good for nothing idle son to inherit, only of course the arrogant little sod happened to pre-decease his dad?"

"Was Tim Eggleton really that rich Pete? I knew he was loaded, but I had no idea at all that he was as wealthy as that!"

"He could have been worth a lot more than that; rumour has it that he has cash stashed away in a number of Swiss bank accounts. The figures I've been able to conjure up all come out of public documents and freely accessible websites. Anyway, let's proceed to question two. Whose great-grandfather married the only daughter of a South African diamond merchant less than six months before the Married Women's Property Act of 1881 came into effect. All her property became his, and it may help you to know that we're talking mega bucks in today's money. If the poor cow had waited a few weeks she would have kept control of the lot. Apparently she was no oil painting, which may help to explain her ill-advised haste in getting hitched. Two years later she was dead, in what might best be described as "suspicious circumstances." Three months after her very convenient death, her husband married his long time mistress: now by all accounts she was a Rubens oil painting with tits the size of rugby footballs and an appetite for sex that can politely described as insatiable!"

"We're talking Tim Eggleton again aren't we Pete?"

"Two out of two, I told you you'd like this game. Incidentally, his great grandfather was also called Timothy Eggleton. What's in a name, eh Gov? A turd by any other name would smell as rank! Now let's see how you get on with question three. Who in the past ten years has been investigated twice by the Serious Fraud Office, and on both occasions has slipped through their net like a Vaseline coated eel"

"I'm guessing that must be Timothy Eggleton again Pete."

"Three out of three, give that man a coconut! Yes, you've hit the nail right on the head. In 1993 the fat prick was arrested on suspicion of involvement in a massive property re-development scam. I don't know all the ins and outs of it but the S.F.O. believed that it involved making illegal payments to council officials and members of the planning committees in several London boroughs and that the anticipated profits to the developers would have been astronomic. It didn't realise its full potential because it was discovered. There were charges, and several people got sent down, but try as they might the S.F.O. couldn't lay a finger on Eggleton, and so the greedy bastard continued to live the life of Riley, while many honest businessmen, who played by the rules were later wiped out in the financial meltdown that followed "Black Wednesday." The other occasion they thought they had him was a big Insider Trading investigation. Lots of people fell foul of that; Nigel Shilton and Roderick Mann amongst them, and they both did time, but Eggleton almost certainly paid them a lot of money to keep their mouths shut about him, so once again he couldn't be tied to anything. So the fattest of fat cats continued to flaunt his wealth over the rest of us and to treat ordinary blokes like you and me with utter contempt. Anyway, from the sublime to the ridiculous! If Timothy Eggleton is one of the most overfed felines in history, can you tell me who it was who sometimes acted as if he was as poor as a church mouse?

"I presume that's Eggleton again Pete, but this time I can't begin to imagine exactly what it is you're suggesting he did."

"Four out of four, you're on a roll aren't you? There were times when Eggleton glorified in being the big show off. He once tipped a teenage waitress with a fifty pound note, just to impress the people he was with, one of whom happened to be your friend, the Assistant Chief Constable! It caused the girl no end of problems because her father simply didn't believe that she had been given so much money with no strings attached. He made her give the money back the next day, and the tight fisted sod nearly snatched the note out of her hand, so glad was he to get the cash back; he never even thought about giving her a lesser amount instead. I know all this because the girl is my niece, but that's not what I'm on about at the moment. In a different restaurant, when he was dining alone, he twice left 10p tips under a plate when he had just spent eighty pounds on a meal for himself; still meanness isn't a crime for us to investigate, so let's move on. Who do you think acquired the well earned reputation for being the most litigious man in Derbyshire if not in the whole of the north of England?"

"The late Mr Timothy Eggleton would be my answer to that one Detective Sergeant Bennett."

"And you would be right Detective Inspector Hobson. My my! There's absolutely nothing getting past you today! Yes Gov, Eggleton was a man who was quick to take offence, and he had the money to employ a whole army of lawyers to put his case for him. I don't think that there was one of his neighbours who he didn't fall out with; certainly none of the local farmers were spared his wrath. He sued Jacob Farrington three times, once for shooting his dog, although that action folded when Jacob subsequently died, once for allegedly damaging a fence which it turned out he had illegally erected across Jacob's right of way, and once for common assault because Jacob shook his fist at him and threatened to rip his head from his body with his bare hands. I can well imagine that Jacob did that, he could be hot headed and stubborn when he chose to be, but the C.P.S. quite rightly ruled that it wasn't in the public interest to prosecute, and when he took out a private prosecution that was thrown out by the judge. Now do you fancy your luck with two final questions?" Hobson nodded his head, he was learning a lot about D.S. Bennett's hated millionaire, and the information was intriguing.

"Question six and I should warn you that this one is a toughie! Who crashed his car whilst drunk into a little Vauxhall Corsa which was being driven by a student from Sheffield University, and then fled the scene leaving her trapped behind the steering wheel?"

"Did Timothy Eggleton actually do that? I'm beginning to understand why you've got such contempt for the man!"

"Nee Nah! I'm afraid you've got that one wrong Gov and the star prize was so nearly within your grasp. The correct answer to that question was Jeremy Sebastian Eggleton; it's such a pity, and you were within a hair's breadth of getting the jackpot too! Do you want to try your luck at one more question to see if you can get a consolation prize?"

"Fire away Pete, fire away; I might as well be hung for a sheep as for a bleeding lamb."

"Ok then. For your final question this round can you tell me who reputedly bought off the girl injured in the accident with a substantial wad of cash, and likewise *persuaded* the two eye witnesses at the scene to say that they both had been looking the other way at the precise moment of the impact and hence couldn't say who was at fault?"

"Would that happen to be Timothy Eggleton Peter? You've already told me that he has bought people's silences before, it would seem to be entirely in character for him to do something like that."

"Bingo! You've hit the nail on the head. Now you've seen what an arsehole the man was, I'll go and make us both a mug of tea, which can be your consolation prize for almost getting everything right."

CHAPTER SIXTEEN

Before I was Lazarus I was Janus, and since death did not claim me I am Janus still. I stand at the threshold of new beginnings and final endings. I am the key to the future and the custodian of the past. I guard the gateway to your soul. One day, if your unhappy fate decrees it, you may see the smile upon my face, but beware the face that is turned away from you, in that face is vengeance and retribution.

You will call me crazy; you will say I am deranged; you will not begin to understand what made me or who I have become. You are enslaved by the present and neglectful of the lessons of history. You do not read, or if you do, you read comic book newspapers or tacky pulp fiction. I read all the time, because I am so often alone. I read history and classical literature. The past is real to me, the myths and legends of ancient Greece and Rome are not forgotten stories, but they are totally unknown to you; the Bible, a book which men have died trying to protect or fighting to suppress is just a rotting tome so far as you're concerned; irrelevant to the way you live your pathetic little lives. My grandfather buried a bible once, a big bible, big as a small suitcase, with a metal clasp and with painted pictures of angels and of demons. The spine was broken through decades of continuous use, and pages had separated from their binding and become frayed and crumpled, yet he couldn't bring himself to burn it. He laid it to rest in a little grave, as he might have lain to rest a stillborn child, and thus he returned the word of God to God. Burn a bible now, who gives a damn? Incinerate ten thousand bibles and feel the chill of apathy it creates. Burn the Koran and unleash the furies of Hell. Once I saw a man, not a young man, killed by a mob, beaten and then burned alive, a car tyre forced tight over his shoulders and arms so he couldn't move and set alight, because the mob believed that he had defiled the sacred texts of Islam. He screamed his innocence, no one believed him, and he was sent on his fiery way to meet the Devil. I believed him. He died, not because he had sinned against his God, but because he had sinned against me. The power of the spoken word when crafted into a well honed lie is the most destructive force on earth. A nation believed a mad man's words once, and he exploited deep seated prejudices with passion and with venom, and six million Jews died. Never doubt that what is said about you makes or breaks your life.

Lies are my stock in trade! I am their creator! I nurture them and I watch them grow, but to understand lies you must first know truth. I knew truth once, a long, long time ago, when I was too young to realise that there was anything else. I thought she was true; the few photographs that survived his rage seemed to show that she loved me. A child in his mother's arms, wanted and protected, knowing nothing of the savage undercurrents that had already wrecked a marriage. I remember her fragrance and her smile, and I think I remember gentleness too. Her father, a fading a memory almost before I could speak was said to have been a good man, a follower of Christ, a lay preacher at a village church: it was he who interred the words of his Saviour rather than commit them to a funeral pyre. He taught her God was good and she believed him, and for a little while before she went away, and when I was just old enough to comprehend she made me say a prayer to Jesus every night. "Gentle Jesus, meek and mild, look upon a little child, pity my simplicity, suffer me to come to the". My grandfather would have approved. No doubt his eyes would have misted over at such Victorian sentimentality, I cringe even after all this time at the very thought of such a pointless incantation.

One morning without warning she walked out of our house, never to return, leaving me alone with my father. I have blotted out everything that happened on that day, but my mind refuses to allow me the luxury of a vacuum, and so ill formed imagined recollections have often laid siege to my sanity. What is true? What is false? I can no longer tell the difference between reality and invention; maybe that's why I have become the person who I am. For a long time I convinced myself that she had tried to take me with her, but he had snatched me from her arms, beating her with his fists and throwing her bodily from the house. I thought, in so far as I was capable of rational thought, that one day she would return to fetch me, but she never did. Years later I saw a picture of her in the paper with a man. I learnt then that she had abandoned me to stand by his side. Nothing had been real except my pain and the tears that I had cried that dreadful day. I swore to myself that I would never cry again, and I never did except on just one more occasion. My mother, the "Whore of Babylon," the "harlot," the "prostitute," the "slut" insults that my father had spat out whenever he mentioned her name had been justly christened by him, and I hated her with every fibre of my being. I hated him too, even though he had been right about her, and I knew full well he hated me; maybe because I looked so much like her. I blamed him for driving her into another man's bed. I'm sure that there were many times when he wanted to disown me, but he knew that to keep me gave her pain. He kept a little boy in misery just to spite his ex-wife; but for that fact I think he would have liked to drown me, in the way that farmers drown feral kittens, tied in a sack and thrown into a water trough; but I was the living proof that he had been wronged and that an unnatural wife and mother had left him to bring up an infant son alone. He kept me: that was my misfortune and his burden, a father and son tied together by bonds of loathing and unable to break free, but break free I did and my words masterminded my escape.

He met a woman, a rich American woman, with a mouth the size of the Grand Canyon whose husband had died after he cleverly piloted his private jet into the side of a mountain. The week before the accident, he had been described by the New York Times as a "high flyer." His tragedy was that he didn't fly high enough, which I thought was really funny. He had money though, he left her loaded, pampered, over-protected and overdressed; who needs five full length mink coats and eight fur stoles? My pathetic, deluded father was dazzled by her, and this mindless Doris Day look alike inexplicably took a fancy to him. She had one son, a tall well scrubbed all-American boy, every American's mom's dream, but decidedly lacking in grey cells. His mother "Gillyanne" with a "G" thought he was wonderful, and dreamed that one day he would become an astronaut or a brain surgeon; a tree surgeon would have been a better bet, except "Junior" was terrified of heights and had all the dexterity of a ham fisted blacksmith. I only actually met him twice: (I wasn't thought fit to breathe the same air as him) and so far as I'm concerned that was two times too many. At all other times he was away in the U.S.A. at one of the best schools Uncle Sam could provide. The first time was at the wedding, I was ten years old. I was so well behaved it was sickening, and just for part of that day my step-mother thought I was "cute." She stopped thinking I was "cute" when I got bored with the vomit making chocolate box production and contrived to get disgustingly and disruptively pissed. (A ten year old puking up on a bridesmaid's dress is apparently not a welcome sight at a wedding, certainly if the bride aspires to have that wedding featured in Hello magazine.)

The second time I saw him was for just a few minutes before "Calamity Jane, Desperate Dad and Einstein" set off for a six week holiday in the Far East. He had flown in from America a few hours before prior to setting out on his long summer vacation. Luxury hotels, five star restaurants, first class travel the order of the day for everyone except me. I resented the fact that "Dumbo" got everything he fucking wanted, and I got fuck all, but at the same time I was glad that they were out of my sight. Also, it isn't absolutely true that I got nothing. When I was sent into exile while they were away it was always here to darkest Derbyshire. I was given money then; it meant that my father's cousin was spared the burden of entertaining me. I could go to hell in a shit wagon so far as he was concerned, I had enough cash to do what I wanted, what more did I need of anybody or anything else?"

Every tedious July and August was the same, and many of the other school holidays were too. I spent seven or eight weeks in this boring backwater, with nothing to do except pick the occasional fight with some moronic in-bred: and the only bit of pleasure I had to begin with, was the pleasure I had in winning. One day Jerry Eggleton saw me smash some yokel's smelly kid to a pulp: you don't piss about when you hit people otherwise you're the one who ends up hurt. He liked what he saw, and I became one of his gang. Maybe it was jealousy, or simmering resentment, maybe it was because I felt that some time in the future it would cause him harm, but when he asked me my name I gave him the name of my father's imbecilic step son. Squeaky clean, dutiful, respectable, God-fearing "Dumbo" running with a pack of hyenas, causing mayhem and ruining lives; It was such a pleasing mental picture that I couldn't bear to let it fade away.

Fat Tim saw my potential and encouraged it to grow, and, in later years, it served him well. I became his enforcer, his iron fist, as you already know, but that was a lifetime in the future when I had matured into the man I am today. The journey was not always straight forward, and sometimes obstacles were strewn across my path. Once for a brief period, very early on, and against my better judgement and any sense of reason I fell in love. She was a pretty girl, although without breeding or intellect, but she was honest enough and she made me smile. I saw her and I knew I would have her, and it was so easy to impress her. I knew from the outset that I should use her as a plaything to be taken at will and then discarded, but on the way it became the real thing. How long it would have lasted I don't know, but I never had the chance to find out. Her friend turned her against me. For the one time in my life I was the victim of an untruth. I felt the destructive force of the lie, and I experienced the pain of false accusation. I felt the rough hand of her father too and the vicious lashing of his tongue. I learnt then the most important lesson of them all. Wrongs must be avenged, and the pay back in kind must be greater than the original offence. Her father's violence upon me was nothing to the violence that was later heaped on him. Others helped me to obtain this just result, but the planning was all mine; and it was me who applied the coup-de-grace. The Gorgeous Gut-Bucket also benefitted from this act of retribution, and he rewarded me handsomely for doing that which I would gladly have done without recompense, and at the time that was enough; but what satisfied me then is no longer enough to satisfy me now. Time does not heal, cancers grow, and the need to settle old score now is greater than it has ever been. She who crucified me with a lie will soon learn how cruel false words can be and she will see her whole world destroyed by my efforts. Even as I seek to charm one widow, I will break the body, soul and spirit of another. Her children will live to vilify her name.

Those mongrel whelps will have a future which is joyless and unhappy, but another unborn child will not live to see the light of day, a grandchild will be lost and a family curse will continue still. Much of this I will accomplish by word of mouth, but there will be a need for strategic planning too.

Word of mouth did for my father. Word of mouth assured him of a terrifying death. He used me as a weapon to beat my mother. I turned my hatred into a weapon to destroy him. A well constructed lie condemned him, and as his flesh roasted I rejoiced in his agony and my victory."

CHAPTER SEVENTEEN

The day was grey and cold. Since Will's death every day had felt grey and cold to Julia, but today, when his body was to be laid to rest, and his too short life was to be remembered, the cold seemed almost unbearable, and her mood was as desolate as the gloomy leaden sky. Julia was afraid that there would be tears, and terrified that there would not be. She had cried alone in her bedroom so much that she felt that there could be no tears left, but if she didn't weep for Will she worried that she would appear to be heartless, but she knew if she shed one tear she would find a hidden reservoir of unhappiness and the floodgates would be opened. How would she get through the rest of the funeral service if that occurred?

None of the usual clichés could be used to mitigate the overwhelming sadness of the occasion. Will's young age and the horrible manner of his death, brought about by his own deliberate acts, meant that the word *celebration*, so often used as a curtain to shut out the sadness of a funeral, was entirely inappropriate in the context of remembering such a tragic end to a life. A rose tinted "retrospective," scattering petals of comfort to individual members of the congregation could not possibly be embarked upon in circumstances such as these. Will's death was not *a blessed relief,* he had been a fit and active young man, not racked with pain, or worn out by a long battle against a debilitating degenerative illness. He had not *lived life to the full,* because his life had ended prematurely, and there were so many things he might have done in the years and decades still to come. Nobody could say *he had a good life* because he had died too soon, although despite anything anybody might say to the contrary, he had been so good to her and to the children. They were his legacy now, and the justification for his life on earth. They were the only good things left in Julia's world; they had to be loved, they had to be protected, and Julia had made a sacred vow to herself that they always would be.

Everything about this day would be hard, but perhaps the hardest thing of all would be the intimate contact with the expressions of grief and the promises of support that would be addressed to her after the funeral service, and from which there could be no escape. Inside the church she was in a bubble, shielded from meeting people, and from having to talk to them, and the only voices she would have to listen to were those of the vicar, and of Will's father who had asked to be allowed to say a brief eulogy. No one would be able to burst that bubble, no unwanted hands could reach for the patient in intensive care, but after the church service was over her shield against the outside world would be gone, and then she would be the centre of the universe to whom every person present would be irresistibly drawn.

The gathering at the restaurant after the interment promised to be a nightmare. Julia wished with all her heart that this ordeal could be avoided, but some people would have travelled a long way to say their goodbyes, and it was unthinkable that they should not be provided for. Some of the mourners would find comfort in togetherness and in shared recollections: their common cause might ease their pain, but for Julia the thought of having to listen to each well meant anecdote was torture.

The number of people present in the church was impossible to guess. Close family could be predicted with near certainty, but who else would attend was completely unknown. There might be very few, in which case the church would be sparsely populated; there might be a great number in which case it would be jammed tight. For Will's sake, and for his parents Julia hoped it would be the latter, for her own sake she prayed it would be the former. Many people meant many strangers, and the thought of talking to strangers filled her with dread: one stranger had already promised to be there; Monty had begged to be allowed to come; what he would say to her, and what she might say to him she couldn't even begin to imagine.

For a few moments she broke away from her depressing anticipations of things to come to deal with the practical needs of the children. They had to be fed and properly dressed, and made ready for her friend Elizabeth to collect to look after them for the day. They were too young to go to the funeral, they wouldn't understand what was going on, but they would understand Mummy's tears and be upset by her unhappiness. Auntie Liz would keep them amused and happy, and at least if they could smile on this the blackest of black days it would be the tiniest of tiny victories over total despair.

Once they had gone, however the misery descended once more. What to wear seemed an impossible choice. The little black dress was chic and sophisticated, Will had liked her in that dress, and he had said she looked "sexy" in it. *Good God!* thought Julia, *I don't want to stand before that wooden box containing Will's mutilated remains looking sexy* and the dress had been returned to the wardrobe with a shudder. After much deliberation she settled on a dark grey business suit which had a sombre dignity which seemed to match the needs of the occasion. She had only worn it once before, because with hindsight she thought it too severe, and on several occasions had regretted buying it, but today it seemed to be just right. For a brief moment she wondered what Will would have dressed her body in if it had been she who had died; she hoped it would have been the little black dress, but she feared it would have been the suit which would have been cast into the flames. She would have preferred Will to have been cremated, so that the fire would have devoured his body and that a damaged skeleton was not left to decay in the ground, but the Inquest was yet to be, and the Coroner had consented to burial, but not to cremation.

For much of the rest of that day Julia's thoughts floated away from her mind in a weird out of body experience. For most of the time it was as if she was looking down on events from on high, although clouds of incomprehension obscured much of what was going on, but there were some moments of total clarity.

The journey to the church in the black limousine following the slow moving hearse seemed to be happening in another world, and the same air of unreality also hovered over the church like a fog. The words of the vicar seemed to come from a place very far away, and they could have been spoken in a foreign tongue for all the meaningful impact that they had.

The words of Will's father came from the heart and were spoken with sincerity and truth.

"I have many memories of Will," he said, "memories of a boy so full of life and with so many friends. He was always smiling then, and his smile lit up the room and made other people smile too. His passion was football and he was very good at it, and if he didn't do too well at school it didn't seem to matter; certainly not to him because God had given him an unusual talent. Then one day he stopped playing football and he stopped smiling, and although he worked so hard and achieved so much, I would have traded everything to see him smile again. I began to think that it would never happen, but eventually I had my wish. He met Julia, and she taught him to smile again, and every time he talked about her he was his old self again. When they had the children he was so happy it was a joy to behold. Why without any warning he again stopped smiling I will never know. He never stopped loving, of that I'm absolutely sure, and he never doubted for a moment that he was loved too. His death has robbed us of our smiles. I know if Will could speak to us now he would beg us to remember his smile and not his anguish. The next time you see a flower in bloom, or a bird in flight, or feel the sun's warmth on your back, think of Will and smile for him, and maybe in a place far, far away Will will smile for us too. He was a good son and a good husband; I can't believe that I will never speak to him again." Julia saw the tears in her father-in-law's eyes and felt the tears in her own, and suddenly she was back amongst the congregation, her feet deeply rooted on the ground and her pain more acute than any person's present.

Like a zombie she listened to the words of committal in the church, like an automaton she followed the coffin out into the cold church yard; black clouds threatened the earth, and there was dampness in the air. Nothing was real; the words at the graveside held no meaning, and every feeling inside her seemed to be dead. Mechanically she scattered a handful of brown earth onto the coffin, but it was empty ritual. Never had she felt so utterly alone. Suddenly a shaft of sunlight ripped through the sombre sky, shining upon the tiny droplets of water in the atmosphere to create a perfect rainbow. "That's Will's rainbow" his mother had said; Julia's face was now awash with tears.

Her tears continued in the car as it travelled towards the restaurant, and for most of the sad journey her head rested on her father's shoulder. His suit jacket clearly showed a patch of damp were the tears had landed: the heavy shower that fell as they walked from the car park to the restaurant entrance was welcome because it disguised the tangible evidence of her unhappiness.

The rattle of the plates and the jumble of sound from a hundred different conversations made the elegant dining room seem like a bear pit, at least so far as Julia was concerned; a bear pit in which she was the bear, confronted by dozens of excitable, yapping terriers, unwilling to leave her alone until their personal condolences had been forced upon her. She wanted to be back at home, alone with her children and her memories, but flight was not an option.

"I know what you're going through, this feels like hell on earth doesn't it? I've been here, I know how ghastly it is, but in the end, it's better to stay and face the music than it is to run away." He was a tall man, too thin for his frame and too old for his years. His hair was short and prematurely grey, his face was gaunt and his skin pale, but he had piercing blue eyes and a presence that suggested that no secret was safe in his company. The stranger extended his right hand. "I'm Charles Montgomery, everybody calls me Monty, I'm so very, very sorry about Will. I know this is hard, and here isn't the right place or time, but please could I talk to you sometime. Nothing can change the past, or bring Will back, but I honestly believe that I may be able to bring you some comfort. I'm staying at the Old Hall hotel in Buxton; if you think you would like to talk to me please give me a ring: I know where you live and I'll be straight over if you do make that call. Now I'd better leave you to your other guests; today will soon be over, and afterwards you'll be glad that so many people came. Goodbye for the moment, I hope we will meet again". Then he was gone. Julia found his sudden departure as disconcerting as his sudden arrival.

Later, on her way home she thought about the things he had said. He had been right about her feelings towards the mourners; now she was no longer among them she was glad that so many had paid their respects, and he had been right when he prophesied that after he left time would speed up. She decided in the car that she would see him. It was maybe taking a risk to allow a complete stranger into her house, but if she didn't do so she felt she might regret her decision in years to come. It was with a sense of resolution that she unlocked the door to her house. The children were not yet back: she had asked her Mum and Dad to give her a little time by herself. She didn't immediately notice the envelope on the floor below the letter box. It was unstamped, it had been hand delivered, it contained a small piece of card. On the card, in bold black type, were written the words,

"Your husband was a murderer!"

CHAPTER EIGHTEEN

They had sat through the inquest with dignity. Grief had been clear to see, and Julia and Will's Mum and Dad often had had to wipe tears from their eyes; but their grief, although deeply felt, had been suppressed within themselves. There had been no beating of breasts or thunderous outpourings of emotion and maybe to some people that might have seemed strange, but their distress had been real and intensely personal, they were not a family given to public show. Mark Hobson compared their restraint with the over dramatic protestations of sadness and anger that he had sometimes witnessed in people who would later become suspects in murder enquiries and ultimately be convicted of the most cruel and heartless crimes committed upon the person they had pretended to care about. Some of those performances had been worthy of *Oscars*. The Hammond's deserved no *Oscars* because they hadn't played to the gallery, but they did deserve to be respected and to have answers, and if there was a need, they deserved to have justice too.

The Inquest had followed almost exactly the pattern that D.I. Hobson had anticipated it would follow. Mr Mayweather had been at his most courteous, listening intently to each of the four witnesses, only ever interrupting their testimony if there was a point he felt needed to be elaborated or clarified, and in a relatively short time he had reached the only conclusion that he could come to given all the evidence that had been set out before him. Will Hammond had killed himself for reasons it was impossible to guess. He accepted that in the period of just a few hours, something had happened either in reality or in his mind that had led him to undertake the most terrible of acts. He was at pains to stress that Will Hammond had been a happily married man, with a loving wife and family, and that there had been no tensions in his relationship with them that could have caused this tragedy. The last postcard that he had ever written, sent to Julia just hours before his death was, as Mr Mayweather stated in terms "a letter of love, not a letter of accusation." No financial or business pressures clouded the horizon, nobody was hounding him for bad debts, and in all respects Will's life had seemed to be an entirely enviable one. Mr Mayweather did not think Will was thinking rationally when he did what he did, although there was no evidence at all of any mental instability, but something had still exploded in his mind driving him to self destruction. It was a tragedy, and the coroner expressed his sadness at that tragedy, and his sorrow for Julia and for all the Hammond family, but there was no doubt. Will had quietly made his way to a place of solitude, and there, away from people and any outside influence, he had very deliberately and very purposely taken his own life. The verdict was suicide; what other verdict could there be?

It wasn't until after the inquest was over that Mark Hobson learned about the existence of the note Julia had found upon her doormat when she returned home after the funeral. She had been reluctant to show it to the police, reluctant to maybe set in motion a train of enquiry that might ultimately damage Will's reputation, but Bob Hammond had told her that she must do so, and at the same time also make the police aware of the unsympathetic biblical text that had arrived at her house along with the letters of condolence.

"What do you make of this Gov?" Pete Bennett asked his D.I. "Is this somebody's idea of a sick joke, or is there more to it than that?"

"I think there's a lot more to it than that Pete. I've got no doubt that both notes come from the same source: I'm hoping we'll pick up something on fingerprints, but realistically that's probably unlikely, but I'm as sure as I can be that there's more to these notes than just simple spite."

"Do you think that there's any truth in what they allege? If Will Hammond had got away with murder for years and years, and had managed to build for himself a pretty comfortable life, then if summat did happen at that funeral to make him believe that the bubble was about to burst it would give him a pretty decent motive for topping himself."

"There could be, and I'm certainly not ruling anything out, but somehow I don't think there is. Nothing about Will's character indicates that he ever had a violent disposition; there are no reports to suggest that he was handy with his fists, and apart from getting Jamie Nadin drunk on one occasion, he never seems to have been involved in any real trouble. He was a quiet family man, who kept himself to himself, and along the way seems to have done a great deal of good. The staff at the hospice all thought he was wonderful. There's absolutely nothing in his background to suggest that he may have had a secret life as a mad axe man!"

"Dr Crippen was a very quiet man."

"And Jack the Ripper may have had royal blood in his veins, but most murderers who we deal with are drunks or druggies, or they're jealous husbands or criminal thugs. None of these profiles fit Will. If he was involved in a murder what possible motive did he have? The first thing we have to do is try to find out who it is that somebody is alleging he actually killed."

" So I take it that the fact that the coroner has pronounced Will Hammond's death to be a grade A, cast iron suicide doesn't mean that our investigation into his death is about to come to an abrupt halt?"

"Not a bit of it Pete, because even if there isn't a shred of truth in the assertions that are being made to Julia Hammond, I still want to find out who is sending her these nasty notes, and discover what his or her motive might be for doing so."

"Well nobody does summat like this for nowt. Could we be dealing with old fashioned jealousy? Julia Hammond has a nice house and nice kids and without doubt a tidy fortune to inherit. Maybe there's an ex-girlfriend somewhere in the woodwork. If Will Hammond dumped her in favour of Julia, and given that she's such a stunner it would be a no-brainer, she might feel that by rights, everything should have been hers. Perhaps she's trying to get her own back by poisoning Julia's life from now on. It could even be his ex-wife; I know she walked out on him and not the other way about, but a lot of women still resent it when their ex's start to shack up with other women."

"It's certainly got potential as a theory, and all that scary stuff about the "sins of the father" does smack of bitter and twisted anger: the trouble is that as far as we know Will Hammond's first wife was glad to get rid of him. I don't actually think she could have cared less about what he did when he was out of her life; she'd got her pound of flesh, and after the divorce, until he met Julia, Will seems to have lived pretty much like a hermit, at least so far as any sort of social life was concerned."

"What about the possibility of financial gain? A rich young widow is driven demented by a series of assaults on the memory of her dead husband. Every untrue allegation is bound to leave her feeling confused and insecure. The person she most relied upon is dead, his memory is being trashed. She wants to defend him, but she's powerless to do so. She doesn't know when the next attack is going to happen, all she knows is that it will happen, and all the time she's getting more and more demoralised. Enter Sir bleeding Galahad in his silver armour and mounted on his milk white stead. She doesn't see the twirling black moustache, or the £ signs reflecting in his eyeballs, she just sees somebody who she thinks is trying to help her. She would be putty in his hands, if he was clever and played his hand well he could probably talk himself into a small fortune."

"Now that's a theory I really do like, and it's well worth considering in more detail. It's a difficult one to know how to play though. There's nobody we can point to at the moment, and there's only so long that I can keep investigating something the coroner says wasn't a crime; and suppose somebody does appear on the scene, what then? There would be some extremely difficult decisions to make as to how and when to step in. If we have suspicions, but no facts to back them up, so we wait until we've got some hard evidence, and in the meantime Julia is taken to the cleaners. We'll be kicked from pillar to post and rightly so. If we leap in early, with all guns blazing, and it turns out this person was completely genuine and might have been very good for her, in her present circumstances, but we ruin everything then we've obviously not done Julia any favours. It's a difficult one to call."

"Fortunately I'm not the one who's going to have to call it; that's why you get your big pay cheque to make decisions, and I get my meagre pittance so I can scoff at you when you get it wrong."

"Thanks for your vote of confidence Pete."

"It's well meant Gov; after all you've got a fifty percent chance of getting it right."

CHAPTER NINETEEN

The man at the door looked to be vaguely familiar, but Jackie Skinner couldn't say why. He had to be local; otherwise she wouldn't have thought she recognised him; but where she had recognised him from, and in what circumstances she had seen him before, she really didn't know. She presumed it was likely that he was somebody she had seen round and about, maybe wandering though Buxton market on a Saturday morning or waiting somewhere at a bus stop to catch the bus to Stockport to do his weekly big shop. He was well dressed, well spoken and very polite. For a horrible moment the thought crossed Jackie's mind that he was on her doorstep trying to sell her double glazing that she couldn't afford and didn't need or worse yet, that he was a Jehovah's Witness trying to sell her a brand of religion which she was sure she didn't want. She recalled one memorable occasion when Mike had threatened to set the dogs on a smartly dressed woman with a briefcase and a well scrubbed young black male, in a crisp white shirt, who had tried to peddle their own brand of salvation to him in the middle of an England football match which was about to be decided on penalties. They had both fled, but the woman had tripped over a rusty tricycle, twisting her ankle and ripping her grey mac. They had called the police on a mobile phone. Mike had pointed to a warning sign on the gate. He said they had refused to leave his property when asked to do so, and all that he had done was to shout at them to make them go. The police had advised him to keep his temper in the future, but they had accepted that he had been within his rights to demand that the couple got off his land, and there had been no charges. Things were different now: with Alan's help her garden was better cared for than it had been before, and there were no "man traps" or even "woman traps" for strangers to negotiate; but never-the-less a look of anxiety must have flashed across her face.

"Please don't worry," the man had said, as if he could read her mind. "I'm not selling anything I promise you, and I'm not offering you any cheap deals on God." Jackie grinned.

"My name is Michael Charles," he continued, smiling as he spoke. "To be honest with you though, I am after something, but it isn't anything that will cost you money, and if you don't like what I say you can shut the door in my face anytime you wish and I'll just go away." From out of his pocket he produced a printed card and handed it to Jackie to examine.

"MICHAEL CHARLES

OFFICIAL COLLECTOR no 1192

N.S.P.C.C."

"That's who I am. I'm going round knocking on people's doors asking for unwanted toys, books, games, videos and C.D's so that we can sell them in an *As good as new sale* that we're holding in a couple of weeks time. I'm not looking for clothing; we've got plenty of that already, but really anything else apart from clothing."

Jackie allowed herself a wry smile: with three active, boisterous boys, shoes and clothes took a constant hammering; there were only their best clothes that would be fit to donate to anybody, and she certainly wasn't about to be giving them away to some do-gooder on the doorstep.

"What I really want are videos and games," he said, sensing her unease, "they always sell well, and I find that a lot of people discover that they do have a stock of films their children have grown out of, or a pile of toys and board games that are no longer played with."

Jackie knew the situation well.

"I'm sure I can find you something," she said, "Can you give me a few minutes to sort something out?"

"I've got lots of other houses to go to. I'll call back in about an hour if that's ok I've got some of our plastic sacks in the van, would you like me to go and get you one?"

"There's no need. I've got plenty of carrier bags lying about thanks all the same. I'm not planning to be out at all today, but if I am, I'll leave the bags on the doorstep so you can just walk right up and help yourself."

As soon as he had gone Jackie set about sorting through the cupboard in the dresser were the games and video tapes were kept. Some of the choices were easy. The games of Monopoly and Cluedo had never been played with: her parents had never understood that Mike had seen himself as "Action Man" or "Rambo", and that he had poured scorn on the presents her mum and dad habitually gave the children at Christmas, so that the whole family could sit down and play together. It was such a pity. Under Alan's influence some deeply held prejudices were being eroded, but he was no miracle worker, and the three boys having once pronounced board games as *boring* had thereafter permanently branded them as *naff*. Jackie looked at the toy guns and light sabres that lay scattered across the youngest's bedroom floor. Even before Mike had died a violent death she had disliked such toys, and after he had been murdered she would have liked nothing more than to collect all these pretend articles of destruction and dump them, without ceremony in the bin, but such would have been the scene if she had removed even one of them, she had long since concluded that she had to leave things well enough alone.

The video collection was much harder to decide upon. She knew if the children had been making the decisions it would have been easy for them, and anything that wasn't an action packed adventure or a Sci-Fi blockbuster would be cheerfully got rid of, especially if it was the type of film that mummy liked. They were their father's sons; gentle, sentimental feel good films didn't get a look in. But, despite their derision, Jackie liked the romantic comedies and the classic Disney films her Aunt Sarah had given them over the years, and it seemed such a pity to throw them out. She picked up the video of the *Jungle Book*, which had always been a favourite of hers and to her surprise found herself singing about the "simple bare necessities of life". Why couldn't her children have a more sensitive streak? But if they had they wouldn't be her boys, and she loved them just the way they were. With similar feelings of regret she grasped the videos of *Cinderella* and the cartoon version of *One Hundred and One Dalmatians*: each video box seemed to glue itself to her hand, and it was almost as if she had to prise open her own fingers before she could drop the cassette tapes into the waiting carrier bags. The real life version of *One Hundred and Two Dalmatians* was spared rejection because the boys still laughed out loud at the slapstick indignities heaped upon Cruella-de-Ville, but that was the only concession to wholesome family entertainment that she made. She did wonder if in real life a series of similar misfortunes had happened to her, and if those misfortunes had been recorded on video tape, would her three little *angels* have laughed like demented hyenas; sadly she came to the conclusion that they would; her only consolation was that she would have probably laughed with them: they were a close family, and the bonds of love were very strong. Her sons were fiercely loyal and protective too; and in the end what more could any mother hope for from her offspring?

In the space of a little over half an hour she had filled two ASDA bags with a sizeable cache of unwanted treasure. She carried the fully laden plastic bags to the front door and set them down on the step alongside the milk bottles. If the charity made money, and some children got pleasure then it was all worthwhile. *If we've outgrown an age of innocence* she thought, *thankfully lots of families haven't.* She closed the door behind her, and set about the tedious task of cleaning the kitchen.

She had not expected the doorbell to ring again. Michael Charles stood outside.

"I just couldn't leave without thanking you for your generosity" he said, "sometimes it's a real wrench to get rid of stuff like this, It's a bit like throwing happy memories on the scrap heap. I know they will sell well, and I know they will bring happiness to children. If only every person I met was as supportive as you, my job would be a whole lot easier than it is."

"That's very kind of you, thank you. I'm just glad I can help."

"And I'm so very grateful for that help. Are there any of these videos that you would really like to hang onto. You've given so much; I wouldn't like to take advantage of your kindness."

"Well the Disney films were the ones that I thought about keeping, but my kids think they're babyish. You might as well have them, they'll only gather dust if they're left here.

"If you're sure then thank you, I've taken up too much of your time already. Goodbye, and once again my heartfelt thanks."

As he walked down the path, Jackie felt an overwhelming certainty that some time in the past he had taken his leave of her before."

CHAPTER TWENTY

"We weren't nice kids at all: most of the members of Jerry Eggleton's merry band, including me, were pretty diabolical. Will and his mate Jamie were different, probably because they belonged around here in a way that none of the rest of us did. Their fathers' had proper jobs; they earned their money the hard way. My dad was a property developer, Eggleton's dad was an entrepreneur, and the others all had fathers who were stockbrokers, merchant bankers or commercial lawyers. They were all Thatcher's disciples: money was their number one goal, and flaunting their wealth their number one pastime. We were the incomers, living in big houses, looking down on the locals, taking the piss whenever we could and being thoroughly, objectionable, destructive, arrogant little pricks!"

"Then why did Will and Jamie want to hang out with you?" Julia poured out a cup of black tea and passed it to Charles Montgomery, who was sat in an armchair in her living room: "I don't think they would have wanted to be part of your gang if you were as horrible as you tell me you were."

"We dazzled them. We had the clothes, the hi-tech gadgets, the money, the whole shooting match. We could just about afford to do anything we wanted to do, and Will and Jamie were only human, they wanted some of what we had, and it amused Jerry Eggleton to throw them the odd crumb now and again. There was a lad called Justin Barnes; I was going to say he was one of Jerry's mates, but he wasn't really anybody's mate; yet somehow there were times when he seemed to be in control. Where he came from, I don't know, he didn't ever say much about himself, but he became the driving force behind a lot of what we did. Jerry seemed to depend on him at times of trouble; I think he was afraid of him; for that matter, I think we were all a bit afraid of him. Jerry would come up with the wild ideas, but it was Justin Barnes, who worked out ways of putting them into practice. Some of Jerry's ideas started off quite nasty, and by the time Justin had finished with them, they were usually a whole lot worse. I'm honestly very much ashamed now of some of the things we did then."

The colour drained from Julia's face, and for a second it looked as if she might shake the bone china teacup right off the pure white saucer edged in gold: the terrible accusation that somebody had anonymously made about Will burnt into her mind. She forced herself to ask the questions that might give her answers that she didn't want to hear."

"What sort of nasty things did you do?"

"We did all manner of petty, vindictive things. Once we nailed the vicar's cat to a yew tree in the churchyard because he had thrown us out of the youth club for smoking "weed." It was a big ginger tom cat; he loved that animal like a child, and he was mortified when he found out what had been done. We got drunk quite often; we were certainly pissed up when we set fire to some bales of hay in a farmer's field. We stole a couple of cars and crashed them, but our parents were always there to bail us out: as I remember it the car incident was hushed up by Jerry's dad. There were a lot of other stupid, pointless things as well, but you probably get the flavour from what I've said already."

"Was Will involved in any of that?"

"I don't think so. I think that all happened before he joined us, but he did get drunk with us a few times, and he did break a couple of windows in the bus shelter."

The look of relief on Julia's face was quite apparent, and Charles Montgomery did not miss it.

"Will was a decent lad Julia. I know Jerry and Justin and the rest of us tried to egg him on to do some really stupid things, but usually he didn't take the bait; they'd done something similar with the Methodist minister's son, and he'd ended up stealing from a local shopkeeper to prove to everyone that he had bottle. After he'd done it they laughed at him, and Barnes grassed him up to Jamie Nadin's dad. The minister was devastated when his son was arrested by the police; he'd always tried to bring up his children properly, and he felt his son had ruined his good name. The family left here to go and live in Manchester. The son took an overdose when he was only eighteen because he couldn't stand the shame."

"So much hate! Why was there so much hate?"

"Because nobody cared what we did and because we all thought we could get away with murder. Will didn't think like that though, but even he was bribed into doing something which he knew to be very wrong."

The look of consternation re-appeared on Julia's face.

"What did he do Monty? I've got to know," and she told him of the card she had received denouncing her late husband as a killer.

"It was something I believe he regretted all his life. Jerry Eggleton's dad had this dog that he was besotted with. It had some fancy Kennel Club name and a pedigree as long as your arm, and Fat Tim (that's Jerry's dad) was always boasting about how much he had paid for it and how good it was. He left it with Jerry to look after for a couple of days while he went off on a jaunt to London. Jerry couldn't be bothered to do it properly, and he let it run wild. It killed some sheep belonging to a local farmer. The farmer shot it with a 12 bore: then there was all Hell to pay. Jerry was wetting himself to think what his father would do to him.

Justin told him to tell his dad that we'd taken the dog for a walk, but that we'd let it off the lead to chase a rabbit. We all swore it was nowhere near any sheep when the farmer shot it and that he was just a trigger happy maniac. His dad believed us and he went mental. He had a stand up row with the farmer, which almost came to blows, but the farmer didn't back down. Fat Tim swore that he'd get even. We all knew that Will was a fantastic footballer and a huge Manchester United fan. His dad was a head keeper as you know. His dad had access to poison to kill foxes, arsenic or strychnine or something like that; gamekeepers never admitted to putting down poison, but we all knew it went on. Anyway, Justin Barnes suggested to Jerry's dad that if he was prepared to pay for Will to go to a cup tie, and to offer him a few other goodies as well, Will might be persuaded to get hold of a little of this poison. The farmer who shot Tim's dog was a champion sheep dog trialist; he was just about to compete in some major championship which he had high hopes of winning; he was also either related to Will's dad in some way, or there was a close family connection. Jerry and Justin doctored some meat, they told Will it was just a mild dose and that all it would do would be to make the animals sick for just long enough to stop the farmer taking part in the particular competition. They told Will that if he fed the meat to the dogs (he was the only one of us who could get access to them) then Jerry's dad would buy him a ticket for the big match. For a long time Will refused, but we all told him that it would be alright, so eventually he agreed to do it. Jerry's dad gave him a genuine Manchester United shirt, not some cheap replica, and he was thrilled with it. He visited the farm and slipped the contaminated beef to the dogs. He didn't wait to see if it had an immediate effect, he was scared of being caught. He went to the match thinking they would be alright, but both dogs died as Jerry and Justin knew that they would: they'd injected enough poison into the meat to kill a bull elephant.

Will was beside himself when he learnt what had happened. He said that they had used him; Jerry told him that it was his own greed that had used him. Will said he would tell the farmer. Jerry said he'd kill him if he did, but Jerry was all mouth, and Will wasn't brow beaten, that much was pretty obvious. Justin Barnes told Will that they hadn't meant to harm the dogs and that it had been a simple miscalculation, but he accepted that the farmer needed to be told. He said the apology and the compensation should come from the man who had sanctioned the scheme. He asked Will to get the farmer to go to a place where he could meet face to face with Tim, but he said Tim was paranoid that the meeting could be taped; he told Will that the meeting had to be outdoors and that the farmer shouldn't know who would be there until he arrived. We all told Will that would be for the best. He was two years younger than most of us, and he was basically honest, and eventually accepted that we were right. He couldn't see that he was still being used. Barnes also tempted him by saying that if he did what we wished nobody need know the part he had played in poisoning the dogs. Will felt so ashamed about what he'd done, and so frightened his father would find out that he allowed himself to be convinced. He would have told the farmer though, and confessed to his father too, if Justin hadn't come up with this plan; of that I'm absolutely sure.

What happened next I don't know. I was rushed into hospital for an emergency operation to remove my appendix. Nobody who was there would talk about it afterwards. Will did persuade the farmer to go to the meeting place; how he did that I'm not sure; I know he didn't go there himself. There was some sort of terrible accident, the farmer fell on some rocks and smashed his skull: well anyway that was the official version. Will blamed himself for his death; I think he suspected that there might be more to it than met the eye, and that he'd been an unwitting party to it. He couldn't change what had happened, and now somebody had died, he was too scared to tell people what he knew.

He never wanted anything to do with us after that. Those few days changed his life forever. He grew up overnight and he saw what a worthless lot we were. Years later I had a massive heart attack. I very nearly died. I had a lot of time to re-examine my life, and I realised how much of it I had wasted. I changed like Will changed. Jerry Eggleton never changed, and in so far as I know, neither did

Justin Barnes. He remained the same right up to the day he died. Even after his death he caused trouble: I know for a fact that his mother threw herself off a high cliff because she couldn't stand the grief; had she known what a vicious little thug he was she might have felt very differently."

CHAPTER TWENTY ONE

Sometimes people bump into each other by accident; at other times a great deal of planning goes into arranging every detail of a chance encounter.

The meeting between Bob Hammond and Mark Hobson had not been planned. Helena had suggested to Mark that as he was on a rest day, perhaps he might like to take her shopping, and that afterwards they could grab a bite to eat. Christopher could be left in the adoring custody of his doting grandparents, and they could have the whole day to themselves. Mark had jumped at the chance, even though he had often been heard to remark that "when God in his wisdom came to regard the concept of Purgatory as outmoded he invented shopping as a suitably joyless replacement for it": he thought with some sleight of hand on his part, the amount of time spent actually traipsing around retail outlets could be surreptitiously whittled away and the time spent eating, talking, being together with his wife, doing anything but shopping could be correspondingly increased. Helena knew that this would be his ploy and, from past experience, she was sure that he could be skilfully played at his own game.

It was as they were in Marks and Spencer looking for a jumper for Mark; (he had long since been entirely out manoeuvred by his beautiful wife) that they were approached by the retired gamekeeper. After an exchange of pleasantries, and a brief chat about the weather, Bob asked Mark if he might have a quick word. Helena smiled.

"You're off the hook, my darling, I need one or two things for myself; shall I meet you in "Enzio's" in about twenty minutes and we'll have a cup of coffee and maybe a cake?"

"Yes, that'll be great love; I'm already drooling at the thought of sticky chocolate gateau."

After Helena had left Mark asked Will Hammond's father what it was he wanted to talk about.

"It's Julia, Mr Hobson; she had a letter from a bloke called Charles Montgomery just prior to Will's funeral, and he actually spoke to her in person after the funeral service. He told her that he was somebody who had known Will as a lad, and that bit's true because I remember the name, but he weren't a friend of his, and as far as I can recall he were an unpleasant little shit. Anyway after the funeral, a couple of days later Julia invited him to the house. He talked about Will, and Julia says he were very nice, although he did tell her that it were Will who poisoned Jacob Farrington's dogs nigh on twenty years ago. If that's true and, it's a terribly depressing thought if it is, then I'm sure he was put up to it by this bloke, or by some of the other clowns who knocked about with Jerry Eggleton, but that isn't why I wanted to speak to you.

Julia said he also talked a lot about himself, and how his life had changed and I think she started to feel sorry for him, which I'm sure is what he wanted; and she's told him he can call and visit her again. The thing is, I was talking to my cousin Tom, we look very much alike, and he told me that he'd met a bloke in the pub who had mistaken him for me. He said this bloke seemed to be a very decent, honest kind of guy, although he looked a bit rough, and he wanted to warn Tom, well really he wanted to warn me, about this chap Montgomery. He said that he knew him. He said that he was devious and two-faced and he was warning Tom, well really warning me, that he was no good and that he represented a threat to Julia. I don't know what to do. Julia's such a lovely girl, and so trusting; if he's a wrong 'un then he could be out to con her in some way, but if I try to warn her off him without any proof then she might end up resenting the interference. I was wondering if you could check him out at all. The chap my cousin Tom met told him that he'd be very happy to talk to Julia or to me and tell us what he knew; but I don't know if that's a good idea. You deal with villains and with suspected villains every day of your working life; what do you think I should do Mr Hobson?"

"It's difficult to know what to say Bob. My sergeant Pete Bennett mentioned Charles Montgomery to me a while back, said he was a "nasty piece of work", but he thought that he'd died of cancer, so the fact that he's still in the land of the living is a bit of a surprise. I'll get him to do a bit more digging, and if he comes up with anything then I'll pay Mr Montgomery a little visit, just to let him know that the police are watching him. If he has been planning anything a bit iffy, then he might just take the hint and disappear once he knows that he's under active observation. I don't think it would be a good idea for the chap your cousin met to speak to Julia just yet, we don't want to upset her without cause, but maybe if you speak to him yourself you could glean a few more facts, and if you do, give me a ring and we'll talk about this matter again."

The meeting between Michael Charles and Jackie Skinner was also unplanned, on her part at least, although it was very definitely intended by him. The kids were all at school, and Jackie was busy tidying the house prior to beginning the task of preparing the evening meal. Nothing fancy would be on offer, just good wholesome food, but Alan was going to join them so she wanted everything to be right.

The knock on the door surprised her: why was it that people always came to the house when you were in the throes of doing something messy and that you had to present yourself to whoever was there, dressed in your least glamorous attire?

"Have I come at a bad time?" he said, seeing the baggy sweater she was wearing and noting the duster in her hand. "I could call back later if you like, but I promise you I'll only take up a couple of minutes of your time. All I really wanted to do was to give you these." In his hand he carried a plastic carrier bag, and before Jackie could enquire further he handed the bag and its contents over to her. Jackie noticed that he was wearing leather gloves. She opened the bag and looked inside. To her surprise she saw that it contained five of the video tapes she had so recently given to him.

"I got our fund raising organiser to price these up, and I paid her the price she said, so the charity hasn't lost out. I thought about how nice you were to me, and how different your attitude could have been. I don't think anybody else that week even came close to matching what you gave to me. I remembered how much you said you liked the Disney tapes, and I thought I'd give them back to you as a sort of little thank you from me."

Jackie smiled. "That's very kind of you," she said, "When the dark nights arrive, and the kids are in bed, and I'm stuck at home with nothing to do, I'll settle down and watch all these films again with a mug of hot chocolate in my hand and I'll remember what it felt like to be a kid myself." She picked out *The Jungle Book* from the bag. "This is the one I'll watch first. I know it's a bit odd for a woman in her 30's to like children's films, and my husband used to think I was daft, but these are so well made and so clever that I really do love them. It's my kind of escapism."

"There's nothing wrong with a bit of escapism. I'm a *Star Wars* man myself, but everyone to his or her own taste."

Jackie laughed and replaced the video in the carrier bag: apart from when she had rummaged in the cupboard to pull out the videos she had given away, it had been years since she had held one in her hands. Recently in a shop she had been looking at DVDs; the shop assistant in a glittery T-shirt, with earrings in both his ears, had reliably informed her that they *were the future*. How light and compact they had seemed; the video tape in her hand felt heavy and chunky by comparison.

"Would you like to come in for a coffee?" she said. "You're very welcome to if you don't mind the mess; it's pretty cold out there. It's always the ends of my fingers that feel the cold first, but I notice that you very sensibly chose to wear gloves."

He shook his head. "No thanks all the same," he said. "I can see you're very busy, and I don't want to keep you from what you're doing. It's actually quite pleasant in the sun. I've got a touch of eczema hence the gloves, and that's probably another good reason why I should say no; I might knock on your door again sometime, and maybe then there will be time for that cuppa and a chat."

CHAPTER TWENTY TWO

The girl waiting to see the nurse looked unhappy. She gazed disinterestedly at the magazine she had picked up only a few seconds before and then threw it back carelessly onto the coffee table; it skidded over the surface and fell onto the waiting room carpet. She looked at it for a moment then left it to lie where it was. The old lady awaiting a flu jab gave her a disapproving glance, she didn't see it; her thoughts were of herself and of the alien intruder inside her body who was already making her life hell.

The other patients in the surgery were a very mixed bunch. The overweight man who had shuffled through the entrance door and who had dragged his fat frame to the receptionist's desk was not long for this world, although the pale youth with a spotty complexion and skin the colour of dirty chalk might yet beat him to the exit turnstile. The small child with the streaming eyes and a penetratingly whinging whine was driving his red faced mother to distraction, while the impatient teenager chatting on her mobile phone in a loud monosyllabic parody of the English language demonstrated ignorance, arrogance and stupidity in roughly equal measures. The only bright spot in this otherwise dismal picture was the young woman who waited patiently to see the

District Nurse and talked gently to the happy toddler who was sitting upon her knee. Helena Hobson could turn heads, and people felt better just for seeing her, but the man sat alone near the tropical fish tank didn't give her a glance: his attention was not obvious, his surveillance was covert, but his eyes and mind were secretly focussed on another person in the room: the moody, miserable pregnant girl filled his thoughts, and slowly he was putting together the finishing touches to a plan.

Detective Sergeant Peter Bennett was also putting the final touches to a plan, although in his case the plan came straight out of the drawer marked *Things to dream about doing* and was destined to end up in the *unfulfilled* waste paper bin, alongside his desire to be the first man to jet ski across the Atlantic Ocean and his somewhat less heroic yearning to grapple naked in baby oil with a gleaming and steaming Pamela Anderson. He had reached the point in his current fantasy where he was about to place red hot knitting needles into the nostrils of Ralph Ambridge prior to deciding how best to insert a shooting stick into his ample rectum when he was disturbed from his appealing day dreaming by the voice of his Detective Inspector.

"How did the interview with Ralph Ambridge go Pete? Did you learn anything useful at all?"

"The man's a self-opinionated, ignorant snob Gov. I knew he would be. He thinks he's so fucking clever, and so much better than the likes of you and me, that he could barely give me the time of day. It were only after I told him that I weren't going anywhere until he condescended to speak to me, and that if he wanted to play silly buggers with me I was a Grand Master at that particular game that he finally granted me a little time. He didn't really say owt even then though. I knew he bloody wouldn't. He claimed to have lost touch with most of Jerry Eggleton's mob, and that the few he did see from time to time were just nodding acquaintances, and that he had no interest in their current activities."

"So it was a complete shut out Pete?"

"It would have been easier for me to prise open the gates of Fort Knox with a tooth pick than it was to try to drag the smallest piece of worthwhile information from his expensively maintained, dentally hygienic gob."

"Do you think that if you'd tried to tease the info out of him rather than being up front and in his face you might have got further? Relaxed conversations are the fount of infinite knowledge, I had a very enlightening chat with Bob Hammond in Marks and Spencer only yesterday, when I was out shopping, and he was under no pressure at all."

"Bob Hammond's a different kettle of fish Gov! He's honest, he wants to help us, and he's not a pompous twat; you can't claim any Brownie points at all for getting him to talk to you."

"No, of course I can't Pete, he wanted to talk to me, he wanted my advice, but in the course of that conversation I did learn something interesting. You like riddles don't you? Well answer me this one. What have a bit part biblical character and Jerry Eggleton's mate Charles Montgomery got in common?"

"Who's the biblical character? If you tell me it's Lot's wife or Salome's handmaiden then I'm telling you now I'll go and seek out a quiet room, and give serious consideration to making an application to join Traffic."

"If I said Lazarus would that stop you making any rash decision?"

"So are you telling me that Charles Montgomery is back from the dead? Well, I'm gobsmacked! Three or four people have all said to me that he died of cancer, and all of them were people with a bit of nous about 'em. Are you sure you've got your facts straight?"

"Well, Bob Hammond swears that it's true, and not only that, he tells me that Montgomery has already met Julia twice and that he's soon going to pay her a third visit; and by the way it wasn't cancer he was supposed to have died from, it was a heart attack."

"Whatever! It does mean that a man who is a total scumbag is sniffing round after Julia, as we feared might become the case; well what are we going to do about that?"

"There's not much we can do at present. He hasn't done anything wrong that we know of; he's not currently wanted for anything, and Bob tells me that Julia says that he's been very nice to her. All we can do is let him know we're watching him, but the fact that one of our cast iron certainties has turned out to be wrong, does make me think that we should recheck all the bits of information we currently have to make sure there aren't any other errors."

" I'm on the case Gov, and I'll start by looking again at all the people we believe have cocked their clogs; we now know that one of Jerry Eggleton's mates managed to dodge the Grim Reaper; it's remotely possible that others might have turned out to be just as slippery. Isn't it always the way? Even in the face of imminent death the rich can wriggle out of trouble. If Charles Montgomery had been a benefit claimant I can tell you now he'd have stayed dead; it's always the bloody same!"

"It's the rich wot gets the pleasure Comrade, it's the poor wot gets the blame, and as the song says, it may be "a bloody shame", but that's how the world is my friend, and whatever you may think that's the way it will always be; but while we're thinking about the deserving and the undeserving dead, there is another death which we need to re-examine. Charles Montgomery apparently told Julia that shortly before Jacob Farrington died Will Hammond poisoned two of his dogs. The Farrington family and the Hammond family were very close, and Jacob was Will's godfather. I've not long since telephoned Bob Hammond to clarify a few points and I understand Montgomery alleges that Will was conned into laying the poison believing that the animals would suffer no permanent harm, but the interesting thing is that after he'd done that, he was put under a lot of pressure to get Jacob to go to a meeting place to talk to Tim Eggleton, who had set up the whole thing as a revenge attack for the shooting of his dog. I know the coroner recorded Jacob's death as an accident, but young Will seems to have suspected that it may not have been, and certainly he was never the same lad after it happened. I want you to find out everything you can about the Farrington death, which won't be easy because it wasn't recorded as a crime, but the anonymous letter Julia received accused Will of being a murderer, and I don't think that accusation relates to the killing of a dog. I also think that the degree of guilt Will seems to have felt wouldn't have been anything like as great if he hadn't believed that he had played a part in causing the death of a man who as a kid he had always called "Uncle Jacob."

"Right you are Gov! While I'm slogging my guts out what are you going to be doing this lovely afternoon?"

"I've got a meeting in Buxton with the Assistant Chief Constable Pete. Like I said, "it's the rich wot gets the pleasure", but the thought of spending two hours in his company makes me wish that I was a struggling P.C. without a brass penny to my name."

CHAPTER TWENTY THREE

Traps have been baited, snares have been set in place, and now at last the hunt begins. Things can't be rushed. The greater the prize, the greater the care needed to stalk the prey. Success takes time, and haste is a sure fire recipe for disaster, but inside me the need for vengeance and for money grows ever stronger; daily I force myself to wait for the moment when I shall have both.

I have been active, and activity speeds the passing of the hours; but much still remains to be done. The building blocks for one part of my plan are now in place, but only the foundation stones have been laid for another; a third refinement to the scheme is barely off the drawing board, and a fourth, the part designed to bring me financial security, is still a vision in the architect's mind.

I have spoken soft words, and I have shown kindness, and I think that trust has been established, but words alone don't get results. Words need to be followed by actions if they are to achieve their goal, and I have carried out effective actions too. Ralph Ambridge was surprised to discover that the secrets of his past were known and it is some of his cash that primed the pump enabling the first part of my plan to take effect. He is a worried man, and he has good cause to be. He doesn't know who threatens him, and my intent is that he never will, although in time he may begin to suspect who it is that has become the thorn that pricks his ample side. His money, and the sink estates of Sheffield and of Manchester, provided for my needs. White powder and blue porn were easy to obtain. Both sicken me; both are the refuge of weak willed fools. Why do some men so willingly poison their bodies and their minds with toxic filth? My mind is razor sharp, it is not dulled by substance abuse or perverse practices, but it is never-the-less damaged. I can no longer feel emotion: my ability to care and to think kindly of others was snatched from me a long, long time ago.

She looks harmless now, and some might say that she is pretty. Pretty and nice with a sweet disposition, but her acts destroyed my life just as much as my uncaring father and disloyal mother ever did. Retribution is encamped outside her door, and even as I write, its forces may be sacking her quiet safe haven. Fear, shame, loss, rejection and despair; all wait just around the corner, and if I have done the spade work well they will soon overwhelm her.

My words to her were kind and gentle; my words about her, spoken anonymously to gullible halfwits were anything but. Social Services have seized upon my disclosure with crusading zeal, and despite its doubtful provenance have already granted it the status of believed truth. My unsigned letters sent to the police from different locations, and in different hands, to give the appearance that several sources independent of each other were making the same allegations have ignited a fuse, and her world is destined to be torn apart by the bombs that I have planted in it.

Her's is not the only world condemned to die, other worlds will perish in the heat of my rage. A family tree, its main trunk already felled by my axe still lives on and side shoots start to spring from its damaged base. I could ignore the saplings, but if I do, they will eventually grow tall and sturdy and a dynasty will survive. I could have created a dynasty of my own, but I was denied the opportunity of doing so. Through lies I lost love, through threats and force I was made to abandon my dreams. If I was deprived of the chance to be happy, I who had had so little happiness in my life, why should the family of the man who caused so much of my misery escape unmolested?

The silly girl means nothing. If it was she who was important then it were better that she be left alone to toil in bitterness, and in despair, to provide for an unwanted brat; but some around her will rejoice in the being of the whelp and will cosset the child as heir apparent to the grandfather. Loss of that unborn child is the only answer, and a broken womb is the most befitting gift that I can bestow. Temptation will be easy. Fear will be soothed away by calming words, but fear will return in triumph with the onset of pain, and the realisation of how wantonly she has thrown away two lives.

As always words will be the cement that binds the enterprise together. Those words remain to be spoken, but in another place words have already been scattered liberally to ferment suspicion. False assertions have been sown to create doubt: Rumour is a mischievous ally; Gossip is a snarling messenger of Hate. What third parties believe is the key. Tell the world that you are great and find yourself repulsed by a shield of scepticism; tell the world that you are good and face loud accusations of insincerity; but convince the wife that your motives are pure, and let her drip feed the message to the husband and at length he will accept the contention as fact, because he trusts the source from whence his information came.

Disclosure through "mistake" is an effective tool. If a secret is unwittingly revealed, particularly if it is then accompanied by earnest pleas to tell nobody of that which was so carelessly let slip, then no-one will challenge the efficacy of what has been said. I met a man who believed that I mistook him for another. I am no such fool, but the deception was convincing. I warned him of a dangerous liaison, knowing that he would pass the message on to the person meant to receive it. That person cares. He worries about another and is protective towards her; he is therefore already predisposed to think the worst and to convince himself that she needs shielding from harm.

When my error was corrected I indicated to my unsuspecting go-between that I would meet face to face the man I mistakenly thought him to be, and that when I did so I would lay bare a history of viciousness and deceit, but I don't intend to keep that promise. I will engineer a situation which will make a meeting impossible. He cannot as yet be allowed to see my face, if he did, that could destroy in an instance everything I strive to achieve.

I won't meet him, but I will speak to him and, in that conversation I'll tell him many things that he is programmed to believe. Lies wrapped in a protective film of truth are elegant lies: they are the best of lies, and the ones most easily digested by a sceptical mind.

In due course, when the time is right, I will no doubt finally be introduced to him, but not as the man who set alarm bells ringing. When that meeting occurs, danger rests in the go-between who is his friend. When I first played him for a fool I took care to stand out from the crowd. My hair was dyed, my clothes were cheap and in bad taste and, the vivid tattoos on my face and arms were my most striking feature. It was all illusion: but who would suspect that any man would be at pains to create such a poor depiction of himself. In good clothes, with natural hair and well-scrubbed countenance and limbs, free from the artistry of the body painter, I will be unrecognisable. When we meet my voice will have changed too, and in accent and in tone will be quite different from the sounds remembered in his head. He won't know me, of that I'm sure, but if he has the slightest inkling his eyes will betray his doubts and I will know. He will not speak until he's sure; and in the intervening time I will have done that which clearly must be done.

Before all this happens I will have been inventive. I will have weaned a lie, and set it loose to feed on raw suspicion. I'll allege vile things about my public character, which later can be conclusively proved to be untrue. First I will be reviled, then I will be redeemed, and when it becomes clear that I was wrongly judged, as an honourable man he will be at pains to ensure that I am not defamed again and his belief in me will become uncritical.

I need his support. If he trusts my motives and believes that I share a desire to safeguard his daughter-in-law's well being he will not fight against me when I start to win her round. I don't deceive myself, it may be a long time before I have her, and longer still before I have what is hers; although her time thereafter will be short. She is beautiful, and so far as I can judge she is good. Oh, how the thought of things to come excite me! Until the day I reveal the carnivore within, I will play the hero and drink in her virtue and her tenderness. My gentle hands will map out every contour of her body and she will forget her sadness and melt into my arms. If I had a heart there is a risk that I might lose it, but my heart and soul were crushed to dust a lifetime ago. If I had any emotion other than hate I could not contemplate the cruel way I will use her, but I am as cold as Arctic ice: I have no warmth, yet excitement burns inside me like a new formed star: I cannot bear the heat. To take a work of art and cast it into the flames is such a thrilling prospect, to smash an icon into rubble is an overpowering thought. I am an iconoclast, a despoiler of truth and beauty and the very thought of how I will outrage the world when I destroy her makes my body shake and my manhood swell.

She is rich, and her riches and her beauty sign her death warrant. I want her money! I want her life! I have considered all the options; for my daily needs at present I can rely on blackmail, but Ralph Ambridge and the others may eventually work out who it is that torments them and they will fight back. My life will have a hefty price put on it: that is a matter of pride. No stupid hired assassin will ever find me and the blood money that is on offer will remain unclaimed. The money I tear from their fingers will suffice for the time being but the money I will get from her is so much more.

This world is full of dangers. Maybe she and her children will have an accident on a country road at night. Loveliness and innocence left bleeding in a mangled heap of metal, the tears of the paramedics mixing with the spillage from a ruptured fuel tank. Perhaps an electrical fault at home will spark an inferno, but not before substantial insurance cover is in place. A walk along high cliffs could end in tragedy, a climactic conclusion to a tragic family opera, but three deaths at the same place would be difficult to explain. If just my wife, as then she will surely be, were to stumble and fall to the jagged rocks below, then I, as the grieving husband, would have to take control of her fortune. A rapid sale of everything she possesses would cause suspicion, and should something then happen to the children the suspicion would grow more acute.

To make me rich, a whole family, bar one, has to perish in a single night leaving just a distraught new husband and father to weep for his loss. I am a monster to plan such acts: I glory in that title. I didn't choose to be a monster; the world made me that and set me loose to prey upon my fellow man. The unkind choices of others gave birth to evil, I did not father it. Others dealt me the wretched hand I hold. My only input to this squalid game of life has been to play the cards Fate gave me fearlessly, and without ever holding back. There is no other way: kill or be killed, destroy or be destroyed, take without asking, give nothing away; I will succeed no matter what I have to do.

CHAPTER TWENTY FOUR

"The baby's doing fine, there's nothing at all to worry about," so commented the practice nurse as she finished her examination of Sharon Farrington. The response to the good news was not what the nurse expected it to be. Sharon's lip quivered and it was all she could do to stop herself bursting into floods of tears: plenty of first time mums lost their babies, plenty of pregnancies ended in disappointment, Sod's Law dictated that her's would not be one of them.

"What's the matter Sharon?" asked the nurse, surprised by the reaction to the glad tidings she had just given out. Sharon didn't reply. Without thanking the nurse, she ran out of the consulting room and, ignoring the calls of the nurse and the doctors' receptionist to wait a few moments and calm down, she rushed from the surgery out onto the street. Everybody in the building saw her leave; most of the people who were present didn't see the man who had been sitting quietly at the back of the waiting room get up and follow her.

"Poor child!" whispered the receptionist. "Isn't it sad when a mother doesn't want her baby?"

The window in the bus shelter had recently been broken by some drunk: glass fragments lay scattered across the pavement and the brown blood stains on the metal frame testified to the fact that the shelter had taken its revenge upon the hand and arm of the inebriated vandal. Sometime in the next millennium the council might send a man with a dustpan and brush to clean up the mess, but until then people would simply have to watch where they stepped.

Sharon Farrington was oblivious to the destruction; her thoughts were all firmly centred on her own predicament. She gazed unhappily at her watch; she had missed the bus by only two or three minutes and now had nearly an hour to wait before the next one came along. But for the vile lump in her belly she would have wandered into town and perhaps gone for a coffee at the Stocks Cafe where maybe there would have been friends to chat to. Not so many months ago such a chance to escape from a domineering mother-in-law and from the claustrophobic atmosphere of the farm would have been welcomed with open arms, but now the only topic of conversation she could expect to have would be about her pregnancy. She had become *a woman with child*, with no identity other than that of a pregnant mother to be. Fashion, frivolity, fun, all of these distractions no longer featured in her world; she was a brood mare, an in-calf heifer, a creature that would get fatter and fatter, and more and more uncomfortable until the moment that her body erupted and spewed out the alien life from within, screaming and gulping down its first lung full of air. When that moment occurred everything was lost, the last vestiges of being a free woman disappeared, and for the rest of her life she would be a slave to the strange life form she had spawned.

She wondered how this fate might be avoided. Half remembered old wives tales came flooding back. She had already tried jumping up and down in the vain hope that this would somehow dislodge the foetus, but all she had done was to make herself hot and sticky, and chronically short of breath: throughout her frantic exertions the baby's heart had stubbornly kept beating.

Lacing her bath with gin had been a futile waste of costly alcohol, and her mother-in-law had gone ballistic when she discovered that half a bottle of Bombay Gin had disappeared. She had accused Sharon of theft and demanded recompense, and for ten days had refused to speak to her. Every cloud had a silver lining, but this one tiny benefit was as nothing when compared with the intensity of the gloom that overshadowed her world.

If I were rich, thought Sharon, there would be no problem; an expensive doctor in a private clinic would administer a drug and all would be well. She had no money of her own, and the money she could beg, borrow or steal would barely pay the train fare: life was so unfair: she stamped on the pile of broken glass in her frustration.

Throughout history desperate women had tried desperate remedies to rid themselves of their unwanted burdens. Sharon knew nothing of Victorian law and of the harsh penalties that had been imposed on the poor unfortunate girls who had taken extreme measures to end their pregnancies, but she guessed that they must have been severe. And arguably the ones who could be punished were the lucky ones because they were still alive, although, perhaps, that made them the most unfortunate creatures of all.

Her grandmother had told a horror story of a sixteen year old girl who had drunk bleach in the forlorn hope it would kill her baby. She had succeeded in doing so, but only at the cost of her own life. She died in unbearable agony, writhing in pain, ignored by her family and without a soul to comfort her.

No doubt there were drugs and substances available today which could guarantee the desired end, and some of them might not have terrible side effects, but Sharon had no idea what they might be, and there was nobody she could turn to to seek enlightenment. She sank down into a corner of the bus shelter, her head in her hands, and a picture of abject misery.

"Are you alright?" The man's voice made Sharon jump; his presence beside her was unwanted.

"I'm fine," she blurted out, "Please just leave me alone."

"I saw you run out of the surgery," said the man. "I could see you were unhappy, I think I might be able to help you."

Sharon forced herself to turn and look at the man. He was a complete stranger, definitely not local, and somebody who she guessed might be a very recent arrival in town. He wore a blue shirt under a black jumper, with black trousers and black shoes, and Sharon wondered if he might be some sort of security guard. The dark glasses that totally obscured his eyes added to the overall impression of authority, and his neatly clipped moustache also gave credence to this initial assessment.

"Nobody can help me," she said. "Just go away and leave me to my own devices."

"I can help you," he said. "I know why you're unhappy, and I can do something about it."

"I ain't got no money, I can't pay you 'owt, so do yourself a favour and just sling your hook."

"I don't want money. I just want to try to help you! Now are you willing to listen to what I've got to say?"

"Why would you want to help me? You don't know me from Adam; you don't owe me no favours. What's in it for you? Nobody does anythink for nothing."

"All will be revealed," said the man. "Do you know anywhere we can go where we can get out of the cold and maybe have a cup of coffee, and I'll tell you all about myself and what I can do for you?"

Brown's Cafe was some two hundred yards away from The Stocks Cafe on the other side of the Market Place to it, and was not nearly so popular with Sharon and her friends. It claimed to have a *cheap and cheerful atmosphere*, but in truth it was neither cheap nor cheerful. The elderly waitress habitually wore a face that would make molten lava freeze, and the coffee on sale was often bitter and overpriced. How it kept going was a regular topic of conversation within the town: the most widely believed theory was that the husband and wife who rented the premises were deliberately trying to bankrupt themselves in order to ensure that no money was left for their estranged children to inherit when they died; but for Sharon and the man in black it offered an ideal place to talk.

Sixties pop music blared loudly from a speaker. The waitress disappeared as soon as she had served the throat lacerating coffee, and Sharon and the stranger had the place entirely to themselves.

"Are you sure you ain't some sort of pervert who fantasises about pickin up pregnant girls and rapin 'em? I've read about weirdoes who like doing that!" This was untrue. Sharon's reading was limited to pop music papers, with occasional excursions into the world of *Hello* magazine. The man looked shocked.

"Look Sharon," he said, "I'm not a sex maniac or an axe murderer; I just feel sorry for you, and I know that I can help you if you'll let me. If I could make that baby inside you go away you'd feel a great deal happier wouldn't you?"

"You ain't a magician, and I ain't takin no poison." said Sharon, remembering her granny's frightening tales about the young girl and the bleach.

"I wouldn't need drugs. I was a medical student for three years; always came top in my exams. I fell in love with a fellow student. She became pregnant. She didn't want the child. I got rid of it for her. I didn't do her any harm, but later she changed her mind and reported me to the Dean. I got chucked off the course, and I spent some time in prison: if I help you, you're not going to change your mind are you?"

Sharon vigorously shook her head.

"You'll need to get away from your family for a couple of days; do you think you can manage to do that? We'll book into a hotel somewhere as man and wife. I'll do the necessary, and I'll stay with you until the foetus has been aborted, and we'll make up some story that you miscarried on the bus or something like that. Nobody need ever know the truth and, I promise you, that within a week you'll feel like a new woman. Now it's up to you Sharon. Do you want to take a chance on me, or do you want to carry the child within you full term?"

Sharon's brain whirled. A thousand conflicting thoughts were flung with centrifugal force to the edges of her mind. Her head spun, she was in a daze, but through the confusion she could see a way to end her unhappiness.

Grabbing the man's hand she looked him full in the face.

"I'll do it!" she screamed. "I'll bloody well do it!"

CHAPTER TWENTY FIVE

Jackie Skinner wiped a bead of sweat from her forehead. The kitchen was hot and sticky, but the heavy rain, driven against the window by a strong westerly gale meant that she couldn't open that to let in a blast of cooling air. Things were just about on track. The vegetables had been prepared and soon it would be time to place the pans on the cooker; two fine lamb shanks were slowly roasting in the oven and, in the fridge the home made panna cotta, which was to be served with fresh Scottish raspberries, was quietly cooling.

Alan would be arriving in an hour's time, and tonight they would be having a romantic dinner for two. He had said that he had something important to ask her; she wondered if it might be a life changing question. If he asked her to marry him what would she do? She knew, without hesitation, that her answer would be "yes".

The children were staying with her mum and dad. It was only the third time in two years that they had agreed to have them, but they were so much better behaved now that there was every possibility that the overnight stay would be incident free; if it was, then in the future, overnight stays might become more regular occurrences.

Jackie looked at the neatly laid out dining table. Best china and best wine glasses; was it all a bit too obvious? She wasn't sure. Maybe the two red candles in the cut glass candlesticks lacked originality, but if it did look *chocolate boxy* did that really matter? How she felt was what really mattered; and today she felt very happy indeed.

There was just time for a shower and a change of clothes. She knew exactly what she was going to wear, (although the decision hadn't been arrived at without a morning's agonising), and further, she had already decided on the jewellery to put on and which scent to dab behind her ears.

Thirty five minutes later, (ten minutes longer than she had expected to be) Jackie came downstairs. The dress was black and sparkly with a lower neckline to that which she usually wore. There was a hint of cleavage; Jackie did wonder if perhaps it was too much. A small gold pendant set with amethyst showed off the shape of her neck, and although she looked critically at herself in the mirror, had there been an honest bystander on hand at that moment, he would have pronounced that she looked very pretty indeed.

Trying not to get flustered, but aware of the time, the potatoes were put on to boil; the vegetables could be left a little longer so that they were not overdone: everything had to be right; nothing could be allowed to spoil the occasion

Bang on time Alan arrived. He brought flowers and a bottle of wine and he told her she looked lovely. "You look pretty decent yourself," she replied and they had kissed and that kiss had felt good.

The meal was as fine as she had hoped it would be. The lamb was perfect and the vegetables were exactly right and Alan complimented her on her cooking. She blushed when he said that it was the best meal he'd had in years, and had tried to play down her achievement. Alan stopped her in mid sentence. "Jackie darling," he said, "You're a wonderful cook and a wonderful person too. Don't sell yourself short. You're an amazing woman, and I really do love you."

After they had eaten a long and leisurely meal Jackie made fresh coffee and they moved away from the dining table and sat side by side on the settee to talk and to drink coffee.

Suddenly Alan became very serious. He put his right hand into his jacket pocket and pulled out a little box.

"Jackie, my darling Jackie, I know I'm going to do this all wrong. I'm not wonderful with words, but the past few months have been the happiest I've known for many years, and it's all down to you.

I don't know if you feel the same way, but I know I can't live without you and I was wondering if you might agree to," and here he hesitated looking for the right words to say.

Jackie thought she knew what was about to happen next. Her heart raced: she felt eighteen again and young and pretty and wanted; the word "yes" hovered on her tongue, awaiting its cue to be released into the open air.

With an almighty crash the front door of the house burst open. Six big men forced their way into the room. The man who lead them in, and who held a piece of paper in his hand, spoke in a harsh and threatening manner.

"Jacqueline Skinner," he said, "I'm Detective Inspector Robert Earnshaw. I have with me a warrant, signed by a magistrate, which permits me to search these premises for illegal drugs and for evidence of child pornography!"

Alan Nadin was on his feet in a split second, anger and anguish etched across his face in equal measure, his temper not helped by a long standing antipathy to the senior drugs officer.

"You've got this one wrong Earnshaw," he snarled. "Jackie Skinner's a decent, honest woman and, if you'd done your homework properly, you'd know that to be a fact. You've been lead up the garden path big time by some malicious bull-shitter, and if you'd come and talked to Mrs Skinner in a civilised manner, instead of doing your usual *Dirty Harry* routine, you'd have discovered that fact for yourself. Before you make matters a whole lot worse, why don't you and your pack of Clint Eastwood wannabes just get out of this house and go and play your Fantasy Island games somewhere else."

"Ex Detective Sergeant, holier than thou, good old Alan bloody Nadin! I might have guessed you'd be hanging round here trying to get a leg over. I'll just warn you once. Don't even think about obstructing my enquiry, because, if you do, you'll be in the back of a fucking police van before you can even blink. Now sit down and shut up while we search these premises; we can do it gently, or we can do it roughly; the choice is down to you and to your glittery bit of stuff on the side."

The arrogance of Earnshaw, his rudeness, his overt hostility reduced Jackie to floods of tears: she shook from head to toe: Alan was beside himself with rage. "You ignorant bastard Earnshaw," he snorted, and for a brief moment it looked as if he might lash out in his fury.

"Alan, please! For God's sake, don't. They'll arrest you and then they'll wreck my home. Please, please just let them get on and do what they've come here to do."

"She's got brains as well as a decent pair of tits; I should listen to what she's saying Nadin. One more wrong move and you're nicked. Now just shut the fuck up and let me get on with my fucking job!"

The search was more selective than might have been anticipated. The police seemed to know exactly what they were looking for and precisely where to look for it. D.I. Earnshaw went straight to the cupboard in which the board games and video tapes were stored. He ignored the action/adventure films and instead concentrated upon the half dozen or so tapes which were the Disney Classics. A smug look of triumph flashed in his eyes as he picked up the cassette box containing "The Jungle Book" video. He shook it gently; a small cellophane bag containing white powder fell onto the floor.

"Oh dear me Mrs Skinner, what have we got here? I'll bet a pound to a penny that it isn't icing sugar!"

Jackie's face drained of its colour, her jaw dropped, she couldn't speak and she was so very, very frightened: eventually words came. "I don't know," she stammered, "I've never seen that before in my life."

"They all say that Love," said Earnshaw, with a self-satisfied smirk: "try telling it to the judge and see how far it gets you!"

In total four of the cassette boxes contained small plastic sachets of powder, maybe more than a hundred all told, but the other two boxes didn't contain any powder at all.

"Can I use your video player Love? I've not watched Cinderella since I were a nipper."

The images that appeared on the screen were disgusting. The children being raped were no more than six or seven years old and the men who raped them, or who masturbated over their naked bodies took extreme pleasure in their perverse abuse.

"And not an Ugly Sister to be seen," sniggered the drug squad inspector, "now isn't that a turn up for the book!"

Jackie shut her eyes in horror. "Dear God!" she screamed "this can't be happening!" She collapsed to the floor, struggling to breathe and, trying to cling onto the last vestiges of reason: Alan wanted to rush to her and comfort her but D.I. Earnshaw barred his way.

"Jacqueline Elizabeth Skinner," he said, "I'm arresting you on suspicion of possessing a Class A drug with intent to supply; I'm also arresting you on suspicion of possessing grossly indecent images of children. You don't have to say anything if you don't want to, but anything you do say will be written down and may be given in evidence against you. In other words Duck I'm going to have to break up this romantic little dinner for two. You're coming with us to the police station where you will be questioned as a suspect. I shouldn't count on getting back home any time soon. Put the cuffs on her Roberts, in case she starts to struggle then stick her in the back of your patrol car, then go and find the dog man and get him in here to see what he can sniff out. The rest of you lot can start bagging up all the video cassettes and then start looking for bank books, dealer's lists and all the usual crap that nasty little drug dealers always possess. And one more thing: one of you escort ex Detective Sergeant Nadin from these premises; God knows what mischief he might get up to if we were to leave him in here on his own.

CHAPTER TWENTY SIX

It was nearly eight o'clock and Mark Hobson was still in bed. The heavy rain and gales of last night had given way to a tranquil sunny day. Christopher was still asleep in his cot, Helena was in the shower, and Mark had nothing to do except plan how best to take advantage of such a beautiful rest day. A trip out somewhere was favourite, somewhere where there were breath taking views and, ideally, wild animals or birds to watch and a place where they could get a fantastic lunch, but which welcomed children. The problem was Mark couldn't think of anywhere that matched his aspirations.

The stridency of the door bell relieved him of the responsibility to think further. *Who could be so insistent at this ungodly hour?* Pulling on a pair of jeans over his pyjama bottoms and throwing on a baggy jumper, in a less than convivial mood Mark descended the stairs to find out; his annoyance increasing with every step when the ringing doorbell finally wakened Christopher from his slumbers.

His state of mind changed dramatically when he opened the door and saw Alan Nadin on the pathway outside. His face was pale, he clearly hadn't slept, there were bags under his eyes and, the smart clothes he was wearing were creased and crumpled It was immediately obvious that something was seriously wrong.

"Good God Alan! What's the matter? Come inside and tell me what has happened."

"It's Jackie!" cried Alan. "She's locked up at Burrdale nick. That cunt Earnshaw's arrested her, and she's going to be put before a court in Chesterfield later on this morning!"

"Jesus Christ!" exclaimed Mark, "It's unbelievable. Tell me what the hell's gone off?"

Alan was nearly in tears as he related the events of the last twelve hours.

"I went to Jackie's for dinner last night and she did us proud. Everything was perfect and she looked bloody gorgeous. I'd told her that I had a very important question to ask her, and I know she'd guessed what it was. Well we were sat down having coffee, and I'd just about picked up the courage to ask her, and I was putting my hand in my pocket to get this," and with tears in his eyes Alan pulled out a small jewellery box which contained a diamond and sapphire engagement ring, "when, that bastard Earnshaw and his marauding band of storm troopers kicked the bloody door in. Earnshaw tells Jackie that he's got a warrant to search for drugs and for child pornography."

"I told him he were behaving like a twat, he and I go back a long way, and he tells me to back off otherwise he'll arrest me, and the bastard would have done so too. So I bites me tongue and lets him get on with it. Jackie was shell shocked, you could see that she hadn't got a clue what was going on, but when you're as tunnel visioned as that pillock is you don't ever allow for the possibility that someone might be innocent."

"Anyhow they search through these video tapes that Jackie's got, you know the sort of stuff you'd find in any normal household and hidden in some of 'em they find little dealer bags filled with Crack. There are about a hundred in total, with a street value of over a thousand quid, and that's not all. They looked in some of the other cassette boxes that didn't have drugs in 'em, and they played the bloody tapes, and when they played the tapes it were some of the vilest pornography you've ever seen. Jackie collapsed on the floor; I'm a hundred percent sure she knows nowt about any of this, but that didn't stop Earnshaw slapping the cuffs on her and sticking her in the back of a police car and then kicking me out of the house."

"I contacted Bob Greenway, the defence solicitor; he's given us a rough ride a few times, but he knows his stuff, and he arrived at the police station to represent Jackie. Not surprisingly she were in a right state. For some reason Earnshaw's convinced that Jackie's got a big stash hidden somewhere, but they turned over the house last night, and they had sniffer dogs but they still didn't find 'owt else. Jackie told Greenway that Earnshaw had told her that she'd lose the kids if she didn't talk to him, but he's never going to admit saying that is he?

"Jackie's told the police that a chap from the N.S.P.C.C. called at her house a week or so ago, collecting jumble or summat, and that she gave him a load of video tapes and games. A couple of days later he brought a few of the tapes back saying she'd been way too generous, and because she'd told him in passing, when she gave him the tapes, that she particularly liked one or two of them it were those that he gave back to her as a sort of thank you present. She didn't have time to look at 'em, so she just stuck them back in the cupboard and she thinks that he must have switched the tapes and hidden the drugs to get back at her for something or other, but she's got no idea why anyone would want to do this to her.

"The trouble is the only fingerprints on the boxes are hers, and although Jackie was able to remember the name that he called himself and even his collector number; he showed her what purported to be an I.D. card with everything on it and she remembered the number because it were the same as the last four digits of her phone number, but guess what! The N.S.P.C.C. has no knowledge of this bloke, it has no person on its books with that collector number allocated to him and, it hasn't collected in the Burrdale area at any time in the last six months!

"Earnshaw doesn't believe her. He's going to push for a remand in custody, and despite Jackie not having any previous convictions Greenway thinks that the prosecution will try to portray her as a liar, and because of the nature of the child pornography and the high value of the drugs, they might be successful. If she's remanded her parents can't look after the kids and they'll probably end up in care because there's nobody else to have 'em. If they take away her boys it'll kill her Mark! I don't know what I can do! It's so bloody unfair! You're my only hope! Please, please help me at the very least to try to get her out on bail."

"Alan you know I'll do anything I can, but what I can do I really don't know. I can't meddle in an enquiry which isn't mine. If I go bleating to Stan Hardy he'll tell me bluntly it's none of my fucking business unless I can prove to him that something's been done which is either incompetent or corrupt, and you know I can't do that. Earnshaw's an arrogant sod with all the sensitivity of a warthog, but he's not daft. On paper he'll be able to justify every single step he's taken."

"I'm not asking you to do that Mark. I'm asking you to help me get her released on bail. You've told me more than once how moved you were by Jackie's courage when she came to the nick less than eighteen hours after her husband had been gunned down with that tin box full of letters and photographs. You told

Jackie the same when we had dinner here a few days ago. Did that mean anything, or was it so much hot air? I thought you were better than that Mark. I didn't take you to be a bull-shitter!"

"Alan that's not fair. I meant every word I said, but I can't go into court and oppose the prosecution; Earnshaw would go ape shit and Stan Hardy would be nuclear. If it was just me to consider then I'd do it, but I've got Helena and Christopher and the baby to think about."

"Jackie's got three little boys to think about, and when she's locked up in a cell and they're being passed from pillar to post by one social worker or another she'll go demented; but that won't be your problem will it Mark?"

The raised voices had disturbed Helena. The sight and sound of Mark and Alan arguing both amazed and distressed her.

"What's the matter with you two?" she cried. "Surely you shouldn't be falling out with each other?"

Alan recounted for her benefit the events that he had previously explained to Mark, and Mark repeated his desire to help, and the fact that he felt powerless to do so.

Helena became very solemn. "Mark sweetheart," she said, "there's no choice: we've got to go to Chesterfield this morning and we've got to give Jackie all the help that we can give her. If you can't stand up in court and support a defence application for bail then I can. I saw how moved you were by her fortitude when Mike was killed, and I've seen her with the kids and I know what a good mum she is. There's no way on earth that she'd do the things that she's accused of; I can stand up in court and say all that. I can also say that if I'm wrong about anything I know my husband will correct me, and you can just sit in court and say nothing. Your silence will confirm the accuracy of my testimony, but at the same time nobody can accuse you of talking out of turn."

"There are two more things I can and will do as well. Firstly, if they want a surety to secure Jackie's attendance at court then I'll be that surety and, if God forbid that they do lock her up, which surely can't be a possibility, but if the magistrates do, then, if Jackie wants me to, I'll look after the three boys. It would be a tight squeeze, but we can manage, and I know you'll both help me to do so if it becomes necessary. And there's another thing you can do Mark. Earnshaw won't look for the man who gave Jackie the tapes because he doesn't believe that he exists, but we do! If Earnshaw's not looking for him, you can, and if you find him then Stan Hardy will have to listen to you. Go and get changed into something respectable. I'll phone Mum and Dad to see if they'll have Christopher for the day then I'll go and make us each a cup of coffee and a slice of toast. While I'm doing that you can give Mr

176

Greenway a ring Alan and tell him what we propose to do and ask him to give Jackie our love, and to tell her we're thinking of her, and say that whatever happens we won't let the children be taken into care and how gladly we'll have them if the worst comes to the worst. Now come on, we haven't got a lot of time: we're going to Chesterfield to be there for Jackie, and we're going to bring her home with us. Now jump to it both of you!"

For the first time since they had met that morning, both men smiled.

"Yes, Miss!" They responded in unison, and they then set about the tasks that Helena had assigned to them.

CHAPTER TWENTY SEVEN

"I hear you've been making a name for yourself Gov, and according to one member of the Angry Brigade here in this building that name is Meddling Moron! I laughed like a demented hyena when I heard what had happened. His expression was an absolute picture; to see that knob head frothing at the mouth, with egg all over his face, was the funniest thing I've witnessed in decades."

"You make him sound like a fizzy omelette Pete, but let's get the record straight. I didn't say or do anything at Chesterfield yesterday, so D.I. Earnshaw can stick his head up his arse so far as I am concerned!"

"Oh, don't get me wrong Gov, I'm with you one hundred percent. Earnshaw was bragging in the canteen early doors about how he'd carried out a major drugs raid the night before and how he'd rubbed Alan Nadin's face in the dirt at the same time and I thought what an arrogant unthinking tosser you are! I've met Jackie Skinner loads of times, usually when Mike had got himself in some sort of trouble; she was way too good for him. She always tried to do the right thing. I don't believe for a moment that she's suddenly turned into Derbyshire's premier drugs baron."

"You may not do Pete, but the magistrates in Chesterfield very nearly did. Group Four brought her into court in handcuffs: they took 'em off before the remand application but to be dragged before the court in chains almost destroyed Jackie. I've never seen anyone looking so scared. She was as pale as death, shaking like a leaf in a gale and then that new prosecutor Plackett set to work. He thinks he's God's gift to advocacy; he'd trample on anybody to get to the top. Well, he really went to town. He described the videos in all their sick detail, he was almost salivating by the time he'd finished doing so, then he launched into a gut wrenching sob story about the lethally destructive power of Crack, and after he'd laid everything on with a trowel he tried to tarnish Jackie with Mike's bad character, until Greenway leapt in to put a stop to that. A lot of damage had been done, though; it was on a knife edge as to whether Jackie would get bail. Greenway told me afterwards that until Helena took the stand he thought he was backing a loser. She was bloody magnificent Pete! I didn't have to say a word. In the end Helena had them eating out of her hand and, with a little bit of help from Alan, and an excellent address from Greenway the Bench decided to grant Jackie bail. It should have been unconditional of course, but a £5000 surety and an 8pm curfew except when she's picking up the kids from a pre-arranged event like a school play or a scout night isn't really too bad. I thought Jackie was going to faint when they told her she could go. She didn't say a word until we got her to the car, then the floodgates opened. She was almost hysterical, crying for her boys, she couldn't think of anyone else but them. We were all nearly crying by the time we got her home. It's going to take her a long while to recover from this and she's going to need a good deal of help."

"And from the look on your face we're going to give her some of that help aren't we Gov?"

"We're going to do our level best. Earnshaw doesn't believe Jackie's story about the N.S.P.C.C. collector, well I do! We're going to find that man and we're going to discover what made him set up a harmless, well meaning creature like her. We won't be treading on anybody's toes because Earnshaw isn't looking for another suspect, never-the-less I think that this is something we should keep between ourselves. You've got contacts Pete, maybe one of them saw a stranger hanging around outside Jackie's house at the relevant time. Jackie says he was driving a small white van, but that's about as much as she can tell us."

"Don't make it easy for me will you! Is there any description of the guy concerned to give me a bit more of a chance?"

"There's the problem Pete. Jackie spent some time with him and she thought he was someone she'd seen before, but apart from being able to tell us he had short brown hair, she's not been able to give us much assistance. She told me his face was like a blank canvas, and depending on the way you looked at him depended on what you saw. Understandably, she was very upset last night so I couldn't probe any deeper, but I think she means that he's like one of those impressionists on T.V. who, without much make up, just by a change of expression or mannerism can become virtually anybody that they chose to be. That doesn't help you much, does it Pete?"

"Not a lot Gov, not a lot, as a certain irritating magician used to say all the time and, talking about men who can do magic; one prick who definitely can't is striding towards this office right now!"

Detective Inspector Robert Earnshaw was not a happy chappie. A volcano was about to erupt, Krakatau would soon explode, and the walls of D.I. Hobson's office would be pebble dashed with obscenities, recrimination and bile. Innocent bystanders should flee the wrath of the Gods, the guilty party was about to be engulfed in flames and, after annihilating a man's reputation, Earnshaw saw himself standing like a colossus over the carnage that this encounter would leave in its wake. It would become the stuff of legend; a Greek Tragedy on a monumental scale, but unfortunately for the Drug Squad officer, Detective Inspector Hobson had no intention of becoming a sacrificial lamb.

"Just what the fucking hell were you doing interfering in my case yesterday, you stupid fucking prat?" railed the incandescent police officer. "You were bang out of order. Because of your intervention a scum bag drug dealer is now free to peddle her poison, and worse than that you've pissed on our chances of recovering a huge stash of Crack. You've blown your career big time over this; I'll bloody make sure of that: If you're still in a job three days from now I'll be fucking amazed; you useless waste of fucking space!"

"Ah! The ever courteous, ever reasonable Mr Earnshaw! Living up to your star billing I see. I'll tell you this just the once. If you ever come rampaging into my office again, you'll be out of that door with my foot up your backside in less than three seconds flat. Before you go anywhere shooting your ill-informed mouth off you should check your bloody facts. If you'd bothered to do that you'd know that I neither said nor did anything yesterday to interfere with your pathetically inadequate investigation."

"No you didn't! But your sodding wife did, and you were sat right behind her when she did it! You're trying to hide behind a woman's skirts, and that really does disgust me Hobson!"

"I'm not hiding behind anybody's skirts Earnshaw. I went with my wife yesterday because she wanted me to be there. It was her choice to go; it was her choice to speak out. Are you suggesting that I should have stuffed a gag in her mouth and then physically dragged an obviously pregnant woman out of court?"

"You should never have let her go in the first place, and if you were too weak to do that, you should at least have had the guts to have disassociated yourself from her remarks when she started to mislead the court. You're a wimp Hobson as well as a fucking cretin!"

"My wife didn't mislead the bloody court. Every word Helena said was true and I'm not going to say otherwise just to give some fig leaf of credibility to your blinkered misjudgement of this case. Jackie Skinner is no more a drug dealer than you are a reasonable man! History will prove me right. Now if you've finished your offensive tirade get out of this office before I throw you out. Your foul mouthed ranting is making the place stink!"

"You haven't heard the last of this Hobson: you won't be laughing when you hear what Detective Chief Superintendant Hardy has to say."

"Stan Hardy will tell you that you've behaved like a moron. If you want to confirm to him that you're a grade A. twat run along and speak to him: my bet is he knows that for a fact already. Shut the door behind you when you leave, and try not to upset any of the office girls, they've all got busy days ahead of them today."

CHAPTER TWENTY EIGHT

"I wish I'd been there Mark, I'd have given a week's pension just to see Earnshaw scuttling out of your office like a punch drunk rabbit, but be on your guard, he's a vindictive swine and he'll try and get his own back any way he can."

"Pillocks like Earnshaw don't bother me Alan; I can have him for breakfast any day of the week. I'm sure we'll have another set to, maybe when I catch the bastard who planted the stuff on Jackie, and I promise you that if we do the outcome will be just the same. And talking about Jackie does she feel any better now she's had a couple of nights at home?"

"She feels like a criminal Mark. She's terrified that someone will try to take the kids away from her and every little noise outside makes her jump. She can hardly bear to let them out of her sight. It was all I could do to persuade her to let 'em go to school. I've told her that she's got to try to carry on as normal, but that's simply not possible at this moment in time."

"Maybe if you asked her the question that you were going to ask her before your good friend and mine put a stop to that conversation it would help to calm her down."

184

"I can't do that Mark. Jackie's head's so screwed up at the moment I don't know what she'd answer. If she said "yes" it might be for the wrong reason and, if she said "no" that might be for the wrong reason too. I've got to wait and to be there for her when she needs me and, perhaps in time, things will settle down and then it will be the right time for me to try again."

"You're probably right Alan, and we are pulling out all the stops to get this matter sorted. I've got Pete Bennett looking for our bogus charity worker. He hasn't had much joy yet, although he has found one person who saw a van outside Jackie's home and witnessed her talking to some bloke on the doorstep. He had his back to the road of course so we're not much closer to getting a decent description, but at least, in my eyes, if not in Earnshaw's, it confirms part of her story. The witness is sure the man is a stranger. He told Pete that he knew just about everybody in town and that he could recognise most of the locals, even from behind; but he didn't recognise this bloke's back. I know Jackie thought she'd seen him before, but obviously that must have been a very long time ago, and my gut feeling is that when we do get our man, which we definitely will, we'll discover that he hasn't been hanging around here for more than a few weeks."

"Is Pete following up any other leads? Is he looking for the video tapes that Jackie gave away and which weren't returned to her by our mystery man?"

"Well he's made enquiries at the tip and at the council depot to see if any of the bin men or the tip workers remember seeing a bin full of video tapes but he's drawn a blank there. When he's got time, his next job is to trawl round the charity shops to see if anybody brought in a pile of tapes shortly after Jackie gave her tapes away."

"I'll save him a job Mark. All the shopkeepers know me. Pete's a damn good copper, but he doesn't have the patience of a saint, and certainly he won't have the time to stand and chat that I've got. The more people talk, the more they remember. If I do find any tapes I'll very carefully stick 'em in a carrier bag and bring' em straight round to you so you can arrange to have the cassette boxes finger printed."

"We'll if you're sure Alan, it'd do us a favour. I know you'll do the job right, and if you do that it will free Pete up to make other enquiries. We're still trying to find out who sent the notes to Julia Hammond that accused Will of murder. I'm convinced that what's happening now is somehow related to Timothy Eggleton's funeral. We know Will Hammond left home a contented family man with apparently no thought of suicide, but after an hour or so in church everything changed and he rushed out of the building seeing no hope for himself except to take his own life. There wasn't any disturbance or unpleasantness during the service so the root cause must pre-date Eggleton's death, probably by a goodly number of years. I think in this case the past holds the key to the future. People are beginning to crawl out of the woodwork. Have I told you that Charles Montgomery has suddenly turned up on the scene when everybody thought he was dead? He seems to be a changed man by all accounts, but unless Jesus Christ popped down from heaven to lay hands on him, I'm not at all certain that I buy that particular story. I've got Pete re-checking all the information that we've discovered to date about Jerry Eggleton and his little gang of ne'er-do-wells just to make sure that we haven't missed something vital."

"That's good thinking Mark, but here again I might be able to be of some use. From what Jamie's told me since and, from what I saw for myself first hand, it were pretty obvious that Justin Barnes were the lad who really ran the show. The others were all scared of him. Certainly when he was running wild he would have been my prime suspect for anything nasty that was going on and things like sending those letters to Julia would have been right up his street: the only problem is that I know for a fact that he really is dead."

"I've got a cousin who was a doctor in South Africa for about fifteen years in the 1970's and 1980's; it was a good life then, before the troubles really kicked in; providing of course that you had money and the colour of your skin wasn't black. Most of his patients were rich ex-pats of English or Dutch descent and at certain times of year there were American and European travellers. Doctor to the millionaires, that was Stewart. I doubt if he saw a shanty town or sniffed the stench of poverty the whole time he was out there. One of his patients were particularly loaded. She had a son in his late teens who I think were knocked down by a hit and run driver, although I may have got some of the details wrong. He were injured but he weren't killed by the car, but before the emergency services could get to him he was set upon by a gang of robbers. They beat him to death with clubs: having white skin didn't do him a lot of good in the circumstances he found himself in. The robbers actually chopped off both his hands with machetes so that they could steal his rings. They probably chucked them away afterwards for stray dogs to feed on after they'd prised the jewellery from his fingers. It were all pretty gruesome stuff as you can imagine. The manner of the road traffic accident and more particularly the brutal manner of his death sent his mother over the edge. Apparently she screamed non stop for five days and then she withdrew into herself and said nothing. She slipped out of the house after midnight, nobody saw her go, and she walked five miles to a local beauty spot. She jumped from a two hundred foot cliff, her body virtually disintegrated on impact; there was hardly a bone that hadn't been smashed. That woman was Justin Barnes' mother, and the lad who died, that was Justin Barnes. There was no problem over his identification, his face weren't badly marked, and he would have been recognisable to anyone who knew him. There wasn't any scope for error and certainly his mum was convinced. Why would a woman go to the extent of taking her own life if there was the slightest room for doubt? You could get hold of the local newspapers if you wanted to see what they made of the story, and no doubt the South African Police still have a file somewhere if you want to look at it, but I think you'd be wasting your time. As the saying goes it's a poor mother who doesn't know her own child, and this one seems to have doted on her son. I'm absolutely one hundred percent certain that Justin Barnes is well and truly dead."

CHAPTER TWENTY NINE

It had been difficult for Sharon Farrington to make her bolt for freedom. She had concocted a hundred excuses in her mind: *She was going away for the weekend to stay with a friend, she had to visit a sick relative, she needed to buy some clothes for the baby,* and dozens of other spurious reasons had briefly flickered in her imagination. The trouble was that nothing she had thought of had credibility. She had no friends now, or at least none who would invite her to stay with them for the weekend. Her near relatives all enjoyed rude good health and, in any event, they all lived locally, which was no use at all. Her officious mother-in-law would insist on coming on any shopping expedition she undertook: since the episode with the gin Brenda had concluded that Sharon was unfit to be let out on her own, particularly if there was the remotest possibility that she would be spending money; and, for every plan that she had hatched there had been a compelling reason why it wouldn't actually work.

Eventually she had decided that silence was the best policy. She had secretly packed a small rucksack with the basic essentials and had slipped away from the farm whilst others were preoccupied with their routine tasks. She left a note for David on the bedside table saying that she needed a little time to herself to get things clear in her mind and that she would be back soon. When she came back there would be hell to pay, and when it was discovered the baby had been lost, the universe would explode. Brenda would certainly suspect the worst, but even she couldn't deny the fact that Sharon had virtually no money of her own to pay for an operation, and that there had never been any talk at the clinic about a termination. It was inevitable that the slight value she had had for her mother-in-law as temporary custodian of the heir apparent would be replaced by the contempt felt for the loser of an irreplaceable jewel. If that occurred Sharon knew that she would be ostracised, but to be ostracised by Brenda was a privilege granted to very few living souls.

She had arranged to meet the man in black on Buxton Market Place near to the Town Hall. She hoped he would be on time; she didn't want to run the risk of bumping into anybody she knew and then having to dodge questions about where she was going, and what she was going to do when she got there. For the *where* she had no idea at all, for the *what* she knew exactly her intent. The prospect frightened her, part of her wished she could talk to somebody for reassurance, but this plan could never be the topic of casual conversation.

Fortunately he arrived on the dot. Strangely, he had not changed his appearance from the time they had first met, and today the sun was so weak that dark glasses were anything but essential; however, if the man wanted to look like Derbyshire's answer to

Johnny Cash then that was his God given choice, and certainly none of her business. She got into his car, a shabby, Vauxhall Astra and, without any exchange of pleasantries, they set off.

"Where are we going?" she asked.

"Wait and see," said the man, "just sit back and enjoy the ride."

"Sit back and enjoy the ride!" That was a particularly inappropriate thing to say. Here she was, in a car with a man she didn't know, at the outset of a journey which would end with a stranger handling parts of her body which should be untouchable except by a doctor or a lover: this man was neither. He was a medical student who had been kicked off his course in disgrace. He had served a prison sentence and he had taken the life of an unborn child; but in what circumstances? Was it possible that that embryo had been the product of rape and that the abortion was a cynical attempt to get rid of the evidence? Could it be that the mother wanted the child, but that an unwarranted assault on a vulnerable woman had taken place to avoid the payment of child maintenance? She was vulnerable. She was at risk. Even if he was everything he claimed to be, and there was so much about him that she didn't know, tonight there would be pain and mess as the premature termination of the embryo inside her womb took place. What would she be like after it was done? Feelings of fear and guilt began to overwhelm her and, at that moment, she came close to abandoning the mission and demanding that he stop the car and let her get out. The man seemed to sense her unease.

"I'm sorry," he said, "that was thoughtless of me Sharon. It was such a stupid comment to make. I know you're frightened, and I don't blame you; if I was in your shoes I would be frightened too. You're being very brave, much braver than I would be. I think that I should tell you now exactly what I've got planned, and then you can decide whether or not you want to carry on."

"We're heading towards a small hotel on the outskirts of Derby; it's very clean and very quiet. Tonight I'm going to perform a procedure upon you. There won't be any drugs and there won't be any surgery. I'm going to very gently insert a sterile knitting needle into your vagina and slide it gently into your womb. There should be very little discomfort. After I've done that you'll need to keep lying down. There might be a little bleeding, and you may feel like you've got a mild stomach cramp, but I promise you it will soon pass. Tomorrow morning you'll start the day a new woman, and one who is back in control of her own body. If you've got any doubts and, you want to change your mind that's fine, but now's the time to do it. I'll turn the car straight round and take you back home if you tell me to, but if you really want rid of the child inside you, today represents your best opportunity of making it disappear. Tell me, do we head south to Derby or north to Burrdale? Whatever you say that's where we'll go."

Sharon bit her lip, she was being silly and in danger of throwing away the thing that she wanted most.

"Derby." She said, "I ain't changing my mind, I want to go to bleedin Derby!"

The rest of the journey was stress free. The man passed Sharon a small box of C.D's and asked her what music she would like to hear. She made her choices. Closing her eyes and ignoring the pretty countryside that flashed by, she listened to her favourite dance tunes. Soon she would be able to dance again. She didn't see the disdainful look on the man's face, or his obvious contempt for her various selections.

At a small village just outside Derby they stopped for lunch.

"This is the last food you'll have for a while," said the man, "so choose something really nice." Sharon looked through the expensively priced menu with its wide range of meats and sauces; without any degree of hesitation she chose scampi and chips with a tiny dish of tartar sauce.

It was late afternoon by the time they arrived at the hotel and Sharon now felt strangely relaxed. The building was a large late Victorian or Edwardian house set in its own grounds, which had been converted into a hotel sometime in the mid 1960's. The overall ambition of the place was modest, but as Sharon's *personal physician* had told her in the car, it looked to be very clean and it was definitely quite secluded. They signed in as Mr and Mrs Browne; it was hardly an inspired choice. Sharon felt sure the receptionist didn't believe them, which was in fact, exactly right; but had they signed in as the Archbishop of Canterbury and Christine Keeler she wouldn't have queried what they had written down in the register.

The bedroom they were taken to was surprisingly large. Two single divan beds had been put together to make up a large double bed, and a third single divan, pushed tight against the wall provided additional sleeping accommodation if, for any reason, that was needed. Unlike the double bed it had not been fully made up and was apparently most frequently used as a depository for suitcases, or as a makeshift settee from which to watch the flat screen T.V. that clung tenaciously to the magnolia painted wall.

"This will be perfect," said the man, testing the single bed by bouncing up and down on the mattress, "not too soft, not too springy, it should be just right." He then proceeded to roll back the counterpane to reveal a thin beige coloured under blanket.

"Oh, that looks a bit itchy!" he said, "and it will show up the slightest degree of discharge, I think we'd better do something about that."

From out of his suitcase he pulled a faded pink bed sheet which he spread over the under blanket.

"I had the choice of pink or bright green when I bought this. The green would have clashed horribly with the paintwork, I'm so glad I picked the one I did."

He looked at his watch, it showed 5.22pm; the digital alarm clock showed 11.17pm: it was wrong now, but it wasn't always inaccurate: in five hours, fifty five minutes it would be exactly right: its triumph however was fated to be of only sixty seconds duration.

"It's a bit too early to start at the moment," said the man. "I've got a bottle of vodka in my suitcase, would you like a drink Sharon? A little bit of alcohol might help you relax; you're not one of those young women who get giggly after just one sip are you Pet?"

"I can take me drink," said Sharon bristling. "I once had sixteen Bacardi Breezers in a single night!" She didn't add that thereafter she had been as sick as a dog and that she had cut both her knees and severely sprained her right wrist when she fell out of the discotheque door and crashed down on the gravel path outside. She had blotted completely from her mind the jeering laughter of the bouncers and the searing indignation of her parents when she arrived home at four o'clock in the morning in a bloody, dishevelled and disorientated state.

"I'll give you a small one to be going on with and maybe another one a bit later on and then, after I've done my bit, you can finish the bottle off if you've a mind to. Now I know how well you can hold your liquor I'm not in the least bit bothered about any adverse consequences."

"Ain't you going to have one with me?" asked Sharon.

"I need a steady hand for what I've got to do," said the stranger. "I don't want to run the slightest risk of anything going wrong. Perhaps when everything's done and dusted then I might just have a glass to drink to you and to the rest of your new life."

CHAPTER THIRTY

Julia Hammond sat alone in the room. The children were in bed and, for the time being, asleep: there was no guarantee that they would remain so. Most nights since Will died had been disturbed. One or other, or frequently both, would awake and cry for their mother; why should tonight be any different? Julia had almost forgotten what it felt like to have a good night's sleep.

There was nothing she could do. The children were too young to understand what had happened to their daddy, but they weren't too young to feel a sense of loss and, although Julia tried hard not to let her unhappiness filter through to them, inevitably it did, and they sensed the despair that at times almost overwhelmed her.

Night time was the worst time because, at night time, she felt truly abandoned. Why had Will done such a dreadful thing? The coroner at the inquest had concluded that he was not mentally ill when he took his own life but, that said, neither was he in a normal state of mind when he so dramatically killed himself. Mr Mayweather had been so kind and he had stressed that it was his view that there was nothing in Will's home life that had caused the tragic events that had occurred. He was sure and, he had stated such as a fact, that Julia had nothing to reproach herself for;

she couldn't be blamed in any way for anything that had happened.

Will's mum and dad had told her many times since his death that she had been the best thing in his life and that he had felt himself to be the luckiest man alive to have found her. Both had said repeatedly that it was only her existence and the existence of the grandchildren that now kept them sane. They were so protective of her and they offered her unconditional support, but were they also shutting their eyes to unpalatable facts? If she had loved him even more than she had, if she had been able to give him greater strength might he still be alive now? More and more she found herself blaming herself for his death.

There was another thing too that intensely saddened her. Will had been dead for a few short weeks, but already it was as if he had never existed. She had photographs of course to prove that he had, and maybe one day when the pain had ceased (if such a day should ever come), she might be able to look at them and then also watch their wedding video and the holiday videos that had been recorded in exotic, romantic places; but that day would be a long time in the future. For now her memories of him all seemed to be unreal and, if she closed her eyes she couldn't visualise his face or hear his speech with any degree of clarity.

The one thing that Julia dreaded was to dream, and yet, at the same time, it was also what she most wanted to do. To dream of Will, of his caress, his kiss, his gentle touch was what she yearned for, but to awake from such a dream would be agony; and what if instead of dreams there were nightmares? If she was to see Will hurtling through space and then recreate in her unconscious mind the dreadful moment the rope sliced his head from his body and to witness the blood gushing from his neck that would be truly unbearable and would surely heighten her sense of desolation.

Postponing the necessity of rest for as long as she could Julia sought distraction by trying to read. That attempt was futile. Time and again she found herself re-reading the same page of the historical novel that she had commenced, with such enthusiasm, just two days before Will's death. Now every word was hard labour and the intricate plot that had at first so excited her had become incomprehensible. Throwing the book onto the coffee table she picked up the remote and turned on the television: there was nothing worth watching. Channel hopping was an irritation. One programme was equally bad as the next; how could so much money be wasted by so many people on producing so much mindless drivel?

When first Victoria and then Robert started crying it was almost a relief, and that relief lasted for nearly two hours before both finally settled back to sleep. It was way after midnight. The moment couldn't be delayed further; filled with apprehension Julia finally made ready for bed.

The dream when it came was unsettling; it was a cold and joyless dream, but to begin with not so disturbing that it exploded the barrier between conscious and unconscious thought. There was a boy; a boy who she did not know but who at the same time looked familiar; a boy who appeared to be both nervous and unhappy. It was going dark. The black and white Collie dogs leapt up at him, pleased at his presence and expecting all the time to be petted by him. He didn't make a fuss of them as he usually did, but they were not to be disappointed. He brought them gifts of food. The raw meat dripped blood and the dogs devoured it eagerly. First they whimpered, then they wailed, then they howled. Their stomachs expanded like overblown balloons until the moment they burst open plastering the concrete yard with foul smelling entrails.

The boy fled with tears in his eyes towards a small group of other boys who laughed at him and mocked his distress. He ran from them into the mist, and suddenly she found herself there screaming at him, begging him to return. He turned for a second and glanced towards her. The boy had become a man. For a brief moment he hesitated, and then he ran on and vanished into the night. She cried uncontrollably: just one more glimpse of his face would have been sufficient; but Will had gone and he was never coming back.

It was barely daylight; the Dawn Chorus was nearing its climax; a gloriously sunny day seemed destined to follow. On such a day people felt better about the world, people felt happy in themselves, people made love, wrote poetry and glorified in being alive; but Julia felt wretched and washed out. Four hours sleep wasn't enough, particularly when it hadn't been followed by the luxury of a slow ascent into reality. One minute she had been dreaming, the next minute she was thrashing about on her pillow, unable to get the images she had seen out of her head. She felt that in some strange way, Will was telling her in death things which he had kept secret from her in life. Was this single episode the beginning of a tragic story? Did it hold the key? She had to know more. Will couldn't tell her, but there were people still alive who could. Charles Montgomery had been the first person to mention the incident and, undoubtedly, his story was the father of her nightmare. Maybe there were gaps in the narrative that he could fill in. She had to find out. He offered her the best hope of piecing together a full history of Will's missing years. She was certain that somewhere within them lay the answer. At a little after 8:30a.m. she telephoned him at the hotel where he was staying.

Monty was cheerful and charming. No, her phone call hadn't come at an inconvenient time. Honestly, it really wasn't too early.

She wasn't interrupting anything important. Yes he had all the time in the world to talk. The full English breakfast that had been set down in front of him just seconds before the telephone bell rang slowly solidified, as it continued to lie unmolested on the plate; if it remained untouched for much longer the kitchen porter would need a stone mason's hammer to chip the uneaten food from the crockery.

He listened attentively to everything that Julia said. He had trained himself to become a good listener and he took pleasure in conversation. Talking on the phone to a beautiful woman was never a chore, even if the beautiful woman was very troubled; but a face to face meeting would be so much better.

"I can be at your house within the hour if you'd like me to come round. I've got a few photographs which if I can find them might be worth glancing at; although it's so long since I looked at them they might be no help at all. I'll bring them with me anyway, just in case they could be of some use. So far as I'm concerned, today I'm at your disposal for as long as you want me; even if we don't find everything out I'm sure we'll make some progress."

In fact it was only twenty minutes later when Charles Montgomery turned up on her doorstep. Julia had barely returned from dropping the children off at Play Group, a journey that took no more than five or six minutes, even on a bad day: she was just taking her coat off when the doorbell rang. She had expected to have had some time to prepare for this encounter, and it unsettled her that he was so very early. Was such haste entirely normal behaviour? She thought not. She knew so very little about this man: there could be a side to his character that was best left undiscovered; but nothing was normal anymore, or ever likely to be.

"I've taken you by surprise," he said, noting the expression on her face. I never thought. Christ, what must you think of me? Shall I go away and come back in a little while? I feel such a prize buffoon!" And he smiled an apologetic little smile and shuffled awkwardly on the doorstep as he waited for a reply.

Julia looked at him; there was something oddly childlike about his appearance: it could be an act, of course, but she didn't think it was.

"No, there's no need. I'm being silly. Come in and I'll make us both a cup of coffee and then we can sit down and talk about Will. Last night I dreamt about him, it wasn't a very nice dream, but it made me realise that until I know the truth about why he killed himself, I'm living in a state of limbo and that isn't helping me, and it certainly isn't helping the children."

They talked for a long time: Julia had so many questions and Monty tried to answer them as best he could, or so it seemed to

Julia; but some of his early optimism now seemed to be misplaced. Apart from filling in the odd detail here and there about minor incidents of anti-social behaviour, which he had touched upon the first time he had been to the house, he wasn't able to help a great deal. In particular he wasn't able to add any more information about the poisoning of the dogs, nor could he throw any further light upon the death of Jacob Farrington.

"I did ask at the time Julia, I really did, but nobody would tell me a thing. I will try to speak to people again to see if, after all these years, somebody will be prepared to tell me more, but I'm not holding my breath; I honestly don't think anyone will be willing to talk to me."

"You mentioned photographs on the phone; would you like to show them to me?"

"Christ! I nearly forgot about them. They may be nothing at all; I just grabbed the envelope before I came out. There aren't many of them, but as I remember them they're all a bit unpleasant. I didn't take 'em, I don't know who did, but Justin Barnes had them. He kept them in a little tin box in his bedroom. Then his uncle, or whoever it was chucked him out of the house after an argument, and chucked his stuff in the bin. Barnesy bullied me into going to recover his gear: his uncle had threatened to set the dogs on him if he ever set foot on his property again, so he didn't dare go back.

I crept into the garden just after dark and grabbed the stuff and ran. I stuffed everything into a rucksack. The lid must have come off the tin and some of the photographs must have fallen into the bag. I didn't realise at the time. I thought I had given him everything I'd got back, but I didn't give him the dozen or so pictures in the bottom of my bag. By the time I realised what I'd done Barnesy had upped sticks so I just hung on to them; why I did that I don't know, they're not very nice pictures.

There were fourteen photographs in the envelope that Monty produced. The nastiest one of all showed Barnes and Jerry Eggleton pointing at an obviously frantic cat, the nail that had been driven through the fleshy part of its tail into the tree was clear to see; almost as bad was the picture of the same two boys standing next to a burnt out haystack with sneeringly triumphant grins on their faces.

"I think these are records of achievement," said Monty. "They're absolutely disgusting; it makes me realise now what little sods we all were then."

The least offensive looking photograph was the one that almost took Julia's breath away. In a pretty churchyard a group of boys, a group which included Barnes and Eggleton stood alongside an obviously new grave. The name on the gravestone could have been written in blood. It burned its way into her brain. Why had

Justin Barnes and Jerry Eggleton wanted to be pictured next to the tombstone of Jacob Farrington? Given the nature of the other photographs, in Julia's mind, there could only be one possible answer.

CHAPTER THIRTY ONE

The thing about charity shops nowadays was the smell, or rather the complete lack of smell, and in some cases also the complete lack of old clothes. Alan Nadin wasn't a regular customer at any of the small shops that were scattered across the Peak District's towns and villages but, occasionally, he had bought second hand books, and once he had acquired an excellent snooker cue, for the princely sum of three pounds. More numerous than his infrequent shopping extravaganzas had been the times he had attended these retail outlets in his official capacity as a police officer on duty. Some little *toe rag* nicked for selling stolen goods at a car boot sale would whinge that he had purchased the offending articles at Oxfam or Cats R Us or Help the Nearly Dead or any number of similar emporiums and some lowly constable would be dispatched to discredit the obviously spurious claim.

Sweat, mothballs and just a hint of piss, these were the scents that once upon a time had seemed to be the norm, but not anymore; except in a couple of tatty back street shops which seemed to have existed in a state of suspended animation for the last thirty years: dowdy Sleeping Beauties clad in the same faded coats and dresses from day one of their increasingly drab existences. Decimalisation had been the fatal pin prick, the demise of pounds shillings and pence had sounded their death knells: both premises now existed in time warps into which only the very brave or the very, very poor now dared to enter.

Today in most of the shops Alan had visited, the story had been a totally different one: bright lights had shone, attractive displays had tempted the eyes, and expensively labelled gear was everywhere to be seen. Tat was banned, Rag and Bone materials were looked at in horror; these places didn't want cheap bric-a-brac or the musty surviving remnants of Great Aunt Florence's wardrobe; but fortunately for Alan, he had eventually found one shop that did at least look at every donation that it was offered.

The R.S.P.C.A. shop bridged the gap between old and new.

"We don't take left over jumble from jumble sales," said the shop assistant, "nor do we touch electrical goods, which is sometimes a pity, but providing clothing is clean and undamaged and china and glass wear has been washed we take practically everything else; it's a slap in the face to peoples' good intentions if we tell them we don't want that which they've so kindly offered; and you never know one day in the future there could be a legacy, and we can't afford to alienate potential benefactors."

Alan nodded sympathetically; no organisation that depended upon public donation could risk upsetting the ordinary people who supported it; that would be economic suicide. A customer approached the till carrying a brightly coloured top and the assistant cut short the conversation and went to deal with her. Ex Detective Sergeant Nadin moved away from the clothes racks and started to browse through the videos on sale which filled an entire shelving unit.

Jackie was still very upset. She hadn't been able to provide a comprehensive list of the films she had given to the bogus collector and almost certainly some had been forgotten, but she had remembered more than a dozen of them, which in the circumstances wasn't bad going. In other shops that Alan had visited he had found the odd title or two, but not in sufficient quantity to cause him any excitement but, on these shelves, there were nine titles that matched the list; this had to be more than just coincidence. Very carefully he removed each suspect video from the display and he took them all to the pay point, explaining his interest in the tapes to the shop assistant, asking her for a carrier bag and, requesting her not to handle the tapes herself to reduce the risk of her fingerprints obliterating any that might be already there. He paid the girl ten pounds for the job lot; it was a little above the asking price but, whether these videos did or did not turn out to be the ones Mark Hobson was looking for it was only right that the R.S.P.C.A. shouldn't lose out financially. He asked the assistant if she could remember anything about the person who brought the tapes to the shop, and he noted down the details she gave him in a small exercise book. It was like old times. Flushed with what appeared to be success Alan headed straight way to Burrdale Police Station.

"We won't know for sure Mark if these are the right ones until they've been fingerprinted of course, but I'm pretty confident they will turn out to be. The girl remembers a chap bringing them in, she said he was a bit like one of the actors out of *The Bill* but she had a feeling he didn't always look that way, which I thought was an odd thing for her to say. There was another strange thing too; she felt that this man was ill at ease, that somehow he thought himself too good to be seen inside a second hand shop, and yet he bought a double sheet which was in a bargain basket of used bed linen: that surprised her: he didn't look the type to make such a penny pinching purchase."

"But nothing surprises us any more does it Alan? Baby faced kids kill toddlers, pious priests turn into paedophiles; it's a mad old world and it's getting madder with every day that passes."

Alan grunted his agreement, and was about to launch into a colourful indictment of charlatans and phonies when he was forestalled by a knock on the Detective Inspector's door and a split second later D.S. Pete Bennett strode into the room.

"Oh hey up Alan! Didn't know you were here. Long time no see. How are you keeping? You're looking good pal. Am I interrupting something Gov? I can pop back in five minutes if you want me to; there's a bit of news just come in which I think might interest you."

"No, there's no need for you to go Pete. I'd better be off. I've been here too long already and I think I should be getting back to Jackie. You're not looking too bad either mate: perhaps sometime soon we could have a couple of beers at The Albert and spend a few minutes putting the world to rights."

"I'd like that Alan. Tell you what give me a ring next week and we'll fix summat up. Give my best wishes to Jackie; I hope she's not too worked up by Earnshaw's fucking insanity. That's the way it's going now Pal, you're well out of the job. Cunts like him are taking over the asylum. In six years time I can put my ticket in, and I can't wait for that fucking day to come."

With these words of support for his decision to retire ringing in his ears, Alan said his goodbyes and left: D.S. Bennett turned to address his D.I.

"It's a sordid little tale I got for you Gov," he said. "It may be nothing at all to do with the case we're investigating, buts my guts tell me otherwise. Yesterday morning Sharon Farrington left home. She didn't tell a soul where she was going. She left a note for her husband saying she needed some time to sort her head out. She's sixteen week pregnant, which is sixteen weeks too long so far as she's concerned, and, by all accounts, her mental state is more than a little bit shaky. Last week she apparently rushed out of the clinic in tears after being told that everything was progressing satisfactorily; the practice nurse was quite concerned about her."

"Yea, I heard about that Pete. Helena was in the clinic at the same time; she told me about a young girl running out into the street in a distressed state; that must have been Sharon. Helena said that she was very, very upset.

"That's right Gov. Anyway yesterday she went walk about. The family claim to have been worried sick when they discovered she'd gone, but they still didn't report her disappearance to us straight away. They don't trust outsiders; they don't like strangers prying into their business. Brenda Farrington rules over them with a rod of iron. She's a scary woman that one: I wouldn't want to be the person who upset her, particularly if I was wearing light coloured pants! They looked for her themselves; they didn't think that she'd get very far because she had no money. Mum-in-law controls the purse strings and Sharon ain't trusted to look after cash. They searched all day but couldn't find her. Eventually they began to fear that she might have done something really stupid, and late last evening they finally reported her missing. The good news is that she was found this morning in a hotel in Derby; the bad news is that she's now in an emergency ward at the D.R.I. and it's touch and go whether she survives.

"So what's happened to her Pete? How come she's ended up where she is?"

"It's still a bit unclear at the moment. She was in agony when the paramedics arrived at the hotel, screaming with pain, not in a fit state to talk to anybody. The room was pre-booked by telephone, and we know she was taken there by a man. They arrived in an old style Vauxhall Astra. The car was a shed and the hotel staff noticed how rusty it was. Unfortunately, none of them had the wit to record the registration number and now the car and the bloke have both vanished from the face of the earth."

"What is certain however is that sometime last night the man carried out an illegal abortion, a primitive knitting needle up the vagina job, and done so clumsily that it missed its target by a country mile; which I think is bloody odd. Sharon ain't the brightest star in the solar system but I'm sure she wouldn't have gone off with a complete stranger if he hadn't at least have been able to talk the talk. It's actions that count of course, and this cretin has carried out a medical procedure on a 19 year old kid with all the lightness of touch of a Victorian slaughter man: even a visually challenged piss head could have done a better job! It's almost as if he did it deliberately cocked it up; he obviously didn't give a shit about what actually happened to his *patient*. There's another thing too. Why did he do it at all? Sharon couldn't have paid him for his services, she hadn't got any money. Unless he's the sickest weirdo I've ever come across, his actions defy all logical behaviour."

"Do you have any sort of prognosis Pete? What are her chances of pulling through?"

"Well she's got peritonitis and it has taken hold. The muscles in her abdomen were so taught it's amazing they hadn't snapped. If she'd been a dog, at the moment they found her you'd have called a vet to put her out of her misery. Right now the odds are worse than fifty/fifty. If she does pull through her inside will be totally fucked up; she'll never be able to have kids that's a racing certainty."

"Do we know anything at all about the man who brought her to the hotel?"

"Well witnesses put his age at somewhere between thirty and forty: an ordinary looking guy with no obvious distinguishing features, except his dark glasses. He didn't say more than a few words so we don't know if he had any kind of accent, but he dressed better than his car suggested would be the case. He had a suitcase with him when he registered, but when Derby police searched the bedroom just under an hour ago it had gone.

Sharon's rucksack and the few pathetic items she'd brought with her were all intact, but every single trace of him had disappeared. If that isn't bad enough, the hotel manager ordered the bedroom cleaned as soon as Sharon left in the ambulance. Sod's law dictated that the chambermaid did a first rate job. Every surface was cleaned, anywhere where a finger print might have been left now sparkles like Gary Glitter's moon boots!"

"So they've recovered nothing that can directly link to him?"

"Not entirely. The Derby police have got an old bed sheet; it certainly doesn't belong to the hotel. He obviously left it behind because Sharon was lying on it, but, it's no good for fingerprints, and I'd be bloody amazed if it had any traces of his DNA: in my view it will turn out to be worse than bloody useless."

CHAPTER THIRTY TWO

A wise man, or a fool, once said "every picture tells a story," which, more times than not, is probably true; but often that story is a mystery; and even on those rare occasions when a tale unfolds that has a beginning, a middle and an end, tomorrow it may all change as new layers of perception and understanding are added to the text by further examination of the image presented.

And while some pictures set out deliberately trying to expose painful facts to the full glare of public scrutiny, others go to inordinate lengths not to reveal a truth: a slap across the face, caught on camera may testify to hatred, but does a kiss always speak of love or maybe just expediency?

The photograph taken in the graveyard that Monty had given Julia took on a different aspect every time she looked at it; and since it had been in her possession that had been on a great number of occasions: the only thing that remained constant was the conviction she felt that in her hand she held a record of pure evil.

The faces of the boys, which on superficial examination all seemed to display identical fixed smiles, as if they had just been called to order by a dictatorial wedding photographer, on closer inspection could be observed to hide a wide range of emotions behind their enigmatic Mona Lisa stares.

Jerry Eggleton and Justin Barnes were triumphant in victory, but even between the two of them subtle differences seemed to emerge. Eggleton was surely glorying in the moment. What happened next he neither knew nor cared; but something in the face of Barnes appeared to suggest that his thoughts had already moved on, and that this scene was just the opening chapter in a story yet to be told.

From behind the set countenances of the other boys less confident expressions seemed to be breaking out. Their lips tried heroically to maintain the illusion of celebration, but in some of their eyes Julia thought she could detect guilt and fear and perhaps even despair. They were still such young lads, not yet on the verge of manhood, but in nearly all of them she sensed a realisation that their own lives were already irreparably compromised by the insane actions they had committed. They would forever have their secrets. Will had lived with a crippling secret for all of his adult life, and, eventually he had been overwhelmed by it. He wasn't in the picture, but did that fact guarantee that he hadn't been present when it was taken? Could he have stood behind the camera? Was it possible he even set up the shot, decreeing precisely where everyone should stand, and in what pose? There were elements to the picture that reminded Julia of team photographs. Will had been a team player; he was very familiar with the composition of such pictures. The anonymous letter flashed into her mind. Only an Animal Rights fanatic would accuse a child who had poisoned a dog, wicked though such an act might have been, with murder, and there was nothing at all to suggest that the mystery correspondent was such a person. The sender of that vile accusation must have meant her to believe Will had killed a fellow human being. She didn't think that could be true, not for a single moment, but now she could no longer completely shut out the voice in the back of her brain that argued otherwise.

Another disconcerting thought ram-raided its way into her consciousness. Like Will Monty was also absent from the photograph, and his omission from it could be confirmation that he had not been present when dreadful acts were undertaken. He had told her that he was in hospital undergoing an emergency operation at the time when Jacob died, but was that really the case? He had revealed things about himself which were to his discredit, and he had accepted joint responsibility for cruel and loathsome behaviour. A man who bares his soul, who confesses his manifold sins and weaknesses, tends to be believed because only a true penitent would expose so much badness about himself: but then if such a person lies, he can rely on the credit he has received from his earlier honesty to help him get that lie accepted as truth. Could it all be trickery and deceit? Was it possible that he had been an integral part of everything that had occurred? She was condemning Jerry Eggleton and Justin Barnes, largely on his say so: maybe he was the string puller, the moustachioed ringmaster, the black caped villain of the piece: perhaps she had been putting her trust in a monster!

The one thing Julia now knew for certain was that she had to find out what really happened all those many years ago. The vitriol that had flowed from the unknown writer's pen was beginning to devour her memories of the decent and gentle man she had married; if nothing was done it would continue to nibble away at her belief in his goodness. She needed Will to be exonerated, but even more than that she needed to know the truth. Guilt would not destroy her love for him but, left to fester and to rot, suspicion might. Uncertain of how to set about uncovering the past she turned to her father-in-law for advice.

The counsel that he gave was strong and clear, but it wasn't what she wanted to hear, and for the first time since Will's death she found herself at odds with Bob: the realisation that they were on different sides of the argument was painful for them both.

"Oh Love," said Bob, "I know how you feel, and I understand what you've been through, and why you're so desperate to find out what happened: but what good will it do? It won't bring Will back, nothing can do that, and surely to God, if he did commit a terrible crime he's paid for it in the most extreme way possible. You lost him in life, don't lose him in death. Hang onto your treasured memories, and when they're old enough to understand, let my grandkids have respect for their dad. How can you break it to them if it turns out he was a murderer? Just think how badly that knowledge would damage them. If you go to the police with the photograph you've got, they will think the same as you. They'll dig and dig and bloody dig, and who knows what they'll find out. If it turns out there was a crime, and people end up being arrested, you know what will happen next don't you? The living will seek to shift blame onto the dead. Will can't defend himself against false allegations: I think that because he committed suicide, he will be seen as an easy target. He'll be smeared with all their excesses, and their lawyers will argue that my son's suicide is tantamount to a clear admission of guilt."

"I know that Bob and I am so afraid of the consequences; and the last thing I want to do is to make you and Anne unhappy; but can't you see that it's got to be this way. I don't know why, but somebody wants to cause trouble for us, especially for me, and I'm certain he's not going to stop. At the moment he can tell me anything, and I've got no defence; and I'll be left trying to shut my mind to the vilest of allegations. I don't think I could cope; it could go on for years and years, and drive me mad in the process. If I can find out, from a reliable source, exactly what did happen then, even if the police never catch the sadist who is tormenting me, at least I can deal with his false claims in the manner they deserve. It's the only shield I possess, the only way that I can have the confidence to rip up his vicious libels, and throw them in the bin where they belong. This way I can keep my fondest memories safe and secure; they're the only treasures I have left; I have to fight to cling on to them!" and quite unable to control her emotions further, Julia sat back in her chair and wept.

"Oh Julia, Julia pet, please don't cry. I only want what's best for you. If this whole can of worms is blown wide open, there will be people out there who will say 'she must have been aware' and 'how could she live with him knowing that he was a killer?' They'll imply that you only stuck by Will because he had money, they'll make nasty comments behind your back. I couldn't bear to see you hurt. You're the sweetest girl I've ever seen, I couldn't control myself if people started saying bad things about you. I don't want you to be damaged, you're too precious to us; we couldn't stand it if you were abused and slandered."

"Bob, listen to me. I know that Will wouldn't have hurt a fly, I know he was brought up to do what was right: it's my weakness that I worry about; it's the sneering voice inside my head that I have to silence. Will couldn't have done the things it says; I have to shut it up. I trust the police, and I know that you do too; you wouldn't have persuaded me to show them the letter if you didn't. Just because something has emerged to suggest that a horrific crime may have been committed doesn't mean that Will was a party to it. Detective Inspector Hobson is a good man, he would make proper enquiries. It won't be easy for us if there are arrests and a trial, and yes, dreadful things will be alleged about your son, the man that I loved more than anyone in the world, which could cause us a great deal of pain; but even that is better than slowly drowning in a sea of poison. Don't be angry with me, but I have to do this my way, I can't begin to face the future while the past is unresolved."

"Tha's right of course lass! So much wisdom in one so young! Go ahead with what you want to do; you've got our full support. I could never be at odds with thee and neither could Anne."

CHAPTER THIRTY THREE

"A bed sheet; a bloody bed sheet! You're so wrong about it Pete! It's the most important find we've had to date. It doesn't matter if there are no fingerprints; it doesn't matter if there's no D.N.A., although it would be bloody fantastic if there was: that bed sheet proves something absolutely vital; it proves that the person who went to such great lengths to set up Jackie Skinner is the same person who has now nearly killed Sharon Farrington."

"How does it do that Gov?" The look on D.S. Bennett's face was one of amazement: "What possible link could there be between Jackie and Sharon? Jackie's a sensible thirty odd year old woman who has faced everything fate's thrown at her head on and buckled down and got on with her life: Sharon's a nineteen year old airhead who reads avidly about boy bands and Big Brother, and who probably wipes her arse on real literature."

"I don't know Pete, but that's what we've got to find out," and Mark Hobson then explained to his detective sergeant the evidence that Alan Nadin had so recently uncovered.

"Our first job is to get these cassette boxes dusted for prints. If we're barking up the right tree they should have Jackie's prints all over them. There could be a whole load of others, maybe too many, there could be none at all, but even if there are lots we won't know who they belong to unless we happen to get lucky and hit on somebody who is already known to us."

"I'll get on to it straight away and, as you say, we may pick out a winner, but I bet you that it's ten to one times more likely that we bloody don't. What I can't understand is what motive there might be for all of this. Do you think he's just spotting random women on the street and deciding on a whim, maybe because of a particular expression on a face, or the colour of her hair, or the clothes that she's wearing that he should set about ruining her fucking life?"

"I don't think that's likely Pete, although we did have a series of rapes and sexual assaults in Sheffield a few years ago where it was the sight of a smartly dressed woman in a suit that drove this chap bonkers. He owned a small bookshop which had got into difficulties. His bank, for very sound financial reasons, refused to bail him out. The adviser who turned down his loan request was a very attractive girl, the type of young woman you see in the building society adverts, and her refusal to offer help had just festered in his mind. Every time he raped or assaulted a girl he was getting his own back on her. We eventually caught him because he finally picked up enough courage to have a go at the girl herself. He followed her intending to rape her and then probably kill her. Luckily for her, her boyfriend was a cop: he'd previously given her a pepper spray that he'd confiscated from a drug dealer to carry for her own protection. She had it in her handbag, and she used it to good effect; his eyes were still streaming next morning when they put him up before the Bench. Ultimately, he confessed to everything, except attempted murder. He's now serving life at H.M.P. Wakefield, probably with pictures of elegant business women stuck up on his cell wall so he can wank himself silly as he dreams about choking them all to death."

"Yeah, I can see where you're coming from Gov, but if there is a specific motive, it's going to be bloody near impossible to work out what it is. Sharon and Jackie don't knock about together; there's a fifteen year age gap between them so it's unlikely there's going to be a disgruntled boyfriend to provide a missing link. Physically they don't look alike, they dress very differently, they ain't got a thing in common that I can see. It's going to be an uphill battle with no guarantee of a victory at the end of it."

"It's a battle we're going to have to fight though Pete; and there's another thing we have to consider. If we're right, and I passionately believe that we are, when we see Jackie Skinner as the victim of a carefully thought out plan, which only became effective because she was persuaded to believe a sob story; and we believe that Sharon Farrington must have allowed herself to be talked into taking a course of action which has left her fighting for her life, it has to mean that a very plausible, very dangerous man is out there ruthlessly carrying out some insane personal vendetta. My big worry is that he may have other women in his sights; there could be dozens of them, he has already earmarked for special attention."

"Not just women Gov. It could also be blokes too, and Sharon's little more than a kid; young, old; sick, healthy; wise, foolish; there's no telling who might be next on his list. Not only that, the consequences of his actions are getting worse and worse: we could end up with a serial killer on our hands before long if we're not bloody careful."

"We could! Shit Pete! It makes my flesh creep just to think about it. If that does happen, nobody will be safe, he could even return to Jackie and to Sharon to deal with them as unfinished business."

"Have we actually got anything at all to go on?

"A bit Pete, a very little bit. Jackie gave Earnshaw the best description she could of the man who conned her. Earnshaw never followed it up because he's a prick and because he didn't believe a word she said. We'll ask her to come in and get an E-fit picture sorted out, but I don't have a great deal of faith in them to be honest! The woman who served Alan at the charity shop was with the man who brought in the tapes for the best part of ten minutes, certainly long enough to feel that there was something odd about him. Alan says she appears to be pretty much on the ball, but the verbal description she gave of him is very different from the one that Jackie gave to Earnshaw; but then of course we still have the hotel staff at Derby to fall back on."

"I take it from the sarcastic tone of your voice they haven't turned out to be of much cop."

"All they cared about was getting paid for the room. Do you know the manager actually asked the ambulance crew which hospital they were taking Sharon to so he could forward the bill to that address? Apparently one of the paramedics told him to "piss off" and he backed down, but it shows the mentality of the penny pinching swine. The girl on the reception desk wasn't much better; she was more interested in painting her finger nails than she was in trying to help the police discover who had violated a nineteen year old girl. The bit of a description she finally came up with could have fitted virtually anybody except, paradoxically it comes nowhere near to matching either of the other two descriptions that we currently have."

"So could we be looking for two different people Gov? It's either that, or one or other of Jackie or the shop assistant is suffering from the onset of premature Alzheimer's, or we've got ourselves a bloody chameleon, and personally I don't believe in fucking shape shifters."

"Neither do I Pete, but funnily enough I think that's the nearest thing we have to an explanation at the moment. What I mean by that is I think we have someone who sets out to make different impacts in different situations. I think our man is a born character actor who, without too much reliance on makeup, which would inevitably mark him out as a phoney if people got up close and personal, can somehow make you see what he wants and not what's actually there."

"So are we about to institute a fucking man hunt for a rubber faced thespian with a personal axe to grind who could be capable of any crime, including murder?"

"That's just about it, but we're also looking for other things too. We need to discover, in no particular order, the whereabouts of his clapped out car, any additional reliable eye-witnesses we can find and, most importantly in my view, something to link the lives of Jackie Skinner and Sharon Farrington. We may have to go back decades, but somewhere in their respective pasts, there must be a moment of fusion. Find that and we're a good way towards finding our motive. That's the next goal, and it's one we have to score quickly if we're going to succeed. Get your arse down to Fingerprints, and I'll get on the blower to Jackie Skinner. I'll probably suggest that Alan comes in with her; there's nobody better than him when it comes to remembering things that have happened donkeys years ago."

CHAPTER THIRTY FOUR

Despite Bob's promise that he would back her in anything she chose to do, which she knew to be genuine, and which did reassure her; after he left Julia sat for a long time considering the situation she was in. Bob and Anne would support her through thick and thin; probably nothing more would ever be said to try to reign her in but inwardly, she would know, that they were scared of what the past might reveal about their son and that their help, although whole hearted, would be given completely against their better judgement and would push them in directions they desperately didn't want to go. Who could blame them? Bob's logic was unimpeachable: she did risk stirring up a hornet's nest and if that occurred they could all be stung by the tiny barbs of venom that she had released into the atmosphere. Common sense screamed at her not to go there: common sense warned her of the dangers; but common sense couldn't help her sleep at night and common sense was no shield against the doubts that had started to make inroads into her mind. She had to have answers, she had to have certainty; without them she was stuck in a joyless eternal limbo.

If she couldn't turn to her parents-in-law, which she felt would be unfair, then who could she turn to for assistance? She hadn't got the contacts, the experience and perhaps even the courage to try to do things all by herself; she scarcely knew where to begin. The police were the obvious answer, and Detective Inspector Hobson had been very kind but, as Bob had so rightly said, if she went to them they would take over the investigation. It was one thing for them to look for the person who was tormenting her with his letters, it was quite another for the full weight of a police investigation to be focussed on Will. Once that juggernaut started it could not be stopped, she would have no control of it at all. If metaphorically she was in the driving seat, she could choose to stop at any time; if she wasn't she would be carried for the ride no matter where the journey lead to. For now only the truth mattered, but tomorrow, standing on the edge of the abyss, self-preservation might gain the upper hand.

Her thoughts turned to Monty. If he was the reformed character he claimed to be then he was the next best choice, and if he wasn't then more than anyone else, he knew secrets that could unlock history. Entrusting herself to him could be fraught with danger, but potentially the rewards could be great. Knowing full well that Bob would disapprove, and that the police would firmly advise against it: deciding to tell nobody, she picked up the telephone and dialled his number.

The response was enthusiastic, perhaps too enthusiastic, mirroring the response that there had been on the last occasion when she had enlisted his help. "No, it was no trouble at all." "Yes of course I'll help in any way I can." "I can come over straight away if you'd like me to." Mindful of the speed with which he had arrived on her doorstep last time and, fearing that unless told otherwise he would be earnestly ringing her bell the moment she put the phone down Julia set a time of three o'clock for the meeting; that gave her two hours to prepare; the children were at her parents and wouldn't be home until at least 5pm; there should be plenty of time to discuss matters before they arrived back.

After she had ended the call Julia set about planning her strategy. There were two objectives she needed to achieve. Firstly she had somehow to try to establish if Monty was genuine or a fake: a shyster or a Samaritan. She didn't know how she would accomplish this; inwardly she felt she would sense it, but intuition had often proved to be a fallible tool: maybe tragic misjudgements of character had lured some of the victims of the Yorkshire Ripper to their grisly dates with death.

On several occasions whilst waiting for him to arrive, Julia nearly changed her mind; twice picking up the phone and starting to dial his number to cancel the visit before abandoning the calls. She wished she wasn't alone, but that was the way it had to be for there to be the slightest chance of making progress. She told herself she was safe in her own home, she told herself she was being silly, but, never-the-less, when the doorbell finally rang it startled her and she felt her hand shaking as she reached for the doorknob.

Monty was all smiles and he had brought flowers, flowers purchased from a proper florist, and not cut price petrol station forecourt flowers. Julia didn't think it was appropriate for him to bring flowers at all, he was not a suitor, but, in reality, if she wanted his help she had no choice but to smile and accept them.

"I thought you sounded a bit low on the phone," he said, "I wondered if these might cheer you up a touch."

"They're very nice, thank you," said Julia, thankful at least that he hadn't chosen roses.

"Well, what's it all about? I'm fully psyched up and raring to go; what would you like me to do?"

As she had done before, but perhaps with a greater sense of urgency, Julia reiterated her need to find the truth.

"I can't help it," she said. "It's become an obsession; I can't begin to get my life back on track until I've laid the past to rest."

"I'll do whatever I can, but it won't be easy. None of Jerry's rat pack have been willing to say a word to me about Jacob; it's been a wall of silence up until now. I'm not sure any of them will ever change their minds, so please don't build up your hopes looking for a miracle because there may well not be one on offer."

"But we've got to try!" and saying that Julia got out the photograph and handed it to Monty. She pointed to each of the nine boys pictured in it. "Please can you tell me who they all are?" she asked, "and as best you can, can you also tell me what's happened to each of them since that photograph was taken?"

"Well you recognise Eggleton and Barnes of course, and they're both dead. The big lad on the extreme right is Ralph Ambridge, he's very much alive, but there's as much chance of getting information out of him as there is of finding a pulse in a corpse. The two lads next to him are the two Davids; one was called Gladstone, sometimes we used to refer to him as the P.M., the other one's surname I forget, but they're both still living in Derbyshire, or at least they were a couple of weeks ago. Gladstone wanted nothing to do with me, you might have thought I was called Disraeli from his attitude towards me, and I don't think he'll change. The other one I couldn't find because I didn't have enough information: if I dig some more I may be able to trace him but that could take time. The little lad kneeling down at the front was called Nathan Curtis, he was always a bit odd, and you can see that in his eyes. About ten years ago he quit a well paid job and joined some weird religious cult; much weirder than my church I promise you. He gave away all his money to them and then discovered they didn't have a hot line to God. He was well and truly conned. They left him practically penniless but on the upside he did meet and marry a nice girl. Of all of the gang of lads you see before you he's the one I think might have been helpful, but he died quite suddenly last spring from a brain tumour. His wife's still around though. She works in a craft shop in Bakewell; I have called in a few times to see her when I have been passing."

"Do you think it's possible that Nathan might have talked to her about his past, maybe when he knew he was dying? I wonder if she'd be willing to meet with me: perhaps if she could see how upset I am she might have some sympathy for me: and no offence Monty, Ralph Ambridge and David Gladstone could easily see you as some kind of threat. If they would consent to speak with me face to face, they would realise I wasn't any danger to them. I'm not Miss Marple trying to solve a murder; I would treat anything they told me in confidence. All I need to know about is the stuff that Will was involved in, I don't need to know anything else. I only want to find out what he did and didn't do. Do you think it's possible you could set something up?"

"I could try Julia, and certainly as regards Ambridge he might jump at the chance of meeting an attractive woman, but I think you'd be mad to talk to him. He thinks he's God's gift to the female sex so a pretty face might do the trick but, be warned, if he gets you alone his mind will only be on one thing. He's got a reputation for being rough. If he can see the chance of a leg over he might just talk, but you'd be playing a very dangerous game and to be honest, I think you're too nice and too soft even to consider playing it. Gladstone is superficially more civilised but deep down he's no different from Ambridge. Stay away from them both. Faith Curtis is gentle enough; you would be safe with her: if you've got to talk to somebody talk to her and give the other two the widest possible berth."

"I don't feel safe anywhere Monty. There are times when I don't feel safe in my own home, I don't feel safe now; so what I'd feel like with two men who have such dubious track records I shudder to think; but something has to be done, and I can't think of another way of doing it."

"You don't feel safe now Julia? Why don't you feel safe with me? Ten years ago you'd have been right, but not now. Near death experiences change a man, I can promise you that. You know that I've got a past I'm not proud of, but what you see now is what you get. I travelled my own road to Damascus; I found my light lying in a hospital bed. If you would like me to leave I'll go now but you're the one who asked for help and I want to help you; I owe it to Will and to you to do that."

The look on his face as he spoke was one of bleak rejection; if he was a charlatan he was a spectacularly good one: Oscars had certainly been awarded for far less convincing performances. Julia felt like she'd just kicked Bambi, and lacerated herself for not spotting his sincerity.

"I'm sorry Monty, I shouldn't have said that. I do feel safe when you're around. Please stay and help me decide exactly how I should go about things from now on."

The die was cast, the gamble had been taken: Julia had tied herself closely to this man who she hardly knew. History would tell if she was right or wrong, hindsight would be her judge, but for now the doubts had to be banished and he and she would have to work as a team.

CHAPTER THIRTY FIVE

It wasn't an ideal day. The grass was still damp from last night's rain but, the weather girl with the brilliant white teeth and the expressive hands of a Geisha, had confidently predicted that it would be the best day of the week. "A brief respite from the showers," she had said: *an opportunity to mow the bloody churchyard* thought Bob. He had other things that he wanted to do that day, but they weren't weather dependant, and so with all the grace of a thwarted bull elephant, he found himself striding out towards the burial ground of St Catherine's church.

When he had got to within a quarter of a mile of his destination a thought suddenly struck him. He stopped, patted his pockets, swore and turned back towards his house: the key to the little brick outhouse where the petrol driven *Flymo* and other assorted garden tools were kept was mocking his forgetfulness from the comfort of his kitchen table.

The young man who had been following him from a distance of around one hundred yards seemed unnerved to see this sudden about face: he also turned the other way and retraced his steps. *That's bloody odd!* thought Bob, but it didn't bother him, and he took no further notice of this stranger.

Ten minutes later he was on his way back to the church, the key was safely in his pocket and the words of his wife, scolding him for being *grumpy* were still ringing in his ears. Suddenly the sun sidled out from behind a shop soiled white cloud. It didn't offer any assurances that the weather girl might be right, but it did seem to imply that if he was quick, there was a remote possibility that it might condescend to wait around until he had finished his task. Its warmth cheered him, he felt less nattered, soon he would be in the right frame of mind to kneel at the graveside and speak to his son. Words didn't come easy; sometimes they didn't come at all, but the conditions were right, bird song hung in the air, the sun caressed his back, he would be at one with Will, and that thought pleased him.

He had expected the churchyard to be empty, it invariably was when he did the grass cutting, but today there was somebody else present. He wasn't bending to put flowers on a grave, or saying his goodbyes to a loved one, he wasn't struggling to come to terms with the capricious nature of fate, he was waiting, waiting for somebody or something, lurking behind a stone buttress, apparently not wanting to be seen.

The world was full of lunatics. Only last month a parish priest in Salford had been hacked to death by a deranged drug addict; mentally ill people were being dumped back in the community every day of the week without any adequate controls being put in place for their proper supervision: voices screamed violence in so many heads. Bob tensed himself and clenched his fists; he wished he'd gone to the shed and armed himself with a weapon, but it was too late to do that now.

"Oi, you over there! Just what do you think you're doing skulking in the shadows?" The young man jumped three foot in the air; it was immediately apparent that he wasn't any sort of fighter, his face lost its colour, and he was obviously terrified. Bob instantly regretted his aggressive approach and softened his stance.

"I'm sorry, I didn't mean to frighten you lad, but you took me by surprise; you can't be too careful these days. Don't be afraid, I don't mean you any harm. My name's Bob Hammond, I'm just here to cut the grass, but I do know a fair bit about this churchyard and the people buried in it; can I be of any help to you?"

"You're Bob Hammond? You're not Will's dad are you? I came here to look for his grave to pay my respects to him. I saw you before when you looked so angry: then I saw you coming back down the road, and you still seemed cross. I thought that there might be a footpath that carried on past the church and I waited out of sight until you were gone, but of course you saw me and found me here. My name's Rupert Henshaw, I used to be friends with Will many years ago: but I don't imagine he ever mentioned me to you did he?"

His voice tailed off into nothing. *"A gentle, intelligent, timid man,"* thought Bob, *"what's the world coming to when I begin to suspect every stranger I meet of being a violent psychopath?"*

"No, he didn't mention you Rupert I'm sorry, but there were lots of things he didn't tell us. His grave's over yonder, next door but one to the one with the big white marble cross: I'm going to give it a bit of a tidy in a minute straight after I've cut this blinking lawn."

Rupert smiled, Bob thought he had an engaging smile, and then he frowned.

"I think maybe its Fate that we should bump into one another like this. I've been trying to make up my mind whether to come and see you for some time, now it's been made up for me. I only knew you by name, not by sight, but I overheard people talking in the park saying how good you were being to Julia and I thought I must speak to him and warn him, but I'm useless at making the first move, and I'm not even sure if I'm right to be worried so as per usual I've done nothing. That's really so pathetic, I wish I was different, but like it or not, I can't help the way I'm made."

"None of us can lad, none of us can. Well, I'm here now, and we have met; the sun's shining, it's a lovely day, let's go and sit on that bench next to the church tower and you can tell me what it is that is clearly bothering you."

Trying to get Rupert to open up was like trying to squeeze Hamlet's soliloquy out of a tongue tied juvenile lead; the spirit was willing; the intent was all too clear; but there were so many false starts that Bob began to lose count of them. It wasn't that the young man stuttered, or even struggled to find the right words to use, Bob sensed his vocabulary was excellent, probably far greater than his own, but his courage seemed to desert him half way through his first sentence, although once he did manage to string three sentences together into a loose fitting verbal explanation before the doubts crept in once more and it was back to square one. The sun sniffed and headed for shelter behind the nearest black cloud; in the far distance thunder rumbled, or perhaps it was just blasting from the quarries; but it was becoming increasingly obvious that unless real progress was made quickly both man and boy would soon be dodging raindrops and the consecrated turf would remain overgrown and unattended to.

"Look, I know you're trying your best Rupert, and if we had all day I could wait until the cows come home for you to tell me what you're trying to get out but, we ain't got all day. It's going to piss it down any minute, and I've still got jobs to get done. I ain't an ogre, I'm not going to bite your flippin head off, so come on, just spit it out and then we can both get on with the rest of our days."

It was as if somebody had turned up the volume on an amplifier which had a loose connection. "It's Charles Montgomery," he said, and then realising he was shouting he took a deep breath and forced himself to speak slowly and quietly; "it's Charles Montgomery; I don't think that he's any good for Julia."

"Charles Montgomery? What about Charles Montgomery Rupert? Come on, just tell me everything you know about that bugger, I've always had me doubts about him. I think you're going to tell me things about him now which will make me realise how right I am."

The story was long and complicated, and at times difficult to follow, but with Rupert telling it, it was never going to be anything else. He went right back to the beginning. He described in too much detail a pretty ordinary childhood, he went on to explain how he first met Will and to stress how much he thought of him and all the time Bob just wanted him to get to the meat of his tale but he knew that any interruption now would be counter-productive: the road to Revelation was being travelled at a snail's pace, but at least it was being travelled.

Through a shared interest in football Rupert said he had become friends with Will; through his father's ambition he had met Jerry Eggleton. He explained, at great length, that his dad had been envious of Timothy Eggleton's wealth, and he had engineered it that they should play a game of golf together. In order to try to cement a friendship he had thrust Rupert at Tim's son. Rupert explained that he didn't really like Jerry but that his father had ignored his mild protests and Jerry, who he felt looked down on him, had recognised that he was clever and had tolerated him and occasionally used him. "That was my big mistake," he said. "There were times when I was flattered by the attention I got, I didn't see the dangers: soon I was part of a nasty little gang of boys, although I don't think I ever had more than a walk on role."

Rupert explained the pecking order in the gang. "Eggleton thought he was number one," he said. "He was full of himself, but the real leader was Justin Barnes. You know all about him, but do you know that in so far as he had any friends, his best mate was Charles Montgomery?

"Some terrible things happened," he continued, "I was mainly a bystander, sometimes with Will stood alongside me; he was the only decent one in the pack. They put him under so much pressure; they told him so many lies, that's why he eventually did what he did. You know all that too, I guess, but I don't think you will know that although it was Barnes who wanted revenge on Jacob Farrington far more than Eggleton, it was Montgomery who came up with the idea of poisoning the dogs. It was him who convinced Will that no real harm would be done; all Jerry did was provide the incentive. He was a glib bastard in those days; he could sell an idea to anyone if he had a mind to: subtlety subterfuge, pathos, flattery, he used the lot. He's still the same today and he's using all his old tricks on your daughter-in-law."

"Is he by gum? He's certainly told her that he nearly died ten years ago and that he underwent some sort of deathbed conversion, then miraculously he got better and found God."

There was firmness and a certainty in Rupert's manner which was striking when compared to his earlier hesitancy; gone was the awkwardness, gone were all the self doubts.

"He's never had a day's illness in his life. It's all bullshit. He's spinning Julia a yarn and there has to be a reason why he's doing that. He wants her, or he wants something from her and he's trying every dodgy move he knows to get it. Watch her like a hawk Bob, watch her like a hawk: he's not the repentant sinner he's pretending to be: he's an evil, two-faced lying bastard. I can't prove anything for definite, but I've met people who say that he engineered the death of Jacob Farrington. I'm sure it can't have been a bloody accident. Don't you find it inconceivable that a farmer with a lifetime of walking these hills in all weathers should simply fall down and crack his skull? I've been told that Jacob was lured to his death and that Will was the unwitting instrument used to get him to go to the place where it happened. Nobody is willing to say a great deal, and stories do vary. One version of events is that the rocks were deliberately coated with grease to make them slippery; another version is that it wasn't the fall that killed him but that a huge boulder was manhandled by two or three youths and deliberately dropped on Jacob's head as he lay helpless on the ground. I've heard it claimed that Montgomery was one of those youths, but he's not going to say sod all about it and no-one else involved will say a word about it either because they're scared of him and of their own guilt.

Somewhere in existence there's a photograph showing the lads who were involved. Montgomery doesn't feature on it, but that doesn't mean he weren't there. I think that's because he's got nous; I also think that he could have been the photographer and if he took the picture and kept it then he's got a hold over every person shown on it. He's a devious swine, capable of doing absolutely anything. If you don't watch out for her he'll get his talons into Julia and drag her down into his own particularly nasty version of Hell."

CHAPTER THIRTY SIX

I was afraid that she was going to die: not because I felt sorry for her, she doesn't deserve sympathy; not because her passing would have left the world a poorer place; but, for several days, I fretted that I had inadvertently handed them a "get out of gaol free card". Everything that happened she brought upon herself, but the silly little cow was so shallow and so self-obsessed that she couldn't see the implications of her actions. There were no drugs, save for a modicum of alcohol and never did I use or even threaten violence. Everything was done at her request; nobody forced her to make the choices that she did: I'm totally convinced that part of her believed it would turn out to be a big adventure, leading to a brave new world in which she would regain control of her sad little life. It was ridiculously easy. Tell people what they most want to hear, offer them what appears to be a way to make their dreams come true and they will believe you: allay their fears, chase away their doubts and you're a God, and one that is trusted to deliver to them their sordid little miracles.

She has had her wish; she isn't pregnant now, nor ever again will be so. A barren womb, a barren life, the one goes hand in hand with the other. The first was once her deepest wish; the second will become her deepest sadness. She knows now that she has sinned and, should she even for one moment forget, she has the scorn of an unforgiving woman to remind her. Every hour of every painful day there will be rancour and discord in that family; that's why I now rejoice: if the infection had taken too great a hold and she had died as it at one time appeared she might well do, her life would have been blanked from their collective memories, like a bad dream shrivelling to nothing in the warmth of a new day.

"A waste of space;" "a brainless little tramp"; "an unnatural mother who conspired with the Devil to rid herself of child": no-one will defend her; nobody will offer her salvation; but she will not be cut loose; it's not their way, it's not their code, and so discord will poison all their lives forever: no second chances will be on offer, no hope of a better outcome with another wife. My plan has achieved everything I set out to do; my gift of misery has been taken to their hearts: I cannot fault the execution of my scheme.

My first endeavour should also have worked like a dream, and would have done so but for interference. She took the bait readily enough as I knew she would and, with misplaced compassion allowed my plan to begin. The foundations were soundly laid and, on those foundations, the arrogant detective set out to build an unassailable case. I love to see men who are ambitious, selfish and vindictive; and that protector of the citizen possesses all those qualities in abundance. He saw a chance to push forward his career, to bask in the approval of his superiors and, with one bound, leapfrog rivals in the promotion stakes who were more deserving of recognition.

Had I been entirely honest with him and offered him this opportunity to succeed, but at the same time warned him that she might be innocent,

I'm convinced it would not have made the slightest difference. A result was all he wanted, and a result is what he most certainly should have got. The evidence was there; the drugs cost more than just a pretty penny and in the eyes of the morally corrupt Drugs Officer, the quantity was sufficient to brand her a serious drug dealer. The videos were repugnant in content and, even the woolliest minded liberal magistrate, and God knows there are plenty of them about, prone to be won over by a pretty woman's tears, would have had their hearts turned to cold steel. No pity for such a monstrous perversion of her sex: I heard the cell doors clang, echoing across the caverns of my mind, and I imagined, with relish, the danger and depravity she would have to face unprotected and alone.

Meddling mischief makers took up her case. Another policeman stood firmly in her corner, his wife spoke movingly in support of the prisoner in the dock and, the solicitor they instructed to act on her behalf, plied his trade well. They achieved the impossible: the balance tilted in her favour and the final outcome fell far short of that which I had intended. Her liberty was to a small degree curtailed but it was not denied, nor was access to her turbulent children prevented, which for her would have been the greatest punishment of all.

Things can still change, of course, there is yet time. At her trial before a world weary judge and a resentful jury, the chance to tug the heart strings will be less, but now I am no longer sure that the prosecution will gain the day.

The picture to be painted must be made blacker, and along the way those who have protected her need to be removed or rendered impotent. My brain spawns a myriad of ideas, but all of them as yet are poor formed embryos. They will grow quickly and reach full term, and I will have my triumph: today must be counted as a defeat; tomorrow I will celebrate a victory.

Thus, as you can see the report on progress to date is patchy; one perfect outcome, one disappointing result; but both are minor shows before the main event. The forces that drive me, aren't hard to understand. A girl lied; a man laid hands on me in public view and used me like a dog: he paid with his life, but that was not enough, and so I had to take more retribution. He left a family in his wake, he destroyed my chances of ever doing that; his family were his key to immortality, I have no such key and so I acted to redress the balance.

Was he or she the main cause of my downfall? I don't think that either can justly claim that prize. Honour should be awarded where it's due, and that honour belongs to someone infinitely more evil. You think my father? You would be wrong; the blame lies squarely on my mother's shoulders. Women who walk away from their young are sluts, unfit to breathe clean air. In my wallet I carry a story of such a heartless trollope; the years have faded the newsprint, and the paper has become brittle but, the tale is still a cautionary one. I interest you now don't I? Shall I begin my disturbing bedtime story?

Once upon a time; all good bedtime stories start this way; the body of a middle aged woman was found naked, dumped in a bed of nettles in woods alongside a disused canal. Sexually assaulted prior to her death, her clothes had been ripped from her body and lay alongside her decomposing corpse. A branch wrenched from a thorn tree had been forced into her vagina and her tongue had been sliced out and then placed on a stump for the flies to feast on. Around her neck a placard hung. "So die all whores" it screamed, and a knife had been plunged into her heart to end her life. Bruising around her eyes and face indicated that she had been severely beaten before the mercy of death had finally been granted to her. The reporter who wrote the article rails against the violence of the age.

Every good story deserves a twist, and this sad narrative can be no exception. The woman denounced as a harlot and a strumpet had never walked the streets in skimpy clothing; nor had she once offered her body for hire to pox marked adolescents or sex starved drunks. She was "very respectable", or so the newspaper claimed, a happily married woman with two grown up children, a member of her local church, a volunteer at the local hospice, a believer in righteousness, the liver of a wholesome life.

"Why her?" wept her unhappy husband; "Why Mum?" cried out her tearful children; "Why She?" intoned her pious parish priest.

"This appalling case bears all the hallmarks of a maniac almost certainly driven mad by mind bending drugs." pronounced the chief of the local

C.I.D.; proving in his arrogance and his stupidity that he knew nothing about the man who had become Satan's executioner. Robbery wasn't the motive, her purse containing cash and credit cards was found close at hand, nothing had been stolen; nothing that is except her wedding ring, which had been wrenched off her finger, her flesh being torn in the process of its removal.

A tame forensic scientist opined that her attacker must have used pliers or some similar tool to grip the gold band and to give him the leverage to force the symbol of eternal love over her swollen knuckle; had such a strategy failed the expert predicted that the next step would have been severance of the finger itself using secateurs or a sharply bladed implement.

"Good people are rarely the victims of violent crime": at least in that claim the local rag was right, but in every other respect they were demonstrably wrong. She had three children, not two, although one had been banished to the wastelands of her mind for over two decades. She was a wicked woman, and so did not turn out to be the exception that proves the rule. Out of the blue she had received a telephone call and memory had been awakened.

She came to meet her son in the hope of forgiveness and reconciliation, but what right had she to assume her tears and her expressions of regret could undo the hurt of half a lifetime. Oedipus made love to his mother not knowing who she was and was cursed by the Gods for his pains; that is called "Tragedy". I knew my mother and I cursed her and that is called

"Revenge". The two people who gave me life and then destroyed it are both dead and that should be an end to it, but it is only a beginning.

I told you I had plans to take by stealth, and by dint of gentle persuasion, the widow of the conscience stricken coward who so messily ended his own life. He realised I had returned and he had recognised that his pathetic gullibility had facilitated murder. That secret was ready to burst forth and shatter his comfy love filled life. His pleas that he knew nothing of the plan would have been risible, and I could have exploited his deep seated feelings of guilt: a craven act of suicide saved him, and cost me dearly, but set me thinking about how best to recoup my loss.

He idolised his wife. I am the great iconoclast, the pitiless destroyer of graven images. I fantasised an outcome that gave her to me, to do with as I willed and even permitted me the possibility of feasting on her beauty; but beauty is evil and distracts men from their purposes. My mother was beautiful and she was vile; had she had the face of a gargoyle perhaps she would not have strayed. His woman reminds me of her, although she is much lovelier than my murdered parent. Much lovelier and much more dangerous, and she knows how to use her beauty to unseal lips. Her quest to discover the truth has begun, and some who were present on the day that Jacob met Jehovah may not withstand temptation. I have to stop her in her tracks and at the same time devise a way to extract from her a substantial wedge of cash. Crude kidnapping might be the answer: a queen's ransom for her little prince and princess, but that would be a highly dangerous plan and would set in train a nationwide manhunt. There will be other ways to achieve the same end, *of that I am sure, but I cannot hope to trick her out of her wealth with the ease with which I collected a bag of booty from a trusting simpleton; yet I will find a solution. I have already access to her mind, the seeds of turmoil scattered with the printed word, but the door is not yet fully opened. When it is I will play tricks inside her head; perhaps she may be persuaded to take part in a fatal game of hide and seek to rescue her husband's mortal soul. I would like to see red blood flowing and to play the role of surgeon one more time, but should she chose to swallow pills, or seek to imitate the last moments of her feeble husband's life both outcomes would be ones that I could live with. The world turns on its axis, the circle never begins and never ends, and if history does repeat itself it would be a tidy conclusion and one that I could not protest against.*

CHAPTER THIRTY SEVEN

The results of the fingerprint examinations of the video cassette boxes were nothing to write home about, but Jackie's prints were present on all but two of them, which made it certain that the tapes recovered from the charity shop were the ones which she had originally given to the bogus charity collector. The criminal records check had produced one positive hit, but as the print belonged to Mike Skinner, who was indisputably and messily long time dead, it didn't take the investigation a great deal further. Eight other full prints and several partial prints had also been lifted; none of these related to known offenders, and all were probably left by legitimate customers innocently browsing through the tapes on sale in the shop.

"A waste of bloody time!" said Pete Bennett; "If this was a T.V. script instead of an actual case file we'd have identified three mass murderers, two serial rapists and at least one old man in a dirty raincoat with a penchant for exposing his cock but, as usual, we end up with sweet F.A!"

"Not quite Pete, not quite. We now know for sure that the man the shop assistant described is definitely our man, and this confirms Jackie's story that she gave away some tapes: if that bit of her story has been proved to be true, in due course a jury may be prepared to accept that the rest of her story is also true."

"I suppose so Gov, but it's still not much when looking at the overall scheme of things, particularly as we seem to have drawn a blank on the other lines of enquiry."

"I didn't expect anything different. The car which took Sharon on her ill- fated trip to Derby is now almost certainly a pile of crushed metal lying in the corner of some back street breaker's yard. He wasn't ever going to make things easy for us was he? There are still too many places where cars can be scrapped with no questions asked; there was never a hope in Hell that in some demonstrably idiotic way he'd slip up and reveal his true identity to a coach load of first rate eye witnesses, or leave gallons of his D.N.A. behind for us to analyse."

The arrival of Alan Nadin temporarily lifted the feeling of frustration that had settled on Detective Sergeant Bennett's none too ample shoulders, and brought with it the hope that he was the bearer of good news. So it proved to be; although, that said, he was not overburdened with that welcome commodity, and after he had left the police station both officers felt that despite the fact a small step had been taken towards a successful conclusion of the case, no giant leap forward had occurred. Some of what Alan had said was already known, some of his revelations were new, and the theory he had put forward had at least been interesting.

Alan had talked to Jackie at length. He had discovered that apart from exchanging the odd word at the supermarket checkout, and brief conversations on the street about the state of the weather, there was absolutely nothing to link Jackie to Sharon. She did know Sharon's husband, but only in the context of him being the annoying younger brother of her best friend Penny, and she hadn't spoken to him for more than fifteen years. She had known Penny Farrington very well indeed when they were teenagers, but contact with her had been lost with the passage of time.

Indirectly through her friendship with Penny she had had a short lived acquaintance with some of the Eggleton gang until she had been responsible for causing the breakup of Penny and a member of that gang when all further association had dramatically ceased. "The boy Penny was going out with was called Beejay and do you remember Jackie saying that she thought his name was foreign?" said Alan; "well, I've been having a think about that. When I was a lad at grammar school they called us all by our surnames, and if two people had the same surname then it was surname and initial. I was always Nadin. A, and I was followed in the register by Nadin. J and Nadin. W. Do you think the same could have been true of this Beejay? Is it possible that his real initials might have been J.B.?"

"It's an interesting thought Alan, and if it's right then J.B. has got to be Justin Barnes hasn't it? But there are a couple of problems with this proposition. Firstly, you'll recall that at my house on the night of the dinner party Jackie was sure that Beejay's family moved away from here to live in the East End of London, which she thought was odd and that was why she remembered the detail. We know that round about the same time Justin Barnes emigrated to South Africa, which puts him thousands of miles away from London. We also know that unless several eye witnesses all saw the same collective mirage, and that Justin Barnes' mother killed herself because a complete stranger had died, which even in this crazy world that we live in seems a touch extreme, it seems to be beyond doubt that he is definitively and permanently deceased."

"But dead or alive Mark, I'm certain he's the key. Obviously, if he's six feet under, or his ashes have been scattered to the four winds, he can't be the man who performed the abortion on Sharon, but he's the reason why it happened, make no mistake about that. I'm not suggesting that you go looking for a dead man, but I am suggesting that you find out every scrap of information you can about Justin Barnes, particularly as regards links he once had with people still living or working around here.

At the self same moment that retired Detective Sergeant Alan Nadin was recommending a course of action to his former colleagues, in a house not far away retired gamekeeper Robert Hammond was counselling his beautiful daughter-in-law to abandon a course of action she had already initiated.

"For God's sake Julia, I know I said I wouldn't interfere but he's a "wrong 'un". The lad I met at the churchyard were frightened of his own shadow, he wouldn't say boo to a blinking goose, but when he got talking about Charles Montgomery it were as if all his inhibitions disappeared. He were adamant that Montgomery were a liar and he were certain that you were dicing with danger in having 'owt at all to do with him. If you could speak to him you'd soon see how sincere he was and, maybe then you'd understand why I'm so bloody worried. I don't want you to come to any harm, and if you continue to meet with Charlie Boy, I'm terrified about what might happen to you. The lad's name is Rupert. He told me that all the talk about illness and a near death conversion is now't but a pack of lies; not a word of it is true. Montgomery's using you for some purpose, he's a shit, a phoney; he'll rob you blind soon as look at you. Steer clear of him: don't give him the time of day; he can't help you in the way you think he can; he can't change one second of the past; but, he can destroy the future. For my sake say to him you don't want to see him again, or if you're too kind to do that, let me tell him for you. He'll get the message clear enough when I tell him to bugger off and never show his face round here again."

Julia held up her hand to stop Bob in his tracks.

 "I know you mean well and that you're only thinking of me, but you have to let me make my own decisions. I have listened, I have been warned and, I will be careful but, phoney or not, he's the only one who can help me find out the truth; and I have to know the truth if I'm going to stand any chance of getting my life back on track. I'm not stupid! I'm not going to take unnecessary risks and, if at any time I come to the conclusion that I'm being strung along by a manipulating fantasist then I promise you I'll drop him like a hot potato but, there is something about him that I believe and, I don't feel frightened anymore when I'm with him; which is very strange because most of the time I'm scared to death about what's going to happen next. I know I could be wrong about him, but I have to be the one to find out. You can't always be watching out for me, I've got to stand on my own two feet; I owe it to myself to do that. But there's more to it than that. I owe it to Will's memory to do everything I can to put a stop to all the horrible rumours which are beginning to circulate about him. My children need to have had a father who they could respect. I know that they had but, for their sakes, the world needs to know that too."

"The world doesn't give a damn about us Julia and, if people want to tittle tattle and peddle smears they will do so, no matter what you or I or anyone else says or does: but I can see I'm wasting me breath. You've got backbone girl I'll say that for you, but, please,

please be careful and don't do anything or go anywhere with him without telling someone where you're off to. You're not a teenage girl going out on a date and I'm not your father insisting on a curfew, but, for your own safety don't keep secrets from Anne and me; it'd kill us both if something dreadful happened to you."

Julia kissed Bob gently on the cheek. "You're like a second father to me and, I'm so grateful for that. I promise there will be no secrets, and I'm absolutely certain I will need your help in trying to understand the significance of anything I discover. I need your strength and your wisdom behind me; I know we have to stick together as a family if we're going to get through this nightmare and. I give you my word that I'll never do anything to put our survival in jeopardy."

CHAPTER THIRTY EIGHT

Ask anyone who has ever watched a crime thriller on television to describe a *grass*, a *nark*, a *snout* and, almost certainly, he or she will start to paint a picture of a shabby, pathetic, dirty individual battling unsuccessfully against drink, drug or mental health problems. *A loner, a man without friends, a dogsbody, a parasite, a petty criminal, a guttersnipe*; these are the mental images people have of police informants and, in many cases, these images may not be far removed from the truth: in many cases but definitely not in all. The informant known to the Greater Manchester Police as *Sherlock* didn't fit that pattern, but only his handler knew of his middle class background and his social standing; and that was the way it would always stay. What was widely known however was that his track record was excellent and, even on those occasions when the information he had provided hadn't led to convictions, because the police could find no usable supporting evidence upon which to build their case, and where any disclosure of *Sherlock's* own evidence would have led to his identification and certain death, the Senior Investing Officers had been convinced that what he said was right. To know everything and to be able to prove nothing; that was the most frustrating situation for any police officer to be in. Over the course of the years Sherlock had sown the seeds of such frustration many times over.

The information that he had unearthed, and which had been passed on to Detective Inspector Hobson was both dramatic and alarming. A Derbyshire business man named as Ralph Ambridge was said to have taken out a contract on the life of an unnamed subject. It was believed that the sum to be paid upon completion of the job was £20,000. This figure was significantly above the odds for a single hit and it was thought that this was because a degree of detective work needed to be undertaken by the hit man before the terms of the contract could be fulfilled. Ambridge, it was thought, might be acting entirely off his own bat, but it was equally possible that he was merely the front man for a wider group of individuals. No indication at all could be given as to the identity of the target, although there was some circumstantial evidence to suggest that his or her eradication was being viewed as the final resolution to a long standing problem. The method of disposal was a matter of conjecture, with shooting being the most likely option; the place of execution was almost certainly to be somewhere within the Peak District of Derbyshire.

The Divisional Commander was a worried man. "We can't let this happen," he had told Mark. "I don't want to see the streets of Burrdale, or anywhere else in the High Peak running with blood, and I especially don't want to see innocent bystanders caught up in the crossfire. This is Derbyshire for Christ's sake! It's not Chicago; it's not even Moss Side. The very idea of a professional hit man hunting the highways and byways of the Peak District is unthinkable: potentially every person he comes into contact with would be at risk, and that includes members of this force. I want him stopped, and I want him stopped now."

"That's easier said than done Sir," Mark had replied. "Ralph Ambridge is an arrogant man who cares nothing for the police. He's got the best legal talent permanently on tap; he's not the sort to crack under pressure, and he's certainly not going to be persuaded by appeals to his better nature to put a stop to this contract, because he hasn't got a better nature to appeal to."

"I know that Mark. I know I'm asking the impossible, but somehow that's exactly what we have to deliver. You've had recent dealings with Ambridge. I know I'm putting you on the spot here, but have you any idea why all of this is taking place?"

"It's a long story Sir, and there are still large chunks missing from it, but I'll tell you what I know, and what I believe to be the case."

The Detective Inspector then explained to Detective Chief Superintendent Hardy his theory that the suicide of Will Hammond arose out of the suspicious death of Jacob Farrington and that that death could in some way or another be laid at Timothy Eggleton's door; maybe through his son Jeremy and the gang of young hoodlums who followed his lead. Unlikely as it might sound Mark Hobson had stated his belief that the shooting of a dog had been the catalyst for the events that had occurred.

Mr Hardy asked for evidence to back up the theory. Mark told him about the extreme distress Will Hammond had exhibited after the death of Jacob, the apparent wanton destruction of a valuable and prized possession; his complete change of personality; and finally, years later, his act of suicide within hours of Eggleton senior's funeral service.

"I'm sure he saw a face from the past which caused memories to come flooding back. What he did wasn't pre-planned: he adored his wife and kids; I think he realised that everything he most cherished was about to be snatched from him, that's why he took his own life; he couldn't bear the thought of that."

The anonymous notes that Julia had received Mark felt added credence to his conjecture and the apparently unrelated assaults on the character of Jackie Skinner, and upon the body of Sharon Farrington culminating in the destruction of her unborn child, all gave support to his contention that a complex game of revenge and retribution was now being played out.

"I had a stand up row with D.I. Earnshaw over Jackie Skinner's arrest, no doubt you know all about that Sir, but we've now recovered video tapes from a charity shop which prove her story at least in part to be true. I know I'm sticking my neck out but, whatever D.I. Earnshaw may say to the contrary, I'm a hundred percent certain that she isn't a drug dealer. If she has been framed, as I believe to be the case, the question has to be why? I can't give you an answer yet, but I'm as sure as I can be that somehow what has happened to her is just one more piece of a complicated jigsaw. And who in his right mind would target a nineteen year old air head like Sharon Farrington? She may have brought things on herself, but she didn't deserve the treatment that was dished out to her. She was cynically persuaded to do something which has ruined her life. You've got to feel pity for her; only somebody with an overwhelming desire for vengeance could have callously subjected a kid like that to the torture she had to undergo."

"If you're right Mark, then it means that there is practically nothing that this man won't do. Have you any idea at all who he might be?"

"Well, I think he has to be somebody who was very close to Jerry Eggleton once upon a time; otherwise I don't think he'd know as much about Jacob Farrington's death as he apparently seems to do. There was a lad who would have been my prime suspect: his name was Justin Barnes but we have checked and double checked and he's dead. He was murdered by a mob in South Africa, there's no doubt about that, we had a file faxed through by the South African police containing all the gory details. His death absolutely destroyed his mother; she threw herself off a cliff because she couldn't cope with the loss."

"And you're sure there's no room for error?"

"It's all well documented Sir. I wish I could say differently, but I don't believe that there's the remotest possibility that there could have been a mistake."

"Is there anybody else then who could fit the bill?"

"Well there is a man who turned up at Will Hammond's funeral after an absence of nearly twenty years. Everybody thought he was dead. His name's Charles Montgomery and, by all accounts, he was a nasty little sod when he was a teenager, but he claims now to have seen the error of his ways and to have repented his manifold sins and weaknesses. Julia Hammond has accepted his change of heart as genuine. Her father-in-law doesn't agree. He's asked me to investigate but, on what I have discovered so far, it could all be true; certainly he disappeared off our radar for more than fifteen years; nothing is recorded against him during that time, not even a parking ticket."

"Once a wrong 'un, always a wrong 'un, that's my motto Mark. He has to be our starting point. He could have come back to town because he has a job to do. The first sign of anything untoward I want him arrested and in the meantime, watch him like a hawk.

The moment we have any evidence at all to justify an application for a warrant, that's what we do. When that happens, I want him, his room, his car and any other possible hiding place searched to see if we can recover a weapon. This murderous plan has got to be stopped and, at this stage, putting it bluntly, I'm not too concerned how we bloody well do it!"

CHAPTER THIRTY NINE

When Julia Hammond answered the phone she was disconcerted to find an unusually cheerful Monty on the other end of the line. Since they had last spoken, she had had the long conversation with Bob Hammond and, thereafter, she had given much thought to what he had to say. In the silence of her bedroom much of the confidence she had expressed to him about Charles Montgomery's sincerity had evaporated. She was no longer sure what to do, no longer certain that the man who was ostensibly helping her didn't represent a huge threat. She knew she had to find out and she knew she didn't know how to do that: she had wanted time to work out a plan of campaign, but time was the one thing that was now being denied her.

"I've got good news", he said jovially. "I've spoken to all but two of the members of Jerry's gang. A couple of them gave me short shrift, but when I told most of them what I was asking, and why I was asking for it, one of them said he would talk to you straight away and a couple more left open the possibility that future conversations could take place. Can I pop round for a chat? I've got quite a lot of information to give you and I think that's better done face to face rather than over the telephone; in any event I would very much like to see you again."

Put on the spot with no more than a couple of seconds to make up her mind Julia had to come to a decision. If she said "yes" and invited him into her home, she could be playing into the hands of a dangerous con man; if she said "no" she might be shutting the door forever on the only chance she had of discovering what really happened to cause her husband's suicide. Emotion battled with common sense, self-preservation struggled with the need for closure; in the end it was no contest: the need to discover the truth was absolutely paramount.

"Give me half an hour to get the place straight, then come on over," she told her ebullient caller. "You can explain everything you've discovered to me over a cup of coffee."

As soon as she had put the phone down Julia's brain went into overdrive. She had promised Bob that there would be no secrets, she had taken on board his pleas for caution, she had acknowledged the need to keep him in the loop and she was sure she would feel safer if somebody else knew that in less than thirty minutes Monty would be knocking at her front door. But, and it was a big but, if she told her father-in-law of the visit he would then come to the house and, even if he didn't enter, which she believed would be unlikely, the sight of him sitting in his car outside the gate, staring into her home, would certainly not help to loosen her visitor's tongue. More likely it would fuel in him a sense of resentment, when he realised that he was not totally trusted. She decided that that was too great a risk to run; this meeting with Monty, for the moment at least, would have to remain private.

Bang on the dot, not a second early or late the doorbell rang and, when she opened the door a relaxed and genial Charles Montgomery almost bounded into the house. His obvious good humour made things difficult. In the twenty five minutes or so that she had had to formulate a strategy, she had told herself that she would listen to what he had to say, and then forcefully accuse him of being a fake. She would have to be nasty to shock him into telling the truth. That didn't come easily to her and, it was so much harder to be aggressive when the person you were about to confront was being so affable and apparently doing everything he could to help you through a horrible period of your life.

"You look so flipping serious Julia, come on now, lighten up a little; go and make that cup of coffee you promised me and then I'll tell you all about my adventures." Meekly she acquiesced, feeling that in some surreal ways the roles of master of the house and casual visitor had been transposed; it didn't auger well; she needed to be in command of the situation but she was doing his bidding, not seizing control of the agenda. She felt like a waitress in an up-market cafe, dancing to the tune of a particularly insistent customer. When she returned with the coffee, scolding herself for her timidity, Monty had let the comfortable armchair in which he was seated envelop him: he looked like a man at ease with the world and with himself; very soon perhaps, all that was about to change.

"I think we've made inroads," he said. "It hasn't been easy, but because I told them I was acting on your behalf and most of them know you by sight, the outcome was a bit different from when I tried to talk to them before."

"The first person I went to see was Jamie Nadin. He couldn't have been more helpful; the trouble is he'd already split from the group before Jacob Farrington died: he'll do anything he can to help you but he's afraid it won't amount to very much. It was useful talking to him though because he remembered a couple of lads who aren't on the photograph but who never-the-less he thinks might have been there on the sidelines. I've added them to my list and I hope to get round to seeing them both in the next couple of days. He also knew the name of the second David, it's David Boswell: so I looked him up in the phone book and then went straight round to his house, just on the off chance that he might be willing to talk to me. I had a bit of a result with him. He remembered me, which was a plus and also, he was never an instigator, and so he may have less to fear. He claims to be doubtful that he can be of much use, but he is willing to speak to you and I think there's a good chance that he will be pretty frank."

"David Gladstone on the other hand was a dead loss, which I feared would be the case; there's more chance of having a sensible chat with a dead donkey than there is of getting any sort of straight answer out of him."

"Ralph Ambridge surprised me; I think it was because I told him that I was merely a front man for you. This time he actually seemed interested in what we were trying to do. He asked me for details of what we'd found out so far. I didn't tell him of course, but he still wasn't unpleasant. He did say he'd think about meeting you in private; he wasn't promising anything, but he wasn't ruling anything out either."

"Finally, I paid a call on Nathan Curtis's wife. She was very sweet. She promised to go through those papers of his that she still has and if she finds anything at all of interest she will happily give you a ring. Overall, I feel we've made a fair bit of progress. If you like I'll set up meetings with David Boswell and Faith Curtis, and then you can take it from there. It's not too bad for a start is it Julia?" Monty looked at Julia, expecting to bask in her approval.

He had anticipated a pat on the head and a warm smile of satisfaction, but he was to be disappointed. Julia's pretty face looked very severe and the clarity and coldness of her eyes shattered any thoughts he might have harboured about enjoying a light hearted chat with a stunningly beautiful woman.

"Is any of this true Monty; or is it just more of your untruths? Someone who knows you of old has told my father-in-law that you're a liar and a charlatan; the actual words he used were that you are an "evil, two faced, lying bastard". He said that you were one of Jerry Eggleton's closest associates; he said you were at the forefront of all the nastiness; he further said that you've never had a day's illness in your life. My father-in-law believes this man and, my father-in-law is a very good judge of character. He thinks you're exploiting my unhappiness for some devious purpose; he thinks that you're a dishonest and dangerous fraud. If you have been using me Monty then that's nothing less than shameless. I want you to look me in the eyes and tell me that none of this is true: if you can't do that I want you out of my house right now and, I never, ever, want you to come anywhere near me ever again."

What Julia had expected she didn't know, maybe vehement protestations of innocence, maybe dramatic denials of any wrong doing, maybe an explosion of anger and a storming out of the house, followed by a thunderous slamming of the door: the one thing she hadn't expected was tears, but tears were what she got.

It seemed as if Monty went into spasm, violent sobbing shook his whole frame and the moisture from his eyes dripped unchecked onto the cream carpet leaving clearly visible damp patches where it fell. If he was an actor, he was absolutely brilliant, so quickly had he dissolved into despair: nobody could have simulated such an extreme reaction: Julia was convinced of his sorrow.

"It's true," he sobbed; "it's all true, but what I've told you today is all true too. I was never in hospital; I didn't nearly die, but I really did change overnight. I knew that without a reason nobody would believe that I had become a new man, but I thought if I told people my transformation happened because I had stared into the abyss then I might be believed. I wanted you to believe me more than anything else in the world. I was helped because I look ill, but that's down to lifestyle not to sickness. I was a total shit. The reason I wasn't present at Jacob Farrington's death was because I was being held in a juvenile remand centre on suspicion of having inflicted grievous bodily harm on a twelve year old child. I was guilty as hell, but my dad could afford a good lawyer and I swore black was white and somehow got away with it. I couldn't tell you that now could I? Not if I wanted to stand any chance of getting to know you. I was a thoroughly wicked kid, I deserved every bad comment people ever made about me, but I swear to God I have changed.

"I'll give you the contact details for Faith and for David Boswell and you can decide at your leisure whether to do anything about getting in touch with them. I'm so sorry I lied about my past, but I promise you I've been truthful in everything I've said today. I'll go now and I'll never bother you again. I hope you find the answers that you're seeking;" and partially blinded by tears he raised himself out of the armchair and started to fumble his way towards the front door. Julia made an instant decision; she was getting quite good at doing that.

"No Monty, Please stay. I believe in you. I need your help. I won't be able to carry on if you're not around to help me along the way."

CHAPTER FORTY

Despite the fact that she faced the sort of charges at the Crown Court that generally led to the accused being shunned by right thinking people, Jackie Skinner had, on the whole, been protected from the worst kinds of public humiliation. One or two so called friends had felt it necessary to break off their acquaintanceships to avoid scandal and, on a few occasions, children had been stopped from playing with her sons for the same reasons, which was very hurtful but, by in large, most people had been very understanding. The public support that Alan Nadin and Helena and Mark Hobson continually expressed had helped enormously; their faith in her was clear and unequivocal, and thus it was that if her forthcoming trial was mentioned in passing in the local pubs and shops, it was generally in terms of the unfairness of the whole process and the short sighted incompetence of the police in not recognising an innocent person when they saw one.

Because she had not been publically reviled, gradually a little of her self-confidence had returned. Venturing out onto the street had become less of an ordeal; meeting other mums at the school gate less of a challenge; but at the back of her mind lurked a constant fear that, in one way or another, the person who had gone to such lengths to ruin her character would try again to achieve his goal; this time to devastating effect. To know that she was hated and not to know the reason why, that was the most distressing thought of all.

The parcel that arrived with the mid-morning post looked harmless enough. It was about as wide as a pencil box, but only half as long: blue, red, green and yellow polka dots decorated the colourful wrapping paper, and even the printed address label was adorned with a smiley face. At first Jackie thought it was an early birthday present for her second son and initially she put it to one side to place with other presents that had already been bought; but the label made it very clear. The addressee was herself; the sender didn't intend this parcel should be passed on to her middle child.

If she hadn't experienced the nightmare of wrongful arrest she would have been intrigued to receive such a gift and, without a second thought, she would have opened the parcel to see what it contained, but now the only thing she felt was fear. Memories of the terror she had experienced when the Drug Squad had forced their way into her home came flooding back: the mocking sarcasm of the lead detective rang in her ears; the forceful application of handcuffs pinioning her arms behind her back, the contempt these men had felt for her plight, the firm belief they had that she was a perverted drug dealer, all of these horrors had been re-awakened.

"Scum" they had called her in the police cell, "an unnatural mother," "the lowest of the low" and they had laughed at her tears. For eighteen hours she had believed that she would be remanded in custody, that her children would be taken from her, that her life would be destroyed; and now, she was sure, it was about to start all over again. Her one desire was to put distance between herself and the package; with tears streaming down her face, she rushed from the house, straight into the arms of Alan Nadin.

"Jackie, Jackie, for the love of God, what's happened? You're shaking like a leaf, I've seen more colour in a corpse; what the hell is the matter?" Although punctuated by sobs and, at times almost rambling, there was urgency in Jackie's voice that could not be mistaken.

"It will contain drugs, I know it will, and if he's sent it to me then as sure as anything he'll have told the police I've got it, and any moment now that horrible man and his team will be breaking down my door and dragging me off to a cell, and I'll lose the children, and they'll lock me up with prostitutes and drug addicts, and they'll pick on me because I'm not like them, and horrible things will be done to me, and nobody will lift a finger to help, and they'll hit me maybe cut me, and I couldn't cope, and I'll go mad, and it's so unfair." With her voice drowning in floods of tears she held onto him as if he was the only thing between her and total annihilation.

Alan had to think fast. What Jackie said about the police being tipped off was almost certainly correct, and D.I. Earnshaw would waste no time in acting on the tip: a jackal cheated of his quarry wouldn't hang about when given a second chance. At this precise moment final preparations for a raid were doubtless being made; every second could herald the arrival of the vengeful Drug Squad Inspector and his team of snapping Rottweilers.

"Get in the car Jackie and lock the door if it will make you feel safer, I'll grab the package. It needs to be properly examined by experts and the best place for it to be is in the hands of a decent police officer. I'll give Mark a ring as soon as we're away from here and we'll meet up somewhere, and I'll give the parcel to him. It may be Helena can help too. If she could arrange to stay here for a couple of hours, maybe together with the solicitor who acted for you in court or one of his clerks, while we sort this mess out, it would mean that Earnshaw's hooligans would have no excuse to break down the door and they'd have to treat the inside of your house properly because there would be witnesses present: and who knows, if we get a move on maybe Mark will be able to persuade Stan Hardy to call off the dogs even before they've been let loose."

Jackie did what she was told; she was too shocked to do anything else. Alan sprinted to the house and grabbed the unwelcome gift and, without a backwards glance, ran from the building and leapt into the driver's seat of the car.

Driving fast, but not stupidly fast, to avoid falling foul of speed cameras, they sped out of town. Soon the built up area was behind them and, a short while later Alan turned off the main road and they travelled down increasingly narrow country lanes until at last he deemed it safe to stop and make a phone call. In a very short space of time a plan had been formulated. Alan would drive to a nearby picnic site and leave his car parked in the car park there: Mark Hobson would meet them at that location in his car and then drive them to the police station at Buxton: Detective Chief Superintendent Hardy would be informed of their intentions and, subject to anything which he might say, Mark would hand over the package for forensic examination and both Jackie and Alan would then make witness statements. There was still an element of risk; if Mr Hardy, on having all the facts placed before him, had any suspicion that Jackie was not telling the truth, he might authorise her arrest and Detective Inspector Earnshaw would then get his way.

The possibility that that might happen gripped every nerve in Jackie's body; the fear was palpable, but Alan convinced her that Mr Hardy was no snarling dinosaur and that he would be fair; he also promised her that he would be at her side every step of the way.

This plan was carried out to the letter. When they arrived at the police station Mark took Jackie and Alan to a small interview room where he left them while he went to speak to the Detective Chief Superintendent; they declined the offer of coffee and waited in near silence for him to return.

Twenty minutes seemed like a lifetime, but when he returned Mark had good news. Mr Hardy had accepted Mark's argument that the last thing a suspected drug dealer would do would be to bring a suspicious package to the attention of the police when it could so easily be disposed of in any number of other ways. He had instructed Mark to arrange for the package to be fingerprinted and forensically examined and for witness statements to be obtained from Jackie and Alan: he was insistent that they should make their statements separately, which meant that Alan could not keep his promise to be at Jackie's side the whole of the time they were in the police station; and, he had added that if conflicting accounts were given by Jackie and Alan, that would cause him to think again and might well lead to both of them being arrested.

In a surprisingly quick period of time all this was done; the two witness statements matched and caused no rumbling of doubt and there was nothing in the parcel to undermine what Jackie and Alan had said. When the parcel was examined the Scientific Support Officer found a pretty little gift card with a message that read "Just a little something to add to your collection" and a cardboard box which contained a small china statue of an owl. The ornament was hollow, the hole at its base had been taped over with a piece of sticky tape; it was also heavier than it should have been. When the tape was later removed the porcelain bird revealed the contents of its ample stomach; more than 20 grammes of white powder spilled out of its gut; unsurprisingly that white powder turned out to be heroin. The gift card was of course unsigned and, no clue could be found as to the identity of the sender.

"He's a clever sod Mark, he doesn't miss a trick. Jackie collects statues of birds, she's got them all over the house, you can see some of them on the kitchen window sill; he's remembered that. The only thing he's misjudged is that he thinks she is just a dumb housewife who would be so pleased at receiving a present that she wouldn't examine it too closely. He didn't allow for the fact that any halfway intelligent person would be suspicious, particularly if she's already been through the ordeal Jackie's been through. I think that shows an innate contempt for women. I don't know whether the man you're looking for is a psychopath, I'm willing to bet that he is; but I'm bloody sure he will turn out to be a misogynist. You won't find any prints on the bird, that I guarantee. He was counting on Jackie picking it up and putting it on display so that when Bob Earnshaw and his Storm Troopers turned up they'd find the statue containing drugs with her fingerprints plastered all over it. That would have been it: the finest advocate in the country wouldn't stand a cat in Hell's chance of getting her bail if the Bench believed that she had committed an identical offence to one which she was already charged with. He's out to get her Mark and I want the bastard stopped!"

"We all want that Alan, we all do. I'm on to it, I promise you. I'll run you and Jackie back to your car and then I'll get straight back to the job in hand."

Helena's phone call to Mark's mobile however, temporarily delayed that process.

 "Earnshaw was here Love and he was pretty obnoxious but, I had one of Mr Greenway's clerks with me, he was brilliant. Earnshaw boxed up all Jackie's ornaments and he's taken them away for forensic examination, but I could tell he wasn't expecting to find anything. He did make an unpleasant comment about me meddling in police affairs and I think he'll have further words with you on the subject, but at least he hasn't caused any damage so Jackie has nothing to worry about on that score. We're not out of the woods yet though Darling; the Burrdale Advertiser was delivered while I was here: one or two fliers dropped out of it and there was a plain brown envelope addressed to The Occupier. It wasn't sealed so I had a quick glance at it. It contained a printed sheet of A4 paper with a photograph of Jackie and a photograph of you and me on it. It was set out as if it was a news story. It's headed "Local Police Chief protects evil child pornographer" and it accuses you and me of telling lies to support a drug dealing paedophile. It's pretty vile stuff Love, as you can imagine, and so far as I can tell, a copy of it has been delivered with *The Advertiser* to virtually every household in Burrdale.

CHAPTER FORTY ONE

"Why would a man like Ralph Ambridge choose now to hire a contract killer to settle old scores? Something must have happened to re-open old wounds; you don't pay a hit man £20,000 to rewrite ancient history., There has to be a current reason why he wants somebody dead right now hasn't there Gov?"

"I'm certain you're right Pete, the trouble is we have no idea at all what that reason is."

"Try this one for size. The word on the street is that a person has crept out of the woodwork to blackmail some of Jerry Eggleton's gang of scumbags. Just suppose for a moment that Ralph Ambridge is one of the intended victims. He wouldn't sit on his arse and do nothing about it, he's not that type of bloke: he'd fight back wouldn't he? And he'd be a bloody dangerous enemy."

"I couldn't argue with that statement Peter, but have we got a shred of evidence to back up the conjecture?"

"Is the Pope a Mormon Gov? Is Tony Blair a socialist? No, of course we don't have an ounce of sodding proof, but it's still the best theory we've got; unless you know something from mingling with people in the higher echelons, that humble jobbing detectives like me wouldn't have a chance of finding out."

"Not guilty on that score I promise you, but as you like to point out, you're nearer to the coal face than me, you know what ordinary people are thinking. How are the good citizens of Burrdale reacting to the *news* that accompanied this week's edition of the *Advertiser*?"

"It's hard to say Gov. I think a lot of 'em still thinks it's a put up job and are dismissing the story out of hand but some of 'em are giving it credence and, if that trend continues, it could make life difficult for you and your missus, and well nigh impossible for poor Jackie."

"I feared that would be the case. It doesn't bother me, I know it's not true; I've got a broad back and I can stand my corner with anyone but I'm worried about the effect these lies may have on Helena and I'm particularly worried about how they will affect Jackie. I want the lying bastard who circulated this rubbish found before he does untold damage, dragging innocent lives through the dirt."

"Detective Inspector *I know fucking everything* Earnshaw has been telling anyone willing to listen that you're the one who's dragging your wife into a cesspit of corruption and that if she gets sucked up into some criminal conspiracy it'll be your fault. I know for a fact that he's gone bleating to Mr Hardy complaining about finding Helena in Jackie's house when he raided the place and he's alleged that you're trying to undermine his legitimate enquiries every step of the way. 'No smoke without fire', that's what he's been saying about the article and he's taking every opportunity that he can to run your reputation down."

"The bloke's a total shit! After last time he hasn't got the guts to confront me man to man; next time I see his smirking, supercilious face I'll be hard pushed not to land one on him."

"That's just what he wants Gov; but you're not thick enough to fall for that one are you?"

Another person who was wise enough not to overreact to Robert Earnshaw's behaviour was Detective Chief Superintendent Hardy but that didn't stop him being concerned, particularly when he received a telephone call on the subject of the fake news report from the Assistant Chief Constable.

"No Sir," he had said, "I don't believe there's a word of truth in it," and he had told him about Mark Hobson's theory that Jacqueline Skinner was the victim of some sort of vicious personal vendetta.

"That's as may be," the A.C.C. had replied, "but never-the-less keep your eyes on Hobson; if he is cosying up to a drug dealer I want the book thrown at him; this force can't afford any bad publicity, particularly just now when we're fighting to remain an independent police authority."

"Yes Sir," Mr Hardy had replied; "I'll certainly do that," and it was with that thought in mind that he telephoned Mark Hobson immediately after the phone conversation had ended and summoned him to his office.

"The A.C.C. has just been on the phone to me. He's not at all happy to see one of his officers being accused of protecting a criminal: you know what I'm on about don't you Mark?"

"Yes Sir, I do. I've read the article and I guess most people in town have done so as well. I know Detective Inspector Earnshaw has spoken to you on this matter and, I'm sure he will have expressed a particularly low opinion of me."

"Which I think is clearly reciprocated," commented the Detective Chief Superintendent.

"Yes Sir, it is. I make no bones about that; but I'm not going to undermine a fellow officer other than to say that if he believes the crap that's been written about me, my wife and Jackie Skinner then he's very wrong indeed. If I was a bent copper Sir, I'd try and get on the payroll of a villain with some clout. Jackie Skinner lives on a council estate, she barely makes ends meet and, it's a full time struggle for her just to feed and clothe her three kids. She's not suddenly come into money, she's never been a big spender and if Detective Inspector Earnshaw would only approach the matter with an open mind he'd see that. She's a decent, honest woman; anyone who knows her will tell you so. She's always tried to do the right thing and if you'd have seen her after just one night in the cells you'd know she'd be too scared to break the law. There is nothing that she could give me which would make me lie for her and she would never want that. Bob Earnshaw has been speculating that she might be offering me sexual favours in return for me impeding his investigation. That's bullshit Sir. I'm happily married to the most beautiful woman on the planet and Jackie has a boyfriend who thinks the world of her: she would never two time him; it's all garbage being peddled by somebody who wants to destroy her and because my wife and I believe in her he wants to damage us too. And just to set the record straight; all Helena has done is to be at Jackie's house when the Drug Squad raided it. That was my idea Sir, I confess it. She didn't say or do anything to disrupt their search of the property and if D.I. Earnshaw felt that in some way his wings had been clipped by the presence of two honest, respectable witnesses simply observing what he was doing, then I would venture to suggest that the problem lies with him and not with the people who were passively watching out for Jackie Skinner's interests.

"Maybe it does Mark, maybe it does; but I'm telling you now, keep your distance from D.I. Earnshaw from now on. I don't want to see two of my senior officers squabbling in public. If there is any reigning in to be done, I'll be the one to do it, do I make myself clear? And while I'm talking to you, if you want to protect your wife from adverse comments then stop her from getting under the Drug Squad's feet. I'm going to give D.I. Earnshaw the same ultimatum that I've given you: if there is any more trouble between you then you'll both be on charges. And one last bit of advice; choose your friends carefully. If you do discover anything about Jackie Skinner that supports Earnshaw's view of this case I need to be told straight away. I hope I don't have to say this, but remember your only loyalty is to the job; if you let personal feelings get in the way of your duty, then you're in big trouble: I won't tolerate it, not for a second, if misplaced compassion gets in the way of any of my officers solving a crime."

CHAPTER FORTY TWO

"It's fixed up for three o'clock this afternoon at his house; I'll tell you how to find it. You've got to go on your own; he won't let me go with you and, there are a number of conditions which he has stipulated. You won't be allowed to take notes. You must agree to leave your handbag and any jacket or coat you might wear in an outer room and, he's insistent that you wear a tight fitting dress that offers no place to conceal a tape recorder. If, at any time, he has the slightest suspicion that you're wired he will stop the interview immediately and you'll be told, in no uncertain terms, to leave the house. It's the only way he'll agree to the meeting: it's up to you whether you accept his terms."

"I'll do whatever he wants Monty. If he's being so cautious it must mean that he knows something pretty significant."

"Which might also mean that he's a dangerous man; I really do think you would be far better staying away."

"I'm going Monty and that's an end to it; and while I'm in his house I don't want you anywhere close by: if he sees your car parked up outside he'll be suspicious and then that will be meeting over. Stay in your hotel, I'll call you when it's finished and then maybe, we should meet up to discuss what I've learnt."

Four hours later and, after a lot of thought, dressed in the sexy little black dress that Will had always loved, Julia arrived at the home of David Boswell. It was raining heavily so she slipped on a long black trench coat to avoid getting soaked and walked up to the front door. Her hand trembled as she pushed the bell; she scolded herself for her timidity: this was *show time* she had to make a big impression.

Mr Boswell himself opened the door: Mrs Boswell had long since fled the marital home and the housekeeper had been dispatched to collect a package from Chesterfield. Julia didn't know it, but he and she were entirely alone. With overstated politeness he admitted her to the house and Julia found herself standing in a large, ornate hallway, more in keeping with a minor stately home than a private residence. Julia placed her handbag on a chair, then she opened the coat and let it slide from her shoulders and onto the floor. Only if she had been naked could the effect have been more dramatic. She looked sensational. It was pure *film noir*; inwardly she felt tacky and cheap: David Boswell gaped at the vision in front of him.

"Charles Montgomery told me of the conditions you attached to this meeting," said Julia. "I hope this dress meets your requirements." It emphasised every curve of her body; Boswell stared transfixed at her shapely figure, he could see how tightly the dress clung; there was nowhere to hide a silk handkerchief let alone the tiniest piece of electronic equipment.

"It fits the bill admirably," he said; his mouth felt moist, he tried not to salivate. "Please follow me into the sitting room, I'll make either tea or coffee, whatever you prefer, and then we'll get started."

Julia did as she was bid. She was ushered into a well furnished room; prints of paintings by Rueben's and Gaugin hung on the walls; the unlamented Mrs Boswell had never approved of the art work. He left her there to go and make the drinks; he came back with coffee in Crown Derby cups; there was nothing cheap about this man, except perhaps his innermost fantasies.

"I'm only going to say this once", he said; "and never outside this room; and if anybody ever asks me about this conversation I will deny it ever took place. I understand you feel you cannot come to terms with your husband's suicide until you know the reason why it happened and I have been persuaded to help you." He didn't add that "if you had looked like an overweight Russian shot putter then you'd have had no chance", but that was exactly what he felt.

"You suspect that Jacob Farrington was murdered and that somehow or other your husband had a hand in his death. I have to tell you that both of those suspicions are well founded."

Julia felt her heart stop, her worst fears confirmed: David Boswell saw her unease.

"It will be a rough ride Mrs Hammond, but maybe not as rough as you fear. Will's involvement was pivotal to the whole scheme, nothing could have happened without him, but he was just the facilitator; he didn't know what was intended.

Timothy Eggleton wanted to punish Jacob Farrington for shooting his Great Dane. He sanctioned a plan thought up by his son Jerry and a boy called Justin Barnes, of whom I'm sure you've heard, to poison two of Jacob's sheepdogs in retaliation. Will was the person responsible for feeding the animals the drugged meat, this bit I think you already may know, and you know I think the reason he did it: he was tempted by gifts, he allowed himself to be bought. He didn't know that the dogs would be seriously harmed; he was told there would be no lasting effect and when that turned out not to be the case he was filled with remorse.

The death of the dogs should have been enough, but it wasn't. Eggleton wanted more and, Justin Barnes, in particular, wanted to see Jacob suffer. Barnes hated Farrington because not long before this episode Jacob had been instrumental in breaking up a relationship between his sixteen year old daughter and Barnes. That bit may not be strictly accurate. The relationship was already over, the girl had dumped him, but Barnes wanted her back.

When he lost her it was the only time I saw any human emotion in him except anger. He tried to re-kindle the affair, but Jacob warned him off big time. He slapped him about the face and shook him like a rag doll. Barnes was humiliated. He wanted vengeance on Farrington: he also wanted vengeance on a village girl who he claimed had poisoned Farrington's daughter's mind against him. He would have killed her if he could have got his hands upon her, of that I've no doubt, but wisely she kept well out of his way: Jacob was however his number one target.

Barnes and Jerry Eggleton came up with a plan. At the time only they knew the full details, but we all knew it would involve causing Jacob physical harm: all of us that is except Will, who had by then turned his back on us but he was essential to the plot. Barnes blackmailed him into helping us by threatening to tell Jacob who it was who had poisoned his dogs and, Jerry Eggleton lied to him and promised, on his non-existent honour, that all he wanted was a meeting to clear the air. They picked a deliberately rainy day and instructed Will to get Jacob to go to Elmton Crags. He wasn't to say who would be there, but he was to say why it would be advisable to go. Provided Jacob arrived Will didn't have to be there and, in fact, Eggleton and Barnes both felt it would be better if he stayed away; which he did. Will didn't know, but the idea was to taunt Jacob when he arrived to get him angry, so he would climb the rocks to get to us. Somebody came up with the idea of covering the rocks with cooking oil, I don't remember who that was, it may have been your friend Charles Montgomery, but if it was he bottled it like he usually did, because he wasn't present to see how his plan worked out.

When Jacob arrived, we all stood at the top of the Crags. We jeered at him; Barnes in particular taunted him about the loss of his dogs and, we threw stones at him. He was like a man possessed: he said "he'd ring our bloody necks". He ran up the rocks, slipped on the oil and fell back to the ground. We all thought the point of the plan was that he'd break a leg, or injure himself in some other way and, that we'd leave him there to struggle back to his house. Jerry Eggleton had arranged an alibi for us all. If Jacob complained to the police, his dad would say we'd all been at his house watching a film; he'd even doctored the CCTV security tape so that it apparently gave support to that claim.

Jacob fell heavily to the ground. I'm sure he broke his legs in the fall. He screamed as he started to fall, but, a split second later he was quiet, almost certainly concussed. Barnes climbed down the slope taking great care to avoid the oil. He picked up a rock the size of a football and smashed it down onto Jacob's head, smiling as he did so, then, he told Jerry to do the same; and, he followed suit except he closed his eyes the moment before the stone impacted. Jacob's skull was split wide open: Barnes shouted out that they'd killed him. He was elated. He told us we had committed the perfect murder and that it was a badge of honour. He said we should be proud of what we'd done. We had proved ourselves capable of doing anything. We were now members of an elite club, bound to each other forever in blood. He swore us to secrecy, and our collective guilt has ensured we keep that secret.

I tell you this history in the hope that it may ease your pain, but I will tell it to no-one else; it will never be repeated.

The rain washed the oil away before the emergency services arrived. An inquest later recorded Jacob's death was accidental. I will never do anything to overturn that verdict and you have no evidence to have it set aside.

Take my advice; let it end here. If you keep digging you may get hurt. You now know that your husband was weak and a fool, but not a killer; let that suffice. You aren't responsible for his death, his shame killed him; you cannot be blamed in any way. You're a very attractive woman Mrs Hammond; you were wasted on a man like him. In this life you can choose pleasure or choose pain. Choose pleasure my dear, delight in the world and let the world delight in you. The choice is not hard and I could help you make that choice: I would be very pleased to be your friend."

It was if a curtain had been drawn back and the *Peeping Tom* at the window had been revealed: maybe the reason for demanding she wore a skin tight dress had nothing at all to do with security, and everything to do with lust. Suddenly the choice of paintings on the wall had become clear. Julia realised this man had an obsession; he was a collector of pictures that aroused him and, right now, he was looking at her in the same way that he looked at his paintings: it was time for her to leave quickly.

"That's very kind of you," she said, "and I will think about your offer, but right now I have to go. I have to pick up my children from the child minder in ten minutes time and I can't be late for that." She lied. She knew that he knew she lied.

Frostiness came over him. "Very well Mrs Hammond," he said; "I'll show you out. My offer still stands, but unless you want to take it up, in which case, of course I would be delighted to see you, please don't bother me again." Julia didn't respond to the instruction.

In the hall she picked up her bag and seized the coat; it had stopped raining but she put it on and wrapped it tightly around her like a burkha; she sensed his frustration; she was sure he was scanning her with x-ray eyes; she had to get away.

For a moment she feared he might not open the door, but he didn't try to prevent her from leaving. She almost ran to the car. She leapt into the driver's seat and slammed the door shut in case he followed her; she forgot to put on her seatbelt and she didn't realise that the hem of the mac was hanging out of the car; it would wet and muddy by the time that she did, but that was not of the slightest importance.

She drove for several miles into the countryside: for some reason she didn't want to return home until she had analysed her thoughts. The thing she felt most powerfully was anger. If David Boswell had been a nicer man she might have felt differently, but his uncaring attitude towards Will had shown his true nature; never-the-less, she had learned a lot from him. Will had been exonerated of major crimes: before this afternoon that would have been sufficient; now she realised it was not. Jerry Eggleton and his callous gang of trouble makers had in truth killed him; they had deceived him, they had used him, they had destroyed his peace of mind and they were just as responsible for his death as they were for the cruel death of Jacob Farrington. Twenty years of guilt and remorse had come flooding back on day of Timothy Eggleton's funeral and no longer able to cope, Will had killed himself; possibly to spare her and the children from danger. Why he died mattered, Julia realised that she had to discover more.

The idea that in someone's warped mind that a brutal killing could be seen as *a badge of honour* disgusted her. The gleeful infliction of pain that Boswell had described appalled her. Both Will and Jacob cried out for justice; Julia realised that she couldn't ignore their call. Something had to be done. She pulled off the road onto the verge, blocking a field gateway in the process, and, bristling with rage, she telephoned Monty.

CHAPTER FORTY THREE

The fact that the woman at the Morrison's check out was not her usual talkative self surprised Jackie: she was never normally short of things to say, but that afternoon she was positively monosyllabic and obviously reluctant to enter into any conversation at all. Jackie put it down to her having a bad day and thought no more about it until she returned to the store, a short time later, to buy the tins of dog food she had forgotten to purchase earlier and, saw the same check out operator talking ten to the dozen with the customers at her till. The penny only dropped when the girl on the fast lane check out was barely civil to her; she clearly didn't want to know her; she didn't even want to give her the time of day: it was abundantly plain that, in the eyes of both shop assistants, she had become *persona non grata*; and the reason for that had to be that they believed the libels contained in the fake news story. Barely managing to hold back tears, and almost forgetting the pet food she had returned to the store to buy, Jackie rushed from the supermarket in a very distressed state.

Her distress was not destined to be short lived. It became a great deal worse when a group of mums waiting at the school gate pretended not to see her and then physically closed ranks to ensure she couldn't break into their tightly knit circle of friends.

Still worse was waiting around the corner: the headmistress sent a message asking Jackie to come and speak with her and, when they met in the school office, she told Jackie that one of her sons had been in a fight with another boy who had been calling his mum names, and that her youngest son had ended up in tears because his classmates had been telling him that he was a drug dealer's son and that someday soon he'd be in a children's home because his mother would be in gaol.

It felt like the whole world was against her and even though one of the teachers and one of the other mums, to whom she was particularly close, both put their arms around her and tried to comfort her, it did no good. She felt unwanted and she would continue to feel like an outcast, a leper a pariah until the truth was out; there was no guarantee that that day would ever arrive.

But Jackie wasn't the only one who was beginning to experience rejection, to a lesser degree so too was Helena Hobson. In her case it was more subtle. The assistants at the supermarket were still overtly friendly, but sometimes little nudges happened or there were quick sideways glances in her direction, occasionally accompanied by slight shakes of the head. A member of the Ladies' Choir was more direct. She advised her, *as a friend*, to be very careful when choosing her acquaintances. The language used was gentile and the warning was wrapped in a sunny smile, but the message was clear. *If you move in the wrong circles you can't then move in the right*. Helena was so angry, but, she kept her cool. She thanked the woman for her concern. She said that as a senior policeman's wife she was acutely aware of her position. She stated that she thought it part of her duty always to try to do the right thing and she added that she would judge people as she found them and that she would not be swayed by idle gossip and ill informed tittle tattle. She made it clear that she felt one hundred percent certain that Jackie Skinner was an innocent woman and she concluded with a wish that the decent people of the town would give her their unstinting support rather than go around repeating what was clearly malicious gossip.

There was also a third person who was at risk. The wave of reaction to the Jackie Skinner story that was threatening to overwhelm her and that was now lapping at Helena's feet was also making ripples for Mark Hobson to cope with. The initial response to the article at the police station had been muted and it hadn't been mentioned, except in the private conversation that had taken place between Mark and the D.C. S. Nobody it seemed wanted to stir things up, nobody wanted to throw mud, nobody wanted to believe the worst, nobody that is except a certain Detective Inspector Robert Earnshaw.

The point of conflict occurred in the station yard. Mark was on his way to the scene of a house burglary when he bumped into Earnshaw, who was returning from a drugs raid.

"We got a good result on this one Hobson," he said. "It's amazing how much my lads can achieve when they're not being obstructed by you and your meddlesome wife. I did worry that you might both be there but then I realised that our suspect was a scruffy old git. Not your type at all; he hasn't got any of the obvious charms of the lovely Mrs Skinner. You like 'em attractive, don't you Hobson? You don't go out of your way to protect the ordinary dross of society, do you pal? I'll tell you this though; with or without your protection, I'll get Skinner and, she will rot in gaol. But never mind. I'm certain that there'll be some big butch lesbian who will be only too pleased to take her under her wing, in a manner of speaking, so you won't have to worry about her being lonely. What you will have to worry about will be if I find that you and your wife have been in any way a party to her filthy dealings because, if I do, then you'll both be playing hide and seek in the communal showers with an assorted collection of sex maniacs."

Mark's reaction was immediate. "You dirty minded, ignorant sod! Open your lying mouth one more time and I swear to God that I will ram my fist down your throat" and, he lunged towards the Drug Squad officer.

"Hobson stay where you are! Earnshaw keep your mouth shut! In my office now the pair of you!" commanded an incensed Detective Chief Superintendent, who had been sitting in his car quietly putting the finishing touches to a speech he was due to make that evening and who had witnessed the entire incident first hand.

Who benefitted most from his intervention it is impossible to say. The answer might be Mark Hobson because, had Mr Hardy not been present, he would have certainly have struck Earnshaw and he would have found himself on a serious disciplinary charge without anyone in authority really knowing the level of provocation that he had had to face.

Few people have witnessed the extreme wrath of Stanley Robert Hardy but, those who have been on the receiving end of his tongue feel like they have been buffeted by a Category A hurricane. Both detectives were verbally bludgeoned by the incandescent Chief Superintendent. When he said they had come within a whisker of being suspended they had no doubt that he told the truth. When he threatened the severest consequences for them both, starting with demotion back to the ranks should there be any repetition of the disgraceful scene he had just witnessed, both men knew he meant every word he said. At the end of the seismic dressing down the two officers were dismissed like naughty schoolboys. A truce hadn't been declared, reconciliation was not an option, but self-preservation insisted that they kept their distance from each other and their lips tightly sealed if they wanted to have any sort of a career with the Derbyshire

Constabulary; and that was how it would always have to be from that day forward.

Privately, though, Mark Hobson seethed. He knew he had been wrong to react but he had been deliberately provoked by Earnshaw and when Pete Bennett spoke to him later he then realised that he had been set up.

"It wasn't a chance meeting Gov. D.C. Steve Langley, you know him, the weasel faced oily little turd who is always brown nosing Earnshaw, was crouched down behind the waste bins and would have emerged just after you'd slotted his boss. You can bet your eye teeth that he'd have had fuck all to say about Earnshaw's behaviour but a great deal to tell about your alleged uncontrolled aggression. It was damn lucky Stan Hardy was sat in his car and caught most of the conversation otherwise, you'd have been out on your ear and Earnshaw would have been prancing about like a fucking lottery winner."

"The devious bastard, I'll..." then Mark stopped himself mid-sentence, "I'll follow Mr Hardy's orders: Earnshaw can go hang himself; he's not worth a second thought: come on Pete, we've got better things to do than worry about a prat like him."

"That we do Gov, and I've got a bit of news that you might find interesting. I've been talking to a couple of snouts and the word on the street is that Ambridge's expensive hit man is experiencing a few problems. He's got a name; my sources can't tell me what that name is and he's got a photograph, but that was apparently taken a long time ago. Currently he's playing a game of *make the face fit* and, at the moment, he's not been particularly successful at it."

"That's all to the good, but we have to hope that he doesn't become impatient; it will be bad enough if he traces the right man, it will be a thousand times worse if the wrong person is selected and an innocent person gets killed."

"At the moment he's seeking *further and better particulars* as the frigging lawyers say so that's giving us a bit of a breathing space. I understand that Ralph Ambridge is throwing money about like confetti trying to buy some up to date info; if he succeeds in doing that then it really will be game on."

"And we'll still be sat on the substitutes' bench not taking part and not even knowing who the main players are. Can none of your sources tell us anything about the hit man himself?"

"Not a sodding thing Gov, unless this next little bit of information has any relevance. Bob Hammond's *bosom buddy* Charles Montgomery has been putting himself about a lot lately. He's been seen going to various addresses in town apparently asking questions and in the process ruffling a few feathers.

"Is it possible that he's the man we want? We've speculated on that before. His record doesn't contain anything to suggest that he could be but..."

"If it is him and he knows his stuff it wouldn't would it? Ambridge is paying top whack, he'd expect the best, and it's not impossible that just what he's got. There's another thing too; he's been seeing a lot of Julia Hammond recently; he must have a reason for doing that; could that somehow also be part of the pattern?"

"I don't know Pete, but if he is the man we're looking for then that means she's in real danger. We've got to keep tabs on him; whatever else occurs, we can't let anything happen to Julia Hammond."

CHAPTER FORTY FOUR

"That lad you met in the churchyard is a rum 'un. He come in here last night acting like butter wouldn't melt in his mouth, had a few drinks then kapow! You'd have thowt he owned the place: I threw him out in the end because he were upsetting me other customers. I didn't hear everything he said because there was a bit of a problem in the kitchen that I had to sort out, but later on I got a telephone call which filled me in with the bits I'd missed. It were from a chap who said he'd been eatin' in the bar, he said he and his missus were going to stay for sweets but they didn't do so because of what were takin' place. He asked me if I knew anybody called Hammond, I said I did and I asked him why he wanted to know. He said that lad had been sayin' crude things about your daughter-in-law, how she had *nice tits* and how she'd *make a fuckin good lay* and then he started on about you and he apparently called you a *knob head* and a *country yokel*. If I'd have been there and heard him talking about you like that I'd have smacked him in the chops for being so bloody cheeky. He behaved like a proper little gobshite; I ain't having him in this pub ever again."

"You amaze me Len, you really do. He seemed such a quiet lad. Well I've learnt me lesson. Next time I see him, he and I will have words. I don't mind the odd drunken laugh at my expense; it's a poor man who can't take a joke but, to drag Julia into the picture and to say vile things about her that goes way beyond acceptable behaviour. By the time I've finished with him he'll have learnt some manners but, he won't get a chance to try them out on me because I shan't be speaking to him again."

At the very same moment Bob Hammond was fuming over Rupert's behaviour and thinking, yet again, how much at risk Julia was and, how great was the need to protect her from a multitude of dangers, Julia herself was embarking upon a very hazardous undertaking. She was a woman with a mission; a mission to place under the spotlight of public scrutiny the lies that had been told about the death of Jacob Farrington and, to bring to justice the people responsible for his murder: but that wasn't all. Twenty years on, one, some or all of these people had robbed her of her husband; they had left his children fatherless and his parents distraught and bewildered. That called for vengeance and, although a few months ago, she would never have thought herself capable of thinking this way, she was now certain that somebody had to suffer for causing Will's suicide before she could ever rest easy. Perhaps it was her intense dislike of David Boswell that fuelled that need: if he had shown some genuine regret she might have felt differently, but not only had he demonstrated total contempt for the man she had married, he had also made a clumsy attempt to *come on* to her and that, in Julia's mind showed arrogance and insensitivity that bordered on the obscene. With the fervour of the crusader burning fiercely inside her brain, she telephoned Charles Montgomery, and it was agreed that she would visit him at his hotel later in the day. She deliberately didn't tell her father-in-law about this meeting; he would undoubtedly have advised against it and, there was a risk that she might weaken and be swayed by his arguments to stay away: she couldn't afford to run that risk.

Monty was waiting for her in the Residents' Lounge; no one else was present and after the waitress had brought the coffee and cakes that he had ordered in advance, they were left entirely alone. He poured out the coffee and Julia began her tale. All the time trying to keep her cool she explained, in more detail than she had already done on the phone, the events that had taken place at David Boswell's house. Monty appeared genuinely shocked. "I never thought he'd treat you like that," he said, "well if it wasn't clear before, it is now. You have to keep well away from him."

"Perhaps I will, perhaps I won't; it rather depends on you."

"On me? What do you mean?"

"Well, quite a lot of what Boswell told me mirrors what you told me, but, obviously being there when it happened; he was able to go into far more detail than you could do. I now know for sure that a murder was planned in cold blood and that it was mercilessly carried out: the people who did it glorified in what they'd done. They didn't only kill Jacob, in reality they also killed Will and he was innocent in all this; I can't let that rest. I want you to do two things for me, but, before I ask you, I just need you to give me an honest answer. Was it you who suggested coating the wet rocks with cooking oil to make them even more slippery?"

Monty shook his head. "I wasn't there to make any suggestions. I was on juvenile remand; remember?"

"You could have made the suggestion before you were locked up. Boswell says it was your idea; is he right or is he wrong?"

Again Monty shook his head. "He's totally wrong Julia, I swear it: whoever came up with that idea, it certainly wasn't me."

"In that case," said Julia, "you have nothing to fear. I said I wanted you to do two things for me. First of all I need you to arrange a meeting with Faith Curtis; there may be stuff that her husband told her that could be very useful to a criminal investigation; and secondly I want you to tell the police everything that you've told me. You can certainly give evidence about the things that were talked about in your presence; if you add to that the things that Boswell told me, it may be enough to persuade them to re-open the case."

The expression on Monty's face was one of utter disbelief; he started to sweat, his hands shook; if Julia had pulled a gun and pointed at his head he couldn't have looked more ill at ease.

"I can arrange the meeting with Faith, Julia but, everything else is impossible; you don't know what you're asking; if I go to the police I'm a dead man: you've got no idea what they're capable of."

"Monty, this is England in the twenty first century: we're not dealing with the Mafia or a reincarnation of the Kray twins; we're dealing with a group of men who together did a terrible thing when they were kids. I can believe that they'll do anything they can to discredit you; I can fully accept that they'll be extremely unpleasant but they're not axe murderers, they're not the Gestapo or the K.G.B. You're over reacting and, in any event, surely the police could protect you if ever the need arose."

"You don't know the half of it Julia. Murder is dirt cheap. Men like David Gladstone and David Boswell and the rest, can afford to buy a whole army of killers. I know what I'm talking about, you don't. I've seen them at work. The police would be powerless to stop them and, given my history, they probably wouldn't even try that hard in any event. "Once a scumbag always a scumbag", that's what they believe. If I tell them what I know they won't follow it up; they'll take the easy option; I'll find myself under investigation as a suspect and at the same time I'll also be dodging bullets. I'm sorry Julia but I can't help you this time; I've already put my neck on the block for you; I can't do anymore; I really can't."

"Can't or won't Monty? I really believed better of you than this. People tried to warn me off you, people said you couldn't be trusted, but I believed your story about having become a changed man, and what good has it done me? You've made everything so much worse. Before I met you I only had suspicions, now I know the whole truth, but, without your help, what use is that knowledge? I can't do anything with it. All my life I will feel that I had a moral obligation entrusted to me which I failed to carry out. You got back a little of your self-esteem when you turned your back on the past, you're condemning me to lose mine by rendering me impotent to do anything; but, if that's how you feel, then fine! If you can live with yourself knowing that you've let me down and let yourself down, then go ahead, but understand this: point one, I never want to see you again and point two, I will keep on trying, with or without your help; and if sometime in the future, something dreadful happens to me you'll have to say to yourself "I left her to make her own way," "I 'hrew her to the wolves because I was a coward", " I could perhaps have saved her"; "maybe if I'd gone with her things would have turned out differently but I turned my back on her and walked away leaving her to her fate". Is that really the way you want our friendship to end?"

It was emotional blackmail and Julia hated herself for resorting to it, but she was learning she had power over men and, by exploiting her God given attributes to the full she could win in situations which a few short months ago would have seemed impossible.

The effect on Monty was devastating. Conflicting emotions battled inside his brain. Anger welled up from the deep recesses of his mind and almost exploded from his mouth in molten fury, but, at the last moment, it was repulsed by sadness and by resignation.

"You're making the wrong call Julia, it's not your fight, and people will get hurt. Your father-in-law's policeman friend is already actively looking for an assassin. At the moment neither you nor I are in his line of fire but if we start rocking boats all that could change in the twinkling of an eye. If you're adamant that you must carry on, I can't let you go it alone; and *yes*, maybe we will succeed, but be warned, there's a better chance that we won't; and along the way there could be terrible danger. You're a beautiful, cultured, compassionate woman, but if you upset the wrong people, none of that will stop you from being dead. If things turn out badly, which they may well do, somebody could have the job of identifying your bodily remains on a mortuary slab. Your children would be orphans; is it worth damaging their live to rewrite a page of history?"

It was Julia's turn to be overwhelmed by emotion, tears pricked her eyes as she fought to prevent them cascading down her face. She breathed deeply to calm herself, finally she spoke.

"No! Of course it's not worth risking everything I care for and more than anything else in the world I want my children to grow up with me by their sides, but every time I think about stopping, I think about Will and about how desperate he must have been in those last few minutes of his life. They killed him Monty, and, if they laughed at Jacob Farrington's death, how much more did they laugh when they heard Will had decapitated himself? I can't rid myself of that thought. I know we must take the greatest care, I know it will be dangerous, I accept everything you tell me but I can't help myself, I've got to see this through to the finish and I have this overwhelming conviction that with your help, we will succeed."

"The confidence of the condemned," sighed Monty, "but if we're going to look forward to a last hearty breakfast, perhaps we should start making serious plans."

CHAPTER FORTY FIVE

"It's bizarre Gov, it's fuckin bizarre. Three sources in the last two days have said the same thing: the person Ambridge's hit man is searching for is Justin Barnes; they're a hundred percent certain that their information is kosher and yet, we know beyond a shadow of a doubt, that he's as dead as a bleedin dodo!"

"Do we Pete? Do we really know? Are we falling into the trap of believing everything we have discovered to be genuine? It could be one gigantic con trick. Death is the perfect alibi. If somehow Barnes has managed to fake his own demise, then that would give him the scope to operate virtually at will. Dead men can't commit murder; corpses can't plan acts of revenge; it's the ideal smoke screen; we must make damn sure that we're not being taken for mugs."

"I was afraid you'd say something like that. You're not backward when it comes to finding people work are you Gov? To pre-empt your demands, I've already done a bit more digging. When Justin Barnes was involved in that R.T.A. in South Africa I discovered that purely by chance, he was being followed by a car load of youngsters who actually knew him. There's a suggestion that the two cars might actually have been racing, but that's pure conjecture; there ain't any clear evidence that that was the case. What is clear is that Barnes lost control on a bend; he skidded off the road, narrowly missing a group of African kids; that did nothing at all to endear him to the local population. They dragged him from his car, and beat him up good and proper; the youngsters in the other car were so shit scared that they just kept on going; they didn't stay to watch any of the real gruesome stuff. When his body was recovered, his clothes were ripped to shreds and, as you already know, his hands had been hacked off so that his rings could be removed at a later time; he were almost certainly still alive when that took place. His face, although a bit of a mess was still recognisable. An old friend of his mum's I.D'd him at the mortuary, his mum were too distraught to do that; but she did see him later at the undertaker's and apparently kissed him in his coffin and then collapsed in a dead faint. She committed suicide less than a week after his funeral. The annoying thing is that his remains were cremated, despite the fact that the South African police were still carrying out a murder investigation: it looks like his mum couldn't stand the thought of a body with bits missing being buried; I think that the fact that she was allowed to have her own way is diabolical. His ashes were scattered at a local beauty spot but they might have well been flushed down the loo as far as we're concerned. Less than a week later, as I've already stated his mum failed to overcome a tussle with gravity and splattered herself over some particularly jagged boulders, thus confirming Sir Isaac Newton's belief that *everything that goes up must come down* was entirely accurate. She landed with a pretty spectacular thud, brains and snot flew everywhere, no doubt you can clearly visualise the scene."

"I can thank you Pete, no need to go into any more detail on my account."

"OK, I'd have never guessed that you were squeamish, that's a real turn up for the books. Anyway they scraped up her remains and what could be poured into a bucket was later buried in a cemetery close to where she'd been living. No doubt, if we put together a convincing enough argument, we could ask for an exhumation and get her DNA, but that would be a pretty pointless exercise, because we don't have any of Justin Barnes' DNA to compare it to."

"What about the P.M. records? Surely there must be something in them to help us and, if Barnes's murder remains unsolved, won't the South African police have retained any exhibits they hold; there must be a good chance of DNA from them?"

"He died nearly two decades ago. We didn't start using DNA to solve crime in this country until 1992; I bet in the 1980's nobody in South Africa would even have heard of DNA. The country was in turmoil: Nelson Mandela was still banged up; sanctions were beginning to bite; the police had a charnel house of skeletons in their cupboards; the last thing they cared about was preserving soiled underpants and dirty bits of clothing: everything seems to have been chucked. The South African cop I spoke to yesterday didn't really give a shit. There's no chance of getting much help from over there."

"So the appliance of science isn't going to give us a magic answer."

"No it's not Gov, but we don't need any sodding magic in this case; the car Justin Barnes crashed was owned by his mother; he was the person who habitually drove it; four people made statements in which they described the accident, they all said they counted Barnes as a friend and that they had known him for at least two years. The woman who identified his body had watched him growing up; his mother sees him stretched out in his coffin, kisses him, then falls to the ground as if she's been pole axed: she turns the whole fucking show into a Greek Tragedy which culminates with her throwing herself off a high cliff. We may not have any DNA, we probably could match blood groups from hospital records, but it'd just be a waste of time and money. There's no doubt in my mind. Even an exceptionally challenged, mentally deficient moron would understand that the case was overwhelming: if you've got any misgivings on that score, see what your *good friend* Bob Earnshaw says about it: he's the nearest thing to a Neanderthal that we can lay our hands on at short notice."

"There's no need to plumb those depths Peter; you've persuaded me: I'll happily agree with anything you say. Justin Barnes is no longer resident on this planet; but, if he has 'shuffled off this mortal coil' why are Ralph Ambridge, and apparently several other people convinced that he's still a fully paid up member of the human race? Ambridge may be many things but, he isn't a fool. He'll have made enquiries in the same way we've made enquiries and he'll know, in broad terms, most of what we know. I accept that some of the people who are falling over themselves to grab his money by feeding him bits of information may have no knowledge at all but, it would be a hell of a risky strategy to pull a name out of thin air and then try to claim the cash prize. If Ambridge thought he was being played for a fool then the shit would really hit the fan. I wouldn't want to be the one who'd tried to con him; at the very least I'd be expecting two broken legs, and that would only be if he was in a good mood. It's too big a gamble; there must be something out there that is causing some people to genuinely believe that, despite all the evidence to the contrary, Justin Barnes is still alive."

"Undoubtedly there is, but I'm not a flamin mind reader Gov so I haven't got a fuckin clue what it might be. Some of the people who have spoken to Ambridge must have known Barnes when he was giving juvenile delinquency a bad name but, unless he's a Time Lord, which somehow I fuckin well doubt, it's unlikely many of them would recognise him after all these years; but, sure as eggs are eggs, something is causing their deluded little brains to slip into overdrive. My bet would be that it's got sod all to do with physical appearance and everything to do with knowledge of historic facts. I think the bloke we want has opened his mouth too wide, and at one time or another has inadvertently let slip something only Justin Barnes, or someone who was very close to him, could possibly have known."

"I agree; and it follows doesn't it that the man who so many people think is Justin Barnes has to be a recent arrival on the scene. Jackie Skinner's continuing ordeal started with the appearance of a stranger and Sharon's Farrington's nightmare was also initiated by an out of towner."

"And despite the fact that we have very different descriptions for those two men you believe that those two apparently different beings are in fact one and the same person, don't you Gov?"

"I'm by no means one hundred percent certain, but yes, I think they could be. I also think that both Jackie and Sharon, who wasn't even born when Barnes was round here, are being punished, in a particularly cruel and brutal way for something that happened a long, long time ago. Even though I am now totally convinced that

Justin Barnes is dead, his life story holds the key; and, I intend to read that story, line by line, chapter and verse, from the very beginning to the very end and, somewhere in that unedifying narrative, I expect to discover just what that key is."

CHAPTER FORTY SIX

"You've got a dirty mouth and an equally dirty mind haven't you Rupert?" The anger in Bob Hammond's voice was obvious; there was no mistaking his rage. Rupert's face drained of its colour; the stammer that Bob had first noticed in the churchyard strangled his ability to speak; his right hand seemed to take on a life of its own, shaking like a rag in the jaws of an over excited terrier.

"But, but, but," he stuttered; the words would not come; he looked to Bob for salvation; none was forthcoming. Like a four year old being told off by his mother, he resorted to tears, hoping that Bob's heart would melt, but the gamekeeper was in no mood for showing mercy.

"It's a nice try Rupert and it nearly had me fooled but I've been taken in by you once before, I'm not going to make the same mistake a second time. You pretend to be so meek and mild; nothing could be further than the truth! You're nothing more than a filthy minded little sod. Well, that's it, I'm through with you! Just get out of my sight! I never, ever want to set eyes on you again!"

"Bob, please don't say that. I don't know what you're on about: for God's sake tell me what it is that I'm supposed to have done."

"You got drunk in the Royal Albert the night before last didn't you Rupert? You were so pissed that you ended up annoying a lot of the customers with your antics; you finished by managing to get yourself barred; which, knowing the landlord like I do, I can tell you is no mean feat; he doesn't bar people lightly does Len, you're probably only the second person he's kicked out of his pub in the last five years."

In an instant Rupert's face changed from ash to fiery crimson.

"You know I did," he said. "I was so stupid. It was the first time in years that I'd had a drink. I can't take alcohol. I honestly didn't have very much, but what I had must have gone straight to my head. I was such a fool. I'm so ashamed. I swear it will never happen again, but surely everybody is entitled to one mistake. I know it was bad, I have written to the licensee to apologise but it's not like I killed anybody, or did any serious harm; I don't understand why you're so very, very angry."

"You got drunk, the mask slipped, and you revealed your true self. I'm not a prude Rupert, I've been bladdered myself on a few occasions and I've said things that I've later regretted but I've never deliberately set out to attack a man's character. I know what you said about me, "an ignorant country clod" "thick as suet pudding" I've heard all about it and do you know what? If you'd restricted your comments to me, I'd have probably given you another chance; but you didn't stop there did you? You started shouting your mouth off about Julia and about all the sick things you'd like to do to her and that revealed the sort of man you really are. If you can think such crude and degenerate thoughts about a decent young woman, who has never done you any harm then you've got a sick mind and I want now't more to do with you. And be warned son, if I see you anywhere near her after tonight I'll break your bloody neck: do you comprehend me? Now just clear off and take your puerile sexual fantasies with you. You're not welcome in this town Rupert. You're scum and as far as I'm concerned you no longer bloody exist."

"Bob I swear I never said any of those things: I wouldn't call you or Julia: I came to warn you remember? I wanted you to try and protect her."

"You're a coward as well as a liar and a louse. Len at the pub wouldn't invent a story like this; I've known him all my life. You've just waved bye bye to the final bit of credibility you had left. Piss off and crawl into a dung heap, you'll find yourself pretty much at home there."

At about the same time that Bob Hammond was charging into battle to defend a lady's honour and expelling the craven hearted black knight from the castle grounds, the fair damsel, who was the object of his chivalry, was beginning the next phase of her own quest. Her latest adventure had started with a telephone call from Monty telling her that he had now spoken, for a second time, to Faith Curtis and that she had agreed to help Julia in her search for justice. Faith had suggested a meeting at her house, just the two of them and she had indicated that she would show to Julia the contents of a battered suitcase which contained all of her husband's personal papers. She promised nothing; she said she didn't know what they might find; she had simply bundled letters, diaries and photographs into the case without examining any of them in detail: one day, when she was less upset, she had promised herself that she would go through them carefully: following Monty's intercession she had concluded that that day might as well be now.

The house that she lived in was small. Built by the local council in the early 1960's it had been sold to its long standing tenant under Maggie's "Right to Buy" scheme. A new porch had been added and plastic double glazing had replaced rotting soft wood window frames but all this had been completed more than a decade ago, at bargain basement prices, which the first purchaser, who fancied himself as a bit of a wheeler/dealer, had bragged about to his neighbours: now the true value of the work done was showing itself in the cloudy, steamed up glass panels and the perished rubber seals. Everything about the property spoke of neglect: Julia hadn't the slightest doubt that she would fail to discover any tell tale signs of affluence when she entered the premises. Almost timorously she rang the doorbell; true to the integrity of the house it didn't work. She knocked; there was no reply. She knocked again, this time a good deal louder and, a few seconds later, the door was opened by a skinny, pale complexioned, nervous looking female, who was probably significantly younger than she actually appeared to be. She looked at Julia with suspicion: to dress well and to look attractive was a mortal sin, but, never-the-less, once her identity had been established, she was admitted to the house without any adverse comment: a sermon on humility and the evils of worldly treasure may have formed in her mind but Faith Curtis eschewed the urge to preach: a blessing for which Julia was truly thankful. She did however feel that smart clothes had been a mistake and that sackcloth and ashes might have been more appropriate attire for this visit and that now she would have to work extra hard if she was going to persuade her edgy, down-trodden hostess to bare her late husband's soul.

The crucifix standing on the sideboard and the painting of the Madonna and child offered hope: here was a house where the pain of religion was real and Julia remembered what Monty had told her about Nathan Curtis's flirtation with an evangelising

Christian sect; if she could display the right level of piety and humility all might not be lost.

"It's so very good of you to see me at such short notice," she said, smiling, "It's been such a struggle to get people to talk to me; I really am so very, very grateful."

"We were put on this earth to help others; if we think only of ourselves there can be no salvation. My husband believed in the Good Samaritan; he gave countless thousands to our church: I owe it to his memory to try to follow his example."

"Did he give the money, or did the church squeeze it out of him?" the question sprang to Julia's lips; a split second after speaking out she realised that that had been entirely the wrong thing to say.

Sidestepping the man trap she had laid for herself, Julia quickly carried on and, without giving Faith time to answer, deftly switched the topic of conversation to Will and the good he had tried to do and how very much she missed his company. The expression on Faith's face softened and Julia had a glimpse of the gentle woman that Monty had described. She gestured towards a faded armchair, inviting her to sit and without a word of explanation she then left the room; a barrier might have been removed but Faith Curtis was far from won over. Two minutes later she returned carrying a small brown suitcase which she set down heavily on the coffee table: the metal edges of the case scratched the surface of the wood. Faith either didn't notice or didn't care that damage had been done. She opened the case and lifted the contents from it and spread the paperwork across the table top. She picked up a photograph. "That's a picture of Nathan taken on our wedding day; he was a fine looking man Mrs Hammond:" a tear formed in her eye; almost angrily she brushed it away.

"I can see that," said Julia, "and please, call me Julia, Mrs Hammond sounds so very formal."

There were so many pieces of paper and so many snapshots it was difficult to know where to start and Faith, who was by now clearly beginning to shed her defensive armour, wanted to talk and to focus the conversation upon the times when she and Nathan had been happy. This did not feel like a rich seam to explore so far as Julia was concerned, but to interrupt Faith's reminiscences now would inevitably send Faith scurrying back beyond a sturdy portcullis of privacy, to a place where Julia would never again be invited to follow. She said nothing and let Faith carry on recalling the good times she had known. More photographs were passed over for comment, many cherished memories were revealed, but at last she turned away from this rose tinted retrospective to the darker times she and her husband had endured.

"Nathan had such a troubled childhood Julia; he was never loved as a son should have been. His parents gave him presents, they never gave him time. He hated himself, particularly when he was a teenager even though to the outside world he had everything that normal kids could only dream of. There was nobody there to guide him and, he admitted to me that he went off the rails: he mixed with some horrible boys; I know you know this and I know that's why you're here; but there was more to his life than resentment and rejection."

"People find it hysterically funny nowadays when a person discovers God, but believe it or not, that's exactly what Nathan did. It wasn't easy for him, there was so much scorn heaped upon him, but it didn't matter. My parents called themselves Christians but they had no passion: Dad could recite whole chapters of scripture but he couldn't live it. Nathan became so intense it was mind blowing. He joined what I now realise was a cynical sect that exploited young peoples' yearnings to find truth: I'd also been seduced into believing that they could light the way to a better way of life. We were both naive and we became victims of a cruel hoax. They took all Nathan's money and eventually he saw them for what they were. He turned his back on them but miraculously he kept his faith and when he left he took Faith with him", and Faith smiled at this simple play on words.

"We started to live together and, although we were practically penniless, we felt rich because we had each other and gradually we found ways to make ends meet. Then just as it seemed like we'd turned a corner, Nathan started to have dreadful headaches. He was diagnosed as having an inoperable brain tumour. They gave him six weeks to live, but, mercifully, he died in just four. He suffered terrible pain; it was pitiful to see his agony. I was so angry with God I nearly stopped believing but, Nathan begged me to stand firm. Three days before he died, while he was still aware of his surroundings, he asked me to fetch the local vicar; he said he wanted to clean his slate with God before the Day of Atonement. He was insistent that a record should be kept of that conversation; everything had to be revealed, there could be no secrets left to be uncovered. He was so brave," and for several minutes the memory of his courage overwhelmed Faith and she could no longer carry on: Julia held her hand and tried to comfort her.

Eventually, when she was a little more composed, she rummaged through the mountain of papers and produced a small black exercise book.

"Everything he said is in here" she said. "This little book contains his last confession. He revealed a secret that he had harboured for more than twenty years. He admitted the most terrible of crimes. Tears poured down his face and he told us of a murder; at times his voice was so low that I could hardly hear what he had to say.

I didn't want to keep writing, but he was insistent that I did. When it was all done he asked for absolution, he begged me to add a sentence stating, in clear terms, that every word of his account was true and then he signed and dated the book; it was such an effort, you can see how shaky his hand was. He implored the vicar and me to sign too, I think we were both crying when we did so, but when it was all done, Nathan seemed more at peace. I've never told a soul until now about the events of that day. I lied to Charles Montgomery and I lied to you when I said I didn't know what the suitcase contained. I can remember every word that I wrote. Nathan said there would come a time when I would know that it was right to let the secret go. I believe that you are now the person to take care of it. Do with the book as you see fit but be careful Julia, a lot of people would do anything that was necessary to stop its contents becoming public knowledge."

CHAPTER FORTY SEVEN

"It's the oddest blinking thing Bob: the day after I told you about that youth shooting his mouth off he writes me a letter of apology. Now, I've had drunks do that before and usually it's just a pathetic attempt at self-justification smothered in a large dollop of self pity: his letter was a bit different. He weren't whining, he weren't pleading to be allowed back in, he weren't looking for sympathy: he said he regretted being a fool, he said he just wanted to set the record straight. I nearly binned it as I have done on every other occasion when somebody has overstepped the mark, but he said that as I personally hadn't seen too much of what he'd allegedly said and done, I should speak to the people who had, to see what they felt about matters. He didn't know names, but, he described two of my regulars to a T so I talked to 'em and, this is where it becomes downright weird. Everybody I've spoken to since I got that letter has confirmed that he behaved like a pissed up twat but, nobody alleges that he said anything bad about you or Julia. In fact quite the contrary: Jim Braddock says you'd have been embarrassed by the amount of praise he heaped on you both. "Laying it on with a trowel" was how he described it and, Jim's about as level headed as you can get so, that being so, why did I get a phone call from an unknown customer saying the exact opposite?"

"I've no idea Len, there are some funny people about, but what you've just said makes me feel pretty bad: because of what you told me I gave the lad a right dressing down and then I fucked him off big time but, now it turns out, that for all his drunken shenanigans he never meant me any harm. He may have behaved like a pillock but I was wrong to treat him in the way that I did; I'll have to seek him out and try and make amends."

"You can tell him I was too hasty as well if you've a mind to. I should have checked all my facts before I barred him. He can come back in if he wants to but I will be watching his every move and if there's another rumpus then that'll be it: whether he's singing your praises or cursing the ground you walk on won't make a jot of difference, he'll be out on his ear and this time it'll be for good."

Unbeknown to Bob and to the fair minded landlord, in addition to Jim Braddock, another potential character witness also existed who could provide a valuable insight into Rupert's character and that witness was none other than a certain Mrs Julia Hammond. She had stayed far longer with Faith Curtis than she had ever intended to do and she had gained much from the meeting. Whether the notebook she had taken away with her had any or no evidential value she didn't know but she had no doubt that every word that it contained was true. Now, she badly needed to make up some time, the children still had to be collected, essential shopping remained to be done but, when she returned to her car she discovered that the front nearside tyre was completely flat; it had also started to rain.

Even as a lone female and thus a high priority call, in all probability a long wait existed before the R.A.C would arrive, and a long wait was something that would cause her untold problems. The alternative to the wait was to change the wheel herself; she had changed a wheel once before when she was a student but the weather had been fine and, at the time, she had been wearing jeans and a T-shirt which were already dirty following a day gardening at her grandmother's house: today she was well dressed; quite inappropriately attired for manual labour, but there seemed to be no other choice. She removed her smart jacket, that at least could be protected from dirt and grime and, inwardly cursing her bad luck she walked to the boot of the car and opened it up.

"Excuse me Luv, do you need a bit of a 'and?"

The man was young, although the oil on his face made it hard to guess his exact age; his hands were black and the boiler suit he was wearing was caked in dust and soot: Fred Dibnah, at his joyful best, would have looked the picture of elegance by comparison; but, guardian angels come in many shapes and sizes and, for certain, Julia was not going to turn this one away.

"Oh yes please," said Julia, "I've got a flat tyre. I don't know how it happened, but I have to pick my children up and I'm already very, very late."

"Leave it to me Luv; I'll 'ave the wheel changed in a jiffy. Give us the key to your locking wheel nut and then go and find yourself an umbrella and try to get out of this flippin rain. You'll be on your way in no time, I can promise you that."

 The man worked with speed and efficiency, he was obviously a mechanic who was used to doing this kind of job and, although his speech suggested an upbringing in one of the less affluent parts of Sheffield, he was cheerful and chatty and Julia was thankful for his presence. A rough diamond perhaps he might be; but a thousand times more useful to her than the Kohinoor itself at this precise moment.

How the conversation started Julia couldn't later recall but as her knight in rusty armour unscrewed the wheel nuts, using a great deal more strength than Julia could ever have summoned up, she said something that made him stop and pause.

"You're not Mrs Julia 'Ammond are you?" he asked, "only a mate of mine is always talkin about you and he'll be dead envious when 'e finds out that I've been able to do this bit of a job for you."

"Yes, I am. Who is this friend of yours? I'll certainly tell him of your kindness when I next see him, but I'll need to know your name so that I can say who it was that I'm so indebted to."

"Me name's John Ashworth Mrs 'Ammond, but everybody just calls me "Ashy". Me mate's name is Rupert 'Enshaw; Rupert's never actually met you, so you won't know 'im but your father certainly does."

"Father-in-law," corrected Julia, "yes, I'm quite sure he knows my father-in-law."

"'E's a good lad Mrs 'Ammond. There's nowt 'e wouldn't for nobody but e's got no confidence, 'e ain't pushy like me, it's as though 'e ain't properly wired up when it comes to relatin with folk. 'E's too trusting; people take advantage of 'im. 'Is heart's always in the right place but 'is 'ead's often in Cloud Cuckoo Land, particularly if 'e's 'ad a few pints of lager"

"Some people are like that," said Julia, "but I tell you Ashy there are a lot worse faults for a person to have. If he cares for his fellow man then he can't go far wrong; there are a great many unscrupulous and cruel individuals in this world who are a thousand times richer and many times more intelligent than your mate Rupert but, take my word for it, they're not fit to hold a candle to honest, well-motivated guys like him."

No more words were spoken on the subject and Ashy returned to the job in hand. It wasn't until the spare wheel had been fitted and he had cleaned the wheel brace and the locking wheel nut with a piece of rag that he pulled from his pocket to wipe off the deposits that his greasy hands had left that he turned his full attention to the deflated tyre.

"It's got a decent amount of tread on it," he said, "You must 'ave picked up a nail somewhere. I'll see if I can see it for you. The tyre certainly ain't knackered: you should be able to get it repaired without too much bother."

But, look as he might, Ashy could find no nail; though finally he saw something else: he frowned and the question that followed the frown caused Julia a great deal of concern.

"I don't want to worry you or 'owt like that Mrs 'Ammond and, I know this'll sound a bit of an odd thing to ask, but is there anyone who might 'ave a bit of a down on you?"

"No, not that I know of Ashy: why do you ask me such an uncomfortable question? It makes me think that you think that maybe there is such a person."

"Well some bastard's driven a knife or some sort of sharp spike into the wall of your tyre. It can't 'ave been done by accident and it does mean despite what I said earlier the tyre is now well and truly fucked; the odd thing though is why did 'e stop at just the one tyre? If all the tyres 'ad been slashed you'd 'ave been up Shit Creek without a paddle, probably stuck here until midnight waitin for a low loader to arrive."

Butterflies crashed into the sides of Julia's small intestine: she had never been marked out for hate before; it was a new and altogether unpleasant experience. She wanted to get away. She tried hard not to let the full extent of her panic show. Maybe somebody had been interrupted before his crime was complete, maybe the intent had been to make the car totally un-driveable; maybe even now, from some vantage point near at hand, somebody was watching her every move with malicious intent: but for the timely arrival of John Ashworth she could have found herself in real and imminent danger of physical harm at the hands of a violent criminal.

"That's a horrible thought Ashy: for some reason it seems somebody round here has taken against me; I think my best move is to get out while I still can. Thank you so much for all your help; I don't know what I would have done if you hadn't been on hand. Please let me give you something for your time," and she pulled her purse from her handbag; she hoped her saviour did not see her hand trembling as she did so.

Ashy shook his head. "I don't want 'owt for doing something any 'alf-way reasonable bloke would 'ave done without thinking about; in any event I've got bragging rights now so far as Rupert's concerned but, maybe there is a favour you could do for me. Rupert's got this thing about a chap called Charles Montgomery: 'e's the only bloke I've ever 'eard him talk bad about. Well, I think 'e's wrong, certainly so far as I'm concerned. Monty did me did me a big favour once, lent me cash when no other bugger would touch me. Without 'im I were getting that desperate that I'd either 'ave topped meself or more likely mugged an old woman for her pension and ended up in Arnley gaol for me trouble. It were just a few 'undred quid, not much by today's standards, but it were enough. I've always intended to pay 'im back but, 'e upped sticks before I could do so. I've got the cash stashed away and I want to settle me debts. I know you know 'im because Rupert's told me that 'e warned your father-in-law against 'im so, I'm thinking that you might be able to tell me an address where I can find 'im.

"He's staying at a hotel in Buxton. I can give you the name, and I've also got his mobile phone number if that's any good to you."

"Well yeah it is, but, what I'd really prefer to do is surprise 'im. I think 'e wants to write off this debt, I don't think it's fair on 'im to 'ave to do that; I'd like to pay back the cash in circumstances where 'e would find it very difficult to refuse it. I don't suppose you could 'elp me, could you?"

A thought flashed into Julia's brain.

"Give me your mobile number," she said; "I've got to fix up a meeting with him tomorrow; when I know where it's going to be I'll telephone you and let you have the details".

"That's a brilliant idea Mrs 'Ammond, let's do that. Now, get yourself out of 'ere, and don't forget to get a new tyre fitted to the spare as soon as you can. I'll see you again tomorrow, and maybe then I'll look a bit less like a bleedin chimney sweep and a bit more like a civilised 'uman being."

CHAPTER FORTY EIGHT

"*The hunter becomes the hunted; the predator becomes the prey; that is his dream. In his mind's eye he sees a stag being stalked by a gillie; the beast is nervous and unsettled, sensing its own death upon the wind. On and on it runs to higher and more desolate places until there is nowhere else for it to run. Exhausted by the chase, it waits. He hears the crack of a rifle, a noble beast is laid low; he watches, with sublime pleasure, its death throes; and he smiles.*

The dream changes; the animal becomes human. A man, his face obscured by the mists of time lies dead upon the ground. Try as he might he cannot see him clearly, but he remembers a face from years gone by. Then for a brief moment the fog lifts, the years are rolled away, the man becomes a boy, though still as lifeless as the adult corpse. He sees a face, a handsome, intelligent face, and the face of one who has suffered and who has learnt from his suffering: it is my poor unloved face, white as the graveyard marble with a slime trail of crimson blood seeping from my lips. He strikes my face with his fists until it is unrecognisable. Now his work is done, he looks upon the wretched remnants of a glorious life and laughs at the carnage he has wrought.

His dream is the product of a desperate obsession to destroy me. The Wanted Dead or Alive posters hang from every tree. The bounty has been fixed and a generous advance payment has been made: I'm flattered that he values me so highly. Should I be terrified by the knowledge that a hired assassin seeks to make my close acquaintance? Should I crawl away on my belly and hope that time will eventually be my saviour? There's not a hope in Hell! I will leave this place when I am ready and I have many things to do before that day comes. He has now added to my work load as I will need to punish him for his impudence before I go. I swear by that which I do not possess, which is a conscience that he will pay dearly for his fault; and not just in terms of cash. His plodding butcher, who thinks himself a match for me, will one day soon regret he ever took on such a cursed contract, but for the present I have need of him. There is a job which he must do for me although, he'll never realise that in trying to do his master's bidding he is serving my cause. He has such vanity: he overvalues his meagre worth: he considers himself a lesser god, with the power to decide who lives and who does not. I am the Avenger, the choreographer of the Dance of Death, that's what he thinks. He believes he holds a winning hand; right now he is convinced that the end game has begun and that all his painstaking enquiries have borne fruit; he doesn't understand that in seeking to harvest the grains of knowledge he has left a trail even a brain damaged Neanderthal could follow. I know him well, but although he thinks otherwise, he does not know me. He is so sure that the final hand has been dealt that he is blind to every other possibility. Tomorrow he will have his eagerly awaited date with destiny and from that brief encounter he will walk away believing he has triumphed; a job well done; a task fulfilled; the final piece of the jigsaw slotted home.

How can that be you wonder! If there is a victor there has to be a vanquished; and surely if he wins you lose! "Oh ye of little faith" do you imagine I can be defeated with such ease? This greedy, sinful world is rotten to the core, intrigue festers in dark places and I am the mother and the father of Deceit.

It is so simple. In times gone by ignorant yokels lived in fear of spells and potions: witches and warlocks terrorised the countryside; shape-shifters caused dread throughout the land. I am a modern magician, with powers far greater than any senile crone. You shake your head and question my grip on sanity, but, know this; shapes can be changed in many different ways. A is changed into B that's magic. A does not change at all but, by false rumour, is widely named as B that's deception; but, if enough people believe the deception to be true, the outcome is the same. A glimmer of understanding flickers in your feeble mind, but let me make things clear. Some time tomorrow I will become somebody else, or rather someone unwittingly will become me.

My death will be reported back to him who most wants to hear the news, but the story will have no more truth than a tabloid expose; never-the-less doubt not that it will be believed.

I did consider adding a dramatic postscript to my Theatre Macabre production. I thought perhaps that a beautiful woman might be cast in a starring role in this delicious tragedy. It would have been the work of a moment to convince the paymaster that he had cause to be afraid: he knows she has been asking questions; for him to suppose that she has received damning answers would need no giant leap of faith; he would then be desperate to stop her revealing all: I too would benefit from her silencing.

What stayed my hand? I saw a reflection of my mother's face in her face. My mother, the Madonna and the Whore of Babylon; her fall from grace and journey into Hell, I have already documented: this woman needs to follow the self same path. To begin with I saw only beauty and the Great Deceiver deceived himself that emotions which were crushed two decades before could be revived. I told myself that there were pleasures of the flesh there for the taking and with the caveat that I could always rid myself of an encumbrance, should it become necessary I formulated a long term plan. I realised very quickly the error of my ways. If I were ever to feel tenderness or compassion, I would lose my power. She would become my Delilah and sap me of my strength and thus, even before she started to meddle in affairs of history, I knew what I had to do. The path that she is following could destroy everything; every time she causes a ripple, sediment is disturbed, grains of truth float to the surface and if enough fragments of concealed fact see the light of day, the police will start to take a new interest in an event they have long thought closed.

Why then did I not let a base butcher ply his trade and, in the process, also rid me of a dangerous nuisance? The answer should be obvious. Would you let a third rate mercenary rob you of a moment of unbridled ecstasy? In the darkness of the night, while others sleep, I have mapped out her future. I have heard her screams and the monotonic sound of clothing being ripped from her body revealing naked flesh and it has been *a symphony. I have seen beads of terror upon her face and her hair matted by her own cold sweat. I have become Tyrannosaurus Rex but, against all accepted wisdom, my blood is molten lava. She cries out and I lightly prick her with a knife. I kiss her lips, she tries to turn her head away, and my fist punishes her heartless rejection of me. The ropes that bind her hold her fast. The tiger penetrates the lamb, and then after the volcano has erupted, for a few minutes I lie prone astride her, exhausted by my Herculean efforts. She whimpers and her sobs assail my ears. My mother begs forgiveness for her; she could not have chosen a worse advocate. I strike with precision and with power. Her body becomes a scarlet pin cushion, each cut and slash spilling her life blood onto the cold floor. The deed is done, I am immortal; there is not a man alive who would hand to another the moment of his greatest triumph.*

Everything thereafter will be anti-climactic, but loose ends still need to be tied up and unfinished business completed before I bring this chapter of my life to an end.

She who told lies about me, although damaged by my actions, still survives and in better shape than I would have wished. I cannot yet be sure of the jury's verdict, but I have a plan which, if successful, will guarantee her destruction. If everything works as I intend, she will be sentenced to serve years of prison time and, if that occurs, within twelve months I'm sure she will become one more grisly statistic upon a mortuary slab. But in her case I have learnt that nothing is assured. If, yet again, my grand design is thwarted by the intervention of others, and she clings on to freedom, then the final solution will be for me to expunge another worthless life: it is a win-win situation, both outcomes hand me a victory: this time there will be no room for failure.

The Fat Cat who wants me dead needs to be punished and I intend that he will suffer for his sinfulness. Before I am done I will have extracted, without anaesthetic, an imperial ransom from his bank account and then, at the very moment he believes he has finally bought peace I will unleash Holy War upon him. The world turns and actions are bound to actions by invisible threads. I won't tell you yet, but eventually you will see how his defeat made possible the Hell on Earth I gifted to the pretty false witness. Wheels within wheels, circles that intertwine, when you understand the simplicity of the scheme you will applaud the skill of he who devised it.

Once the main players in my carefully staged drama have made their final exits I will create a suitable gory swansong for the bone-headed butcher of this epic tale but all this still awaits, and you must be patient and wait to see what will eventually come to pass."

CHAPTER FORTY NINE

Sharon Farrington stared out of the rear window of the farmhouse; she was entirely alone, but, there was nothing new in that experience. Even when everyone was at home her presence didn't register. Ever since the botched abortion she had been treated like a leper by Brenda and Brenda ruled the roost; her influence was corrosive: now even David largely ignored her, her wants and needs no longer important to him.

When she cried, and she cried nearly every day, she was told to stop whining and, if she didn't stop, Brenda would explode with anger. Her misery was a "punishment from God" that was how her mother-in-law saw it. Her opinions of her daughter-in law were carved in stone, they would never ever change.

"You've ruined our lives and you've destroyed your own" that unforgiving judgement was restated day after day after day after dreary day. Joy didn't exist anymore; fun had been banished from her world; drudgery and contempt were her lots in life: the certain knowledge that this would always be the case was an unbearably painful thought.

"I wish I were fucking dead," she screamed, knowing that nobody was around to hear her anguish: for once Brenda's oft repeated, bitter retort of "*I wish you were fucking dead too*" would go unsaid.

In the silence that followed suddenly everything became clear. Here was an opportunity to show them all: surely *suicide could be painless* as the song said, if the act was done properly. Will Hammond had made an error and had unintentionally severed his own head from his body; she knew better, she would not make that same mistake. It would be quick and easy. A step stool, a length of washing line, a low beam, a confident leap into the void and it would all be over. They would regret it when they returned to find her body hanging in the kitchen; a sad end to a tragically short life; that would pay them back for their cruelty; that would punish them for their lack of understanding.

What mattered now was the final impact. She had to look her best. Quickly she changed into her prettiest dress: she glanced at herself in the mirror, it would be the last time that she would see her own reflection. The thought almost stopped her in her tracks, but what was the alternative? She smoothed down her hair, one final touch was needed; an angry, unsightly rope burn would destroy the beauty of the scene. With her hand shaking slightly, she opened the dressing table drawer and took out a pink silk scarf. Carefully, she wrapped it round her neck, then she took a deep breath and counted down from ten. She was composed. She was ready. She had the courage to proceed.

***

"Poor stupid little Sharon!" Detective Sergeant Peter Bennett's sympathy was genuinely felt: underneath an outspoken and sometimes crude exterior was the heart and mind of somebody who cared. He didn't often let his feelings show but when weak and vulnerable people were victimised, abused or attacked; the ferocity of his anger would sometimes reveal itself.

"They did her no favours when they cut her down Gov: it's impossible to say how long she'd been unconscious, probably at least seven or eight minutes, a few seconds longer and they'd have been too late, which would have been a good thing: as it is they've saved her life but her brain's totally shot: fifty years of slobbering, gibbering and having your arse wiped by a nurse ain't a life that's worth living: if she were my daughter I'd smother her with a pillow while she slept rather than let her endure that. And it's all his bastard fault. He's deliberately sacrificed a silly clueless little girl to make a point. What harm did she ever do to him? She were too wrapped up in schoolgirl fantasies ever to be a threat to anyone. He must have known when he intentionally messed up her innards, that at one time or another in her life, an attempt at suicide was always on the cards. If he can treat a kid like that with such callousness, it's only a matter of time before he turns his attention towards the people he really hates and when he does that God help 'em. Jackie Skinner could well be one of them; we've got to stop the sod before there's a fucking bloodbath."

"Nobody's arguing with that Pete. I don't use the word lightly, but I'm convinced we're dealing with a psychopath. Sharon's tragedy has destroyed a whole family. The one who's been hardest hit is Brenda. She found her, she cut her down, she gave Sharon the kiss of life, and she tried repeatedly to revive her and, for better or worse, her intervention saved her life. She was often exasperated by Sharon's attitude, and the destruction of her unborn grandchild did cause a huge rift, but now she blames herself for Sharon's pathetic state and its hit her hard: the son's not much better, and both of them will be plagued by feelings of guilt for the rest of their natural lives."

"And they may not be the only ones with feelings of guilt to contend with. If something happens to Jackie Skinner when we should have prevented it how will we feel? The odds should be stacked in our favour but they're not. Even when we seem to have found a bit of a lead it ends up not taking us anywhere: the only name in the frame we have is of somebody who no longer exists, but that seemingly insuperable obstacle doesn't appear to be a problem: he still seems able to commit crime at will. The only way we look remotely like getting a result on this one would seem to be if a professional hit man does our job for us and that's something I couldn't fucking stomach. The trouble is I think that I am going to need Milk of Magnesia; half the scroats in Burrfield are convinced that something is going to happen soon. Most of 'em wouldn't know how many blue beans made five, even if you gave them a colour chart, but the belief is so widespread that I believe it has to be taken seriously. The problem is, even if we get lucky and the right man bites the bullet, we won't know for sure that that's the case and, in any event there'll still be a killer on the loose. People like Bob Earnshaw will be going round telling every prat who is daft enough to listen to him how we've cocked things up big style and just how crap he thinks you and me are."

"You can bet your pension on that Pete; we've just got to make sure that we don't give him the satisfaction."

"Then we have to get this sodding case solved Gov, we have to get this sodding case closed!"

In a luxury house less than two miles away from the police station another person was feeling many of the same emotions as the two Derbyshire detectives. Julia Hammond had slept badly: in the early hours of the morning she had thought she heard the sound of the garden gate closing and then the outside security light had come on. Seizing the cordless phone from its stand she had made her way, in total darkness, to the front bedroom window and peeped through a gap in the curtains to see if she could spot an intruder. Eventually a dog fox had arrogantly strolled into view and the panic was over, but the incident had brought home to Julia how badly she had been rattled by yesterday's events. She had slept intermittently after that and as a consequence had woken up late. Everything had been one mad rush, but now her children were in Play Group and, at last, she had time on her hands. She picked up the diary that Faith Curtis had given her and re-read, for the hundredth time, the words Nathan had signed. What should she do? She had to show the journal to Monty, she badly needed his advice. At shortly after 9:30am she telephoned him at his hotel; his mobile was switched off so she used the land line. He was still at breakfast and had to be brought to the phone. She apologised for interrupting his meal and then explained to him, briefly, some of the occurrences of the previous day and stressed how urgently she wanted to meet him. Fearful that their conversation might be overheard, she suggested as a meeting place a public car park in the centre of Buxton; the children were back at school, the tourist season was largely over, the weather was grey and gloomy and, at midday, it was unlikely that there would be very many shoppers about.

Monty agreed the choice of venue and, for Julia's sake, was happy to go along with her cloak and dagger precautions, which seemed to set her mind at ease. After the arrangements were finalised, she put down the phone. It was only later she remembered the promise she had made to John Ashworth; an hour before she left the house she telephoned him to give him details of the meeting place. Monty would soon be pleasantly surprised; he deserved a bit of good fortune for all the help he was giving her.

The car park was less than half full and the cars which were there were concentrated in the spaces nearest to the entrance. When it was that something in our national psyche had decreed that to walk half a yard further than was absolutely necessary was an onerous burden Julia didn't know but, on this occasion, it suited her purposes well, as it meant that she had the whole of the rear of the car park from which to choose a space.

She was a little bit early and, as she waited, she started to scold herself for being so melodramatic. The incident with her car yesterday had been an act of pure vandalism or, at the very worst, a blind attack on a symbol of wealth. The person responsible neither knew nor cared who the driver was. His, or maybe even her, actions were rooted in working class political ideology and tainted by straight forward envy: it wasn't a personal vendetta, she wasn't being singled out for special treatment, and it was ludicrous to imagine that she was at risk.

I've become paranoid, she thought. *I'm seeing threats that don't exist. Right now* she taunted herself; *I could be sitting in a comfortable chair in a nice hotel or alternatively in my own home, discussing what to do next with a man who wants to help me.*

Why hadn't she simply invited him to come over? Why had she gone to such ridiculous lengths to choose a place that could be categorised as neutral ground? He wasn't the enemy, there was no danger to her in him visiting her house, nor was there the remotest possibility that an expensive 4 Star hotel had been electronically bugged to eavesdrop upon her private conversations. *I have been silly* she thought, *I'll suggest we go and find a quiet coffee shop and then our discussions can take place in warmth and comfort.*

She double checked that the diary was in her handbag, despite the fact that she knew for sure it was there; even this she felt was a sign of how jumpy she had become. It was exactly where it should be; it hadn't been spirited away by the Tooth Fairy to a secret hiding place in Never Never Land. She got out of the car and walked over to the ticket vending machine. She bought a three hour ticket and placed that on the dashboard of the car, then she turned around and saw Monty; he was about to cross over the road and enter the car park. She signalled to him to wait where he was, and when he acknowledged her signal she hurried down the car park to meet him.

Two cars travelling down the road at speed forced her to delay her crossing for a few seconds; the car park might have been quiet, but traffic on the streets was unusually heavy for that time of day. A vehicle following the two cars visibly slowed down and Julia crossed in safety, turning her head momentarily towards the driver and mouthing the words '*Thank You*' at him.

"I've had a change of plan," she said to Monty, "rather than sit cramped up in a cold car I...."

The sound that interrupted the sentence was not loud; a gentle sneeze might have made more noise, but the blood that spurted from the wound in Monty's forehead splattered her face and the sound that gurgled from his throat was unintelligible in its horror. There was a second *pop, but* Julia didn't hear it. The bullet grazed the fabric of her unfastened coat before entering Charles Montgomery's heart. That shot was unnecessary, the job was already done, but experienced professionals leave nothing to chance. Red blood spread slowly across the grey pavement; Julia sank to her knees alongside Monty and screamed like a vixen in her terror.

People came running to the scene. The young man with the mobile phone frantically dialled 999 and stutteringly told the police and the ambulance service about the shooting. He too was shaking like a leaf. "I saw the driver," he kept saying, "I saw the driver; it was that bastard John Ashworth!"

CHAPTER FIFTY

The cold blooded murder of Charles Montgomery sent a shiver through the whole town. In Buxton there wasn't the grief that a community feels at the loss of one of its own; Charles Montgomery wasn't a local man and there was nobody in town to mourn him, but still people felt regret. In Burrdale the mood was different; there Charles Montgomery was known, but wasn't liked; his name carried with it too much baggage; and there were some of the older residents who were not at all distressed by the news of his violent death. But, in both places there was fear. Shootings in broad daylight in pretty Derbyshire towns were almost unheard of, and this was not a crime committed in the red mist of anger, it was the cynical extermination of a human being such as might happen in Chicago, or Bogotá, or Sao Paulo or in a thousand other places where life was cheap and the gun was king. The belief of many of the inhabitants of the two towns had been that they were immune from the kind of brutal killings that blighted Moss Side and Toxteth and too many other places in Great Britain but that belief had now been blown apart by this terrible event.

Julia Hammond was distraught. It wasn't the realisation that she had been inches away from a lethal bullet that appalled her, it was the knowledge that she had been taken in by a killer and that unwittingly she had provided him with the information that he had needed in order to be able to carry out his dreadful act of slaughter. The police had asked her for a description of Ashworth; all she could remember was the oil on his face and his dirty boiler suit. They had taken away the wheel brace and the locking wheel nut from her car to test them for fingerprints, but to no avail. The reason why he had meticulously wiped clean the tools before he replaced them was now abundantly apparent.

The only things to link Ashworth to the crime was the conversation he had had with Julia and the crucial fact that he had been recognised as the driver. His great misfortune seemed to be that, purely by bad luck, Rupert Henshaw had been walking down the street at the time of the shooting. A large amount of hope was pinned on the fact that Henshaw was believed to be a good friend of Ashworth and therefore potentially able to provide much valuable information; but when he was interviewed as a witness by murder squad detectives, it turned out that much of what Ashworth had told Julia about their close friendship was a lie. He had certainly met the man and he certainly believed he was called John Ashworth, but their acquaintance was very limited and they had not been close in the way that Ashworth had told Mrs Hammond that they were. In Rupert's mind they could hardly be described as "mates." He did admit that he had a strong dislike of Charles Montgomery, so that part of the story Julia had been told was true; but, his violent death had shocked him and caused him to re-appraise his assessment of him: he now believed that his apparent reformation, which he had previously dismissed as a sham, might have been entirely genuine and his efforts to become a new man entirely real.

One thing that was becoming clearer by the hour was that virtually nothing was as it seemed about John Ashworth. Every garage, tyre depot, smithy, engineering works, car breakers and welding company in North Derbyshire had been checked, to no avail. Not one of them had a recently disappeared employee and, although one John Ashworth was found, he was a fifty five year old mechanic with a grey beard and an impressively large beer gut. The man Julia Hammond had met looked as if he had just slipped out of his place of work for a breath of fresh air or a quick infusion of nicotine polluted smoke, but enquiries had now established that that couldn't possibly have been the case. A totally false image had been created, but one that was good enough to have completely fooled an intelligent, perceptive, clear minded woman.

Rupert Henshaw tried to help the police in every way he could, but everything about the man who claimed to be his friend and who he had witnessed driving the assassin's car was turning out to be untrue. No address for him could be found, no social contacts could be unearthed, the oily faced Samaritan had vanished into thin air and, in a very real sense, it was becoming more and more apparent that he had never truly existed.

This turn of events was bad news, particularly for the Derbyshire Constabulary: a ruthless killer had disappeared into the ether, but there was no guarantee that he was gone for good: nobody could exclude the possibility that he might re-emerge at any time and strike again, at will, against whoever he intended to be his next target. The hotel room of Charles Montgomery had been searched, nothing of interest had been found and, although the police had taken away bank books and a laptop computer, there was no suggestion that a £20,000.00 mystery payment had ever been received: the nearest thing to a weapon that was discovered was a nail file and there was absolutely nothing to suggest that this bedroom might have been the temporary hideout of a vicious killer.

The death of Charles Montgomery was a major blow to D.I Mark Hobson and D.S. Pete Bennett as it meant that an event that had been foretold, at least in general terms, and one which should have been prevented, had never-the-less occurred; and although, when the full facts were put before Detective Chief Superintendent Hardy, he accepted that everything that could have been done had been done, it didn't stop the two officers feeling that somehow or other they should have done more. That belief was overwhelmingly endorsed by Detective Inspector Bob Earnshaw, who took great delight in taking every opportunity that was available to him to declaim loudly and at length about the incompetence and bone-idleness of some of his *so called professional colleagues.* Every black cloud has a silver lining and the Drug Officer's enjoyment at the discomfort of his two adversaries was the one ray of sunshine in an otherwise universally gloomy picture.

Outside the police station other people were also becoming extremely concerned; one such person was Alan Nadin. He already had had to witness the distress of the woman he loved when, at the most romantic moment in both of their lives, their hopes had been ground into the dirt by the juggernaut that was Robert Earnshaw. He had heard Jackie being verbally abused and seen her being physically manhandled and later, he had learnt of the psychological pressure that had been piled upon her to try to make her confess to a crime that she hadn't committed. Through the intervention of true friends, against all the odds, she had been saved from a lengthy spell in prison custody, but those few hours in a police cell had terrified her. Even now, she still didn't begin to comprehend why dreadful things were happening to her; it seemed to her that Fate had chosen to heap misery upon her without reason or rhyme. With over thirty years experience as a police officer behind him, Alan knew this wasn't so; somebody was deliberately trying to destroy her life and in that person's mind, there had to be a specific reason why: he wouldn't in time be moving on to inflict his misery on another randomly selected individual; his quarrel, real or imagined, was with Jackie; and, he wouldn't stop doing what he was doing to her until he achieved his goal.

The man was obviously clever; the timing of the second attack on Jackie's reputation was precise; just at the point at which Alan had been able to see a little of her self-confidence being restored, he had struck again to discredit her.

Jackie was now almost a recluse; she was frightened to go out unless he was by her side and she could never settle until all the children were safely back at home. She was too scared even to allow him to hold her and it seemed that the moment when they should have been able to secure a lifetime of happiness together had been forever lost.

The murder of Charles Montgomery had upped the stakes even more. The man who was slowly destroying her mind had shown himself capable of murder. Having come so far in his campaign to wreck her life there was no reason to suppose that he would stop now; a savage, brutal end to an innocent, honest life was very much on the cards. The weapon of choice might be the gun or the knife, but a speeding car, a baseball bat, a length of razor wire couldn't be ruled out: all Alan could see was that the danger of something happening was very, very real. How could he protect her? How could he urge her to take every possible precaution against imminent attack without sending her already distraught mind into a state of meltdown? He had thought long and hard about what he should do but, to be honest, he had no idea about what to do for the best.

CHAPTER FIFTY ONE

That there had been a shooting in Buxton town centre was beyond doubt. The presence of T.V. reporters and the blanket coverage the story received in the daily papers testified to that fact: that the man demanding payment from Ralph Ambridge had carried out the assassination was also not in dispute: that the man who had died was the man Ambridge wanted to see dead was less clear cut, and he demanded proof before he would be prepared to hand over any money.

The killer was interrogated. He admitted to Ambridge that in the beginning he had found it difficult to locate the person who was blackmailing the business tycoon and several of his acquaintances and he accepted that, initially, many things had pointed him in an entirely different direction to the one he had finally settled upon. He had found himself chasing shadows and had searched several blind alleys but latterly, his fortunes had changed. Details that could only have been known to the extortionist were being reported as having been let slip by the man calling himself Charles Montgomery: one or two utterances could have been coincidental, but recently there had apparently been so many that there could only be a single conclusion. When he was sure he had acted: he had acted to devastating effect: he had entirely fulfilled his contract: he was entitled to the remainder of his fee.

Ambridge had been convinced. He wanted to keep contact between himself and his *employee* to a minimum. He was adamant that the man should never come to his house or be seen anywhere in the vicinity of it. He didn't trust anybody enough to get them to act as a go-between and he didn't dare entrust £20,000 in used bank notes to the vagaries of the G.P.O. Eventually, after much deliberation, he had arranged a meeting place where he was sure that what passed between them couldn't be overheard, and the *giving and receiving of gifts* could take place unobserved.

The 18th Century church on the outskirts of town was a monument to the glory of Christ and to good architecture; but on a weekday it would be empty apart from perhaps a curate pre-occupied with higher things, or a cleaner, polishing the brasses so that they shone with sacred light, or maybe some lost soul pleading for divine help to an entity that didn't exist. All these people, in their different ways, would be immersed in their own thoughts: a visitor who had wandered into the building to put to death a moment of unwanted time would be instantly ignored and, when he or she left, would be immediately forgotten.

Everything had come to pass as the tycoon had imagined. When he entered the House of God only two other people had been inside the church. The man he had come to meet sat in a pew next to the centre aisle, his closely cropped head bowed down as if in prayer. To someone in the know, nothing could have seemed more false than to see a cold blooded killer wrapping himself in the trappings of piety, but Ralph Ambridge was the only person with such knowledge and he was about to hand over a fortune in money as a reward to a man for committing a cardinal sin. Where was Jesus when the temple needed cleansing these days? Ambridge decided that he must have slipped outside for pie, peas and gravy at the local chip shop; the absurdity of the idea almost made him laugh out loud.

The presence of the other person in the building was unwelcome: clinging desperately to what Ambridge presumed was a bible, he wandered around the periphery of the church like a man in a spiritual trance, sniffing or sobbing as he dragged himself across the floor. Finally, he shuffled towards the exit door. Ambridge saw it open and heard it shut with a loud bang: he wondered if the wretch was as weak in the arm as he was in the head: a pathetic specimen of humanity; he didn't give him another thought.

The satisfaction of being a winner lasted for a whole seven days; that was long enough for Ralph Ambridge to collect reimbursement from the others who had benefitted from the silencing of an enemy and to drink a toast with some of them at the success of a risky venture. For all of them the experience had been a salutary one; nobody wanted to see a repetition: talking out of turn could have devastating consequences; all of the surviving members of Jerry Eggleton's little gang were resolved that their shared secret would never see the light of day.

The buff coloured envelope that arrived on the eighth day looked harmless enough and initially it was thrown on to a pile of correspondence that the elated entrepreneur expected to occupy a micro-second of his time at some future date, prior to being tossed into the waste paper bin with all the other items of junk mail, but the longer it lay there, the larger the envelope seemed to grow and the louder it seemed to yell for immediate attention, and to dominate his desk to such a degree that it could no longer be ignored.

If it had contained a death warrant signed in blood and against which there was no appeal, the contents of this thin package could not have been more unwanted: the truimphalist tone of the letter was mind destroying in its gloating simplicity and the photographs, *those bloody photographs*, were the incendiary bombs that could burn his world to the ground.

"My Dear Ralph", the mocking missive began, "I know that you never expected to hear from me again so I'm sure this letter will be a big surprise. As you can see I am still an active resident of

Planet Earth and if anything, I feel invigorated and strengthened by recent events.

A week ago I know you felt exhilarated when the news of my death reached you and that you and some of your nasty little friends celebrated with champagne. It may please you to know that I now feel the exhilaration that you felt and it would surely be churlish of you to begrudge me my Verve Clicquot moment.

Your man in black, with the less than golden gun, was so easy to manipulate. If you chose him he must have come well recommended and I do not doubt for a second his technical proficiency but, you must admit, that his intelligence was sadly lacking. He swallowed every lie that was fed to him and, although you thought it was you who pulled the strings, I was the puppet master; in your name he did everything I wanted.

It's not all bad news for you. The killing of Charles Montgomery removes a man who could have harmed us both; but this is the only crumb of comfort I will feed you and I do expect to be paid handsomely for that morsel

I knew that after he had done your bidding a reckoning would follow and that you would gladly pay your dues. I do hope when I present you with my bill, which you can well imagine will be far greater than the paltry sum you paid to him, I will be paid my just deserts with similar alacrity.

The church was an inspired meeting place, I cannot fault your logic in choosing it and I congratulate you on your reasoning. The only flaw in your plan was that you didn't expect that your hired assassin would be followed; that was a significant mistake. He saw no need to take precautions, his job was done, and the world believed that he had vanished without a trace; only by behaving suspiciously could he attract suspicion: confidence and arrogance would not demand a second look.

As soon as I saw him step through the churchyard gate, I knew that had to be the meeting place; why else would such a man seek out a place of prayer? Unchristian, un-holy unforgiving, the antithesis of every virtue the followers of the Christ Child claim as their own. I watched him enter the building and, moments later, I shuffled in behind him. I'm certain when he heard the door clang he thought that it was you and, when he realised it wasn't, he must have resented the presence of an intruder but, a closer examination of his new companion convinced him that I was a religious cripple needing the fantasy of an afterlife to survive the pressures of this world. He saw me clasping what he thought was holy writ, you saw the same when you arrived to keep your sordid date with him. You were both mistaken; the pictures I enclose bear testimony as to its true nature. You and he, each one smugly contented in his own way; your moment of victory captured for posterity; please accept this gift as a memento of that joyous occasion. The camera can lie, but its lies can be detected by experts; it can also tell the unvarnished truth and, on this occasion, I can assure you that its honesty is painful.

But look now how the scene has shifted. Is that the image of a soon to be dead man caught in friendly conversation with a beautiful woman? Yes, I believe it is! Now who is that driving the car? Is that your friend? Yes, it is, without a doubt. What is he holding in his hand? Does it look like a gun to you? Merciful heaven who is he pointing it at? The man falls to the floor, the woman sinks to her knees beside him, mouth wide open: is she screaming? I rather think she is.

You hold in your hands the history of a crime, and should that history fall into the wrong hands it would spell disaster for the conspirators captured for eternity by the camera's lens. What could prevent such a calamitous outcome? Now, now Ralph use your head; what do you think the answer might be? I'm not a greedy man; two million pounds will buy you the universal rights to do with my low budget documentary what you will. I think with your connections 5 days should give you ample time to raise the money; I will be in touch shortly to give you your final instructions.

Just one further word of warning: if you try to injure me again, I promise you, you will regret it. Like Samson in the temple I will bring down the whole rotten edifice that is your world crashing onto your head. I know that you know that I never make a promise that I can't keep. Do what I tell you, and all will be well. If you're sensible, as I'm sure you're going to be, I may reward you with a parting gift. The woman in these pictures is hell bent on causing trouble and her questions, or more accurately the answers she may have received to those questions, represent a danger to both you and me. I have made plans to ensure that that threat is neutralised in a very final way, but time may not permit, and, if it doesn't, I will pass the baton on to you so that you can finish the task that I have started.

There may perhaps be one more pest to be controlled and "Rent-a Kill" will be my final option. With luck, I will rid the world of this vermin by myself, but out of kindness, if I fail, I will pass a name to you so that the last threat to your security can be erased.

See how I mellow Ralph. Rejoice that you are being let off so lightly.

Sweet dreams until we talk again.

CHAPTER FIFTY TWO

The way in which Jackie had taken the news of Charles Montgomery's death and had listened to him as he had attempted to explain to her the danger she might be in, had caused Alan Nadin a great deal of concern. He had tried hard not to frighten her, but, at the same time, he had wanted her to be on her guard. He had been prepared for panic or distress and he had told himself that by being confident, but also being gentle and by showing the tenderness he felt, he could allay her fears; but she hadn't reacted in that way at all. He had been ready for a superficial display of self-confidence, probably masking deep seated concerns, but there had been none: what he had in fact witnessed had been a weary disinterest and a feeling that the woman he loved was about to be overwhelmed by forces that she could neither understand or control and in a terrible way was resigned to her fate, and that thought truly terrified him.

His one crumb of comfort was that she showed no desire to venture out by herself; she was a prisoner in her own home, not daring to emerge into the real world unless he was by her side: that gave him hope, yet at the same time it was clear that by allowing her life to shrink in on itself, a vital spark of humanity was slowly dying.

He went with her to collect the children from school and he took her shopping to an out of town supermarket where there would be few, if any, familiar faces, but that was it. Nights at the cinema and late night meals at local restaurants were prohibited by the unfair curfew the court had imposed, but even an early evening drink at a country pub was off the agenda and until the weight of anxiety could be lifted off her shoulders, any thought that he might have about them enjoying a social life together was a none starter; and that was the way things seemed destined to stay. For the foreseeable future Alan had rescheduled his life. Any meeting he had to attend, any appointment he had to keep had to be fixed for the times of day when Jackie didn't need him and, even then, his mind was often with her and rarely fully focussed on the job in hand.

Another person who was forever thinking about Jacqueline Skinner was Detective Inspector Robert Earnshaw. The drugs raid on her house had delivered the evidence, but, thanks to the intervention of Mark Hobson and his meddling bitch of a wife, everything had gone pear shaped. It wasn't right that smooth talking lawyers could bamboozle pea brained magistrates into releasing scum back on to the streets. He felt cheated and bitter and resentful and he was beginning to believe that this case was ill-starred. A pretty face, a flood of tears, a procession of *holier than thou* character witnesses and the jury at the Crown Court would think that they were being asked to convict Snow White of dwarf bashing! More had to be done if he was going to get a result; but how, and where, the evidence came from to achieve a successful outcome he didn't give a damn; providing it bloody well came.

The photographs that arrived in the post were a God send. They didn't show a great deal: pictures of a cheap family saloon car parked outside a neglected looking council house don't score highly in the visual impact department, but, this wasn't any cheap car, nor was it any badly maintained council house. To any experienced drugs officer the building was instantly recognisable. The entrance door, with its peeling paint looked flimsy, but the quarter inch steel plate on the inside made it almost impregnable: the rear door was similarly re-enforced to prevent unwanted intruders gaining access to the property, and the windows all had metal grilles fitted to make entrance virtually impossible. Amongst the police this house was universally referred to as "Fort Cox" and its owner Winston Milton Cox was known to be the biggest dealer in heroin in the High Peak and for many miles beyond. People didn't visit Milton to exchange pleasantries or talk about the weather or the price of coffee in the supermarket; he wasn't a man for casual conversation: people visited him to buy drugs and their money funded his frequent trips to the Caribbean and the million dollar lifestyle he lived over there.

But to Bob Earnshaw the most exciting thing about the picture was not the fortified house; it was the presence of the car: the registration plate was clearly visible and it showed a number that was well known to him. He had no doubt; the car belonged to a certain local resident who he was convinced dealt in hard drugs. If Jackie Skinner had gone to that address there could only be one reason for it. Obviously he needed more evidence, obviously he needed to catch her in the act of dealing, or at the very least in possession of a large quantity of drugs, but this was the encouragement he had been waiting for: these photographs could be the start of a new case against her. If, at a later date, he was asked about the source of the pictures he would assert that they had been the product of covert surveillance: he would refuse to name the photographer or pin point the observation post on the grounds that this was *Sensitive Information* and that to reveal details would put lives at risk; he had no doubt that he could make such a story stick. All he needed now was to catch Skinner with the stuff, and as he pondered the best way of doing this, miracle upon miracle: that was the moment when the anonymous tip off was received.

The person who telephoned Jackie on the other hand was not at all anonymous. He introduced himself as Andrew Wainwright, and explained that he was the latest recruit to the management team at the school two of her three boys attended. He was most apologetic. "It clearly shouldn't have happened." "The headmaster had already taken steps." "The two boys responsible had been immediately suspended, and decisive action would be taken to ensure nothing like this happened again." "He isn't badly hurt, but he is quite shaken by the experience." "His class teacher feels he needs to be at home with his mum." "Why the attack had happened, they couldn't yet say, but the root cause of the problem would be uncovered." "The school operates a strict No-bullying policy." "Appropriate punishment will in due course be meted out, but today, as a damage limitation exercise, we feel it's better if you come straight away and collect both your sons and take them home." He was "very, very sorry". He "hoped that the school would be allowed to deal with the matter internally, but that was a matter for her to decide upon after mature reflection." Alan had gone to Stockport, as he did most weeks at this time to visit a former colleague who was recovering from a serious illness and to do any shopping for him that needed to be done: it would take him at least forty minutes to get to the school.

Without stopping to think, she had told the school administrator that she would be right over; her thoughts were entirely with her son: he had probably been beaten up because of what people thought his mother was. She burst into tears, grabbed her car keys from the kitchen window sill and set off in haste to retrieve her younger children; not knowing what state they would be in when she arrived.

"It's all been a cruel hoax Mrs Skinner!" The headmaster was very kind. "We don't have anybody called Andrew Wainwright working at this school. There hasn't been a fight. Both your sons are absolutely fine; if you look through my office window now you can see them playing happily with their friends: do they look to you as if they've been bullied or are unhappy?" Jackie had to admit that they definitely did not.

The callousness of the joke that had been played upon her struck her with the force of a Mike Tyson punch. She rocked back on her heels, she couldn't take the punishment and she began to sob uncontrollably. The headmaster tried to re-assure her, he sent out for coffee, he implored her to report the matter to the police, he asked if there was anybody who could drive her home. He even offered to take her home in his car and suggested that her car be left on the school car park until it could be picked up later when she was less upset. Jackie declined the offer. She told him that she would be alright, which wasn't strictly true and, resisting all further offers of help, she returned to the car to drive it home: it had been left unattended and unlocked for the best part of ninety minutes.

She was less than a mile from home when she realised she was being followed. The unmarked vehicle was glued to her rear bumper. She accelerated, it did likewise, she slowed down, it declined to overtake; it was like a scene from "Cagney and Lacey" or innumerable other American cop dramas and it became spectacularly more so when another unmarked vehicle, travelling in the opposite direction, suddenly veered across the road, tyres smoking and squealing, totally blocking the carriageway in front of her and making any further progress impossible. Jackie slammed on her brakes but couldn't prevent the front of her car impacting with the side of the other vehicle. The collision took place at slow speed, but never-the-less it gave her a severe jolt: she was hysterical, and feared that every second would be her last.

Fearsome looking men with unshaven faces and muscular bodies leapt from both cars. Jackie tried to lock the driver's door but, before she could do so, it was wrenched open and she was pulled bodily from her seat, and flung, with some force onto the pavement. A big man pinned her to the ground. She was helpless, she couldn't move a muscle: then she heard the unmistakable sneering voice of Detective Inspector Robert Earnshaw.

"You've been rumbled Mrs Skinner! We know you've got a shed load of drugs hidden in that car. This time I've caught you red-handed and neither Mark bastard Hobson, nor his trouble making shrew of a wife, nor Jesus bloody Christ himself can do a fucking thing to help you."

CHAPTER FIFTY THREE

"She looked like a zombie Mark! You saw her! She didn't stand a chance. I know that lying bastard Earnshaw's verballed her; she'd never have sworn at him, I'd stake my life on that, and she'd never ask him "Which bastard grassed me up?" but the magistrates believed every untrue word he uttered. Even if he hadn't over-egged the pudding there wasn't a hope in hell that she'd get bail this time: ten thousand quid's worth of heroin is a big haul, if you're caught with that much gear in your vehicle you haven't got a prayer. There was only ever going to be one outcome, particularly if you're already on bail for a similar offence, and none of its true! She's completely innocent but this time we can't do a thing to help her. This will kill her Mark, it'll kill her, and what about the boys? I know you and Helena will take care of 'em, but their lives have been turned upside down and it's all so bloody unfair! I swear to God that next time I see Earnshaw, I'll break his bloody neck!"

"You won't do that Alan because you're a thousand times better man than he is and, right now, more than ever before, Jackie needs you to be strong and to use your head."

"We can prove the fact of the phone call; we can also prove that Jackie arrived at the school in a highly distressed state; we can't actually prove that her car was left unattended and insecure, as she claims; but nobody can prove that it wasn't. Earnshaw got what he wanted; he clearly made no attempt to find out if anybody saw anyone behaving suspiciously near the car. We can establish that after she left the school, she headed straight home, Earnshaw's own timings don't allow for anything else and, surely, any judge would see some mileage in an argument that says what drug dealer worth her salt would make up a ridiculous story about her child being bullied and become so upset by the fiction that she leaves a fortune in class A drugs at the mercy of any passing sneak thief for well over an hour and a half?"

"But Earnshaw's got photographs of the car outside *Fort Cox*, that's the other piece of damning evidence: if he hadn't got them we'd have a bit of a shout but, with those pictures, and with Cox's previous, we're stuffed; there's only one reason why people go to that address, and it isn't to admire the bloody view."

"We need to get copies of the photos, and we need to examine the originals. I don't trust Earnshaw farther than I could throw him, and we need experts to check 'em to make certain they haven't been tampered with; I'm sure Bob Greenway will have got that in hand already. It's tragic that Jackie's in gaol, it's terrible that we can't just wave a magic wand and get her straight out but, I promise you, we will find a way; and in the meantime we must let her know that we all believe her and that we're doing everything we can to put right this appalling travesty of justice."

"But why's this all happening to her Mark? If she'd ever done anything really bad I might understand it, but she never has. None of this adds up; and because there's no rhyme or reason to it that I can fathom, I can't see any way we can end it."

"There's always a way; we've just got to find it. I still believe that in some bizarre way all these recent events are linked. Sharon Farrington wasn't a random target, neither was Jackie, and the murder of Charles Montgomery was a specific hit. The only connection I can come up with is the one that leads from Jacob Farrington's death, through Jerry Eggleton's gang, to Sharon and to Jackie and now to Charles Montgomery. If the lad Justin Barnes were still around, for sure he'd be my number one suspect, but, I've checked, and I've checked, and I've double checked and it's a hundred per cent certain that he was murdered in South Africa; yet even knowing that to be true, try as I might, I still keep coming back to him. I'm sure I'm missing something, but for the life of me, I don't know what it is; there is an answer out there, although just at the moment I seem to be too dumb to find it."

"Well keep on trying Mark, keep on trying. Right now Jackie desperately needs that answer, and you're the only one who can find it for her."

***

Now she had got over the initial shock of Monty's death, Julia Hammond was also seeking answers. She had listened to her father-in-law's remonstrations about the madness of meddling in matters which were the prerogative of the police. "She had put herself in great danger." "The second bullet to strike Charles Montgomery could just as easily have hit her". "Did she know that detectives investigating that murder thought it likely that Rupert Henshaw, who had rushed to her aid, had unwittingly in the process placed himself in the line of fire, and maybe prevented a third shot from being deliberately aimed at her?" The man who Bob Hammond had banished from his sight, might have proved to be the human shield that had potentially saved his daughter-in-law's life: he owed him a debt of gratitude that couldn't be repaid; she owed it to herself and to her saviour, never to put her life at risk again.

She had agreed with everything he said and had promised that there would be no more dangerous excursions. There had been hugs and tears and her intent had been real, but now she had had time to recover and to think, anger was once more building up inside her. Will had been a good man, yet he had been driven to take his own life: another good man had tried to help her, and he had been brutally murdered: the police seemed powerless to act against Ralph Ambridge or any of Jerry Eggleton's coterie of friends and, in the meantime, extreme evil remained unpunished: that state of affairs couldn't be allowed to continue, but what could she do? Miserably she gazed out across the empty garden, her mood as gloomy as the day; surely the world couldn't carry on as if nothing had happened, surely two men's deaths must count for something; but it was beginning to look more and more likely that they counted for nothing at all.

A hesitant knock on the front door distracted her from her morose contemplations: without any enthusiasm she made her way to it. She looked through the spy hole and saw a man standing outside; her first reaction was that he was a stranger, and she reached for the security chain to fix that in place before opening the door; then she realised that it was the man the police believed had probably saved her life: she opened the door wide, and admitted Rupert Henshaw.

"I'm so sorry to bother you Mrs Hammond. I've not come at an inconvenient time have I? I need to talk to you sometime, but I can always come back later if you'd like me to."

"No, no, please come in Rupert, I'm so pleased that you're here. I understand that you may have saved my life and I'm so very, very grateful."

"I didn't do anything special Mrs Hammond; I just happened to be in the right place at the right time. Anybody else would have done the same thing."

John Ashworth, or whatever his real name is, might be a professional killer, thought Julia, *but he was right in his judgement of the character of the man standing before me.*

She led Rupert to the kitchen and made coffee, then she listened to what he had to say. In a manner which her father-in-law would instantly have recognised from his meeting in the churchyard, he told her his story and then asked for advice.

He had *misjudged* Charles Montgomery, he realised that now. He was ashamed to admit it, but he had been following him for several days prior to the murder in the hope of finding out something which would discredit him. He had totally failed to find anything. Monty had visited several houses; he had visited them too. More often than not, the door had been slammed in his face, but, the day before Monty was shot, he had followed him to an isolated cottage near to Elmton Crags. Yesterday he had gone back there and, after much difficulty, he had persuaded the elderly occupant to tell him what he and Monty had talked about. Rupert now believed that this man, although a little confused, might have witnessed some of the incident that had led to Jacob Farrington's death all those many years ago. He wouldn't say much, and had disintegrated into a state of abject terror at the mere mention of the police, but, Rupert believed that, to the right person, he might reveal a great deal. He thought that Julia might be that person. Would she like to go with him to talk to this man? Without a second's thought, or a moment's hesitation, her unequivocal answer was "Yes."

CHAPTER FIFTY FOUR

"You imagine that it's difficult to be somebody else; it's not, it's really very easy; much harder by far is to be a version of yourself that isn't wholly false, nor yet completely true. When I present a counterfeit face to the world, I become that person, and his actions, thoughts and deeds are not my doing, but are his. If he's cruel, that's a choice he makes; if he's brutal can I be blamed for the hurt he inflicts? When I present my own face to the world, even though partly concealed by a lie, I cannot hide behind another's personality: I feel the pain, I sense the odium, I suffer in the knowledge I have sinned.

"Then why step out of character?" you ask; "why wipe away the grease paint to reveal the face behind the makeup?" These are good questions. The answer to them both is simple. Sometimes it's just too dangerous to pretend; sometimes you have to re-enforce duplicity with truth. A forged document runs the risk of being pronounced false, an imaginary identity can be revealed for the shallow pretence that it is; therefore occasionally it is safer to be honest.

For a brief period I have been forced to use that strategy, but soon the need will have passed, and I can once again play my games and turn my back on the history that God gave me.

For one thing, I'm now rich. I knew Ralph Ambridge had no backbone. Five hundred thousand pounds, in used bank notes, is a tidy sum, but it fitted easily into a rucksack. How thick do you think a twenty pound note is? Shall we guess at perhaps a millimetre, and let's suppose, for argument's sake, that it is about five and a half inches long. Three or four columns of flimsy printed paper twenty or twenty five inches high can easily be carried on your shoulders. I won't bore you with the details of the merry dance I led poor, frustrated Ralph before I relieved him of the cash; but he provided me with rare sport. Later, when I slipped into a ramblers' bar to celebrate my good fortune, I experienced the most incredible euphoria. A man, to all intents and purposes, scrabbling in his pocket to find the paltry bits of change to buy half a pint of bitter, and all the time I knew I had a fortune strapped to my back. I could have bought and sold the landlord ten times over, and yet he mistook me for a pauper. And of course that wasn't all the money: one and a half million pounds had already been transferred electronically into a bank account under my control; and from there it had commenced a circuitous journey, the money barely registering in one set of financial records before being snatched away into another. I'm not so stupid, or so vain, to pretend that a trail couldn't be followed, but only by acknowledged experts, and even then with great difficulty; but I can guarantee that that will never happen.

Why, you might wonder, did I chose to demand such a large quantity of hard cash, which can always be lost or stolen, if perverse Fate decrees that that be so, when a much safer option already existed? Again the answer is a straight forward one. I needed the money to buy goods and services. Ten thousand pounds has already been well spent, and the drugs the money purchased have been used to good effect. I finally have my revenge; there will be no need for Ralph Ambridge to tidy up the pieces. The bitch is suffering now because she slandered me. If, by the benign intervention of some lesser deity, her tongue could be ripped from her mouth by a monstrous metal claw, that would indeed be justice, but in this imperfect world that can never happen. Degradation, despondency and despair, these are my legacies to her, and although wholly insufficient to erase the memories of her crime, they must satisfy my modest desires.

Another, even larger sum has also been put to good use. Ralph Ambridge did not pay me willingly, he demanded guarantees: he sought unequivocal assurance that there would be no more acts of blackmail, and that no photograph in my possession, would ever be used against him, before he was willing to pay me a single penny. In truth, he was in a position to demand nothing, but I gave him the pictorial record of his murderous conspiracy and, I promised freely, that I would never do anything to point the finger of suspicion towards him. He knew, from times gone by, that I never fail to keep my word and so, believing the threat of exposure to be neutralised, and with extreme bad grace, he handed me the cash. I am a man of honour; I will not back away from that which I have sworn to do.

But is it right that a man who plotted to see me dead escapes so lightly? The answer is an emphatic "No!" For that reason, I have been a spender. A small part of his cash has purchased me the services of an assassin; one far more proficient than the clown he gave blood money to, to ease my passage into Satan's furnaces. He has bought and paid handsomely for *his own death, he now lives on borrowed time, his own money guarantees his murder; there will be a sublime irony when this outcome is achieved.*

Nor should the plodding psychopath, who followed me like a demented bloodhound, escape unpunished. He doesn't have the benefit of my word, I have given him no promises, and I will never do so. The pictures that inextricably link him to a shooting are already in the post, and soon the police will have all the evidence they need to convict him. He will be arrested, he will stand trial, and he will be sentenced, unless of course he exchanges fire with police marksmen; in which case there can only ever be one outcome. Everything is coming to its rightful conclusion and, as my sweet mother used to say, before she was forever corrupted "God's in his heaven, and all's well with the world."

Yet one more thing must yet come to pass. My mother gave me life and then condemned me to a life of pain. She travelled down the rough road that leads from Devotion to Depravity. I thought that when her death throes ended, I would be free, but somehow her grip upon me tightens, and she is squeezing the life out of me. When I see Will Hammond's wife, I see an angel with a demon deep within. The Whore of Babylon, who gave birth to me, was such a creature, and I of all people know the havoc that she wrought. Her spirit taunts me and every time I look at Julia I see her image staring back at me. All living creatures are in peril. My solemn duty is to save the world from mortal danger. The date, the place, the hour are set in stone, an act of ritual slaughter will take place, and when the deed is done the curse will finally be lifted. She will know terror, and for a short while she will live with the certain knowledge that violent death awaits her. At the blessed moment when blood is spilt I must have been cleansed of all unclean thoughts and so before the sacred knife does its holy work I will have emptied my manhood into her vile body. To rape a condemned woman on the steps of the guillotine, while being watched by the leering eyes of her soon to be executioner, and cheered on a baying crowd, that would be a thrilling experience. Alas, I cannot have an audience applaud the rigours of my sexual appetite, but after it is fully sated, I will slay my dragon with cool headed deliberation, and in my ears I will hear a hymn of praise from a grateful multitude.

Lazarus will become St George; my search for freedom will be over. What new quests lie ahead, I can't begin to imagine, but a tormented, bitter past will have been left far behind along with a bloody, unburied female body."

CHAPTER FIFTY FIVE

Never, not even for a single second, had Helena imagined that looking after Jackie's three unhappy little boys would be easy; and not once had she regretted her decision to help; but, at times, the pressure she felt herself to be under was immense.

Her own state of health remained good and, although now very noticeably pregnant, she was still suffering none of the complications she had had to endure before Christopher was born. He was a two and a half year old bundle of energy, into everything, and in need of constant watching; only when he was asleep in his cot at night, could she allow herself time to relax. Now, imported into her demanding world, were three bewildered, distressed children, who couldn't begin to understand why their mother was locked up in prison and how it had come about that they were being forced to live away from their own home. All this was almost impossible to cope with, but sometimes things became even worse, when unkind and hurtful comments were made at school: it was perhaps inevitable that resentment and anger would, on those occasions, boil over and that stupid, naughty, irrational reactions would follow.

The most serious event to date had happened that day. Jackie's second son, Michael, had responded to some cruel name calling by breaking a window in one of the Year 8 classrooms. A teaching assistant had seen the incident, and had grabbed hold of the boy. She had demanded to know his name; he had told her he was his younger brother, and had then wriggled from her grasp and ran away. The pretence had been maintained for the remainder of the school day and, because the two boys looked so much alike, it had been the younger boy who had been on the receiving end of the headmaster's tongue. Helena had been summoned to the school in lieu of a parent, and she had had to cope with the tears of the younger child, and the sullen protestations of innocence from his elder brother. Eventually the truth had been established and Helena had pleaded with the school for them to understand the turmoil both children were experiencing and the matter had been resolved: in due course a bill for the repair would have to be settled, but, for now, so far as the school was concerned, the matter was at an end.

"It was incredible how he stuck to his story," Helena later told Mark. "Michael was adamant it wasn't him, and even though Matthew was sobbing his heart out, and Michael's usually so good with him, he wouldn't admit the truth to save his little brother from distress. I think that he'd almost convinced himself that he wasn't lying. Even you, with all your training, would probably have believed him. It was only when I asked him would he still be saying the same things if his mummy was present, that he started to cry, and then he confessed what he'd done. I couldn't be angry with him, he looked so absolutely desolate, but from now on we've got to be on our guard. They're so frightened at the moment that any one of them could lash out in pain at the slightest provocation. They were still distraught when I drove them home; it really upset me to see them sobbing together in the back seat. Down by the phone box I saw Bob Hammond talking to a very attractive young woman, who I assume must be his daughter-in-law. She was standing alongside a parked car, and I think she was about to get into it; for some reason, maybe it was Bob's body language, I got the impression he wasn't entirely happy but, he looked up, obviously recognised our car, and he waved to me. I was so wrapped up thinking about the kids that I drove straight past without acknowledging him. Next time you see him Love, please give him my sincere apologies and tell him I had a few things on my mind. I'm sure that if you say to him it was just one of those dizzy blonde moments, he'll have no difficulty in accepting that to be true.

"He'll not believe that of you in a million years Love, but he'll be fine; he knows damn well you'd never deliberately ignore anyone. I'll give him your apologies, but I know he'll tell me they aren't necessary. He's got enough on his mind in any event; he'll totally understand why you were pre-occupied. An awful lot of people would be a hell of a sight better off if we could just get this bloody case sorted out but, we seem to be permanently stuck in reverse gear, and now on top of all that, you and I have taken on the responsibility of looking after three emotionally disturbed children. Where we're going to end up with them is anybody's guess."

"We had no choice Darling, and it won't be forever. Michael reacted in a totally predictable way. And so what if he lied; maybe deserted, distressed, abandoned children are just unable to cope with the truth; perhaps they all invent worlds in which they can be happy, or at least escape the misery of their daily lives: I'm afraid it's likely that we'll be seeing a lot more of this type of behaviour."

Helena's words seemed to switch on a light in Mark's brain: it flickered dimly, like a lone candle, in a dark, draughty room, but it was the spark that lit the touch paper of knowledge.

"The answer may have been staring me in the face, and I've been too stupid to see it. If I'm right, then I need kicking from John O'Groats to Lands End for overlooking something so obvious. I've got to get back to the office to check out one or two things; I don't know how long I'll be, but you may have just given me the answer that I've been searching for for weeks and weeks."

***

It was more than four hours later when Mark returned; Helena knew immediately that a breakthrough had been made.

"You're looking at the biggest imbecile on the planet Love. If I'd just used my brain, I could have had this whole thing wrapped up by now, and Jackie would never have ended up in gaol and, in all probability Charles Montgomery might still be alive. I was a fool you see. Everything I learned about what happened in South Africa to Justin Barnes was absolutely correct; that's what threw me. He was mutilated and murdered by a mob; his mother did throw herself off a cliff less than a week after he died: there's no doubt about any of that."

"So how does the fact that you now know you were right about everything help you then Darling? I mean none of this is new information."

"I didn't search beyond the obvious; I didn't go into her family history because I didn't think that mattered: I just crossed a name off my list of suspects and deluded myself that I was making progress; but I wasn't!"

"Justin Barnes's mother married twice; her first husband was killed in a plane crash. She then met and married an English man whose wife had run off with another man; he had sole custody of their only child. It seems to have been the case that step-mother and step-child hated each other and, the relationship was probably made worse by the fact that the family emigrated to South Africa. They originally settled in East London, which is a holiday resort in Cape Province. Jackie misheard you see; it wasn't *the East End of London*, it was *East London*, but it was an understandable mistake to make. Even when we later discovered that there was a South African dimension to the case, I still didn't put two and two together."

"I think that just like little Michael, the stepson told lies, but he took everything much, much further. I believe he started to tell people that he was Justin Barnes, probably intending to get the real Justin into trouble or, maybe, to try to grab some of the status that Barnes had and that he lacked. My intuition tells me that he probably suffered severe psychological damage when his real mum deserted him and, I think that explains, at least in part, why he behaved as he did, when he was in Jerry Eggleton's gang. Nobody liked him, he was an outsider, an interloper, but everybody was afraid of him; and anecdotally, with very good cause. Then he had a crush on Penny Farrington, who was an extremely pretty girl, and I'm sure that that crush would have been intense: I don't think he ever did anything by halves; and this is where all the pieces begin to fit.

Jackie told Penny that the boy we have been calling Justin (or Beejay as she believed him to be called) was seeing another girl, which as she freely admits was untrue. She did this to protect Penny. She didn't trust Beejay, she thought, almost certainly correctly, that he would be bad for her. Penny believed everything Jackie told her and promptly broke up with him. To make sure that the relationship was over, Jackie also told Jacob about it. He hit the roof; he gave Beejay a beating, and threatened him with more violence if he ever saw his daughter again. The next thing that happens is that Jacob is dead; rumours abound that his death wasn't an accident; and I agree with the people who think in this manner. Shortly after this incident Justin Barnes or Beejay as people around here believed him to be called disappears, only to re-appear at a later date in South Africa. Tragedy strikes his family; first his step-brother, then his step mother both come to violent ends, and then later his father is also killed in a particularly appalling manner. I think that either by default, or inertia, and certainly against the wishes of his step-mum, a large part of the joint estate eventually settled on him."

"I can't prove any of this yet, but I believe the man people in town still think of as Justin Barnes, came back to this country to settle old scores. It may not be the first time he did this; Pete Bennett says that one of his informants believed the man Ralph Ambridge wanted dead was a onetime enforcer for Tim Eggleton."

"You will probably think I'm losing my marbles, but I'm convinced that the person who tricked Jackie into giving him the video tapes is the same man who warned Bob Hammond's cousin in the pub about Charles Montgomery and I think he is also the stranger at the bus stop who persuaded Sharon Farrington to go with him to the hotel in Derby where he carried out a deliberately botched abortion. I even think that the man who was Julia Hammond's Good Samaritan, and who used the name John Ashworth, is also the same person. I know I'll struggle to convince people that I'm right, but if you look at all the very different descriptions the police have been given, the things that stand out are the unsightly tattoos on the man's forehead and arms, or the mud and grime that virtually obscured his face, or the spectacles that he wore, or his neat moustache: they're all camouflage! This man has been play acting all his life, he's got a natural talent for it, and he seems to be blessed with a face that is easily transformable. I'm sure he could pull off any number of deceptions without anyone realising that they were being taken in.

"The only times when he hasn't tried to be somebody else were when he sought out Bob Hammond in the churchyard, and crucially, when he made a witness statement to the police following Charles Montgomery's murder. I'm sure he didn't lie to us because he couldn't be certain that we wouldn't start asking awkward questions, and he didn't dare run the risk that his false I.D. might be exposed.

"There's just one more thing Love which I haven't yet told you. The Englishman who met and married Justin Barnes's American mother was called Victor Clement Henshaw. His only son was christened Rupert, apparently after his paternal grandfather. Our star witness Rupert Henshaw, who supposedly heroically saved the life of Julia Hammond, is exactly the same age our Justin Barnes would be, if Jackie is correct in her remembering. Taking everything together, I'm utterly convinced that he is the man who we have been looking for, for a very, very long time."

CHAPTER FIFTY SIX

There was still not a day went by when Julia didn't think of Will. She hadn't realised it of course, but life had been easy when he was around: they had been friends as well as lovers, happy together in a secure marriage, until that dreadful day when the whole world changed forever. The hardest thing to bear was that there had been no advanced warning; no opportunity to steel herself to face the horrors that were about to come. Will had been fit, strong and healthy, and Julia had imagined a long lifetime of being together, but, in a few short hours, on a single day, she had lost forever the husband she adored. Now memory played strange tricks. She remembered, often with tears in her eyes, the good times and how much she still loved him, but he was no longer there to hold and to kiss and to snuggle close to in bed. The pain of loss was like razor wire slicing into her heart and sometimes now she almost hated him for the agony she endured, day in, day out, knowing that she would never see him again. When those thoughts came, she tried to convince herself that he wasn't to blame and that evil, wicked men had caused their joint tragedy: sometimes she almost succeeded in doing that.

Sadness had changed her, as it changes everyone. Honesty had been the bedrock upon which her marriage to Will had been set. She had never lied to him and, although he had kept a part of his life hidden behind dark screens, she was sure that everything he had told her about himself was absolutely true. Now there was a new order in place: today she was actively planning to deceive. She had faithfully promised Bob that there would be no more meddling in police affairs and she had assured her father-in-law she would take no more risks, yet here she was, getting ready to go with Rupert Henshaw to meet a complete stranger in the hope that she might learn something that could help explain why her husband had taken his own life. A little while ago, a similar expedition had initiated a chain of events that had culminated in the execution of Charles Montgomery on a busy Buxton street; who was to say that history could not repeat itself?

Not without a degree of self-deception, she convinced herself that this time she would be safe; after all she was going to meet a poor old man who was too nervous even to talk to the police and she would be accompanied by the man who had already saved her life: she couldn't possibly be in better hands; surely nothing could go wrong this time?

But, in one sense, things were already starting to unravel. She had hoped to meet the reluctant witness in the early afternoon, which was free from any other demands on her time, but when Rupert

Henshaw telephoned him to confirm the time, he discovered that the man was resolutely refusing to see them until after dark. This had meant that frantic phone calls had had to be made to her parents to arrange for them to have the children in the early evening. They were pleased to help, but both had to go into Macclesfield to see their dentist for their six monthly check ups; that wasn't a problem the dentist had a crèche where the children could play with toys and one or other grandparent would be able to watch over them, but it did mean Julia had to hand them over by two o'clock at the absolute latest.

Worse had then followed; Rupert had suggested going to the cottage in his car because it was known to the old man. He had arrived late to pick her up, explaining that he had been delayed by a phone call from the old man telling him that he'd ordered one or two bits and pieces from the hardware shop in town and asking him to collect them for him.

"He's got an account there," Rupert told Julia, "I didn't think he was switched on enough to do business like that nor that he had enough gumption to get some mug to run round after him; but it seems that he's not backward at coming forward if it's going to save him a few pennies."

When they got to the shop Rupert had left Julia in the car saying that he'd only be gone for a few moments; but while he was gone she had grabbed the opportunity to dash into the nearby newsagents shop to buy a local paper. That had been a mistake. The fat shopkeeper had been in animated conversation with a middle aged man about the respective merits of two Sunday League football teams, and had been slow to serve her and to give her her change. By the time she returned to the car Rupert was already back in the driver's seat and, calamity upon calamity, he was engaged in friendly dialogue with the one person she hadn't wanted to see, her over-protective father-in-law.

Thinking quickly on her feet, and hoping desperately that Rupert had said nothing to Bob about their planned itinerary for the day, Julia explained that she had been unable to start her car and that she had phoned Rupert to ask him to take her shopping. It wasn't a good explanation, and of course Bob asked the obvious question "Why didn't you phone me? I know a fair bit about cars and, if I hadn't been able to get you going, I could always have given you a lift to the shops myself and maybe there'd have been time for a cup of coffee and a chat, which would have been very nice." Try as she might, Julia couldn't come up with a convincing answer; weekly she replied "I just didn't think; I'm sorry." She could tell that he was upset by her response.

Fortunately, at that very moment, a car drove past which her father-in-law clearly recognised and his attention was briefly switched to that motor vehicle. Julia took her chance: she gave him a kiss on the cheek, and promised she'd be in touch again very soon; and she climbed into Rupert's car before Bob was able to continue the awkward conversation. She felt herself untrustworthy and not very nice; she was pleased when Rupert set off straight away. Anxious not to dwell on her feelings of shame, she asked Rupert to tell her more about the man they were going to meet.

"Well, I have to say he's very odd indeed; he's almost a total recluse. Ever since his mum died, over twenty years ago he's lived by himself in the house he was brought up in. Part of him wants to break away, and the property's been up for sale or rent for more than two years. The trouble is he's never made any attempt to modernise it and it's stuffed with the sort of furniture most people chucked out forty years ago. He's also chronically shy, which has meant that on the few occasions the estate agents have brought interested clients to view the property, more often than not they haven't got beyond the front door. We've got to be realistic; there's no guarantee that he'll let us in today."

"But you've got his stuff from the hardware shop," said Julia, poking the white carrier bag that lay in the passenger foot well, with her shoe.

"That's probably our best hope," said Rupert. "I think he will let us in because he will want his stuff. Once inside, it's up to you. If he likes you he'll talk to you; if he doesn't we might as well just pack up and go home."

It was starting to go properly dark when they arrived at the cottage. It was set on a hillside about a quarter of a mile from the road: the deeply rutted track that led to it seemed designed to deter visitors, as well as threatening to break Rupert's rear axle, so deep were some of the potholes. The For Sale sign, nailed to a rotting gate post had long since been beaten into submission by the autumn gales: Cold Comfort Farm could not have looked less inviting than this battered farmstead; not a light could be seen anywhere in the house.

"Oh Rupert, he must be out! We've bounced our way down this appalling driveway, and it's all been for nothing;" and Julia felt tears of frustration pricking her eye balls.

"Don't be so sure Julia; let's go up to the house. You bring the bag with you so that we've got a peace offering if it's needed. I'll go on ahead."

Julia did as she was told and followed Rupert to the front door. He knocked loudly, there was no reply. He knocked a second time, with no better result, but then he tried the door handle: it turned without difficulty.

"He's in," whispered Rupert, "he's just hiding. When he sees it's us he'll be fine. Follow me inside; I know where the light switches are; and, as soon as you're in, shut the door behind you; he's got cats you know; if one of them escapes we'll be lucky to leave here alive; one thing is for sure, he'd never talk to us again; that's a racing certainty."

Julia did as she was bid, and once inside the building she immediately turned to fasten the door. She did not see the baseball bat, or hear the rush of air, as it hurtled towards her head, but she felt the impact of the heavy object which knocked her off her feet and left her spread-eagled and unconscious on the grimy concrete floor.

CHAPTER FIFTY SEVEN

Mark Hobson's intention had been to do further research and then to discuss his findings with Pete Bennett before laying the matter before Detective Chief Superintendent Hardy, but circumstances had dramatically changed his plans. A telephone call to Bob Hammond to see if he could give the police up to date information about the current whereabouts of Rupert Henshaw had elicited the fact that a few hours earlier he had been seen in company with Julia Hammond and that she had willingly left with him in a car. What now caused Bob Hammond concern was that she had told him she was going shopping but, four hours later, she still hadn't returned home: her mobile phone was switched off, she had left no messages for her parents and, for the time being, nobody knew where she was.

The high ranking officer listened to what his Detective Inspector had to say and accepted much of the logic behind the theory, but there were certain things which clearly bothered him.

"I can accept Mark that Rupert Henshaw has a motive, albeit a seriously flawed one, to want to harm Jackie Skinner, and to a lesser degree Sharon Farrington, because of her family connections, and those two cases could indeed be linked. What I find more difficult to understand is where the murder of Charles

Montgomery fits into the equation. Intelligence tells us that it was Ralph Ambridge who hired the hit man, not Barnes, or Henshaw, or whatever his name is; and one thing that is beyond dispute is that he couldn't have been the man who shot Montgomery. He was seen by several witnesses to be walking down the street as the killer's car was driving down it. Seconds after the first shot he was right by the body, his presence may well have saved the life of Julia Hammond so, unless he can be in two places at one and the same time, he can't be the murderer. But even if none of these obstacles existed, we still couldn't treat him as a suspect. Two hours ago, an anonymous letter was received. Somebody captured Montgomery's assassination on camera. The photographs show the driver of the car pointing a handgun out of the window; there's also a clear shot of his face. I'm hopeful that very soon we'll have a name, but I can tell you now the man in the picture is not Rupert Henshaw."

"It doesn't mean he wasn't involved Sir. I accept that he didn't hire the assassin; indeed, I suspect that he was earmarked as the victim, but I believe that somehow or other he set up the wrong man. Charles Montgomery was helping Julia Hammond to uncover what led up to her husband committing suicide: we don't know why he did what he did: to date, my best theory is that everything that has happened stems from the violent death of Jacob Farrington. I think he was almost certainly murdered and I think that Justin Barnes, as people then believed him to be, planned and carried out that crime. I believe that by asking questions Charles Montgomery was starting to worry a number of people, as of course was Julia Hammond herself. One of those people feeling threatened could well be Henshaw himself; it's quite likely he has good cause to wish Montgomery out of the way; but Sir, there's still more that you need to know.

"Some time ago, I discovered that Henshaw's father was murdered in South Africa, in a particularly gruesome way, but I've only just learnt that his natural mother was the victim of a brutal sexual assault, before being slashed to pieces by somebody wielding a butcher's knife. How many men are unfortunate enough to have both their parents murdered, on different continents, in particularly revolting and nauseating ways? I venture to suggest that the odds against that happening purely by chance must be astronomic. The murder of the mother was almost demonic. We know his mother ran off with another man; what if he hated her for doing that? The manner of her death was so appalling that it speaks to me of deep seated anger; I think that he killed her and I believe her desertion of him turned him into a psychopath.

"And now we come to the most worrying thing of all. Just before I came up to see you Sir, I asked Pete Bennett to find out everything he could about mum and he's come up with a couple of pictures of her. The crime scene photographs don't really help; all they show is a naked, savagely mutilated corpse that looks barely human; but he also managed to get a copy of her passport photograph. It doesn't flatter her, passport photographs never do, but you see a bright, attractive young woman; and here's where my worries leap into overdrive: she may not be the spitting image of Julia Hammond, Julia's a lot more glamorous, but they do look remarkably similar. They're not identical as I've already said, but they could easily be taken for sisters. I'm a hundred percent certain that that fact isn't lost on Henshaw and right now Sir, Mrs Hammond has disappeared and when last seen she was in company with Rupert Henshaw. I don't think he's rational. I think he believes himself to be so clever that he's untouchable. My fear is that, in his eyes, Julia has become his mother, and I think there is a very good chance that unless we find her quickly, she is likely to suffer the same sickening fate his mother did."

CHAPTER FIFTY EIGHT

It took Julia a long time to realise what had happened. Like a patient coming round after anaesthetic, she had wandered, in a daze, into the No Man's Land that lies between the worlds of Reality and Imagination. Now, bit by bit, things were starting to become clearer. She felt sick and her head ached in a way it had never ached before. She knew that there had to be a swelling, probably the size of a duck egg, on the back of her skull, and that her beautiful hair was almost certainly matted and caked in blood. Her instinct was to try to touch the injury with her hand, but that was impossible. She could turn her head from side to side and no doubt if it hadn't been so painful even to move, she could have shifted her body position by a few inches left or right, but that was the extent of her mobility. Her hands and feet couldn't do her bidding: leather straps cut into both her ankles, and her wrists were denied movement by the cable ties, which bound them tightly to some unforgiving piece of ironwork.

Gradually, by a process of deduction, the gaps in her memory were filling themselves in. That she had been struck a violent blow to the back of the head was self-evidently true: whether the person who had hit her was Rupert Henshaw or the strange old man he had taken her to see she didn't know. In a sense it mattered not. If

Rupert was her attacker, then he was capable of any outrage; if it was the old man it probably meant that Rupert was dead and she could take no comfort knowing that she was in the hands of a homicidal maniac.

Whoever had rendered her unconscious had obviously then carried her to a sparsely furnished room, whether on the ground floor or the first floor, she couldn't say, and had placed her senseless body on an ancient wrought iron bed. It had no mattress, just a bare metal grille to lie on, and through the corroded mesh of metal, leather straps had been threaded, which now bound her ankles so tightly to it that the flow of blood to her feet was severely restricted. Her arms had been unceremoniously stretched out behind her head, and her wrists had been tied to the rusty scrolls of a Victorian bed head: her gaoler had been thorough; he had used a thick cable tie to hold each wrist in place and he had then added a second tie, to eliminate completely the remotest possibility of escape. Mercifully, she had been unconscious while he carried out his work and she had been spared the sight of his flushed face, his mouth drooling with excitement at what was yet to come. Once he had tied her down onto his butcher's block that state of ignorance hadn't been allowed to continue: Julia's face was wet; she guessed that she had been wrenched from the protection of oblivion by cold water being flung into her face.

"I think you've made me wait long enough Julia; there's only so much eager anticipation that a man can be reasonably expected to endure. I've been incredibly patient; I think that now it's about time we made a start."

The voice was one she knew well, but now it had a harder, more strident tone. Rupert Henshaw walked to the head of the bed and looked down at his victim; he was smiling.

"I thought about several ways of waking you up, most of them involved using bodily fluid, but that wouldn't have been at all gentlemanly. My late mother would have called it *wicked*, and she knew all about *wickedness*; she embraced the way of sin when she left her only child with the fiend who was my father."

A look of total disbelief spread across Julia's face. The meek young man with the stammer who had so impressed her father-in-law in the churchyard and who the police had told her might well have saved her life, had turned into a sneering torturer. Tears filled her eyes. She tried to speak. Words wouldn't come. Eventually they tumbled from her lips in an avalanche of despair.

"Why are you doing this to me Rupert?" she sobbed. "What harm have I ever done to you?"

"You remind me of her Julia, you remind me of her. I saw you at the funeral of the fool that you married and I knew that I could have loved you. Maybe I was gazing on you in adoration, as I once gazed on her, with a child's eye. I saw only beauty; I didn't see the maggot in the peach. I couldn't help myself. I started to dream as I had dreamt as a little boy, but all dreams turn bitter with the coming of the light. You set your mind on another. You couldn't wait to work your charms on poor old Monty. He became your poodle and I realised then that you were a witch; a black, ugly witch, just like her and I knew you had to be punished in the same way that she was punished".

"She came to me in the hope of reconciliation; she begged me for forgiveness. I threw her rancid pleas back in her face: I convicted her on all counts. She pleaded for mercy; her pleas fell on deaf ears. I tore the clothes from her back, just as I will tear the clothes from you, and because she had cast aside her only child to have sex with another man, I paid her back by raping her. She knew, because I spelled it out to her, that after venal sex, the corrupt blood that flowed through her arteries, pumped by an uncaring heart, must need be spilt and I didn't disappoint her expectations. Shallow cuts were followed by incisive thrusts, scratches became slices, and the green grass turned brown when contaminated by her life's blood. She died a whore's death; I can promise you a similar introduction to eternal damnation."

"But be honoured! In your case I have had more time to plan, and what makes this act of closure so special is that it ties together all the loose ends of my life. The final cut that will sever your whimpering soul from your body will also be the cut that that frees me from a painful history: evil will be purged; a new life will await me."

"You were so gullible! There never was an old man with a story to tell; he existed in my imagination and nowhere else. This house has been on the market for years: nobody has ever been stupid enough to make an offer for it. The estate agents were ecstatic when they thought they had found a mug. They couldn't do enough for me. I asked to make a second visit on my own, "to help me make up my mind": they knew there was nothing of value to steal and so they happily lent me the keys. I didn't come back here then, I had no need, but at the hardware shop a polite young man called Michael Charles got a new set of keys cut. From then on I could visit here at will. The trap was baited; you were such an easy prey: you even carried the implements of your own torture into the building for me, which is the final irony".

"Undoubtedly the police will try to piece together what took place here. Maybe the estate agent will tell them about a plausible potential purchaser called Mr Charles, and if they do their job well they may discover that the said Mr Charles had keys cut in a local shop. If the right officers handle the investigation, they may even work out that Michael Charles features in another case that the investigating officer already regards as solved; but when they start to look for him they will never find him."

"I, on the other hand will remain available, at least for the short term; no suspicion will be roused by a sudden departure. I'm glad that your father-in- law saw us together. After my work is done here, I intend to seek him out and tell him how worried I am about you. I will say that in the supermarket car park you saw Ralph Ambridge and, that despite my pleas and exhortations to the contrary, you went away with him in his car. He will never deny that story because he lives on borrowed time; a sniper's bullet is the legacy that I have left to him. It's a foolproof plan and if you have any sense of fairness, you'll admit that fact to me"

"But now, my sweet Julia, the time for talk is over. Shall I show you what was inside the bag you carried into the house? This Stanley Knife is razor sharp, so too is the boning knife I hold in my other hand. Both will have their uses. Let the play commence! You're overdressed for your part in this unfolding drama; I think some necessary adjustments are required."

Without saying another word, Rupert inserted the blade of the Stanley Knife under the top button of Julia's coat and, as delicately as a skilled surgeon performing an intricate operation, cut it cleanly from her jacket. He repeated the operation twice more, and then peeled back the fabric of the coat to reveal the shirt underneath.

"A skirt and a blouse Julia; I must say you have made things easy for me: a jumper and trousers would have proved a great deal more difficult to remove."

Julia lay rigid with fear. She felt the hem of her skirt being lifted; she saw Rupert slice through the double layer of material with the knife and then, seizing the skirt with both hands, on either side of the cut, he tore the fabric of the garment down its full length. Another deft stroke of the knife severed the waist band and Julia was left lying on top of the once smart piece of clothing. She was now shaking like a leaf and in a state of blind panic. Rupert, on the other hand, seemed outwardly calm, but the redness of his face and the manner of his breathing betrayed his inner excitement.

"Just one or two more small incisions and then we can move on to phase two," he said exultantly, cutting off every button of the shirt with an exaggerated show of precision. She was totally at his mercy; any second now her bra and pants would be attacked, and then rape and murder would be at hand. Dread held her in a vice like grip; she would never see her children again; she was now moments away from abuse and minutes away from death: nothing could save her: Fate had decreed that she would perish alone, and in abject terror. She closed her eyes, but that only heightened the awareness of her other senses. She sensed the movement of Rupert's arm, and clearly heard the metallic rasping of his zip as he undid his trousers. His erect penis was no doubt exposed: any second now he would launch himself upon her. She felt him slide his finger into her panties; she knew her final ordeal was beginning.

The faintest of faint noises momentarily distracted her. She knew she was imagining it, and certainly it hadn't reached Rupert's ears, but for a brief second she thought that the door to the room had opened. Rupert's mind was a cauldron of lust and vengeance; he mounted the bed, he ripped off her silk panties, all thoughts of compassion and restraint had perished in the white heat of his anger.

The first bullet struck him at the back of the head; he rolled to the right and crashed down onto the floor, the second bullet hit him mid forehead and drilled its way into his brain; a third shot was pumped into his heart, and then just as suddenly as he had arrived, the killer was gone.

Rupert's blood spread quickly across the floor. Julia had been saved from death, but the man who had ended Rupert's life had totally ignored her plight. She was on her own, imprisoned in a cold bedroom with the bleeding remains of psychopathic killer lying at her feet, naked and afraid, with no way of knowing when, if ever, she would be found. Rescue might not come for days, in which case it would be too late. She had been granted a lifeline by a murderer's intervention, but how tenuous that lifeline was, it was impossible to say.

CHAPTER FIFTY NINE

A story on North West Tonight highlighted a case in which an empty property, left insecure by incompetent estate agents, had been invaded by a gang of drunken teenagers. Drugs had been taken, damage had been done and, most harrowing of all, a thirteen year old girl had been tortured and seriously assaulted. The judge, when sentencing the offenders to long custodial sentences, had made scathing comments about the criminal negligence of the agents, and queried whether any right minded vendor, would want in future, to entrust the sale of his or her house to such a cavalier company. Alarm bells had rung in the head of the woman who had lent the keys to the property at Elmton Crags to the nice Mr Charles. She was probably being silly, he seemed so pleasant and so inoffensive, but although the cottage contained nothing of value, it was so remote that it could be seen as a safe haven by drug users. She had disobeyed company instructions, albeit with the tacit approval of her boss; she had granted a client unsupervised access to a property to facilitate a sale. What if he had forgotten to lock up? What if he had left the lights on or the water running? Her's would be the head on the block if there was a problem, she would be the one singled out for blame: she there and then determined that next morning, on the way in to work, she would make a detour to check upon the security of the house, and so it was, purely by chance, Julia Hammond was found alive, with the body of her attacker lying on the floor beside her. She had been strapped to the bed frame for over fourteen hours, much of the time in total darkness, so cold and so painfully stiff, that at times she had wanted for nothing more than sleep, even if that sleep was one from which she would never awake. Hours had become years, years had become decades; and by the time the shocked estate agent burst into the room Julia felt as if she had already spent a lifetime in solitary confinement in a condemned cell.

The picture that the police first gained when they arrived at the scene was, by dint of circumstance, quite confused. Julia was in no state, either mentally or physically, to answer questions. Hypothermia had set in, and given the ordeal that she had been through, it would be inappropriate to speak to her for many hours to come. The best estimate that the police pathologist could come up with was that Rupert Henshaw had been dead for approximately twelve hours and that therefore Julia Hammond must have been a prisoner in that room for longer than that period.

The discovery of Henshaw's body did however open up a whole new line of enquiry, and ultimately persuaded a prisoner in custody to reveal the truth. A man called Michael MacDonald had been arrested by the Derbyshire Police driving a grey Vauxhall

Cavalier along the A6 towards Manchester on the late evening of the previous day. A farm hand had reported that he had seen a car parked in a field gateway on a narrow country lane and that the driver of the vehicle had been standing outside the car observing a house, which had stood empty for several years. He knew that there was still furniture inside the building, and he had heard a rumour that the old man who had lived there had reputedly concealed a large quantity of cash somewhere inside the cottage. He had suspected the chap was "up to no good", so he had memorised part of the registration number and then passed the information on to the police. The story about hidden treasure they dismissed as idle gossip, but the description of the car interested them greatly: in a number of ways it matched the description of the motor car driven by the killer of Charles Montgomery. All police mobiles had been alerted. They had struck the jackpot. They had stopped the suspect vehicle near to the village of Furness Vale and carried out a search. Hidden under the driver's seat they had found a handgun. MacDonald had been arrested. Forensic tests had soon matched the weapon to the bullets recovered from Montgomery's body. Macdonald had remained stubbornly silent, but later when the bullets that killed Rupert Henshaw were also found to match, suspecting that he had been betrayed by his *employer*, he had then completely opened up to his interrogators.

"If I'm going down I'm taking that bastard with me!" Those were the opening words of his diatribe against Ralph Ambridge. He confessed to the police that Ambridge had hired him to kill a man known to him many years ago as Bee-Jay or Justin Barnes. The price set for the job had been generous. Ambridge, it seemed, wanted him dead because he was blackmailing him about his role in a murder that had taken place many years before. The problem with the job had been that the exact whereabouts of the target were unknown and that the only photograph that Ambridge had of the intended victim was over twenty years old. The man he mistakenly took to be the intended quarry didn't look exactly the way he imagined the youth in the photograph would have aged, but with other information that came to his ears from an unknown source he had become convinced that he was the correct target. Only after he had been killed, when Ambridge then received a letter from the supposedly dead man, had the error been discovered. The only mistake the real target made was to suggest to Ambridge that there might be some *tidying up* for him to do in respect of Julia Hammond. MacDonald admitted that thereafter he had kept Julia under close observation because Barnes had told Ambridge that his involvement would only ever be a fallback position and that the task of silencing a troublesome woman was one he hoped to perform himself. He had watched her for a number of days; finally his persistence had paid off. He had seen her leave her house in Henshaw's car, and had rightly suspected that the driver might be the man he was looking for. He had followed the vehicle, at a discreet distance, and had tracked the car to Elmton Crags. He had waited for about thirty minutes, and then had got out of his car, to check that there were no signs of movement within the cottage; he had then made his way, in stealth, to the property, and there he had completed the job he had been hired to do. The woman was no concern of his, no price had been agreed in respect of her, whether she lived or died wouldn't benefit him a penny; therefore he had left her as he had found her and gone on his way. He had telephoned Ambridge to report the kill and indeed his mobile phone had a record of that call. Because of the extra work that had been involved, he had asked for some more money, but he had been contemptuously refused. He assumed it was then that his reluctant paymaster had tipped off the police, seeking to rid himself of an encumbrance and, confident in his arrogance that his word would carry far more weight than that of a common criminal and that he could talk his way out of any police investigation.

Every word MacDonald spoke in that interview was believed by the police to be true; especially when they discovered that Ambridge had gone away for a few days "to stay with friends" at an allegedly unknown destination. A hunt for the missing business tycoon had then begun in earnest.

For over three weeks he remained undiscovered; but in the world outside the bubble which is Criminal Investigation, important events did take place.

Jackie Skinner was released from custody and all charges were dropped. The experience had terrified her and shattered her self-confidence. Alan Nadin never left her side; and one night, without any great romantic gesture, but quietly and tenderly, he asked her the question that Detective Inspector Robert Earnshaw had previously prevented him from asking. Offering only to protect and love her, he asked her if she would marry him; clinging to him, her face awash with tears, she said "yes." The news was greatly welcomed by Mr and Mrs Mark Hobson and by all of Jackie and Alan's true friends.

Finally, after four weeks, two other events occurred in quick succession. News was received that Ralph Ambridge had been shot whilst waiting to board a train at Manchester's Piccadilly Station. It had been a clean kill. There was much CCTV evidence, but none that showed a clear shot of the gunman who, after firing the fatal shots had melted into the crush of commuters and simply disappeared. While the police were not exactly writing off the possibility of one day catching the assassin, they were extremely down beat about the chances of ever getting a positive result.

The other incident happened nearer to home, in the Royal Albert public house. Alan Nadin, Mark Hobson, Pete Bennett and a number of Alan's friends, including Bob Hammond, met to celebrate Alan's engagement. An enjoyable evening was made even better by the news that Bob could give about the state of Julia's recovery: the ordeal she had been through would never be forgotten, but she had been showered with so much kindness and compassion that now, at least, she was beginning to see a brighter future secure in the knowledge that two guilty men were now dead and that three others were awaiting trial: and most importantly of all that it had been publically acknowledged by the police that Will had not been a party to the dreadful crime of murder.

The evening nearly took a downturn when, at approximately 11pm police officers attended the public house claiming that they had reason to suspect that Alan Nadin had confronted D.I. Robert Earnshaw, earlier that evening in the toilets of the nearby Swan Hotel and, after an exchange of words, had punched him in the face, giving him a black eye. The only witness was the complainant himself. There was no CCTV, and nobody in the Swan admitted hearing or seeing a thing, although a slightly inebriated petty criminal called Bob Leather had been adamant that ex Detective Sergeant Nadin had been nowhere near the premises. It was a fact however that the alleged attacker was very well known to his accuser and the officers who followed up the complaint, didn't see how D.I. Earnshaw could have made a mistake.

Mark Hobson, Pete Bennett and all the other people present swore that Alan had been with them all evening, and taking into account this alibi and the unsolicited comments of a witness who was not thought to have any reason to lie on behalf of the suspect, the investigating officers accepted the truth of their combined testimony. It was only some time after the officers had gone that Pete Bennett turned to Mark Hobson.

"You know Gov, I've just remembered something. Alan did say he were nipping to the toilet round about 10pm, and he were gone for the best part of fifteen minutes; I was beginning to think he'd fallen down the pan, when he comes back with a self-satisfied smirk on his face"

"Funny, I've just remembered the same thing as well," said Mark; "still as some character used to say on a T.V. programme a few years back, "Oh dear, what a pity, never mind." Are you ready for another pint yet? I think it's better if this moment of temporary amnesia remains our little secret, don't you? We wouldn't want Stan Hardy thinking that two of his best detectives were losing the plot, now would we Peter? We could start a collection to get

Earnshaw some flowers, but somehow I don't think that there would be too many contributors."

THE END.

CPSIA information can be obtained at www.ICGtesting.com
Printed in the USA
LVOW11s1934011015

456528LV00007B/952/P